CARYL PHILLIPS

In the Falling Snow

VINTAGE BOOKS
London

Published by Vintage 2010

6 8 10 9 7 5

Copyright © Caryl Phillips 2010

Caryl Phillips has asserted his right under the Copyright, Designs and
Patents Act 1988 to be identified as the author of this work

First published in Great Britain in 2009 by
Harvill Secker

Vintage
Random House, 20 Vauxhall Bridge Road,
London SW1V 2SA

www.vintage-books.co.uk

Addresses for companies within The Random House Group Limited
can be found at: www.randomhouse.co.uk/offices.htm

The Random House Group Limited Reg. No. 954009

A CIP catalogue record for this book
is available from the British Library

ISBN 9780099539742

Penguin Random House is committed to a sustainable future for
our business, our readers and our planet. This book is made from
Forest Stewardship Council® certified paper.

Printed and bound in Great Britain by Clays Ltd, St Ives plc

IN THE FALLING SNOW

Caryl Phillips was born in St Kitts and now lives in London and New York. He has written for television, radio, theatre and cinema and is the author of twelve works of fiction and non-fiction. *Crossing the River* was shortlisted for the 1993 Booker Prize and Caryl Phillips has won the Martin Luther King Memorial Prize, a Guggenheim Fellowship and the James Tait Black Memorial Prize, as well as being named the *Sunday Times* Young Writer of the Year 1992 and one of the Best of Young British Writers 1993. *A Distant Shore* won the Commonwealth Writers' Prize in 2004 and *Dancing in the Dark* was shortlisted in 2006.

www.carylphillips.com

ALSO BY CARYL PHILLIPS

IN THE FALLING SNOW

I

He is walking in one of those leafy suburbs of London where the presence of a man like him still attracts curious half-glances. His jacket and tie encourage a few of the passers-by to relax a little, but he can see that others are actively suppressing the urge to cross the road. It is painfully clear that, as far as some people are concerned, he simply doesn't belong in this part of the city.

As he turns into Sutherland Road, he reaches up and peels off the dark glasses. There is no sun to speak of, and autumn has long ago dispatched the lukewarm summer for another year. The wind suddenly rises and dislodges a flurry of leaves from the over-hanging trees, and he feels a chill ripple through his body. Despite the cold, the dark glasses make him feel more comfortable on these streets, for he is able to look at people without them being able to see his eyes. He fishes the slim plastic envelope from his inside jacket pocket and folds the glasses into their case, before tucking the envelope back into the same pocket. He stops by the small gate and takes a deep breath, and then he reaches down and lifts the latch. He passes through and watches as the wooden contraption swings back into place with the assistance of a tightly coiled iron spring. The half-dozen steps along the crazy-paved pathway are undertaken joylessly, and then he pushes the bell, which sings out with a lyrical two-toned peal whose lingering echo suggests that nobody is at home. He hears footsteps padding down the stairs, and he listens as she fiddles with the bolt and chain before throwing open the door.

'Keith?'

He is never sure what to make of the greeting. It is not really a question, for they both know who he is.

'You all right, Keith?'

He says nothing in reply. She tosses back her tangle of black hair and tilts her chin upwards, and then she quickly tips her head to one side and invites him to kiss her on the cheek. He leans in and dry-kisses her, and then as he stands tall he lets the end of his tongue draw a wet line against the side of her face.

'Dirty sod.'

'What do you mean, "dirty"?'

She laughs out loud.

'I'm only kidding. You look good, babe.'

He steps through the door and notices her looking anxiously over his shoulder to make sure that there are no prying eyes, and then he hears what he imagines is a businesswoman hurrying by whose footsteps click primly against the pavement. She slams the door shut and he resigns himself to the fact that once again he is marooned in her dismal hallway, at the bottom of her stairs, in her small terraced house in north-west London.

He watches as the late afternoon light fades behind the sky blue curtains. She should use heavier fabric in the bedroom. At first he stayed overnight, and in the morning, as the birds started to sing, he would lie quietly beside her and wonder if his wife was also waking up next to somebody else. And, if she was, where was their son? Who was looking out for Laurie? In the mornings he tried hard not to move as the last thing he needed was Yvette talking to him, but because the curtains didn't block out the light it was impossible for him to sleep beyond dawn. He thought maybe she liked it this way, with nature giving her an automatic wake-up call, but he didn't want to ask any questions because that would be to suggest an intimacy that he was keen to avoid. A forty-seven-year-old man and a twenty-six-year-old girl. He understood the detached role that he was playing, and he was determined to stay in character.

These days there is a predictable pattern to these more acceptable afternoon visits. Yvette likes to take charge. She carefully turns out the light in the downstairs hallway, and then she leads him upstairs. Once they reach the top landing she lets the silk robe slip to the floor. Initially he found the drama arousing, thrillingly so, but after his third or fourth afternoon visit (or 'service call' as she likes to refer to them) she abandoned the black lace corset that he relished and replaced it with a red push-up bra and a matching thong. Clearly she imagined this to be an improvement – more of a 'turn on' – but he couldn't find the words to fully express his disdain for the crass vulgarity of this silly piece of string. Yvette continues to wear this tart's uniform, and as her robe pools on to the floor his eyes drop down and focus first on her legs and then on her ankles (which he knows are cocoa butter smooth), but try as he might he can't bring himself to look at her underwear. Once inside the bedroom, Yvette locks the door by sliding a small brass bolt into place, and then she eases her hands into his jacket and up towards his shoulder pads, stripping the garment from him as though peeling the skin from a piece of fruit. He may not have found a way to talk with her about the underwear, but he has been forced to tell her that scented candles make him gag. After the second coughing fit, Yvette quizzed him, and although at first he denied that there was a problem he eventually confessed, and she laughed and assured him that a hint of jasmine or honey peach was something that she could happily live without. Having removed his jacket she allows him to undress himself while she lies on the top sheet of the bed and unclips her bra so that her breasts, while not totally abandoning the infrastructure of the wired cups, perch mischievously on the threshold of liberation.

Yvette's enthusiasm is almost theatrical, but she is genuinely aroused and achieves a climax with speed and great vocal excitement. He used to worry about the neighbours, but she assured him that they seldom returned home from work before nine o'clock. Besides, she and Colin never had any complaints from them, and she never hears *their* lovemaking, so she assumes that the walls between these houses must be quite thick. She closes her eyes, lies back on the bed and continues to catch her breath, while he props himself up on one elbow and carefully tunnels his free hand through the rough nest of her hair. He knows that she 'relaxes' it, for he has seen the full artillery of creams and lotions in the bathroom, but her heritage is most evident in the battle between Europe and Africa that is being waged on her face where full lips and emerald green eyes compete for attention. Under the most intense scrutiny she could easily pass for white and suntanned, but her penchant for kente cloth scarves and wooden beads speaks eloquently to the fact that she has never tried to deny her mixed background.

When she is ready, Yvette opens her eyes and smiles gently. Then she jackknifes her leg and runs her instep against his thigh, which is his cue to mount her again and this time slowly tease her by conjuring pleasure out of gestures so subtle that only those locked together in the most claustrophobic of embraces might sense movement. Rather than quickly capitulate in one furious yelp of gratitude, Yvette punctuates the 'second round' with a continuous low burble of half-whispered imprecations and throaty gasps which diminish in volume as she approaches climax, and then she falls silent before releasing a cry of distress and shuddering against his body. For a minute she holds him tightly, as though she might burst into tears, and then she slowly spurns him and rolls to the far side of the bed and curls into a tight foetal ball. He watches as she loses herself in what he imagines is the familiar entanglement of female feelings of guilt and vulnerability, but he is untroubled by her temporary plight. Annabelle has left him yet another urgent message about Laurie and the problems he is experiencing at school, having fallen in with what she likes to call, 'the wrong set'. He knows that he should have called her back, for she has been insisting that their seventeen-year-old son is growing increasingly 'bolshy' with her, although it is unclear what Annabelle expects him to do about it. After all, they are both fully aware that Laurie seems somewhat indifferent to the idea of spending any time with his father.

On the second message, the anxiety in Annabelle's voice had alarmed him. Since their separation some three years ago, she has made it her business to carefully construct a steely façade around her emotions as a way of distancing herself from him. These days she is usually meticulous about keeping both her wit and her levity of spirit well out of sight. For his part, he is fully aware that through nobody's fault but his own he now lives alone in a small flat, and his wife and son have every reason to be annoyed with him and every right to protect themselves emotionally. However, he is still not sure why he told Annabelle about sleeping with his annoying co-worker at the office New Forest retreat, for it was a nothing encounter, semi-drunken, and not pleasurable in the least. It was the first time that he had even thought of cheating on his wife, and once it was over he knew immediately that there would never be any repetition of his infidelity, yet two weeks later, and after he imagined that he had successfully negotiated the awkwardness of the workplace situation, he suddenly felt some foolish compulsion to confess everything to Annabelle as she stood ironing tea towels and watching *Newsnight*. He is unsure what kind of a reaction he expected, but having heard him out she calmly replaced the upturned iron on the ironingboard and told him that in the morning she wanted him to leave her and their fourteen-year-old son alone in order that they might get on with their lives. 'Go away and sort it out,' she said contemptuously, 'because after everything you and I have been through I really don't deserve to have to put up with your pathetic midlife crisis. So just go, okay?' She abruptly unplugged the iron and left the room, and he realised that he would be spending the night alone on the sofa. In the morning he would do as she suggested and leave, but three years later he still questions himself as to why he felt the urge to put in jeopardy everything that they had worked so hard to build. What he is sure about, and doesn't have to question, is the reservoir of resentment that Laurie is drawing upon whenever his mother suggests spending any time with his father. He turns over on his side and looks at the late afternoon light behind the thin curtains in Yvette's bedroom, and then at his jacket which lies in a discarded bundle on the floor. He hears the roar of a passing aeroplane and he imagines the thin, wispy trails of departure in its wake. There is no longer any escaping the fact that today he will have to talk to Yvette and end their arrangement.

While she is in the shower he surveys the small, cluttered, bedroom and wonders about the young woman whose bed he is lying in. He knows that her ex-husband Colin was her lecturer at college, and that he is twelve years her senior. She shared this piece of information the first time they went to the pub together.

'He left me for an older woman,' she said, 'somebody more his own age. But at least I got the house.' She paused, moved the plastic stirrer to one side, and then took a noisy sip of her vodka tonic. 'Well, we never really argued. It just became clear that we didn't have that much in common and we'd even stopped, you know. Well not completely, but I had to ask for it.' She blushed slightly and then tried to smother her nervous laughter with her hand, but she coughed as though something was stuck in her throat. He gallantly climbed to his feet and went to the bar for a glass of water, which she drank in a series of rapid gulps. She paused, as though eager to belch, but eventually she simply swallowed deeply then reached up and began to stroke and flatten her hair with the palm of her hand.

'Too much information, right?'

He smiled and shook his head.

'Don't say much, do you?'

He laughed as he took in the gentle curves of her young body. Since Annabelle had put him out of the house there had been no other women. It's not that he'd lost interest. He would still sit on the bus and try and sneak a look without being seen, and he would frequently follow a girl down the tube escalator and make sure that he got into the same compartment and casually sit opposite her. But he was too old to go to the places where he imagined men went to meet girls. Visiting clubs or going to parties lacked a certain dignity, and the idea of internet sites or, even worse, singles evenings with all that speed dating business filled him with dread. Computer porn was all right as far as it went, and he'd somewhat resigned himself to the reality that an occasional furtive log-on would have to do for now. At his age, it was better than making a fool of himself by going out on the pull, or gently soliciting friends for introductions. However, as he sat in the pub opposite her, he realised that Yvette could solve a problem for she had a vibrant personality and a well put together body, and she appeared to be interested. He liked her energy, and the fact that she didn't seem to be afraid of saying whatever came into her mind, but Yvette worked for him. Unlike the New Forest encounter with the co-worker who was his professional equal, he was actually Yvette's boss and, although she appeared to be unfazed by recent developments between them, he kept reminding himself that he was the one who ought to be responsible. Of course, what made their situation even more complicated was the fact that it was actually Yvette who was determining both the pace and the nature of their courtship.

By the time she strides out of the shower and back into the bedroom, with the towel tubed tightly around her body, she expects him to be dressed and sitting on the edge of the bed ready to watch her step into her clothes. She walks from one side of the room to the other and makes a performance of turning on all the lights, including the bedside lamps. He knows that this part of the encounter is all about her vanity, for she simply desires him to concentrate on her. He observes as she gently powders her body, then eases into her lamentable lingerie, then her jeans, and then she rolls a sweater down over her chest before arching her back and stretching her arms up towards the ceiling. His job is to study the supposed object of his passion as she declares herself now unavailable, and the expectation is that he should tightly rein in his lust and wait patiently until she is ready to lead him downstairs to the kitchen. Today she prolongs her performance, and poses as though unsure if she should wear the white turtleneck that he knows, from previous experience, to be an expensive cashmere and silk mix, or simply pull on a blue cotton blouse that looks disconcertingly like a working man's shirt. She removes the turtleneck sweater and holds the blouse up as she twists and turns in front of the full-length mirror that stands to the side of the wardrobe door. She makes a decision and tosses the blouse to one side where it catches the arm of the wooden rocking chair.

'I was right the first time, wasn't I?'

There is no point in replying for the sweater is once again halfway over her head, and she begins to wiggle and squirm like a music hall performer escaping from a sack. By the time her head plunges through the neck hole, and her startled face readjusts itself to the glare of the bedroom lights, there is no need for him to answer. She crosses quickly to the door.

'Well, you coming, or what?'

He doesn't like reality television, finding the humiliation that is visited upon the contestants embarrassing. Whether they are stuck in a house, or on an island, or whether they are encouraged to sing, model, diet, cook, or dance, it all seems to boil down to the same thing: laugh at other people and then feel smug about yourself at their expense. Yvette, on the other hand, loves these kinds of programmes, but she has given up trying to persuade him to sink into the sofa and relax with her in front of the telly. The one time he agreed to do so she turned on the television, ordered an Indian meal, and then began to text in her vote as she decided whether successive male contestants were gay, straight, or taken. He knew that if he said anything critical she would just accuse him of being boring so he remained silent, but by the time the meal arrived he was desperate to leave. She took the food into the kitchen and quickly spooned it out of the containers and on to two paper plates, before dashing back into the living room, practically dropping the two plates on to the coffee table, and once again picking up her mobile phone and starting to text. She idly removed the Indian restaurant's plastic forks and paper napkins from her back pocket and tossed them down next to the two plates. He looked at her, but she did not meet his gaze.

'It's all right, Keith. You can have some of my chicken vindaloo and fried rice if you like. I'm not that hungry.'

These days they don't bother with the television. They sit in her remodelled kitchen on the two designer barstools, and he opens a bottle of Sancerre from the case of wine that he arranged to be delivered to her house. He has tried to tell her that she should put a couple of bottles in the fridge, but she doesn't seem to listen. He passes her a long-stemmed glass of warm wine and realises that in her own way Yvette is trying. However, he recognises that their relationship must occasionally be difficult for her, for he can be private to the point of being hermetically sealed and, in the past few months, Yvette has been offered little more than enigmatic smiles and semi-educational gestures, such as an introduction to the world of wine. As a couple they have shared nothing, except the temporary convenience of her former marital bed, and no matter how attractive he finds her he knows full well that there is no substance to their relationship. He worries that the wine might be too dry for her, but she takes another sip and appears to be waiting for him to say something. They can't even listen to any music together for she finds his passion for Stevie Wonder, and for American soul music of the seventies in general, as tedious as he finds her love of independent northern bands, particularly the Arctic Monkeys. Once it was clear that the television was not going to work she did attempt music, but why anybody would choose to listen to the mindless lyrics of a song called 'Balaclava', or a discordant cacophony with the unlikely title of 'Fluorescent Adolescent', was beyond him. When he finally expressed his distaste she simply shrugged her shoulders and turned off the CD player. She has never again suggested that they listen to any music, for which he feels a mixture of relief and guilt. He has tried to talk to her about the social significance of soul music, and he did confess his desire to one day write a book about music, but he quickly recognised that their conversation was rendered positively one-sided, and somewhat uncomfortable, by the undeniable fact that the music he was enthusing about was recorded before Yvette was born. Indie bands, or hip-hoppers with acronymic names, suggest to him not a new generation of music, but the evidence of a general cultural malaise. This being the case they have accustomed themselves to sitting in silence on the steel and chrome barstools and drinking their warm white wine before he is once again ushered out of the door.

'You know,' he begins, 'I'm not sure that we should continue to see each other.'

Yvette puts down her glass of wine, making sure that it is centred on the circular wooden coaster that she imagines will protect the kitchen work surface. He doesn't wait for her to say anything, choosing instead to press ahead with his unrehearsed words.

'I don't want things to become difficult for either of us and, to be honest, I'm beginning to feel as though we either have to take it to the next stage or accept the fact that we're not able to move forward. Am I making sense?'

'What do you mean by "the next stage"?'

Yvette runs her tongue along the full length of her bottom lip and stares at him.

'No, it's just that well, for a start, you work for me. Or with me. Whatever, you know what I mean. And then we don't have *that* much in common, do we? I'm a bit of a downer compared to you. It's not like I can come with you to some Club 18–30 in Spain, or on a piss-up to the Canary Islands.'

'You're worried about the age difference? Is that it?'

'Yvette, that's part of it. I'm just trying to be sensible about everything. I don't like mess, and so I'm just thinking that it's best to be honest.'

'And what about how I feel? If it doesn't feel right to you, that's one thing, but how about working together to fix it? You know, saying, "okay, it's not perfect" and then just trying to sort it together, or do you just want out?'

He moves to top up her wine, but without taking her eyes from his face Yvette covers the glass with her hand. He pauses, unsure whether to prolong this encounter by pouring himself another drink. He lowers his eyes and looks at the canary yellow and white label on the bottle, and then he pours himself a small amount.

Two hours later he is on a Hammersmith and City train to Shepherd's Bush. He peers through the window at the low horizon, which is ragged with rusting fire escapes and abandoned buildings, as the train passes quickly through the desolate parts of the city. He changed at King's Cross, but luckily he didn't have to spend any time on the platform. These days it doesn't pay to linger anywhere in the city, and being dressed as he is only serves to mark him out as prime mugging material. As he reached the top of the second escalator, he called Annabelle but the line went almost immediately to voice-mail. He thought about leaving a message, but the idea that she might be with her friend Bruce annoyed him so he closed the phone. Then he realised that he was being petty, and this was really about his son, and so he opened his phone and for a moment he was rooted to the spot with indecision. It was then that he heard the dull roar of an approaching train so once again he flipped the phone shut and tumbled rapidly down a neighbouring escalator and squeezed through the carriage doors as they were closing. Three teenagers sit opposite him, and when the train plunges into a tunnel he can see his reflection in the window behind their heads. He can see that, like his son Laurie, all three kids are partly white, but it is clear from their baggy dress sense, and from the way that they slouch and speak, that they identify themselves as black. Gone are the days when, sitting on the tube at night, he would feel perfectly safe if a posse of black youths got into his carriage. Back then he often took silent satisfaction in seeing how their exuberance made older white people somewhat uneasy, but today's teenagers no longer respect any boundaries. Black youths, white youths, mixed race youths, to them all he is just a middle-aged man in a jacket and tie who looks like he doesn't know shit about nothing. He lowers his gaze and tries to figure out the genders of the gang of three, whose faces remain shrouded beneath oversized hoods. A few seats away, an elderly white lady with a blue silk print scarf, and wearing expensive designer flats, sits by herself with two carrier bags of groceries balanced delicately between her feet. Bloody hell, couldn't she find a better time to do her shopping? By the time the train sways and lurches its way out of Paddington station and back into the evening gloom the three teenagers are on their feet. The smallest one, who he now realises is a girl, has had her iPod snatched by the older of the two boys. She begins to chase him, but the boys toss the iPod to each other and the girl's frustration mounts.

'Give me my fucking iPod you pair of cunts.'

The boys laugh and throw it to each other like a cricket ball, the earpieces and cord trailing like a cartoonish jet-stream, and then one of the boys fumbles the iPod and it bounces on to the seat next to the old lady. He feels his body tense, as though suddenly understanding that he might now have to be drawn into this conflict, but the old lady simply looks at the iPod, and then at the teenagers, and then back at the iPod. She picks it up, wraps the cord around it as though balling wool, and then offers the iPod to the girl.

'Might I suggest that you take better care of your personal property.'

For a moment the girl looks at her, as though genuinely shocked that this apparition has the power of speech. As the train slows and pulls into Westbourne Park station the two boys begin to kick the carriage doors, but the girl does not take her eyes from the old lady. The doors eventually open with a well-rehearsed clatter and the two boys leap out on to the platform.

'You coming, or what?'

The girl begins to move off, but she has not finished with the old lady.

'You better keep your fucking hands off people's stuff, all right?'

The girl turns now, and as the doors begin to close she quickly jumps and joins her friends on the platform. Through the window she gives the lady two fingers and mouths 'fuck off'. The train speeds off again, but this part of the Hammersmith and City line is overground and so there are no longer any tunnels to plunge into. He glances at the old lady, who seems totally unruffled by the encounter, and he wonders how this woman is able to maintain such poise with these hooligans who are probably the same age as, or even younger than, her grandchildren. Does she understand and maybe pity them, or does she simply feel contempt? Though only a generation removed from the brutes, he finds their ill manners mystifying. As a child, Brenda would never have allowed him to get away with such behaviour. After his father was readmitted to the hospital, and it was just the two of them alone, she drilled him in the importance of always saying 'please' and 'thank you', and if his tie wasn't straight, and his socks pulled up all the way, and his shoes properly polished, he wasn't allowed to leave the house. 'There's people out there, Keith, who think they're better than you, but never mind what they say, they're not. However, I'm not having you giving them some reason to think they are. Keep your chin up, love, your clothes nice and tidy, and your language decent, and you'll be a credit to yourself and your mum and dad. Now get yourself off to school and mind you come back with As on that report card or don't you bother coming back at all.' Brenda knew that good manners were important, and he had tried to pass these values on to Laurie who, as a small boy, was so timid that at times he wondered if he had not overdone it with the manners thing. In fact, once boys started to bully him, he was sure that he should be encouraging his son to be more assertive, but Annabelle disagreed, and insisted that Laurie was right to walk, or even run, away when boys pelted him with stones and called him a 'halfie'. He and Annabelle had words, and he tried to explain to his wife that his own understanding of how to survive an English childhood had involved knowing that there was a time when it simply didn't make sense to run, and that you sometimes had to stand up and fight. While he could not persuade his wife that Laurie should be encouraged to occasionally scrap it out, it was, ironically enough, his father-in-law who ended up agreeing with him, for the man's military background meant that the idea of his grandson backing down from a scuffle filled him with something akin to shame.

The subject of Laurie and bullying came up on the only occasion that Annabelle's father actually met his grandson. It was an uncomfortable encounter, but Annabelle had been both courageous and unambiguous about where her loyalties lay. If her parents disapproved of her choice of a partner, then her relationship with them would have to change radically. She was still at college when she first found herself trapped awkwardly between her boyfriend and her parents, and although she had no desire to be disrespectful towards them, her parents' intransigence eventually forced a choice upon her. Some years later, but before the uncomfortable encounter between her new family and her father, Annabelle made the mistake of attempting to keep something about her relationship with her parents a secret from Keith. Annabelle was in the middle trimester of her pregnancy, and her mother had met up with her for their regular lunch at Harvey Nichols, followed by a walk in Hyde Park. After six years of post-college non-communication, when he and Annabelle had lived first in Bristol and then in Birmingham, actual face-to-face relations had been re-established with her mother once they moved to London and Annabelle started working for the theatrical agency. After three years of monthly lunches, during which time Annabelle's mother was always careful to ask after her son-in-law, but without ever expressing any interest in spending any time with him, Annabelle waited until they were strolling by a stand of beeches near the Serpentine before announcing her pregnancy. Her mother's anxious smile collapsed, and the well-disguised wrinkles began now to spider around her eyes. Annabelle helped her mother to a seat on a bench and watched as the older woman began to cry. Then she sat next to her mother, and for a few moments she looked helplessly at the space between her feet before slowly placing an arm around her mother's heaving shoulders. The occasional walker ambled by, and a small group of children on the grass continued to play with their kites, but the mother and daughter were largely oblivious to any activity. They sat together for nearly an hour before the older woman finally reached into her handbag for a handkerchief and carefully wiped her nose then dabbed at her eyes. Annabelle tightened her arm and pulled her mother an inch or so towards her.

The following month they met at Harvey Nichols as usual, and over lunch her mother shared with her the village gossip, energising each trivial tale with the drama and intrigue of an international incident. Annabelle smiled knowingly and nodded at the right moments, although it was almost ten years since she had last seen the family cottage in Wiltshire, or set eyes upon her father, and her pre-college, pre-Keith, life had long begun to fade into the general mélange of hazy childhood memories which included attempting, and failing, to learn how to ride a bike, and falling into the stream at the end of the garden. Once her mother had paid the bill and retrieved her credit card, Annabelle gathered up her belongings and made ready to leave the restaurant, but her mother did not immediately get up from the table so Annabelle sat back down. After a few moments of inelegant silence, her mother asked if she would mind sharing a taxi with her to the train station as she really didn't feel up to a walk in the park today. Having ascertained that her mother was not suffering from light-headedness or about to faint, she offered her an arm and the two of them flagged down a black cab whose driver seemed to know all the backstreets and soon dropped them at Paddington. Once they passed into the loud and cavernous station concourse, her mother reached into her bag and produced a train ticket. 'I'm sorry, darling,' she said and then she held on to her daughter's arm and began to sob. Annabelle led her mother to a coffee bar, and left her at the only free table, which was uncomfortably close to the door, while she ordered two herbal teas from the counter. When she returned to the draughty table her mother had calmed down somewhat, and she appeared to be eager to talk. 'It's your father,' she began. 'He needs to see you and find a way for you two to make up. He won't admit anything, but you know he's always been a stubborn so-and-so.' Her mother picked up the tea and blew on it, then immediately placed it back on the saucer. 'Darling, I really don't know what else to do about it. I suppose I'm begging you.'

That evening, Annabelle arrived back home at just after eight o'clock. She had left Keith a message on the answerphone explaining that the agency had asked her to attend the dress rehearsal of a play that she had read and recommended, and which was opening in Watford later in the week. She had let him know that there was food in the fridge and she would see him in the early evening. He was sitting at the kitchen table reading the review section of the paper, and he looked up at her as she took off her coat and draped it over the back of a chair. He noticed that small threads of silver were now embroidered into her bob of brown hair, and he anticipated that at some point they would have to sit down for the 'to go grey or not to go grey' discussion.

'You look knackered,' he said. He put down the paper and stood up. 'Shall I get you a coffee?'

'That would be great.' Annabelle didn't meet his eyes as she pulled out a wooden kitchen chair and sat down at the table.

'How was the play? Presumably you did the right thing recommending it?'

'It was all right. Not bad at all. I think it will come into town.'

'Which masterpiece was it?' He opened the cupboard which held the various jars of coffee and boxes of tea. 'What do you want, instant?'

Annabelle nodded. 'Thanks.'

'Well, what play was it?'

'Look Keith, I didn't go to a play.'

He spooned the granules into a cup and focused his full attention on the task at hand. The water in the kettle started to make a slow, steamy gurgle, and as the mist began to rise the light from the halogen fixtures passed through the vaporous cloud and created a strangely ethereal pattern on the granite counter top.

'I went to see my father.'

He turned to look at her. 'I see. Why did you lie to me?'

'I don't know. I think I was just a bit scared.'

'Of me?'

'I don't know, Keith. I didn't want to hurt you, but I shouldn't have done it.'

'You shouldn't have lied, or you shouldn't have gone to see your father? Which is it?'

'I don't know, I'm confused. Both, I suppose.'

'So how long has this been going on?'

'How long has what been going on?'

'Don't play games with me, Annabelle. How long have you been saying you're having lunch with your mother, but secretly traipsing off down there?'

'Look Keith, I *have* been having lunch with my mother. This is the first time I've been down there since university. Jesus, I've not seen Dad since he took us out for that awful meal just before graduation.' He pushed the cup, with the granules still in it, away from him so that it slid some distance along the counter. 'Keith, don't you believe me?'

'You've lied to me once already, what's to stop you lying again?'

'Come on, you can't be serious, Keith. I'm not a liar. Look at this situation, I can't even keep it up for a few hours.'

He picked up his jacket from the back of the kitchen chair that he had just vacated.

'Where are you going?'

'Out. I need to clear my head.'

'Look, I know you're upset and I don't blame you, but I won't be going back again. Not ever, if I have my way.' He moved past her and walked towards the door. 'Keith?'

'Annabelle, that doesn't help. I wish it did, but right now it doesn't, okay.'

He slammed the front door as he left, rattling the letterbox. Annabelle listened to the exhausted splutter of the boiling kettle as the switch eventually tripped off, and she lowered her head and closed her tired eyes as the kitchen fell silent.

On the train journey to Wiltshire few words were exchanged between mother and daughter. Annabelle was relieved when her mother finally stopped sobbing, but as they left London behind, and accelerated out into the countryside, she had to fight hard to keep her memories of this journey from overwhelming her. She smiled to herself as she recalled schoolgirl Saturday outings spent browsing the trendy, but overpriced, shops along the King's Road, followed by clandestine meetings with boys in Chelsea pubs, before hurriedly dashing to the tube so that they could get to Paddington and catch the eight o'clock train back home. It had all been very innocent, even the time she went off with an Italian boy and they sat together on the sofa in his parents' London flat and listened to Duran Duran while he tried, and failed, to roll them both a joint. In the end they settled for a menthol cigarette, and later in the day, when she met Gemma and Lisa at the train station, they didn't believe her when she said that nothing had happened. In fact, nothing happened until she went off to university and introduced herself to Richard Coombs at the university drama group's stall at the freshers' fair, and he asked her if she'd ever written any sketches. She lied and said 'yes, of course', and three days later she trekked up Crowndale Road to his digs and the pair of them sat on the floor while she read out a spectacularly unfunny piece about Chaucer manning the gates of heaven and choosing not to admit various people from *The Canterbury Tales*. Richard Coombs was a third-year, and well known in university circles as somebody who was probably going to end up at the BBC. Apparently there were rumours that he had already been approached by a script editor from Birmingham's Pebble Mill studios. When he laughed at her unfunny jokes she felt grateful, but as she continued to read, and self-consciously switch voices, she could feel herself turning crimson. Then she felt his hand on her leg and she heard him say 'put down the script,' which she did. She raised her arms above her head so that he could peel off her jumper, and then she lay back on the scatter cushions and closed her eyes. It was over in minutes, and he hurriedly asked her if she would like to use the bathroom first. 'No,' she said, 'you can go ahead.' Once she heard the door close she sat up and was relieved to see that there was only a small trace of blood on the inside of one thigh, and it was possible that he might not have even noticed. It had hurt, but at least it was over, and she already knew that it was unlikely that Richard Coombs would ever contact her again. All she had to do now was nego- tiate the awkward conversation about her sketch, and then endure his clumsy request for the phone number of her hall of residence, and that would be it. In fact, that was it with boys and sex, until the end of the academic year when she found herself sitting in the next seat but one to an awkward-looking boy at a semi-professional production of *Sweet Bird of Youth*.

As the train pulled into Ashleigh station she scanned the platform for any sign of her father, who she expected to be waiting eagerly for them. Her mother seemed to have retreated further into herself as they drew closer to 'home', so Annabelle decided not to ask her how best to handle the forthcoming encounter. She assumed that if her mother knew then she would have said something, but the silence between them was eloquent and so she opted to leave her mother to her reverie and resigned herself to dealing with the situation as it unfolded. There was a single taxi waiting outside the small country station, and she was surprised to see that the driver was an Indian. She looked around and blinked slowly, in an owl-like fashion, as she took in the full reality of where she was. 'Magnolia Cottage', said her mother, 'off Willoughby Lane.' The man smiled and started the engine, and as the taxi gently crested the stone bridge which spanned the river her mother slipped her gloved hand into that of her daughter.

Her father was standing by the window when the taxi pulled up, and he watched impassively as his wife and pregnant daughter passed through the wrought iron gate and began to make their way up the garden path towards him. He showed no interest in waving to them, or in any way acknowledging their presence. For her part, Annabelle looked at the newly planted flowers and plants that edged the path, and she blocked out her mother's twittering voice which rose and fell with a feverish anxiety. The door was never locked so her mother simply ushered Annabelle inside. They moved into the living room where her father continued to stare out of the window with his back to them both. She noticed that the antique occasional table was set with three cups and saucers and a cake stand which held a half-dozen scones and three slices of Madeira cake. Carefully arranged around the base of the cake stand were delicate glass dishes containing various jams, and one that held two dollops of clotted cream, so she could see some evidence that she was expected. 'William?' said her mother. Her startled father turned around and blinked, as though only now becoming aware of their presence.

'Annabelle, it's so good to see you after all this time.' He came towards her with his arms extended and kissed her once on either cheek without seeming to notice her protruding stomach. 'Please, take a seat. Goodness, we have so many.'

He gestured in the direction of a number of comfy chairs with overly plumped cushions, and he continued to seem somewhat disconcerted, and a little embarrassed, that there was so much choice available to his guest. Unfortunately, her father seemed to have aged cruelly, and there was little evidence of the military man with whom she was familiar. He had not only lost his hair and his posture, but she could clearly see that his hands were shaking.

The civilised gentility of tea offended Annabelle, who soon understood that this was a world that, inadvertently, her husband had helped her to escape from. The fact that she had called their home from Paddington station, and left her husband a deceitful message about a play opening in Watford, made her feel sick. Her mother tried to keep a tight grip on proceedings by repeatedly bringing the conversation back to the subject of flowers, but then the kettle began to whistle and she hastily stood up and announced that she would make another pot.

'Mint? Jasmine? Or should I just bring more of the same?'

Annabelle smiled and shrugged her shoulders. She watched as her mother retreated to the kitchen.

'Your mother likes to blather.'

Annabelle looked at her father, who was staring intently at the scones without showing any real inclination to pick one up. Her mother returned almost immediately and began to flutter nervously about as she served the tea, and then she asked Annabelle if she wanted to see what they had done with her old room, or perhaps she would like to see the new conservatory, but all Annabelle wanted to do was go back to London and resume her life with her husband. Eventually, the conversation touched upon urgent matters relating to local efforts to block the motorway extension, and her father's success with turnips and beetroot at the county's agricultural fair, and then her visibly fatigued mother asked her when exactly the baby was due, although she knew full well, practically to the hour, when she was likely to become a grandmother.

'Do you know what it is yet?' asked her father.

Annabelle shook her head. 'No, we're not sure.'

'Well,' said her mother, 'it will be one thing or the other, that's for sure.'

Her father pursed his lips. 'Yes, quite. I'm afraid your mother and I had no idea what you would be, that is until we had you, of course.'

'I had her, William,' smiled her mother.

'Yes, yes, of course you did, but I *was* involved,' insisted her father.

'I think Keith would like a son.'

'Would he, indeed?' mused her father. 'I see.'

She looked at her father and could see his mind working rapidly, so much so that his lips began to move as though he were rehearsing the opening of a sentence. Then he hummed reflectively and knitted his fingers together in what she assumed to be an imaginary golf grip.

'You see, Annabelle, I received a note, anonymous of course, shortly after we last saw you in Bristol. In your salad days, as it were. Your mother may have mentioned something to somebody at bridge, or perhaps I blabbed to Walter or Barry in the pub, but some chap, or woman for that matter, wanted to know what it was like to have a "nigger-lover" for a daughter. He wrote that he hoped I would never have the ill manners to pollute our village with my mongrel family. Now then, what do you make of that?'

After the unscheduled visit to Magnolia Cottage, she resumed meeting her mother for monthly lunches at Harvey Nichols, which were only interrupted by a break shortly before she gave birth to Laurie. Her husband had forgiven her for lying to him and 'sneaking off,' as he put it, to Wiltshire, and when he returned after his door-slamming exit he told her that he'd sat in the pub and thought about things and he could understand why she might have wanted to go and see her father after all this time. When she told him what had transpired, and that she had shouted at her father and told him that it was his responsibility to deal with racist abuse, and not wait for a decade and then dump it in her lap, her husband shook his head and bent over and kissed her on the forehead. 'Fucking wanker,' was all he said, before announcing that he was going upstairs to get ready for bed. She had asked her distraught mother to call for a taxi to take her back to the station, but her father seemed genuinely annoyed, as though he had made some huge effort that had gone unrewarded. He reminded her that she hadn't even bothered to have a scone or a piece of cake.

The taxi wound its slow way through the narrow country lanes that were walled on both sides by seemingly ancient bowed trees. Annabelle noted that, according to a neat billboard by the roadside, an archaeological dig sponsored by Cambridge University had recently unearthed evidence of pre-Roman settlement, a discovery which her parents had failed to mention. Once she reached Ashleigh station, Annabelle realised that she had just missed a London train so she would have plenty of time to think about how she was going to deal with this mess when she got home.

Sitting alone on the empty platform, Annabelle suddenly felt herself convulse into floods of tears. She hated these people, the women with their starched hair and silk scarves, and the men in blazers and slacks, making conversation about nothing, smiling 'yes, yes', laughing nervously at their own jokes, trying to be decent, but beneath the façade full of contempt and wanting only to be among their own. What the hell was the matter with them? Jesus Christ, she was pregnant. She was having his grandchild and he wanted to know what 'it' was as though he was talking about a dog? Really, what the hell was the matter with him?

It was only after Laurie was born that she felt inclined to ask her husband if it might be all right for her mother to sometimes come to the house instead of them always meeting in town. Twice now, Laurie had screamed down the restaurant at Harvey Nichols, but she also saw no reason why her mother should continue to be inconvenienced simply because of her father's ignorance. Her husband had no problem with the suggestion, but when she brought this up with her mother, as they sat together in Hyde Park, her mother's eyes remained focused on the carry-cot and she continued to play with her grandson. Annabelle held out a hand for rain was now falling through the trees, but in drops so fine that it felt as though they were being sprinkled with dew. Eventually her mother looked up at her and told Annabelle, in a semi-whispered voice, that she didn't think that this would be a good idea, and so Annabelle decided not to pursue the topic. When Laurie was five, and had started to go to school, mother and daughter began once again to meet without the child being present. It was then that she noticed that a considerable loneliness seemed to have descended on to her mother's shoulders. At first she thought it was just age, and that doting upon her grandson had been keeping her young. However, it soon became clear that, beyond the subject of Laurie, there was nothing occurring in her mother's life that she might transmute into the raw material of conversation. She worried about her, but realised that the best thing that she could offer her was time with her grandson, which suited Laurie for he loved being spoiled by his grandmother. During school holidays, she often let them spend an afternoon together at the zoo or at the pictures, and before Grandma got on the train to go back to the country she always made sure that her excited grandson was laden down with sweets. As he grew older, Laurie began to wonder aloud why Grandma never came to the house, or why Daddy never came to wave goodbye to Grandma at Paddington station, and then he began to ask his increasingly frail grandmother questions about her husband which she found difficult to field. By the time Laurie was ten, his grandmother's trips to London were becoming infrequent, and Annabelle decided that she had to talk with her husband about the situation. Much to her surprise it was he who suggested that they should make a daytrip to Wiltshire and give Laurie the chance to meet his grandfather before it was too late.

That evening, Annabelle called her mother and said that they were thinking of motoring down on Sunday. There was a long silence on the other end of the telephone and then Annabelle heard her mother's hesitant voice.

'Sunday?' She paused. 'This Sunday?'

Again Annabelle repeated the plan, stressing the fact that Keith would be driving the car so that there could be no misunderstanding as to what she was proposing. There was another long silence and a worried Annabelle felt compelled to ask, 'Are you there, Mummy?' She heard her mother cough quietly and then pull herself together.

'Yes, dear, of course I'm here. And Sunday should be fine, but I've been meaning to tell you, Annabelle, that things with your father are a little difficult. Apparently the doctor thinks he might have the dreaded big "c". She paused. 'Cancer. Of the lungs, he says, but that doesn't make any sense for your father hasn't smoked a cigarette since he left the army, and that was aeons ago.'

On the journey down from London, Annabelle kept twisting around in her seat and dabbing Germolene on Laurie's bruised lip where the boy who had called him a 'halfie' had hit him. Clearly, Laurie didn't like his mother's attention, so he kept squirming away from her and jiggling the packet of sunflower seeds that he had bought as a present for his grandmother. He was excited that they were finally going to visit Grandma's home, where he would also meet his grandfather, but even happier to know that she had a big garden, as opposed to their own tiny one, and lots of space in which she could plant flowers. Annabelle had just helped Laurie with a school project on the different uses of sunflowers, and because the teacher had told him that sunflowers needed a lot of space to grow Laurie had decided that he wanted to bring sunflower seeds for Grandma. When Laurie dropped off to sleep, Annabelle finally had the opportunity to tell her husband what she had wanted to say since he had suggested that they make this trip. First, she wanted to apologise again for what she had done all those years earlier when she had lied to him about going to the theatre, but more importantly, even at this late stage, she wanted to let him know that she really didn't need to see her father again. His use of the term 'nigger-lover', while knowing that she had an unborn child in her body, had irreparably broken something between them. As she sat and cried on the platform at Ashleigh station, and waited for the train that would take her back to London, she had finally come to accept that her father was weak, pathetic even, and she felt not a jot of hostility towards him. In fact, once the flood of tears had subsided, she finally understood that what she felt towards him was a remote indifference, which she knew she could cope with. However, what caused her a real shock was the realisation that she was experiencing a rising tide of admiration for her mother who stoically, over the years, had been living with a man she feared, and for whom she clearly had little affection.

Annabelle looked across the table at her gaunt father, who was propped up under a heavy blanket that reached to his chest, then at her husband, and then she stood up and left the two men at the table and joined her mother in the kitchen. Her mother passed her a wooden mallet and Annabelle slapped a bulb of garlic and watched as the cloves collapsed into a flower. Through the window they could both see Laurie on the expansive back lawn, wheeling around in circles and chasing butterflies. Back in the living room, neither man would look at the other. Annabelle's father pointed out of the window towards Laurie.

'How old is the boy now?'

'Ten. He was ten last month.'

'I see.' Annabelle's father began to nod as though approving of the fact that his grandson had crossed this threshold. 'And the name, Laurie. Is that with a "w" or with a "u," because there are two ways of spelling the word, or so I'm led to believe.'

'It's with a "u". We named him after Laurie Cunningham.' He paused and looked at his father-in-law, whose strangely dull eyes seemed to have lost their ability to reflect light. He felt sorry for him, for the man seemed to be permanently thrashing about in his mind. 'He was a footballer who I used to like a lot. He played for England, but died young in a car crash. In Spain in the late eighties, I think.'

'I see. Did you know the chap?'

'Know him? You mean personally?'

'Was he a chum?'

'I didn't know him, but Annabelle and I both liked the name.'

'Well, given the bruise on the boy's face perhaps you should have named him after a boxer. Henry, maybe. He's got to learn to stand up for himself. No feather-bedding. People can be very cruel, you do understand that, don't you?'

Through the window he could see his son charging happily about the vast expanse of the cottage's neatly manicured lawn.

'Yes,' he said, transferring his attention to his ailing father-in-law. 'I have some understanding of how cruel people can be.'

'Well jolly good. I'm pleased to hear it.' For a moment they were enveloped in a cheerless silence that was punctuated by the sound from the kitchen of clean cutlery being dropped into the appropriate sections of the silverware drawer. 'Now then, you do love my daughter, don't you? I mean really love her.'

As the train leaves Ladbroke Grove station and begins to sweep left in a wide arc towards Latimer Road, he notices that most of the empty carriage seats are covered in discarded crisp packets, empty cans of Coke, and abandoned free newspapers. Kids, he thinks. Every day now he witnesses packs of these youngsters on the street, or on the tube, or on the buses, swearing and carrying on with a sense of entitlement that is palpably absurd. Each of them seems to believe that he or she is an 'achiever', and that they deserve nothing less than what they call 'maximum respect'. Thank God, Laurie isn't like this, although Annabelle appears to be increasingly concerned by his behaviour. He has tried to explain to her that all teenage boys go through some form of rebellion, and that she shouldn't take Laurie's surliness as evidence of anything more than his ongoing, turbulent, passage out of childhood and into the no man's land of young adulthood. The urgency of Annabelle's recent messages speaks both to her disappointment with him as a husband and father, and to her concern for their son, although he senses that some other anxiety is troubling her which she will most likely never reveal to him or, he suspects, to this new friend, Bruce. He stands to get off the train and he glances again at the old lady, who appears to have neither accepted nor totally rejected the ill-manners of the teenagers, but rather to have achieved an enviable place of quiet serenity. She raises her eyes to meet his own, and she smiles. As the train pulls away he can see her, still smiling at him, through the filthy carriage window.

He steps out of the tube station and into the frigid November air. It is Sunday evening, so the traffic is not nearly as heavy as it might be on a weekday, but he assumes that there must have been a gig at the Empire for people are impatiently sounding their horns and he can see that there's some kind of bottleneck at the round-about. Across the street he sees the blue and white neon lights of the new Cineplex that he once went to with Yvette. He cannot remember the name of the romantic comedy that they sat through, for he fell asleep soon after the opening credits. After the film, her sullen silence at Pizza Express spoke volumes about her sense of disappointment. The trip to the cinema took place before he began visiting her north London terraced home, so in a sense she had no right to be irritated with him. As he forked the last slice of margarita into his mouth, he looked across the table at her but she would not meet his eyes. For Christ's sake, he thought, these things happen and it was hardly a criticism of her. She, more than anybody else, should understand that he has been working hard, and he was just tired, and that's all there is to it. End of story. As the waitress placed the stainless steel tray which held the bill to the side of his now empty plate, he reached for his credit card and wished that she would get over her disgruntle-ment and grow up. Her sullen demeanour had managed to cast a cloud over a perfectly nice evening and a pretty good pizza. He turns towards Uxbridge Road, and wonders how the atmosphere will be when Yvette comes to work in the morning. He had tried to explain to her that all he wanted was for things to return to how they used to be before they got involved, but as he nervously redistributed his weight on the designer barstool, then sipped at his warm white wine, the look on her face made it clear that she was in no mood to end their arrangement amicably.

He dashes across Uxbridge Road before reaching the pedestrian crossing, and moves towards the building society cash machine. He really doesn't need any hassle at work, especially not now when the local authority seem determined to make his life an administrative nightmare by merging his Race Equality unit with Disability and Women's Affairs. He was pleased when Clive Wilson called him in and told him that as the chief executive he had decided that a certain Mr Keith Gordon should be the one to head up the merger, for it meant more money, a bigger office, and double the number of staff to manage. He soon discovered that it also meant learning about the problems of wheelchair accessibility, understanding why rape crisis centres could not be funded if they excluded male rape, coming to terms with the irony of being an able-bodied black man speaking on behalf of disabled white people, and being the highly visible male spokesperson for feminist groups, many of whom appeared to despise men. The workload was such that it was no longer possible for him to leave the office early and go back to the flat and work on his book. These days it was also unlikely that having surreptitiously scanned *Time Out* or the *Guardian* and discovered that some refugee from the seventies such as George Clinton or Sly Stone was playing in Tooting or Brixton, he could just shoot off early from work and go down to the gig with his notebook. After the announcement of the merger, most evenings were taken up with his trying to digest the contents of thousands of pages of printed policy reports, and then adding to the rubbish with short directives of his own. Then he noticed Yvette, who had recently been recruited as a research assistant in his unit. As he tried to tell her over pizza, he didn't fall asleep at the cinema because he was bored, but because these days he simply has too much work to do and he often finds himself still awake at two o'clock in the morning trying to make sense of endless reams of local government bureaucracy.

He grabs the five £20 notes and tucks them into his wallet before slipping the thick wad back into his pocket. A sudden gust catches an abandoned newspaper and it begins to fly in all directions. He kicks away a few pages that are swirling around his feet and begins to move off in the direction of his flat. There are very few people out walking on this windy Sunday night, and he imagines that most folks are sensibly at home watching television or already safely tucked up in bed and getting ready for another week of work. For over twenty years he shared a front door with Annabelle, which meant that there was always a good chance that he would not be coming home to an empty house. The lights would be on, and the smell of cooking would have permeated the flat or the house, and perhaps there would also be the sound of music blaring out. After graduation they had decided to stay in Bristol, and so they moved out of their respective halls of residence and into a slightly damp one-bedroom flat in the supposedly respectable Clifton district. He accepted a job in the black community of St Paul's, and Annabelle also successfully applied for a position in social work, although her own particular focus was single women and violent men. After a difficult pre-graduation dinner with her mother and father, Annabelle had decided not to apply for any jobs in publishing, which would have meant moving to London and perhaps spending the occasional weekend in Wiltshire with her parents. At the dinner, she finally introduced her boyfriend of two years to them, but having witnessed her father's behaviour Annabelle had decided that there was nothing further to be gained by trying to be diplomatic. They had forced a choice upon her, and so she had chosen. The idea of moving into social work interested her, and it seemed practical given her boyfriend's vocation but, after four years in Bristol, Annabelle felt burned out and in need of a change.

They were offered a husband and wife job in residential care in Birmingham and, without even thinking about it, they went one morning to a registry office in Bristol and asked two guests who were there for the wedding before their own if they would stay on for a few minutes and be witnesses. The registrar would not look them in the face, and the man's hand shook as he turned the book around for them to sign. Having blotted the ink dry, the registrar handed the certificate to the husband, who quickly folded it in half and gave it to Annabelle, who pushed it into her handbag. They then drove out to a country pub for a celebratory lunch that soon descended into silence. He knew that as happy as Annabelle was with him there was no getting around the fact that Annabelle's parents had 'let her go', and that he had no real family to offer her as a substitute. After two difficult years in Birmingham, a city they both loathed as much for the grating accent as the labyrinth-like city centre, it was he who suggested that they move to London and that Annabelle might consider switching careers and trying to get a job in the media. They had saved enough to put down a small deposit and buy their first property, a tidy Victorian terraced house by the village common in an unfashionably scruffy part of west London, and while he took up his new job as a community liaison officer for the local authority, Annabelle found employment reading scripts for a theatrical agency who, as though already anticipating how her life would develop as both she and her husband now closed in on thirty, suggested that she could work some days from home. Three years later, and only months after Mrs Thatcher was finally removed from office, Laurie was born. In addition to the house being filled with the aroma of cooking, and the sound of music, there was now the babble of a newborn child and the breathless gunfire of his excitable laughter.

By the time young Laurie found words, his father was pouring most of his energy into the local authority's nascent Race Equality unit, which he one day hoped to lead. Laurie's words soon took the form of a mild interrogation as he learned to ask, 'Where have you been, Daddy?' and 'What did you do today, Daddy?' and then eventually, 'You're not going out again are you, Daddy?', and Annabelle would shush him while chopping carrots, or basting a chicken, or pushing her fingers into a batch of buns to see if they were ready. As he invested increasing amounts of time in his work, Annabelle's supply of scripts and freelance work started to dry up, but it appeared to him that she had plenty to occupy herself with coping with Laurie and trying to be a pillar of support for her mother whose devotion to her grandson was genuine but, according to Annabelle, masked an increasingly obvious gaping void at the heart of her own life. He could see that Annabelle was struggling to cope with her own family situation and he was actively looking for an opportunity to help her to heal the rift. In the meantime, although he occasionally felt guilty for not being around the home more often, he had to admit that he was enjoying the new work opportunities to travel to conferences and make presentations, junkets which gave him a sense of having reclaimed some of his independence.

The wind continues to gust, and as he makes his way along Uxbridge Road he turns up the collar on his jacket and leans slightly into the gale. He can hear dustbins being turned over, and up ahead of him a row of decorative plastic pennants which have been strung up outside a petrol station look as though they, and the flimsy piece of rope to which they have been affixed, are about to fly clear of the forecourt. Then he feels suddenly overwhelmed by panic and checks that the wallet with the five £20 notes is still in his pocket. As he nears his street, he rues the fact that, having left the family home, he has found it difficult to enjoy his new freedom for he has never been able fully to reconcile himself to the fact that each time he arrives back at the rented flat it will be a cold beginning. He has to switch on the lights, he has to turn on the heat, draw the curtains, warm up the place, select the music, and create some atmosphere. He has almost forgotten what it feels like to slide into a body-warmed bed. Three years ago, it was entirely up to him to transform the empty flat into a place that he could relax in, but it soon became apparent that there were aspects of the shared responsibility of marriage that he was going to miss desperately. Before turning into his street, he decides to stop at the pub for a quick drink. His local is one of the few pubs left in west London that has refused to capitulate to the sawdust-on-the-floor and alcopop trend, so at the best of times there are only a handful of ageing drinkers in the place. However, the melancholy, almost nostalgic, ambience of the Queen Caroline seems, these days, to match his own mood.

He carries his pint of Australian lager across to the jukebox, rummages around in his trouser pockets for some money, slots in the £1 coins, and then taps out the song numbers. The jukebox is a relic from an earlier period, as are the singles that will eventually swing into place. Bob Marley, Barry White, the Isley Brothers, the Clash, the Specials, and Stevie Wonder. He smiles to himself realising how helplessly he has become a creature of habit, for these are probably the same six songs that he chose the last time he ventured into this pub. As 'No Woman, No Cry' begins slowly to crescendo and energise the musty atmosphere of the public bar, he picks up his pint and tucks himself behind a circular wooden table in the furthest corner of the empty room. The upholstered bench is dirty, and the shabby fabric needs to be either cleaned or replaced, but from this vantage point he is able to monitor the door and observe everything that might occur in the pub. In this sense, he is in control, which is precisely what Yvette accused him of needing to be.

She covered her glass with the top of her hand, and then she watched as he decided to pour himself another drink and quickly took a sip. She pulled at the collar of her turtleneck sweater, as though suddenly afflicted with a flush of heat, and she smiled and told him that the one thing she had learned from her break-up with Colin was that men who rigorously police the boundaries of their lives are always looking outwards. According to her, such men don't seem to understand that whatever it is they have inside is most probably wilting, or even dying, because they are refusing to take the time to nourish their inner selves.

'You think I sound like some new-age imbecile, don't you? You don't have to say anything, I can tell by the way you're just staring at me.'

He put down the glass of wine and reached out to cup her hands with his, but she withdrew so abruptly that her whole body snapped away from him.

'What's the matter? I only want to hold your hands.'

'Keith, don't treat me like I'm stupid, okay. All this bullshit about how I'm too young, and I work for you, and we don't have enough in common. You've got it all worked out in your head like it's some bleeding presentation that you're giving. Doesn't it matter to you that I really care, and that I'd actually like this to work out? It's not as if I've been with any other blokes since Colin left. And, in case you've forgotten, it was you who asked me out, remember?'

'Listen, I'm not arguing with any of what you're saying. And you're right, since I split up with Annabelle I have been a bit more stand-offish and vigilant, if you like. I suppose it's only natural that once you get your freedom back you want to protect it.'

'So what are you saying?'

'I suppose I'm saying that policing my borders is a good way of putting it, but I don't want to be like that.'

'So what's the problem?'

'The problem is I can't just suddenly let my guard down and get involved in something serious.'

'So you don't think I'm serious?'

'Of course you are. Listen, Yvette, I think you're great.'

'But you're finishing with me.'

'I told you, it's not going anywhere, how can it?'

'Well why didn't you think of that before you fucked me?'

For a moment he thinks about refilling his glass, for she has finally hit a nerve.

Yes, he had been secretly looking at her, but it was actually Yvette who had asked him if he wanted to go out to the cinema, and a week or so later, when she had finally forgiven him for falling asleep, it was she who suggested that he visit her north London home. He could have said 'no' and not gone to the cinema with her, and he could have made up some plausible excuse and not visited her home. But he liked her and he wanted to sleep with her, and he was curious to know if she wanted to sleep with him, which it soon transpired she did. It was a bit much suggesting that he was the only one responsible. Rather than give voice to these thoughts, he deemed it best to leave while there was still some vestige of civility about their discussion. He pushed his glass away from himself, then slid from the barstool and started to edge his way towards the hallway.

'Listen, it's getting late so I'd better go.'

Yvette shook her head in disbelief.

'So that's it then, you want to just end it like this?'

He quickly licked his dry lips and then shrugged his shoulders. This degree of indignation was not something that he had anticipated.

'Listen, let's just leave it. We can talk about it later, okay? I probably need to do some thinking.'

Yvette held on to the counter top with both hands, and then

she stepped down from the barstool and caterpillared her bare feet into her fluffy carpet slippers.

'So what do you think's going to happen now, Keith?'

'Listen, Yvette, I've no idea what you're talking about.'

'Well you had better go then, hadn't you.'

'Look, I'm really sorry about everything.'

Yvette moved swiftly past him and into the hallway, where she yanked open the door.

'Just fuck off, Keith. I don't like being used. Colin tried and it didn't work.'

He could hear birds twittering in the small front garden, and then a sputtering car attempted to change gears as it passed by. He looked into Yvette's fiery green eyes, but it clearly didn't make any sense to linger.

'I'm sorry, Yvette. Really.'

He felt the rush of air behind him, and then he heard the crash of the door as it slammed shut. He stood still, shocked at the fury that he had unleashed. Carefully buttoning up his jacket against the early evening chill, he began to walk quickly back in the direction of the tube station.

The music has stopped, so he feels in his pocket for more change and then stands and crosses towards the jukebox. He selects the same artists, but different tracks, beginning with Bob Marley's 'Exodus'. He sits back in his corner and nurses the third of a pint that he still has in his glass, having decided not to bother topping it up with another half. The music is good, but there's no escaping the fact that the pub is dismal. His mind revisits the problems of work, and the policy report on trans-racial adoption that his department is supposed to produce by the end of the week, and he shakes his head. After many years working in the Race Equality unit, during which time he has contributed to drawers and cabinets crammed with spurious material associated with countless quickly forgotten initiatives, he has no appetite left for reading, let alone producing, these meaningless policy reports. Twenty-five years ago, when he was leaving Bristol University, he thought differently. The urban insurrections, or riots as the media liked to call them, which punctuated his days as a student, convinced him that staying on and doing graduate work would almost certainly prove to be a frustrating waste of time. He already understood that while he would be bashing the books in the university library, out there on the streets there were youths who looked just like him who were being brutalised and beaten by Maggie Thatcher's police. His generation of kids, who were born in Britain and who had no memory of any kind of tropical life before England, were clearly trying hard to make a space for themselves in a not always welcoming country. Back then that's how it seemed to him, and that's how he tried to explain it to Annabelle's father when he and his wife took the young couple to dinner at the Madras Bicycle Club shortly before they graduated.

He had been warned, for when he and Annabelle went for coffee after the Tennessee Williams play, she had confessed to him that her father could be a 'difficult' man. She told her new friend that her father was an ex-army officer who had resigned his commission because he was distressed at having to associate with fellow officers who he regarded as being a cut below by birth, but who behaved as though they were a cut above by divine right. Her father had used his old school tie contacts and forged a successful career for himself in banking, but he had recently retired to the tranquillity of the countryside. 'I'm it,' she said, 'the only child they were able to have so they dote on me, but they also kind of resent me a little for not being two, or even three, and that way they wouldn't have had to put all their eggs in the potentially disappointing Annabelle basket. Of course, he wanted a boy, so the daddy's little girl thing never really worked for me.' He listened to Annabelle, but he found it difficult to hear anything that she was saying for he couldn't take his eyes from her stunning, almost perfectly oval face. Her wispy brown hair was tied back with an elastic band, although unruly strands sprouted out from all sides so that the overall effect was a weird bohemian self-possession. When he entered into the second year of the sixth form he had a girlfriend of sorts, but that solitary relationship was more about sexual confidence-building than any kind of affection, or even attraction, and once he was accepted at university their friendship gradually petered out. For most of his first year at university his energies had been thoroughly invested in football and drinking, and the notion of pulling a bird seemed so vaguely remote that he spent a great deal of time affecting a lack of interest. However, from the moment during the interval of *Sweet Bird of Youth* when the girl looked up from her theatre programme and leaned across the empty seat between them and asked him if he was enjoying the play, he was intrigued. At the end of the performance, as they were both putting on their coats, he found the courage to ask her if she was a student, and she not only told him 'yes', she also scribbled down her name and the number of the phone in her hall of residence and handed the piece of paper to him saying, 'I thought I was the only one who went to see Tennessee Williams's plays on my own.' As she smiled and turned to leave, he heard the words emerge of their own volition. 'Would you like to have a coffee?'

Two days before the end of his first year at university, he waited for Annabelle outside Lecture Theatre One in the English department, and showed her the letter which effectively undid his summer plans. Despite Brenda's urgings, he had consistently made it clear to her that he had no interest in spending the summer building any kind of a relationship with his father, for he felt that the effort should be coming in the other direction. In fact, he had already made plans to spend the late summer travelling around Europe on the trains. The university authorities had agreed that he could stay in the halls throughout the early summer, and so he had set himself up with a part-time job pumping petrol in a garage on the edge of the campus. He reckoned that by mid-August he would have saved enough money to fund a month of Inter-Railing, and perhaps have enough left over to be able to spend maybe another two weeks in Spain, or Portugal, or anywhere that was warm and cheap. After he and Annabelle had shared their first hot and stuffy night squeezed up tight in his single bed, he asked her if she wanted to join him 'on the road'. She laughed and wondered if he was deliberately trying to sound like a hippie, but before he could answer she said 'yes,' she would love to join him but she would have to meet him in late August as her father had fixed up a job for her as a lowly dogsbody at the *Wiltshire Times* so she could acquire some journalism experience. However, just as he was beginning to feel happy and safe with their arrangements, everything came apart when he got the letter from Brenda. He walked over to the English department, and once Annabelle had read the letter he explained to her that this woman had pretty much raised him by herself and that if she needed his help then he had to be there for her as she didn't really have anybody else in her life. Annabelle nodded and smiled. He assumed that she might be annoyed because he was changing their summer plans, but she slipped her arm through his and laughed. 'Listen,' she said, 'we can do it next year. Europe will still be there. If she's become ill then you must go and be with her. Maybe you could take me too, or maybe I can come and visit when it's convenient?'

Two years later, as they stood on the threshold of graduation, they were an inseparable couple. They both realised that it wasn't going to be possible to go forward with their lives until the situation with Annabelle's parents had been confronted. It was Annabelle's mother who telephoned her hall of residence and suggested that they would like to come up and take her for a pre-graduation dinner, and when Annabelle made it clear that she would not be alone she heard her mother's flustered voice agree wholeheartedly that she must, of course, bring her 'friend'. She left the choice of restaurant up to Annabelle, and then began to babble unceasingly, leaping from one topic to another, as though terrified to submit to a lull in conversation. The young couple decided upon the Madras Bicycle Club which was Indian colonial in décor, but the cuisine was far more eclectic. As he sat on the bed in Annabelle's room, and watched as she put on her lipstick in the mirror, he had a sense of foreboding about the forthcoming meal with her parents for he knew that his girlfriend had been struggling with a kind of double life for the past two years. 'Well,' said Annabelle, dropping the cylinder of lipstick back into her handbag and then turning to face him. 'I'm ready if you are.' They had been in the restaurant once before, when Annabelle's Wordsworth and Shelley tutor had missed two tutorials because of a three-week fellowship in California and wanted to make it up in some way. While that meal had passed off pleasantly enough, and Dr Stewart had treated them more like colleagues than students, the evening with Annabelle's parents began ominously with Mr Johnson, having limply shaken hands with him, being visibly reluctant to make eye contact with anybody at the table. However, by the time he had downed his third Scotch and water, and the servers had cleared the main course plates from the table, he had introduced finger-wagging into his conversational style and decided to redirect his hostility away from his daughter and towards her boyfriend. Her father practically demanded of him that he take responsibility for his people's 'ill manners'. 'You're rather like the Irish aren't you, with loud voices that get on one's nerves and always protesting about what exactly? Mind you, at least you people are not bombing innocent civilians. Well, not yet.' When he tried to explain to Mr Johnson the frustrations of his generation, the man laughed in his face and signalled to the waitress to bring another drink. A mortified Annabelle attempted to intervene and support her boyfriend's argument, but when she was shouted down she simply removed her mother's hand from her arm and left the table. Having neatly folded his napkin, he asked to be excused and climbed to his feet. He found a distraught Annabelle outside, standing bareheaded in the rain on the pavement in front of the restaurant. 'I can't believe my bloody mother. She actually leaned over and whispered to me, "He seems like a nice boy." I mean, in the face of his ranting and raving, that's the best she could come up with? Whispering to me.' He held Annabelle's hand for a few moments, and then he dried her tears with the back of his hand and realised for the first time that Annabelle was more than just a girlfriend. Standing in the rain outside the Madras Bicycle Club it occurred to him that he was probably going to know this young woman for the rest of his life. He looked at her, then slipped an arm around her shoulders and tried to persuade her that she should return to the table.

Although the rest of the meal was a predictable failure of communication, he now clearly understood why local authorities up and down the country had started advertising for race relations liaison officers, people who could help explain black anger to white people, and white liberal do-gooding to disgruntled black people, although he knew that anybody reckless enough to attempt to explain anything to Annabelle's father risked incurring the full force of his smug indignation. Had he not been in a hurry to leave the table and comfort his girlfriend, he might well have continued and calmly explained to Mr Johnson that because he believed that he might be able to help people understand one another, he had put aside all thoughts of a Ph.D. and had recently started to apply for jobs in social work. While most of his fellow students had no idea of what they were going to do upon graduation in a couple of weeks' time, he was suddenly aware that he had the opposite problem.

He had filled out six application forms and had been offered six jobs, which was far too much choice, for location aside, the job descriptions and the respective starting salaries seemed pretty much the same. That night, after Annabelle's parents had left, and she had come back to his room and finally stopped crying and apologising, he gently changed the subject so that they were soon talking about where they might relocate after graduation. It soon became clear that Annabelle would go wherever he wanted. He told her that now that he had a selection of jobs from which to choose, his only restriction was that he didn't see any reason to go north and back in the direction of his father, particularly as he no longer had Brenda. By the time they cuddled up together in his single bed, they had pretty much decided to stay where they were and accept the job that he had been offered in Bristol. Not only was it a place they both knew, but things being what they were in the city they assumed, rightly as it turned out, that Annabelle would have little difficulty in also getting a social work traineeship with the local authority. As he drains what remains of his pint, he now remembers that rather than spending his Sunday night in the pub he should be at the flat reading up and preparing notes in order that he might begin drafting his department's policy report regarding the supposedly ethical question as to whether or not a white couple should be allowed to adopt a black child, but he knows that this is a banal place, intellectually and professionally, for him to find himself marooned in after all these years of white collar bondage. The lilting strains of Stevie Wonder's 'Living for the City' start to fade, and then he listens carefully as the clanking arm levers the seven-inch disc back into place before he stands and eases his way out from behind the circular wooden table.

In the fridge at his flat in Wilton Road, there is an apple, a carton of yoghurt, and two bottles of white wine, one of which is uncorked but still three-quarters full. He balances awkwardly on one leg and holds open the fridge door with his knee while he pours a glass. When he bought the fridge he failed to notice that the door was hinged on the left-hand side. The two Nigerian guys from the superstore had already finished installing it, and were lingering by the front door waiting for their tip, when he saw what the problem was. He asked them if they could help him out and change the door around, but they laughed and said, 'it ain't our job, mate' and then insisted that they were in a hurry because Arsenal were playing at home. He had left his tools at Annabelle's house so he had no choice but to make an excursion to the local hardware shop and buy a small screwdriver kit. When he returned he cleared a space and wrestled the fridge down and on to its back. To begin with he carefully followed the instructions in the manual, but after a while, feeling that he had got the hang of it, he stopped looking at the small booklet. Eventually he hoisted the fridge back upright, and although the door was now hinged to the right it didn't stay when opened: slowly, but determinedly, the door began to swing back closed. However, he judged the operation to be something of a success and decided that later on, if it didn't settle down, he could always look again at the manual and if necessary troubleshoot the problem.

But he has never re-read the manual, and occasionally when he goes to the fridge he has to practise what feels like a yoga position in order to return an item to a shelf. He sits on the sofa in the semi-gloom and sips at his wine. A car alarm begins to wail beneath his window, but he assumes that it has been triggered by the wind. The flat was unfurnished, so he had to buy everything at Ikea, although Annabelle did offer him one or two pieces from the house. He politely refused, for once he realised that Annabelle was not going to change her mind and take him back he decided that he would rather make a clean break. However, he did take the two poster-sized black and white photographs of Billie Holiday and Miles Davis, even though they had bought these items together. After a week living in a Travelodge out towards Heathrow, and attempting, and failing, to work out how to operate the toaster oven in the kitchenette section of his suite, he was relieved to be given a lead on a flat that was less than a mile from Annabelle and Laurie where he might finally establish some kind of domestic order. The lettings agency down the street from his office had called to let him know that a clean and tidy new conversion had just become available and, as long as he was willing to pay slightly above market rent, and three months' key money in advance, he could move in at the weekend. When he telephoned Annabelle, she announced that she and Laurie would be visiting her mother on Saturday afternoon, so this would be a good time for him to come round and get his things. During the following few weeks he worried that she might question him about the two missing posters, but Annabelle never mentioned a thing. She would eventually redecorate their home, and he imagined that framed photographs of American jazz musicians would probably play no part in Annabelle's design scheme. On their final night under the same roof, as he lay on the sofa and tried again to fathom what on earth had made him 'confess' to his only act of infidelity, he pictured Annabelle upstairs busily planning her Keith-free life. He lay awake for hours hoping that she would miss him, but he had no confidence that she would. In the morning, a resolutely silent Annabelle drove Laurie off to school in her hatchback, and then presumably continued on to her new job at the BBC. Meanwhile, he knotted his tie and took one final look around what had been his home before pulling shut the door behind him and heading off towards Hammersmith Grove and in the direction of the office and then, at the end of the day, on to a depressing Travelodge.

That was three years ago, and as he cradles the wine glass in his hand, and stares out through the uncurtained windows at the dark shadows of the trees that line his street, he thinks once more that he may have cheated on Annabelle for the flimsiest of reasons; perhaps he simply wanted to know what it felt like to be single again. Of course, most men in his position have the common sense just to have an affair and keep quiet about it, or arrange to go on a trip by themselves for a week or two. He knows this now because in the past couple of years he has felt moved to flip through the problem pages of *GQ* or *Esquire*, or whatever men's magazine happens to be handy while he is killing time in the waiting room of his doctor or dentist. The magazines address the surprisingly common occurrence of male forty-something panic by insisting that the victim keep his big mouth shut and simply wait for the storm clouds to pass. However, the fact that he actually confessed suggests to him that a deeper malaise was being expressed by his single act of infidelity, and his confusion might well have benefited from some constructive discussion with his wife. But Annabelle's unforgiving response would admit no conversation, and she immediately closed down any possibility of dialogue on the subject of how he felt or what had motivated him to sleep with his co-worker. His wife had been betrayed and clearly she was in no mood to compromise. Having ushered him out of their house, Annabelle not only secured a promotion and landed a production assistant's job at BBC Television Centre, she began to repair her relationship with her mother and became a regular weekend visitor at her mother's assisted-living home. Then, about a year ago, she announced to him that she was seeing a film editor named Bruce who was four years younger than her and who might, from time to time, be spending the night at the house. This being the case, she wanted her estranged husband to meet the man who might have some kind of a role in his son's life, and she suggested that all three of them have dinner.

He remembers standing at his own front door, clutching a bottle of wine and feeling apprehensive about how the evening was going to unfold. Eventually a flustered Annabelle opened the door and ushered him through and into the kitchen where he could see three fish crisping in a skillet, their silver skins curling at the edges and the flesh browning quickly. Annabelle had waited until half-term, when she knew that Laurie would be away on a geography field trip in Swanage, before announcing that she would make supper for them all and keep things simple and informal. He looked closely at her as she grabbed the skillet from the stove and recoiled slightly as oil began to spatter up towards her face. He noticed that she seized the pan with her now empty ring hand and he felt a brief surge of resentment. Annabelle didn't seem to be ageing, in fact if anything she appeared to be getting younger and he wasn't sure how he felt about this. Bruce, however, looked decidedly older than forty-three, and as the man stuffed a handful of peanuts into his mouth he realised that his wife's friend had a very unappealing habit of speaking with his mouth full. Bruce's shirt was open at the collar and his sleeves were rolled up, and he noticed that the man had deliberately left a pile of papers and some DVDs scattered on the kitchen table. Bruce was marking his territory, and before either man had a chance to refill his glass he began to do the same thing conversationally. Annabelle's friend leaned across the table and picked up one of the DVDs, announcing that he was editing a major documentary series about the three waves of immigration to Britain during the past decade. He confessed to Bruce that he didn't know that there had been three waves, and Bruce seized the opening and began to explain. What felt like an age later, Bruce concluded his lecture with a flourish. 'You see the asylum-seekers, and those migrants from the subcontinent who come here to marry their cousins, they have every right to be here no matter how hard some of us may find it to accept them. But this cheap Eastern European labour in the wake of EU expansion, well to Old Labour men like myself this just doesn't seem fair.' He listened to Bruce but said nothing, and then he glanced up at the clock as he tried to work out what time they might be eating. Annabelle rescued the situation by picking up the grater and handing it to the speechmaker. 'Bruce, you're on cheese duty. Come along, chop, chop.' Not only did this intervention have the desired effect of sidetracking Bruce out of his conversational comfort zone, it also allowed the man the opportunity to demonstrate his inability to grate Parmesan cheese. However, what really caught his attention was the fact that Annabelle had obviously recently acquired a kind of singsong delivery to her speech, and as he listened to her he realised the degree to which his wife was slowly, despite her youthful looks, becoming her mother.

Outside in the street a car backfires, and then he hears the sound of breaking glass. A visitor might be perturbed by these noises, but he has become accustomed to such nocturnal intrusions. He knows that he is safe in the flat, although sometimes he feels lonely. However, he was never lonelier than the night following dinner with Bruce and Annabelle when he had to walk home by himself and try hard not to imagine Annabelle in bed with her film editor friend. She never again suggested that all three of them get together and, in fact, these days she seldom mentions Bruce. Laurie never mentions him at all, and the one time he pressed his son on the subject Laurie just sucked his teeth and called him 'the dry guy'. Again he hears a car in the street backfire, and it occurs to him that perhaps this was not a car backfiring after all. When he last travelled north to see his father he told him about the rise in gun violence on the streets of London, but his father had just turned away from him and shrugged his shoulders. That was four years ago, and in the interim their infrequent phone conversations have been similarly frustrating. It was Annabelle who had encouraged him to be more understanding, and who had sought to remind him that for the greater part of his father's adult life the man had been either hospitalised or struggling in his mind. Despite Annabelle's entreaties, he has found it difficult to be always sympathetic towards somebody whose stubborn behaviour so successfully obscures whatever sensitive or vulnerable qualities he may possess. Most of the time it simply doesn't seem to be worth the effort. He puts down his glass on the coffee table and goes into the kitchen to the fridge, where he tugs open the door and removes the open bottle of wine from the top shelf. He returns to the sofa and refills his glass and then puts the bottle on the floor so that it won't mark the table. Were Brenda still alive he feels that she would be sympathetic with regard to some of the recent decisions, and mistakes, that he has made in his life, but he is reasonably certain that his father's response would be judgmental. This being the case, he is right to be cautious in his dealings with his father and share little, for even though he is content once again to be in contact with him, it is exhausting to constantly negotiate the emotional mood swings of this unpredictable man and his demons. He notices that there is only a little wine left in the bottle so he decides to drain it. The wine will help him sleep and encourage him to forget the unpleasantness of being exposed to Yvette's fury. He hears shouting and hands clapping, and he slumps back into the sofa as he realises that it is just the young couple in the ground floor flat hoping to send a cat scurrying into the night.

The following morning he senses that something has changed. As he walks into the office, his secretary glances up at him from behind the computer on her desk, but she doesn't say anything. Ruth looks alarmed, and she furtively clicks the mouse and changes the image on her screen.

'Morning, Ruth.'

'Yeah, good morning, Mr Gordon.'

'Everything all right, is it? You look like you're up to no good.

And before you ask, I haven't finished the trans-racial adoption thing, so if anyone asks feel free to give them the runaround.'

Ruth picks up a pencil and begins tapping it nervously against the side of her desk.

'Mr Gordon, I think you should check out your email.'

'My email?'

'I'd check it out if I were you.'

He shrugs and walks past her and into his office, swings the briefcase up on to the desk, and then punches on his computer and watches as the screen flickers and buzzes to life. He shouts through the open door.

'Ruth, any messages?'

'Not really.'

'Not really? What's that supposed to mean?'

'Mr Wilson said he'd like to see you. In his office.'

He clicks on his email account.

'Any particular time?'

He does not hear if Ruth answers or not, for he is scrolling down the list of one hundred and twenty-seven messages that decorate his screen. There is no reason for him to open any for he has read them already. Yvette has copied their entire correspondence, including his appreciation of her attentiveness in bed, to everybody in the department. He sits down and stares in disbelief. When he looks up, Ruth is standing before him.

'Well, if it means anything to you,' begins Ruth, 'we all kind of knew that something was going on between the pair of you. It was pretty obvious to me, but other people soon guessed, but what's the big deal here? You're both single, right?'

He rubs his face in the palm of his hand.

'The big deal here is that Yvette seems to have it in for me.'

'Did you two have words?'

'Well, sort of. Last night I told her that we should cool it a bit.'

'Oh, I see.'

'What do you see?'

'Well that's it then, isn't it?'

He pauses and looks again at the screen. 'What time does Mr Wilson want to see me?'

'He said after you've had a chance to read your email.'

He looks up at her. 'So she sent this to him too? Bloody hell what good does she think is going to come from this? Okay, so I'm embarrassed, is that what she wants?'

Ruth shrugs and throws out a helpless arm.

'I'm sorry, Mr Gordon, but I don't know what she wants. I haven't got a clue.'

He opens the door to Clive Wilson's office and sees him sitting at the rectangular conference table with Lesley Thornton, his deputy, seated to his right. He sits at the table opposite them, although this makes him feel as though he is being interviewed, and he loosens his tie and undoes his top button. Lesley is careful to betray neither a smile nor a scowl, but her coldness has been a feature of their exchanges since the fateful policy-making retreat in the New Forest. On the third and last night, they had both slipped into the village for a Sunday nightcap, careful to choose a different pub from the one which they had been frequenting as a group. Over a dry Martini she complained about the rudeness of the staff that she inherited on being promoted earlier in the year, and how the table manners of the last guy she dated seemed to have been picked up from the chimps at Regent's Park Zoo. She even did a quick impression of him eating spaghetti which was genuinely funny. Like many country pubs, come eleven o'clock the place officially closed, but the curtains were simply drawn and the drinks continued to be served and so they both decided to stay on.

Once they returned to the conference hotel, she invited him to her room for a quick raid of the mini-bar, but as soon as she closed the door they began to clutch and paw at each other, tossing clothes in all directions until he pushed her back on to the bed and unzipped her brown leather ankle boots. He didn't stay the night, although she made it clear that she wanted him to. She pointed to the small digital alarm clock on the bedside table and insisted that it had never let her down. She was sure that if they set it for six in the morning he could easily get back to his own room without being seen by anyone. But he sat on the edge of the bed with his back to her and pulled his belt an extra notch tighter before standing up and turning around. It had not been in any way satisfactory, her lust being more desperate than sensual, which made him feel slightly used. She was now wrapped in a white cotton sheet, and much to his embarrassment he realised that he didn't even feel particularly attracted to her. Before leaving, he placed his hand against her cheek, and then he crossed the room and quietly closed the door behind him. Early the next morning, he called the room of the colleague who was giving him a lift back to London and asked if they might leave an hour ahead of schedule as he had an emergency to attend to. Back in the office, Lesley smiled in his direction and offered him every chance to ask her out, but after a week had passed, and it had become clear to her that he was unlikely to do so, she cornered him by the Xerox machine. She announced that her sister had let her down and was going to Crete with her husband, and she therefore had two tickets to see a revival of a Pinter play at the National Theatre. For one moment he thought about making up a plausible excuse to spare her dignity, but in the end he could think of nothing to say and so he simply shook his head.

'I'm sorry,' he said, 'but I can't.'

A surprised Lesley Thornton smiled weakly and slowly nodded, and then she gathered her composure and said, 'Oh well, I tried.' She turned and walked away, and for a week or so her icy silence in his presence made him feel uncomfortable. And then he told

Annabelle what had happened and his life changed. During the nightmare week in the Travelodge, Lesley began again to smile in his direction, having heard the rumours of his changed circumstances. But once he moved into the flat in Wilton Road, and studiously refused to meet her eyes at work, or reply to her email messages with anything but the tersest of responses, their frosty relationship was once again re-established.

Clive Wilson begins.

'Keith, Keith, Keith. What have you got yourself into now?'

Clive Wilson is the chief executive of the council, and effectively his boss, and these days he works increasingly closely with his boss. However, he has come to understand that Clive Wilson loves only Clive Wilson and the thrill of wielding both actual and imagined power. He is generally quite good at reining in his smug bonhomie, but occasionally he gets a glint in his eye and crosses a line, at which point his tone becomes both over-friendly and admonitory.

'Tell me, Keith. Why would she want to do this to you?'

'I wanted to break it off and I suppose this is her way of trying to slap me in the face.'

'And, as it were, shoot herself in the foot.'

'Well I don't know if she's bothered about that.'

'Quite.'

Clive Wilson steals a glance at Lesley, whose detached demeanour betrays no emotion, and then he rocks back in his chair.

'She's been a researcher in your department for three months now, right?'

He nods.

'And how long has your affair been going on?'

'It's not an "affair". That makes it sound like there's been some kind of secretive thing to it. We've been having a relationship. It's all there in the emails.'

Clive shakes his head and stands up. He turns and walks a few paces, then he stares out of the window.

'Well, Keith it's a bit of an awkward one.' He turns around to face him. 'What do you want me to do about this? I can have a word with her and tell her not to wash her dirty linen in public or something like that, but I don't think I've got any grounds for dismissal.' He laughs now. 'I'd have the bloody unions all over me like a Bangkok rash.'

'Technically,' says Lesley, corkscrewing her body around to face Clive, 'she hasn't done anything wrong. She's been stupid, yes, but she's obviously feeling hurt and rejected.'

'Well I don't know what she's got to be hurt about.'

For the first time, Lesley looks directly at him. She uncrosses, then crosses, her legs and he can hear the rasp of her tights as she does so.

'Well maybe you should find out.'

Clive Wilson takes his seat again.

'Lesley's got a point there, Keith. Maybe you should talk to her and try and bring her to her senses.'

'According to Ruth, she's not come into work today. I can go and see if she's at home.'

'Have you called her?'

'No point. I know her. She won't answer her phone. I'm pretty sure I'll have to go round and see her.'

'Good.'

'What's good about it?'

Clive laughs now. 'Take it easy, cowboy. We're all working to get a resolve here.'

Clive stands again, but Lesley remains seated and with her right thumb she nervously pops the nib in and out of a cheap office biro.

'Let's have a drink and a chat at the end of the day, Keith.

By then you should be able to reassure me that everything is fine, okay?'

The walk from the tube station to Yvette's house has lost whatever thrill it once possessed. Without the prospect of a sexual encounter, he can now see that this part of London is bleakly suburban, and even the temperature seems to have dropped a few degrees in the space of twenty-four hours. It is positively freezing, but he resists the urge to draw further attention to himself by donning the sunglasses that he likes to wear when walking these less than friendly streets. Today, he doesn't care if people see him staring back at them, he just wants to get this business over and done with, and then hurry back to the office. It suddenly occurs to him that from Colin's point of view, not contesting the terms of the divorce and leaving his estranged young wife in a mortgage-free terraced house might have been the price he had to pay to escape this dreadful location. He crosses the road and can see that Yvette's blue curtains are closed. He presses the annoying bell and then waits. He presses again and although he is tempted to open the letterbox and demand that Yvette stop messing about and come down and talk to him, he knows that there is little point in becoming aggressive. He backs up a little along the crazy-paved path and looks at the upstairs windows to see if there is any movement of the thin curtains, but nothing stirs. He closes the gate behind him with a clatter, and then pauses to let a young woman, who is wheeling a child in a pushchair, pass by. He knows that he is imagining it, but he is sure that the young woman looked at him disdainfully. He watches as she wrestles the pushchair down off the pavement and crosses the road, before moving on purposefully in the direction of the local park. Eager to flee the site of what is fast beginning to feel like a crime scene, he walks quickly away from

Yvette's house and back in the direction of the tube station. He knows full well that at the office his colleagues will have spent the greater part of the day studying the one hundred and twenty-seven emails, and he will most likely have already become the elderly Lothario at the centre of a dozen risqué jokes.

Clive Wilson returns from the bar and slides into the chair opposite him. He hands him a glass of Pinot Grigio.

'There you go, mate. Bottoms up.'

Clive tips his own glass of red to his mouth and swallows deeply, and then he places the half-empty vessel on the table between them.

'So how about going on leave for a while? It'll give us a bit of time to work out what to do about the girl.'

He looks quizzically at his boss but says nothing in reply.

'Come on, old man, she works for you. It isn't going to be easy with the two of you in the same office.'

'Why not send her on leave? How come you're asking me to step aside?'

'Whoa, hold on a minute. This is paid leave, Keith. No hint of censure or anything like that. We can even call it a research break.'

'And what about her? Doesn't she even get a rap on the knuckles?'

'Lesley's going to sit down and talk with her. Better if it comes from a woman. She's going to make it clear to her that she's bang out of order and that whatever the emotional distress that she might be feeling, she has no right to copy your private emails to the whole department.'

'And that's it?' He stares at his boss, who shrugs helplessly. 'Oh come on, she was attempting to humiliate me.'

'Undermine you, perhaps. I can work with that, but I'm not

so sure about the humiliation thing. Look, give it a few weeks and then maybe it will have all blown over and you two can re-establish some kind of working harmony.'

Clive Wilson drains what remains of his wine in one gulp, and then he leans in closer.

'To tell you the truth, Keith, I don't want to push the girl too much. What if she starts sending these emails to head office or to the local press? At least at the moment it's all reasonably under control, wouldn't you say? Right now, we both know what we're dealing with. Another drink?'

He watches as his boss gently shoulders his way to the bar. On the positive side, a few weeks' leave means that he won't have to write the stupid policy report on trans-racial adoption. He assumes that Lesley Thornton will be put in charge of his depart-ment, which makes perfect sense given the fact that before her last promotion she used to run Women's Affairs, and so she at least has some knowledge of his newly expanded responsibilities. Race Equality initiatives will, presumably, be put on hold. Maybe Clive is trying to ease him out, or perhaps he is seeking to increase Lesley's portfolio? However, the more he thinks about Clive's motives the more he realises that he simply doesn't care. Time away from the whole Race Equality, Disability and Women's Affairs circus is what he needs, and if temporary humiliation is the price he has to pay to escape the clutches of the local authority for a few weeks, then he is ready to pay. A grinning Clive Wilson walks triumphantly towards him clutching two more large glasses of wine, one white and one red. He decides that he will drink his wine quickly and leave Clive Wilson alone in the bar where, as the evening wears on, his boss will no doubt run into old friends or simply make new ones.

II

II

For the first time since his student days, he is living without a daily structure. Clive Wilson's suggestion that he take a research break has enabled him to ignore the alarm clock. During his first year at university his erratic sleeping habits inconvenienced nobody for he had no girlfriend and, aside from his lectures and the odd tutorial, his main focus was football training, and that did not start until four in the afternoon. During his second and third years his involvement with Annabelle meant that he had less time for football but, much to his girlfriend's frustration, he remained unpredictable with regard to the time when he went to, or emerged from, his bed. Thanks to Clive Wilson he has been able to resume the indulgent sleeping patterns of his youth, but after just one unstructured week he realises that he is simply wasting his time. He has filled a yellow legal pad with notes for his proposed book about music, but most of the so-called notes are copied from earlier ideas that he had initially scribbled on Post-its before transferring the nuggets of wisdom into the back of old diaries. The one thing that he has achieved in the past week is to create an office space in the corner of his living room where he has arranged everything in an orderly fashion. The books on the two shelves are neatly divided into fiction and non-fiction, the A4 writing pads are neatly stacked, the Post-its and brightly coloured paper files are easy to reach, and the newly purchased laptop computer and printer-scanner-fax, while not the absolute top of the range, suggest a man who is serious about his home office. He stares at the screen and resists the urge to listen again to David Ruffin's recordings as a solo artist and then compare Ruffin's voice to when the singer was lead vocalist of the Temptations. He has replayed 'I Wish It Would Rain' three times already, but his written thoughts amount to two sentences. 'Once he liberated himself from the Temptations there was a new tonal flexibility to his voice. One can sense both pain and elation co-existing in a raw and vulnerable fashion, whereas loyalty to the group had previously reduced his voice to harmonic decoration.' Would he really learn anything new by listening to this song for a fourth time?

He checks his email. Ruth wants to know if he will be attending a disability workshop in Milton Keynes next month because, if so, she will have to book a hotel room for she's heard that the non-smoking doubles are going fast. There are two emails from Annabelle, who is clearly still annoyed that he hasn't made time to meet her and have the 'urgent' talk about Laurie's behaviour, but in the meantime she wants to know if he is coming to parents' evening. Her second message, some-what sarcastically, reminds him of the date of parents' evening. He clicks out of his email account without answering and pulls up the chapter headings and wonders if he should reconfigure the structure of the book. Maybe this will get him started. During the course of the past week the book has shrunk in scope as he abandoned the chapter to do with gospel music, and then the one about the blues, having finally admitted that he knows precious little about either genre. With regard to jazz, he agonised and wondered if it was even possible to write a book about contemporary music without including something about this tradition, but he finally convinced himself that there were already hundreds of respectable volumes on the subject and, quite frankly, he didn't need the hassle of adding his opinions into the mix for even the most level-headed people tended to become either very defensive, or unusually aggressive, when explaining their convictions about jazz.

He is now contemplating a three-part study of the music of the sixties, the seventies and the eighties. The first part of the book, 'Motown and the Suburbs', will specifically concern itself with soul music, the middle section, 'Rebel Music,' will address itself to the rise of reggae as a global phenomenon, and the final third of the book 'Whose World?' will look at the implications, musically and culturally, of the emergence of so-called 'World Music'. This new structure seems more manageable to him, but he still has the problem of not being entirely sure of how one actually starts to write a book. He wonders if this is what people mean when they talk about having writer's block, but he quickly reminds himself that, up until this extended research break, he has had little chance to seriously address himself to the project, having had to be content to snatch writing time at weekends, or on bank holidays. Annabelle often consoled her husband by telling him that his responsibilities at work meant that he obviously did not have enough free time to do anything other than simply plan a book, and he should not be so hard on himself. In her less supportive moments, his exasperated wife would point out that if he really wanted to write then he should stop bleating and just get on and do it, but within the hour she would be apologising and literally, and metaphorically, stroking his back and encouraging him to keep trying. For his part, he remains undecided whether or not the issue really is time, or if he fundamentally lacks motivation. Conjuring with the idea of writer's block is a new option, and while he remains tempted by the ease with which he might claim to be afflicted with this malady, the more rational part of him is fully aware that in order to be stricken with this condition he would first have to be able to provide tangible evidence that he has gone beyond the planning stage and actually written something.

The local library is undeniably dingy. People toting heavy shopping bags often step inside its vaulted entry hall simply to shelter from the rain, and stubborn local vagrants have to be regularly ushered out and back on to the street. In the centre of the reading room are two large wooden tables surrounded by orange plastic chairs, which are generally vacant. Should anybody inadvertently leave a book on top of one of the tables then the eager librarian will swoop and swiftly return the volume to its rightful place on a shelf. It is over a year since he first scanned the popular music 'collection' and discovered that, apart from a paperback biography of Nat King Cole, and a semi-academic book which claimed to be an investigation of the influence of religion on the musical development of Sam Cooke, Wilson Pickett and Curtis Mayfield, there is no material in this library that is going to be of any use to him. Nevertheless, he has temporarily abandoned the neat desk at his Wilton Road flat in the hope that a change of atmosphere will stimulate him to begin writing. This is the second afternoon that he has sat in a plastic chair at the far end of the larger of the two tables with his back to the window. From this vantage point he need only raise his head slightly to see who is coming through the door. However, in two days he has barely set down a word that he has not immediately scratched out with his cheap blue biro, having deemed the writing to be either derivative or so trite that, were he to be brutally honest, his advice to himself would be to give up.

At four o'clock she comes in, and again she sits at his table and reaches into her rucksack and pulls out a carefully folded copy of today's *Evening Standard*. She takes out a small notebook and a battered paperback dictionary and she begins to read the newspaper. Every few minutes she carefully writes a word into her notebook, and then she reaches for the dictionary and quickly leafs through it until she finds the appropriate dog-eared page and meticulously transcribes more words into her notebook. Her face is strangely angelic, and he guesses that she is Slavic. She is certainly pretty, despite the fact that she is wearing no makeup, and her blonde hair is bunched untidily on top of her head and loosely fastened with some sort of bulbous plastic clip. The previous day their eyes met briefly as he stood up to leave, and she offered him the faintest of smiles before lowering her gaze and returning her attention to the clutter of material on the table. As he passed behind her back he noticed that the newspaper was open at the international news section, but he didn't know if these pages were of particular interest to her, or if the girl just systematically worked her way through the tabloid.

He folds the flimsy piece of paper in half and then leans over and slides the note towards her. She looks up before he has time to withdraw his hand, and he self-consciously pushes the message the last few inches. It rises up and momentarily butterflies open before coming to rest, closed, in front of her. He smiles and shrugs his shoulders in a gesture of fake helplessness, and he watches as she ignores him and picks up the note and begins to read. She reads it again, and then again, and he worries now that either her English is bad, or his handwriting is unclear, but after what feels like an age she reaches for her pen and begins to write. Without meeting his eyes, she slides the note back in his direction and continues to read the newspaper. 'In one hour, please.' The letters are carefully attached to each other with anxious loops and curls as though this is a child's first attempt at joined-up writing. He remembers that Laurie's first sentences betrayed a similar deliberation, and he accused Annabelle's mother of interfering with what the boy's teachers were doing. Annabelle admitted that, on the afternoons that her mother spent with Laurie, she often sat him down on a bench at the zoo, or in a café, and helped her grandson with his writing, but Annabelle failed to understand what harm her mother was doing. When Annabelle asked him what exactly he meant by 'middle-class writing', he tried to explain, but he soon gave up, realising that he was beginning to sound ridiculous. He looks again at the four carefully inscribed words, then across in the girl's direction as she continues to read, then back at the note. Okay, one hour it will be.

The girl looks around at the shabby interior of the Queen Caroline and gestures with one hand, palm turned up.

'But this is an ugly place. For old men and tramps. Why does somebody like you wish to come here?'

'Well, because it's never full and it's never noisy. I suppose I can think in here.'

'And what do you think about?'

'The same as everybody else. What I'd like to do.'

'And what is it that you would like to do, Mr Keith? Do you have a big plan?'

He looks at her closely as she picks up her gin and tonic and takes an unconvincing sip. She wants to appear confident, but he wonders if behind the bluster she is perhaps unsure of herself. However, he can't imagine an English girl reading his note and then agreeing to come for a drink with him.

'Smoke?' She offers him a freshly opened pack of twenty but, as she balls up the cellophane and places it in the ashtray, he simply shakes his head. He watches as she knocks the box against the side of the table and loosens the cigarettes, then she pulls one clear and prepares to light it with a blue throwaway lighter.

'I'm afraid not. No smoking any more.'

She tosses down the lighter, but keeps hold of the cigarette. 'Stupid country with crazy rules.'

'Are you from Poland?'

'What do you know about Poland? Have you been there?'

'No, I've never been there.' He smiles in what he hopes is a reassuring manner. 'It's just that in the library I noticed the dictionary. "Polski". That's Polish, isn't it?'

'You are a detective?'

'Of course. I am an extremely smart detective, which is why I worked out that "Polski" might mean Polish.'

'And you think you are also a funny man?'

'Yes, but only in my spare time. The life of a comedian is very demanding. And you, you are a student?'

'Very good, Mr Keith. In the day I learn English at a language school in Acton. It is not far from here.'

She points quickly with her cigarette in the direction of Acton, and then carefully slides the cigarette back into the pack.

'A twelve-week course but I have to practise as well, which is why I go to your library. To learn English words.'

'And after your course you will go back to Poland?'

'For sure, I will go back to Warsaw.'

He wonders if he is irritating her, for she is speaking to him with an exasperation which suggests that she thinks he is an idiot. In fact, her ironic tone seems calculated to remind him that his questions are somewhat tedious. He is curious to know about her family, and he would like to raise the subject of whether or not there is a boyfriend. Perhaps there is a small flat in Warsaw that she intends to return to, or maybe she has a clerical job waiting for her, or a junior university position that she has been paid to take leave from in order that she might improve her language skills, but he dare not risk these questions. She is a little overweight, but it suits her. However, the angular bones of her face do seem slightly at odds with the graceful curves of her hips and breasts. The truth is, it looks as though her body has recently put on weight but her face has yet to catch up. Probably fast food, he thinks. McDonald's, KFC, Burger King, deep-fried garbage that will quickly ruin a slim body. He wonders if she is hungry. Perhaps she would like to go for an Indian, or maybe to his flat for another drink if she doesn't like this pub? He thinks carefully about how to pose the question for he doesn't want to come over as tacky. Who is he trying to fool? She has to know that he likes her, for she will have felt the weight of his gaze in the library, and then again here in the pub, and she will undoubtedly have measured it and made her calculations. In fact, the more he thinks about it, the more he realises that the girl will already have anticipated both his question and his uncertainty as to how to frame it.

He opens the front door and steps to one side, enabling her to pass out of the spitting rain and into the communal hallway. The light comes on automatically, the management company having installed a motion detector both for safety and to save money, for the young couple in the ground floor flat were in the habit of leaving the light on all night. As she squeezes past him she lets her rucksack swing down from her shoulder and it now dangles from her hand. He closes the door then stoops to pick up some mail, which he places on the small glass-topped table that stands beneath the ornately framed mirror.

'It's upstairs. Let me go first.'

He begins to climb the stairs, conscious of the fact that she is behind him and watching his every movement. Just as he reaches the top landing the light snaps off and plunges them both into darkness. He fumbles for his keys.

'A sixty-second delay's not really very much, is it?' The girl doesn't answer, so he concentrates on unlocking the door and then he ushers her inside. He gestures in the direction of the sofa, then excuses himself and passes into the kitchen where he leans against the cooker and wipes his brow with a piece of kitchen towel which he then pushes into the tall swing bin. He shouts through.

'Would you like some food? I've got crackers and cheese, or I can even make you some soup. It's not much, but it's all that I've got.'

He pours two glasses of Sauvignon Blanc and wonders if she minds the fact that it's a screwtop bottle. Some people like to hear the cork pop, but her silence is making him uneasy so he has chosen the quickest option. When he walks back into the living room she is sitting forward on the edge of the sofa and apparently gawping at the blank television screen. However, he soon realises that in the absence of a mirror she is probably staring at her own reflection. She has removed the plastic clip, and spilled her blonde hair so that it now reaches down to her shoulders. However, he can see that the roots are dark brown. He hands her a glass of wine and then crosses to the CD player.

'I said I could put together some food if you're hungry.'

'I am not hungry. But if you are hungry then you must eat.'

He puts on some Wynton Marsalis, the music being neither too abstract nor too difficult, and then he sits opposite her on a plain wooden chair. He thinks of Marsalis as the prime exponent of light jazz, for his graceful music is perfect for background atmosphere as it never seems to disrupt a private train of thought or hijack a conversation. The skies have opened, and rain is now lashing against the windows. Add a view of a Paris skyline, and the cliché would be complete. She sits back and raises her glass.

'Cheers, Mr Keith.'

'And cheers to you too. And to learning English in Acton.'

'Now that is quite funny. Very good. Cheers to learning English in Acton.'

They listen in silence to the end of the track. Her black woollen winter tights represent the triumph of common sense over style, but he notices that her shoes are both scuffed and badly worn down at the heels. He looks up at her pale, slender face, and decides to ask the question before Marsalis has a chance to blow the long mournful notes of the next ballad.

'Are you married?'

She laughs.

'No, of course I am not married. Are you married?'

'I used to be, but three years ago we decided to go our own way. It was reasonably amicable.' He pauses. 'Friendly.'

'I understand "amicable".'

'Sorry, I didn't mean to be rude.'

'And so you are a social worker who lives by himself and who likes to try to pick up girls in strange places.'

'Have I picked you up?'

'I am curious about you, Mr Keith. You like lonely pubs, and this is a lonely flat.'

He understands that being occasionally talked down to is the price an older man has to pay for the privilege of having a young girl flatter him with some attention. If he took anything from his disastrous relationship with Yvette, he took this much. He is learning to tolerate a disrespectful aggression that women of his own age would never resort to, but he suspects that this is because women of his own age no longer possess the gift of youth to embolden their behaviour. The confidence of most older women has usually been undermined by the harsh reality of accepting that their stepping into a room no longer results in heads being turned, but not this girl called Danuta who behaves as though she has never suffered a single moment of self-doubt. He imagines that her parents are most likely still alive, and he suspects that she has probably never endured the sudden, heart-wrenching loss of friends or loved ones. The girl in the black woollen tights remains untouched by life.

'Do you have a job in Poland?'

'I work with young children. Before they go to school.'

'Kindergarten. That's what they call it here. A kindergarten school.'

'The word is similar in Polish. I am a teacher, but I want to open an international kindergarten, for foreign children too. Children of businessmen and diplomats.'

'More money, right?'

'Of course, more money. But first I must improve my English. It is good to have conversation.'

'Is that why you agreed to have a drink with me? For my conversation?'

'Perhaps this is the reason.' She grins, and then she bursts out laughing as though unable to contain herself any longer. 'You are a very stupid man.'

He smiles quickly, and then he stands and takes the empty glass from her proffered hand. In the kitchen he refills both glasses, and then replaces the nearly empty bottle in the fridge. He catches a glimpse of himself in the dark kitchen window. He should know better. Where is all of this leading to? A quick fumble on the sofa, and then into the bedroom, leaving the lights on in the living room, the music playing, and the wine glasses still full? Perhaps they will scatter a trail of clothes behind them, or will they both have the discipline to wait until they get into the bedroom before they start peeling off the layers? And then what about all that confusion with the lights in the bedroom? Will they go for dim lighting, which will mean a quick time-out and crossing to the bedside lamp; or no lighting at all, which is maybe too weird; or perhaps a compromise and leave the door ajar so that some light from the living room is able to leak in? And then immediately afterwards, the sudden panic about contraception and disease. And she is probably the type of girl who after sex likes to roll up on to her elbow for a cigarette and talk. And will she be staying the night, or will he want her to leave straight away so that he can read or watch television? And what will she expect? A relationship? A phone number? Dinner? Suddenly it all seems extremely complicated, and as he continues to stare at himself in the kitchen window he wonders if indecision really is a sign of ageing.

'Would you like to stay?'

He hands her the refilled glass of wine.

'What do you mean "stay"?'

'I mean longer. We could order some food. Chinese. Indian. Whatever you like, they'll deliver.'

'I think I have to go now. But I like this music. It is very nice. May I know the name of the man who is playing?'

'Wynton Marsalis.'

He crosses to the CDs that are neatly stacked in a revolving tower. Skimming down from the top he identifies, and then plucks out, seven CDs by Marsalis and shuffles them like a deck of cards. He squares their edges, and then hands them to the girl. He wants her to be fascinated by the music, to ask him more questions, to give him the opportunity to share his knowledge with her. The more he gazes at this Danuta's mop of blonde hair, and her chewed nails and nicotine-stained fingers, the more he wants to know about her. She looks at the artwork on the covers and then, one at a time, she places them down on the coffee table before eventually reclaiming her glass of wine.

'You say you do not have a wife, so who is this woman in the photograph?'

She points to a small headshot in a stainless steel frame that is tucked away on the windowsill behind the television. He is surprised that she has spotted it, but he is coming to terms with the fact that she seems far more interested in her surroundings than she is in him.

'That's Brenda. She's my father's wife.'

'But she is not your mother.'

'No, she's not. To be more accurate I should say she used to be his wife.'

'But you do not have a picture of your mother, and you do not have a picture of your father, but you have a picture of your father's wife?'

He has noticed that she likes to phrase her questions as mildly accusatory statements of fact, but he is unsure if this reflects her combative character or if it is just evidence of her inexperience with the English language. He shrugs his shoulders.

'If you do not wish to talk about these things then this is good with me.'

'I'd rather talk about you.'

She laughs now and reaches both hands up to the top of her head, where she bundles her hair together and then holds it in place with one hand as she takes the plastic clip from her pocket. The girl then pulls her hair back and secures it so that her whole face seems brighter and more attractive. The young can do this. He has noticed it on the tube, in the street, in his office, young women who by undoing a button, or putting on some lip gloss, or hooking in a pair of earrings can suddenly, and dramatically, transform themselves as though they have plugged themselves in to an energy source. She walks to the window where she picks up the small framed photograph and looks closely at the image of Brenda, before replacing it and then peering down into the darkness. He notices the irritating flicker from the faulty street-lamp that is clearly visible through the window. Last month he urged Ruth to write to the appropriate department of the local authority and suggest that they immediately send somebody out to fix the problem. Apparently, either Ruth forgot to write, or the email landed on the screen of somebody who must have deemed his request low-priority. Danuta turns from the window and appraises the small flat as though considering whether or not she should buy the place. And then her eyes alight upon the present occupant.

'You like women or you like men, or both?'

'I have no interest in men.' He pauses. 'Well at least not in that way.'

'Never?'

'Never seen the point. I have enough trouble with women.'

He realises that she has teased out of him a little more than he intended to say. He will have to be careful for, until the night he told Annabelle about the encounter in the New Forest, he had no idea that the urge to confession played any part in his character. She leaves the window and sits back down.

'I have to go.'

'Are you sure? I'd like you to stay.'

'I work, Mr Keith. I have to go to work or how else do I pay for my English lessons.'

Well, he thinks, you've just had a free conversation class. Perhaps you can skip work tonight and keep me company.

'One for the road?'

He stands, picks up her glass, and gently touches her shoulder as he passes behind her. He tops her up and then quickly washes out the bottle and puts it by the sink with the empty Perrier and Gatorade bottles ready for recycling. The metal cap he pushes into the tall swing bin, and then he carefully carries her glass back into the living room. As he hands her the wine, he ignores the wooden chair and sits next to her on the sofa. They clink glasses, drink, and then he replaces his glass on the table and turns to face her. He reaches over and gently cups the right side of her face in his left palm and feels the softness of her skin.

'You know, you're quite beautiful.'

She looks at him, but says nothing. He stretches out his other hand so that her face now sits in the chalice that he has created. His eyes lock with hers, but he is conscious that he must not hold this pose for too long. He leans forward to kiss her, but at the last moment she twists her head offering him a cheek and withdrawing her face at the same time.

'I'm sorry,' he says. 'I didn't mean to do anything to cause offence.'

Suddenly, the confidence seems to have drained out of her and she stares at him, her eyes moist with what he imagines is disappointment.

'At night I am a cleaner. I work in an office building so I must go and do my job.' She puts down her glass of wine and stands. 'I do not wish to be late.'

To be misunderstood, and thereafter disliked, is always hurtful. At work he is a boss, and his colleagues have not always appreciated his gestures of authority, no matter how sensitively he has tried to bestow them. Clive Wilson has occasionally reminded him that he is not paid to win popularity contests, and the discomfort of being misunderstood comes with the privilege of being a decision-maker, so he just has to ride it out. Sometimes he can repair the damage of a comment or gesture that is offered in innocence and received with indignation, but more often than not he has learned to say nothing further and trust that time will heal any temporary distress in the workplace. However, as far as women are concerned, he has little experience of how to navigate such awkwardness, and the unfortunate episodes with Lesley and Yvette speak eloquently to this fact. Really, he asks himself, why push it and cross a line with this young woman? He could have waited and seen how things developed and discovered how she wanted to play it, but instead he stupidly does something which makes him feel like he is taking charge and now she is rightly outraged. She moves quickly to pick up her rucksack, and he finds himself stricken with anxiety. Okay, he does want to kiss her, and yes he doesn't want her to leave, but he also doesn't want to have full-on sex with her, at least not yet. Jesus Christ, he's already seen the mess that can get you into. Perhaps some kissing and fooling around, but her eyes indicate that she thinks he wants more than this, and maybe she is even a little saddened that their promising friendship should have been sabotaged by his pitiful impatience.

'I am sorry, but I must leave.'

He stands and walks with her to the door.

'Will you be getting a cab? There's a minicab place on the corner, I can walk you there.'

'No, it is not necessary.'

'I'm sorry,' he says. 'Sorry.'

She silently follows him back down the stairs and he scrambles around in his mind for something to say. He unlocks the front door and holds it wide open so she knows that she is free to go.

'I don't have a car. It's just too much hassle in London.'

He wants to reassure her that he earns more than enough to have a car. That he is a respectable middle-class professional man, not some leering jerk who preys on women. He wants her to know that the attempted kiss wasn't a clumsy gesture of foreplay, with the next stage already programmed in his seedy mind. He likes her, even though she is a little bit chippy. She is a single woman from another country, on her own, learning English. Of course, she has to be a little bit chippy to survive. He understands, he gets it, it's fine.

'Thank you for the drink, Mr Keith. And the conversation.'

She tosses her rucksack up on to her shoulder and deliberately avoids any eye contact as she sweeps past him.

One hand holds the edge of the open door, while his other hand is jammed flat against the wall as if to steady himself. She doesn't look back as she turns right at the gap where there should be a gate, and he watches as she walks up towards the main road. No hug, no peck on the cheek, no wave, just withdrawal and retreat. Poland. Back at college watching Wajda's *Man of Steel* and *Man of Marble*. Solidarity buttons. Lech Walesa as a cool guy before it became clear that he was an anti-Semite. But it's Poland, right. Home of Treblinka and Auschwitz. You don't change people's minds in a couple of generations. What else did he know? Kielbasa sausage, but he'd never tasted it. And Chopin, the man she probably thinks of when she imagines a real composer, not Wynton Marsalis. He closes the door and listens as the metal letterbox rattles noisily, and then he is suddenly enveloped in darkness as the sixty-second delay expires and the light clicks off.

Back upstairs and in the privacy of his flat, he opens another bottle of wine, this time with a corkscrew, and pours himself a fresh glass. He then scatters a few crackers on a plate and cuts off a hunk of Gruyère, before carrying everything through into the living room. He kicks off his shoes, and puts his feet up on the coffee table, then reaches for the remote control and turns up the volume of the CD player. Strange, but the flat suddenly seems empty without the girl. He again notices the framed image of Brenda's face on the windowsill and remembers that it was Annabelle who took this portrait. Although Brenda was clearly ill at the time, there is a serene aspect about her in this photograph which he has always liked. At the end of their first year at university, and before Annabelle went back home to do the work experience job that her father had set up for her at the *Wiltshire Times*, they travelled north together. He had telephoned Brenda as soon as he got the letter and insisted that he would be spending the summer with her, and although she had tried to persuade him just to go ahead with his Inter-Railing plans, his mind was made up. When Annabelle said that she would like to meet Brenda, he called again and having asked her what medicines the doctor had prescribed for her, and checked if she would mind if he did some university work at the city library from time to time, he eventually raised the subject of his previously unmentioned girlfriend. Brenda laughed, then coughed long and hard, before finally asking, 'Well, is she coming with you or not?'

Brenda lived in the same modern terraced house in which she had raised him. When his father went into hospital, and it looked as though he might not be coming out any time soon, the West Indian man to whom Brenda and his father paid rent made it clear that he did not want her in his property. He came to collect the rent on a Friday night, and he stood on the doorstep and told Brenda that she had no right to do what she had done so she had better take her white arse out of his place by the end of the month. Brenda slammed the door in the man's face, but on Monday morning she presented herself at the housing office of the local authority who, having listened to her situation made it their immediate business to find a place for Brenda and her charge on their proud new development. Back then the Whitehall Estate featured tree-lined pedestrian walkways, grassy communal spaces for kids to play in, and concrete benches and tables for parents to sit around and talk with each other. However, within weeks the rope swings and carefully assembled mounds of tyres had been slashed and vandalised, and the sitting areas were defaced with graffiti. Glue-sniffers and clusters of youths with cider bottles seemed now to dominate every underpass and footbridge, and although the model estate was no longer visited by enthusiastic groups of studious-looking men with clipboards and cameras, he never once heard Brenda complain. Their house had underfloor heating, a bathroom upstairs, and out back there was a small fenced garden with a tiny lawn surrounded by a thin border of soil in which Brenda showed him how to plant daffodils and bedding flowers. Brenda couldn't stand the smell of cat piss, and she was terrified of the neighbour's Staffordshire bull terrier which occasionally got over the fence, but this didn't stop her from dragging out a chair on a sunny day, and lighting up a cigarette to accompany her cup of tea, and simply staring contentedly at the world.

The Brenda who opened the door to the pair of them was not the same Brenda he had last seen almost a year earlier, shortly before he went off to university. The new Brenda seemed stooped, and her hair had been cut short and was styled in a lifeless pageboy cut, but the old Brenda always dressed and looked like she was about to go out on a hen night. Where, he wondered, had her energy gone, but she gave him no time to speculate for right there on the doorstep she immediately folded him into her thin arms and attempted to squeeze him. She eventually let him go and then cast her bright eyes over his companion.

'This is my girlfriend, Annabelle.'

Brenda smiled and ignored Annabelle's hand. 'Well, young lady, don't I get a hug or don't you want to crease your fancy togs?'

He moved to one side and Annabelle stepped forward and leaned in to embrace Brenda, but as they uncoupled Brenda kept hold of Annabelle's hand. He noticed that the hem was hanging down from Brenda's housecoat.

'Well, as Keith has no doubt told you, it's not much of a place but come on in. It's all I've got so if you don't like it you'll just have to lump it.'

She sat them on the sofa opposite her, and she then took up her perch in the armchair that she always occupied to do her knitting, or to watch television.

'I'll get you a pot of tea in a minute, but I just want to look at the pair of you.'

As she glanced back and forth from one to the other, he looked around and could see that the house was uncharacteristically slovenly, with unwashed dishes and newspapers littering both the tabletop and the floor. According to Brenda's letter, after she was discharged from the infirmary the local authority had apparently provided her with a home help who came in a few times a week, but it was clear to him that Brenda was still struggling.

'Well, isn't either one of you two lovebirds going to tell me how your journey up here was, or how your first year at university has gone? I *am* interested, you know.'

Annabelle stood up. 'Mrs Gordon, can I make the tea?'

Brenda laughed. 'Nobody's ever called me that, love. Well, not in a good while. How old are you, if you don't mind my asking?'

Annabelle blushed. 'Nineteen.'

'Well, I reckon you're old enough to call me Brenda. And yes dear, my throat's as dry as a dog biscuit, so I'd be grateful if you could make us all some tea while I look at my boy. Everything's through there in the kitchen.'

Once Annabelle had passed out of sight, Brenda eased back in her chair and relaxed.

'Have you seen your father?' He shook his head but wouldn't meet her eyes. 'You should give him a call.'

'For what?'

'Because, sweetheart, he's forty-one years old and he's still full of anger and confusion in his head. You're only nineteen. Have a bit of compassion for the silly sod.'

'When he came out of hospital he didn't have any right to take me away from you or this house.'

'Change the record love, that's all in the past. He's your father and he had every right. Anyhow, he was just trying to do what he thought was best, but he's not perfect. None of us are.'

'Well, he's not that for sure.'

'Look, we got through it, didn't we? And he didn't say no to your spending the weekends and school holidays here, did he?' He looked at the space between his feet and didn't answer. 'Oh come on, don't give me the face. As far as I know, he's still doing the same boring janitor's job, and no doubt drinking with his mates. But look at you. You've made it to university, and you've got a lovely girlfriend, and the whole world is in front of you. Be kind to him, love. What's to lose?'

Annabelle put the tray down and began to pour the tea. Then she realised that she had forgotten the sugar, but Brenda waved a dismissive hand and said that she'd probably run out so not to bother.

'Sugar's bad for you anyhow. Ruin your teeth and rot your stomach, or so they say.'

Annabelle finished pouring the tea, and then she handed Brenda her cup before sitting back down next to her boyfriend.

He watched Brenda closely and could see that the suddenly aged woman was merely wetting her lips before slowly setting the cup back down on the saucer with a nervous clatter. Her hands were shaking and the loose-fitting housecoat could not disguise the fact that she had lost a shocking amount of weight. She asked Annabelle where she was from, and questioned her about her parents, and Annabelle answered politely and told Brenda more than she had ever told him. For the first time, he learned that her father was a keen golfer who had actually won some amateur tournaments, and that her mother had never worked for a living but apparently had earned a degree in French and Spanish from Durham University. As he listened to the pair of them, he realised that it was difficult for him to gauge the degree to which Brenda was genuinely interested in his girlfriend's history, for he had never before introduced anyone to Brenda. The one relationship he had at school had never been serious enough for either one of them to risk family introductions. However, Brenda was not one to indulge in any pretence, and she seemed to be listening intently to Annabelle and so, as far as he could tell, she really did like his girlfriend. Annabelle edged forward and began to pour some more tea, but Brenda shook her head and covered the top of her cup with her newly frail hand.

'No thanks, darling. However, I was wondering if you'd be a love and help me up to the bathroom. All a bit of a struggle for me these days.'

He listened closely as the two of them made their slow way up the stairs, and then he heard the sound of the bathroom door closing. He looked around the room and noticed a child's potty behind Brenda's chair and his heart sank. Although she was only thirty-nine, her health was worse than he had imagined, but after a year at university he was simply relieved to be returning to a home which held only good memories for him. He was just six when his grieving stepfather took him by the hand and led him to a house where he was deposited with the man who was his real father. At this time his father and Brenda were living in a small back-to-back whose door opened directly on to a cobbled street. He remembers that people hung their washing out like bunting on lines that crossed the roadway, but they propped the laundry high so that if a car went by it wouldn't dirty the clothes. But very few cars went by, for this cobbled street was effectively a cul-de-sac as three iron bollards had been installed at the far end to prevent any through traffic. For two years, the three of them lived in this rented house, but there always seemed to be arguments between his father and Brenda which sometimes grew so loud that Brenda was forced to turn on the radio or tele- vision set in an attempt to drown out his father's raised voice. The problems invariably occurred at night, when his father had returned from his job as a cleaner, and their heated disputes frequently concluded with his father curled up in a corner and steadfastly refusing to listen to the pleadings of Brenda, or his son's childish entreaties that he should put aside his book and acknowledge their presence. Eventually, he learned to leave his father alone once he picked up a book, but when his father gave up on books and began to conclude arguments with Brenda by stripping off his shirt and shouting at nobody in particular, even the eight-year-old son realised that something was seriously wrong.

He remembers that it was a Monday. He came home from school an hour later than usual, for he had to stay behind for football practice. As he turned the corner at the end of the street, he saw Brenda on the doorstep talking with a small congre- gation of neighbours. They looked up and noticed him and, still in his football boots, he began to show off and he started happily to slip and slide from one smooth stone to the next. However, by the time he reached Brenda the neighbours had disappeared, and Brenda draped an arm around his narrow shoulders and ushered him inside. She didn't waste time. 'Listen love, your dad won't be coming back for a while. He's in hospital.' He felt momentarily ashamed for he had almost forgotten the confusion of the previous night when the police had come and taken his father away.

'Are we going to visit?'

Brenda ran her hand across the top of his head and assured him that they would visit. 'Maybe over the weekend.' However, when Saturday came she dressed him neatly in his school clothes, and combed his hair in silence, and he had a feeling that this wasn't an ordinary hospital that they would be visiting.

The pair of them were finally escorted into the sterile visiting room, but his father didn't recognise either of them, or if he did he pretended not to. His father sat stiffly in a chair by the window and stared out into the garden. He remembered that the man looked old, and that while his hair was still black he seemed to be growing a grey beard. He tried to see what he was looking at, but apart from a line of tall trees in the background that blocked the view, and an empty lawn in the foreground, there was nothing. Nobody playing or relaxing, no birds or animals, and he didn't understand what the man was staring at. He and Brenda stood together, and she talked enthusiastically to his father, and asked him how he was, and if he needed anything, while the male nurse who had escorted them hovered impatiently by the door and began to tap his foot against the linoleum floor. After a few minutes, he felt the tears beginning to well up and he started to cry, although he was careful not to make a sound. Brenda pulled him closer to her side and looked down. 'Okay, honey, don't worry we'll go now.' His nose had started to run, and he didn't have a handkerchief, but he didn't want to wipe his nose on the sleeve of his school blazer. Brenda reached into her handbag and pulled out a small packet of tissues which she pushed into his hand. When they reached home he told her that he didn't want to visit again, for this silent man didn't know who he was. Brenda listened sympathetically, and tried hard to persuade him to accompany her on the Saturday excursion, but once they were settled in the new house eventually she too stopped visiting, which made him feel better about everything.

The man who knocked on their door on his thirteenth birthday was a stranger to him. He enjoyed living with Brenda, even though his friends at school thought it a bit odd, but he soon accustomed himself to telling everybody that his parents had gone back to the West Indies. According to his story, they wanted him to stay in England and get an education and so they had decided to leave him with a close family friend. Unfortunately, the sudden appearance of the cold-looking man standing at the door, who silently handed him a thirteenth birthday card in an envelope, and then a watch in a long, thin, transparent box, suddenly complicated his life. Brenda shouted through from the living room and asked who was at the door, but he just stared at the stranger and neither one of them said a word. 'Well?' shouted Brenda. He heard her walking towards him, and he turned as she stepped into the hallway. She had a half-washed saucepan in her hands.

'Earl?' The man said nothing in reply. 'Bloody hell, why didn't you tell me they were letting you out?'

'I have to report to you?'

He looked at Brenda, then back at this man who was his father, and he realised that even after all these years there was still animosity between them.

'Look, do you want to come in?'

'I just want to wish my son a happy birthday and let him know that I want him living with me.'

'Well, I'm not sure that this is the best time to be talking about all of this.'

'And who are you to talk to me about my own son?'

Brenda sighed and gathered herself. 'Earl, I am the woman who has clothed and fed Keith for the past five years.'

'Well, if you didn't lock me up then I'd have done my duty by him. I don't have no desire to come into your place, but I'll soon be back for my son.'

He watched as his father turned and strode down the short path to the pedestrian walkway before disappearing in the direction of the bus stop. He looked up at the sky, where the clouds were high and heavy with snow, and followed a flight of birds which dropped and fell, one after the other, as their leader banked and led them in the direction of a warmer climate for the winter. The birthday card and watch felt clammy in his hands. After what seemed like an age, Brenda slowly closed the door.

Annabelle came downstairs so quietly that he didn't hear her. She startled him as she opened the living room door, and he rubbed his eyes and realised that he must have drifted off. She flopped down on to the sofa next to him and hooked one leg over both of his knees.

'She's gone to sleep, poor woman. She's exhausted. Does she have any friends or family that can come over and maybe just keep her company? Besides you, that is.'

'Well I imagine she's got friends from the hairdresser's.'

'Hairdresser's?'

'I told you, she's a hairdresser.'

'Well there's irony. You know she has no hair. She's wearing a wig.'

He looked across at Annabelle. 'I thought her hair looked strange.'

'I know you've told me, but you used to spend weekends with her and the weekdays with your father, right?'

'That was the arrangement they came to. He's never forgiven her for having him sectioned in the mental hospital, but once he got custody he never tried to stop me seeing her.'

'That's good.' Annabelle looked at him. 'Well, it is good, isn't it?'

'So what do you want me to do, give him a medal?'

'Well, from what you've told me she probably did the right thing getting him packed off to a hospital.'

'Try telling him that.' He unhooked her leg and stood up. 'Are you hungry? I can see if there's anything in the fridge.'

Annabelle shook her head. 'Don't bother, I've already looked. If you tell me where the shops are I'll go and get something. When she wakes up I'm going to ask if she minds my taking a picture of her. She's got an amazing face. And then I should probably get going.'

'Don't you want to stay the night?'

'I wanted to meet Brenda and now I've met her. The two of you should be together. And you know, the sooner I get started on the summer the sooner it will be over. Then I can join you again. Make sense?'

He sat back down and leaned over and picked up both of her hands. He kissed the back of one, and then the other.

'Thanks. I'm glad you're here.'

The Wynton Marsalis CD comes to an abrupt end and for a moment he thinks about going back into the kitchen and slicing off another hunk of Gruyère. He has not eaten dinner, but the truth is he isn't hungry. It is still mid-evening, so there is time to do more work on the book, or at least re-read his notes. He looks across at his neatly organised desk, but he does not leave the sofa. He reaches out a hand and picks up the remote for the television.

The book can wait. That's enough work for one day, and the truth is he doesn't wish to be reminded of the library or the girl. Tomorrow morning he will get up early and resume work on the book. He won't set the alarm, but if he goes to bed at a reasonable hour he should be able to make a timely start. That much he is sure of. He points the remote at the television set.

The following afternoon he waits in the doorway of Dewhurst's, the butcher's. It is half-day so the shop is locked, but the red plastic awning protects him from the drizzling rain. Cars slosh by, throwing thin sheets of water towards the pavements and causing young and old pedestrians to move quickly away from the kerb. He ought not to be here, he knows this, but he sat up until three o'clock in the morning with a notepad in his lap making notes about Wynton Marsalis and wondering if he should not at least consider including a jazz epilogue to his book. Something brief, a nod in the direction of the field, a half-dozen footnoted paragraphs that suggest familiarity without expertise. Around the edges of the pages in his notebook he found himself writing her name in neat black capitals: DANUTA. There was no surname to root the romantic, French-sounding, Danuta in Polish soil, but for some reason he was sure that hers would be the most jaw-breaking of Polish names; a chain of late consonants strung together with a total disregard for vowels. By the time he put down his notepad, and began to slouch his slow way towards the bedroom, he realised that the girl held some kind of grip on his imagination, although he was too fatigued to try and fathom the source of his fascination.

The first students begin to walk down the steps of the bleak stone building, their bulky bags hooked over one shoulder, their hands forming visors against the rain. Somebody should tell these foreigners that it is always raining in England, and that they should buy an umbrella before they even think about a travel pass, or cheap jeans, or a copy of *Time Out*. After all, an umbrella is a key part of the English uniform. He glances at his watch. Four o'clock precisely, and so he seems to have guessed right. And then he sees her talking to a tall blond boy who is Germanic in appearance, but he could also be from anywhere in Scandinavia, or from one of the former Soviet countries. The boy is smiling, but there does not appear to be anything intimate about their encounter. As they reach the bottom of the half-dozen steps the boy punches her playfully on the arm and then peels off and dashes towards the bus stop where a double-decker bus, its headlights already bright in this late afternoon gloom, is about to depart.

He steps out from beneath the red awning and strides across the road, and he can now see that she is dressed in the same clothes as yesterday, including the uninspiring black woollen tights. Her rucksack dangles casually from one hand, and he notices that she has about her a distinct air of general dishevelment that he is beginning to believe is carefully cultivated.

'I thought you might like to go for a coffee. Or a drink if you prefer.' She turns to face him and is unable to disguise her surprise. 'There are quite a few pubs around here. I can't guarantee that they're much better than the Queen Caroline, but we can try.'

Confusion clouds her face, as though suddenly the English language has abandoned her. He can see that she has no words to place on her tongue.

'Think of it as another free conversation class. Better than going through the *Evening Standard* in that grubby library, right?'

She waits at a table by the window while he loads a handful of pink sachets of sugar, and some small plastic containers of milk, on to a tray. He edges around the crush of uniformed school kids and slides into the bolted plastic chair. He shakes his head as he lifts both coffees clear of the paper-lined tray, and then he unloads the sugar and milk on to the table before shoving the tray to one side.

'Let's be honest. It's all McDonald's is good for. Coffee and the bathrooms. At least they try and keep them clean.'

'The bathrooms do not clean themselves. Somebody has to clean them, do you know this?'

'Okay, fair point. At least somebody keeps them clean.'

He watches as she rips open first one sachet of sugar, then another, and eventually she pours the contents of three envelopes into her cup. She finds a thin red straw among the superfluous sugar and milk, and she quickly stirs with it and then tosses the straw on to the tabletop. Like him she takes no milk, but unlike him she takes sugar; plenty of it.

'How was the language school today?'

'It was the same as yesterday.'

'And how was it yesterday?'

She shrugs her shoulders and stares out of the window. It has begun to rain heavily and the raindrops tattoo loudly against the window. Umbrellas have mushroomed everywhere, but he is sure that she is looking at nothing in particular.

Has he made a mistake? If so then he is sorry, but he is keen to make everything all right, that is all. He knows that he should not have tried to kiss her, but right now he just wants to spend some time with her. Yes, in a sense, win her over. She takes a loud sip of her coffee. What should he say? Danuta, I like you, but I am sorry. She glances at him, then quickly turns back to the window. The words are in his head. Danuta, I just want to say sorry for last night, but if you want to finish your coffee and leave then that's fine with me. I'm not being pushy or anything. She turns from the window and looks at him quizzically, as though baffled by his uncharacteristic silence. He feels compelled to speak.

'Was the blond guy your boyfriend? I didn't want to embarrass you, or cause you any difficulty, so I backed off until he ran for his bus.'

'You were spying on me?'

'I wouldn't call it spying. I'm not the secret police, you know.'

'You are not funny. In my country this is still not a joke, Mr Keith.'

'Ah, so at least you remember my name.'

'Of course I remember your name. I met you yesterday. How can I forget your name?'

She shakes her head and once again stares out of the window. The puddles reflect red and white light from the cars, and red, amber and green from the traffic lights. The slack water rainbow is surprisingly beautiful. He has to take charge, yet be sensitive, otherwise he realises that the whole encounter will quickly descend into argument and she will leave. She seems to like it when he leads, for this perhaps gives her the space to be quirky and witty. This being the case, he understands that now is not the time to let the conversation drift. He takes a sip of the bitter McDonald's coffee and then he places the plastic cup back on the tray. He stares at her, but still she will not meet his eyes, so he picks up the discarded red straw and drops it into his abandoned coffee.

'Shall we go back to my flat? I've got better coffee than this, and at least it's more comfortable.'

'Comfortable?'

She picks up her cup and takes a noisy sip.

'Well, this is McDonald's. You know, everything is secured to the floor, no reclining allowed. It's not exactly relaxing in here. And it's cold, particularly every time someone opens the door, so that's what I mean by more comfortable.'

He points through the window.

'We can get that bus and be at my place in five minutes.'

The following day he works well on the book. His only inter-
ruption is a call from Ruth, who wants to know if he has taken
home a file about racial violence in Cardiff. Apparently, she needs
to give the file to a researcher who is putting together a piece
about the cultural insularity of South Wales. He asks Ruth which
researcher, and is relieved when she does not mention Yvette's
name. There is a pause and then, lowering her voice, Ruth asks
him how he is doing. She seems embarrassed.

'I'm all right, Ruth,' he says. 'Recharging my batteries. You
know I haven't had a break from work in over twenty years. I
don't mean holidays or anything like that, I mean a real break.
So I'm just exploring other things. I'd almost forgotten that I
had any other interests or talents.'

Ruth says nothing, and awkwardness overtakes them both. He
realises that he probably sounds immodest, but it is too late now.
Suddenly he is conscious of the presence of the telephone in his
hand, and he longs for her simply to ask him what he is doing
with his time, or make a joke, or tell him that the photocopier
in the office isn't working, but she remains silent.

'Has Clive asked after me?'

Ruth seems momentarily surprised.

'Mr Wilson?'

'Yes, Clive Wilson.' He laughs now. 'The boss.'

'No, he's not said anything. You know what he's like.'

He regrets having mentioned Clive, for it makes him appear
anxious and weak. However, this is not how he feels, nor is it
the impression that he wishes to convey to his secretary. Having
closed the telephone he finds it difficult to reapply himself to
the words on the screen. He would still like to write a few

paragraphs on Gil Scott-Heron, but he wonders how much, if anything, his potential British readers will know about the chocolate cities and vanilla suburbs of the United States? If they don't know anything then it will be impossible for him to develop his thesis about how black cultural heritage is passed on from one generation to the next. After all, he can't illustrate the principle by pointing to Liverpool or Birmingham. Okay, so the Romans brought black soldiers to build Hadrian's wall, and there were black trumpeters and pages in the sixteenth-century courts of England and Scotland, and everybody knows that eighteenth-century London was full of black people, but that was then. He is trying to write about a deeper and more substantial tradition of cultural inheritance, and this means that he has to look across the Atlantic for his models. Of late he has found that the same is also true in the race relations business. Increasing numbers of social policy papers seemed to cross his desk arguing that one can only understand Bristol or Leicester or Manchester by looking at Oakland or Detroit or Chicago. He switches off his computer and admits defeat for the day, but he had worked well until Ruth called. Now he has time on his side.

By quarter past four it is apparent that everybody has left the building. There are no longer any students ambling down the steps before peeling off to the left or right in search of a bus, and nobody else appears to be emerging from inside the school. It is not raining, but he stands beneath the red awning, although he now admits to himself that he is wasting his time loitering on this far side of the road. Today he will use the pedestrian crossing. He waits until the beeping begins, and the little green man appears, before dashing quickly in front of the idling traffic. There is still no sign of her and so he decides to go inside and see if he can locate some kind of administrative office. Yesterday she chose not to come back to his Wilton Road flat, and having walked her to the bus stop, and thanked Danuta for having coffee with him at McDonald's, he watched her get on the bus. It was his bus too, but he decided to walk back in the rain, without an umbrella, and think about what a strangely pleasant distraction the girl was. However, when the skies really opened he realised the extent to which rain could hurt, for the heavy drops felt like needles of glass. By the time he reached home he was drenched to the skin, so he took a long hot shower to prevent himself from catching a chill, and then he kicked up his legs on the sofa and spent the evening continuing to think about Danuta, or his book, jumping nimbly in his mind from one subject to the other, happy to be able to focus on something other than the situation with Yvette and the frustration of not knowing when he will be able to return to his job.

The unfriendly woman looks up from her desk and peers at him over the top of her glasses.

'Can I help you?'

It is the end of the day, and it is apparent that she is the only one left in the reception office of the language school.

'I'm looking for somebody. A friend.'

The woman peels off her glasses and places them on her desk. She stands and crosses to the hatch. He guesses that she is in her late fifties, and almost certainly a spinster. There is no sign of a ring, and no hint of sensuality to her.

'And does your friend have a name?'

'Danuta.' He pauses. 'She's Polish.'

'I take it you're not with any official organisation? Immigration? Housing?'

'I told you, I'm just a friend.'

'Then I'm afraid I can't help you. Students come and students go, but we have to respect their privacy.'

He smiles and nods.

'Yes, of course, I understand what you're saying, but it's just that I arranged to meet her. Today at four o'clock, and I'm worried because she's not here.'

'Have you tried calling her?'

He stares at the woman.

'Well? You do have her number, don't you?'

In the evening it starts to rain hard, lashing, stormy rain. He sits at his laptop and types 'Danuta', then 'Polish', then 'London', then 'language school', then 'cleaning agency,' and hits the return button, but he is offered a choice of an expensive maid service near Marble Arch or two escort agencies. There are some websites in Polish, but these are of no use to him, so he tries again, but this time for an image search. There appear to be many Danutas of all sizes and ages, but nobody that he recognises. Then it occurs to him that perhaps Danuta is not even her real name. He cut the conversation with the unfriendly woman short, for she clearly regarded herself as the commissar of the language school and there was nothing to be gained by arguing with such a woman. Once he abandoned the office hatch, and left the language school, he caught the bus to the library where he sat for nearly two hours staring at the door in the hope that she would walk in. He thought about simply asking the librarian if she had seen the strange Polish girl who usually arrived with a dictionary and a copy of the *Evening Standard*, but he worried that the woman might regard him as some kind of stalker. He was sure that the librarian would know who he was talking about, and if Danuta had signed up for a reader's ticket then her real name and address would be on file, but by the end of his second hour of gazing at the door he had convinced himself that her 'disappearance' was not his problem, nor his fault, and he should just get on with his own life.

He tries another web search, this time typing in 'Danuta' and

'Warsaw' but again there is nothing. He logs into the wine ware-house site and types in his username and password. Clicking on past orders he deposits a dozen screwtop bottles of Sauvignon Blanc into his basket and then quickly checks out. She seemed to like this wine, and he wants to be ready. As he waits for the order to process, he stares out of the window into the black night where he can see that the few leaves that remain on the trees are now falling like confetti. The rumble of distant thunder is now comple-mented by lightning, which sporadically illuminates his living room, and he can hardly believe that a second storm is brewing.

The following morning the sun is out, although a stiff wind blows litter so that the empty crisp packets and plastic Coke bottles swirl crazily about the Acton street. He leans casually against the wall at the foot of the steps that lead up into the language school, and then he sees her. Danuta is walking slowly and is bent forward into the head wind. When she reaches the school he moves away from the wall and blocks her path.

'I was worried about you.'

She looks up at him and scrutinises his face.

'You didn't show up yesterday. Neither here nor at the library. I was working on my own stuff but I was finding it hard to concentrate.'

She continues to stare at him.

'Look, I'm not weird or anything, I'm just concerned. I care.'

'Why should you care? Who are you to care?'

He puts his hand gently on to her shoulder, but she pulls her body away from him so that his hand now hovers foolishly in midair.

'I know you've got your classes so why don't I just see you back here at four o'clock. We can talk then, when we've both finished what we've got to do.' He smiles in a manner that he hopes will put her at ease. 'Okay?'

At four o'clock he hands her the travel-size umbrella, which is immediately blown inside out by the powerful gale. She lowers it and begins to struggle with the contraption, so he takes it from her and pushes it back into shape.

'You can hang on to it like this and stop it from popping up on you.'

He places her hand in the right position, then folds his own hand around hers to make sure that she has the correct grip before quickly releasing both her hand and the umbrella.

'Bloody hell, I can't believe that it's raining again.'

Rain is now trickling down her angular face, and her damp, unclipped, hair hangs limp.

'You're going to catch your death of cold in those clothes.'

'I should go home. Tonight I must work.'

'But I'm just down the road. At least come by and get dry before you go to work. You can wear some of my clothes while we put yours in the tumble dryer. Then you can get a minicab to work. I've got to go out tonight anyhow so I'll just take the cab on.'

He stands in the darkness, his back against the trunk of a tall oak tree. He doesn't know anything about flowers and plants, but many years ago an overly keen young supply teacher once tormented his class for a whole afternoon with silhouette shapes of various trees until they became imprinted on the pupils' minds. The windows of the office building are illuminated like square portholes on the side of a ship. Occasionally a figure drifts into view, then retreats into the room and out of sight, but as yet he has not seen her. The security guard sits only twenty feet away in his small hut staring intently at a tabloid newspaper. The man is perusing the sports section, and so far he has turned only one page. Clearly the rest of the newspaper holds no interest for him.

He guesses that this heavy-set man with a peaked cap set at a jubilant angle, and a blue blazer that appears to be bursting at the seams, is probably only a few years younger than him. He seems to have settled contentedly into his life as a watchman who does not watch, and the man probably has no ambitions beyond his weekly wage packet and his food being on the table when he gets home early in the morning. But who is he to feel superior? He envies the man who has organised his life so that he has no desire to elevate himself. The overweight guard is a Buddha of tranquillity in his heated shack, with a newspaper for company and silence all about him.

And then he sees her. She has a cloth duster in her hand and she is running it along the windowsill, first to the right, and then to the left, and then she disappears as quickly as she appeared. Once again the lighted box is empty. He cranes his neck, sure that she is going to appear in another window, but all sixteen are empty and for a moment he imagines that the building has in some way swallowed her whole. Perhaps she is in danger, but he cannot leave the safety of the tree's shadow and show himself. Suddenly, in a window on the floor above, he sees a tall blond boy, and she joins the boy in the window and says something to him, and then as quickly as she appeared she is gone again leaving the blond boy by himself. And then he too is gone.

He is sure that this is the same boy that he saw her with the day before yesterday on the steps of the language school. In fact, the same boy he had asked her about only a few hours earlier when she came back to his flat to dry her clothes.

'Your roommate is called Rolf?'

'Is there something the matter with his name? Perhaps it is a popular name in Latvia?'

He didn't know how to explain that to most people in England, Rolf is a strange Australian man with a beard and glasses who draws cartoons and sings kids' songs very badly. He is a figure of fun from down under, a man who bears absolutely no physical resemblance to a tall young Latvian.

'Rolf is harmless, but he has an interest.' She paused as though expecting a response. Realising that none was forthcoming she continued. 'In me.'

'And do you have an interest in him?'

She looked momentarily startled and then she began to laugh, and although he understood that she was to some extent laughing at him he felt relieved that he had finally connected with her. He wondered if there were other buttons he might push that would encourage her to relax and perhaps believe that as a couple they were actually quite good together. But maybe he was the one who needed to unwind and take things easy. Obviously, to some extent, she trusted him. She had come back to his flat and accepted a large towel and gone into the bathroom and removed her clothes. She emerged with the towel wrapped tightly around her, and in her arms she cradled a damp pile of garments like a newborn child. He took them from her and tossed each article separately into the dryer.

'Because a man is interested in me, this does not mean that I have any interest in the man. Are you interested in every woman who is interested in you?'

He wanted to keep the conversation alive, but suddenly he was aware of the loud hum of the dryer as the cylinder lumbered its slow way around the fixed circle. Once the buzzer signalled the fact that her clothes were dry she would no doubt leave, unless they were deeply involved in this, or some other, conversation.

'Of course not. But you said that he had an interest and so I thought things might be difficult for you. But obviously they're not, which is good.'

'And why is it good?'

He shrugged his shoulders. 'I don't know.'

'You don't know? Then you should maybe say nothing. I am happy with silence. Unlike you English, I do not have to talk to fill in the silence.'

'I see.'

He watched as she reached into her rucksack and pulled out a book whose title was in Polish. She began to read and he understood that, at least for the moment, this peculiar young woman had nothing further to say. He stared at her collarbone, which was unusually prominent beneath the thin layer of skin, and which curved left and right like the bow of an archer, and then she looked up from her book and he quickly averted his gaze.

Half an hour later, she emerged from his bedroom in her warm clothes and handed him the neatly folded towel, which he placed on the arm of the sofa. He stared at her petite and perfectly formed feet which, unlike her nicotine-stained and somewhat scrawny hands, appeared to be so smooth they might be waxed. Her toenails were cut short and not painted, and for a moment he understood why, in some cultures, women are encouraged to walk delicately on the bodies of men. But presumably not in Poland. He stood and offered her a glass of wine, which she refused by simply looking at her girl's watch and insisting that she could not afford to be late. She informed him that Rolf would be upset if he had to make up an excuse on her behalf, and this is how he discovered that Rolf was not only her roommate, but they also worked together as cleaners. She asked him to please call the minicab, and so he eased by her and passed into the kitchen where he had left his mobile. 'Two minutes, mate.' It was then that he heard Danuta close the door to the bathroom and then immediately flush the toilet. A few moments later she tiptoed back into the living room and he watched as she clumsily pushed her feet into her scuffed shoes, seemingly oblivious to the fact that she was breaking down their heels. They both heard the doorbell.

The rain had stopped at some point, but the streets remained damp and strewn with puddles into which drivers seemed to be deliberately steering. She held her face close to the window, and whenever they passed beneath a lamppost he was able to catch a fleeting glimpse of her pensive reflection.

'Near the BBC, you said, mate?'

The minicab driver had a heavy West African accent and he was wearing a lime green dashiki, which made his attempt to speak cockney come across as vaguely absurd.

'You'll be wanting this side of the Westway, or just over the other side?'

'Just before, please.'

The African driver nodded to let him know that he had heard, and then he signalled and took the last left before the motorway. Danuta turned from the window and pointed through the front windscreen.

'The building there.'

The driver ducked into a space by the night-watchman's hut, but the man kept the engine running and his eyes focused straight ahead.

'Perhaps I could see you tomorrow? I'm not working this week.'

She smiled, and then gathered up her rucksack and opened the door in one smooth continuous movement.

'Thank you for my dry clothes.'

She slipped out of the car and slammed the door behind her. The minicab then began to move off in the direction of the West London Boys' Club by Wormwood Scrubs, one of the community centres that fell under his jurisdiction. As they passed under the Westway he asked the driver to stop.

'You have changed your mind?'

He reached in his pocket for his wallet and took out a £10 note which he handed to the driver.

'I'll get out here.'

'Sir, I must charge you the full ten pounds, even though you have not completed your journey.'

'It's all right. It's cool.'

He could see the driver staring into the rear-view mirror and looking closely at him as he slipped his wallet back into his pocket.

'Cheers, my friend,' said the driver. 'Please take care of yourself.'

He momentarily met the driver's eyes, and then he stepped out of the minicab and slammed the door shut.

Rolf reappears in the window, and this time he finds himself inching forward, out of the shadow of the oak tree, and he looks up. The blond boy scans the distance and raises a hand to his face as though attempting to see more clearly. He continues to look up at Rolf, and then he hears a man's barking voice.

'I said, what are you doing here?'

The night-watchman has left his hut and is slowly waddling towards him with his newspaper dangling from one hand.

'You, over there. Are you deaf?'

Between Rolf in the window, and this man walking towards him, he has no choice now so he turns and begins to run in the direction of the main road. He hears the night-watchman shout something further, but he cannot make out the man's words. As long as a dog does not come chasing after him he will be fine. He has done nothing wrong. He has broken no rules.

He is fully awake before he opens his eyes. He likes it this way, lying perfectly still in the dark and choosing not to move, and then he remembers. He feels nauseous, and he wants the bed to swallow him whole so that he can disappear and then, after a decent lapse of time, he can reappear and pretend that none of this has happened. He is wrong, he knows this. Wrong to have passed her the note, wrong to have waited for her at the language school, wrong to have invited her back to his place. He opens his eyes and looks around his cramped bedroom. Last night he ran all the way back to the flat and then closed the door behind himself and double-locked it. He slumped down on to the sofa and kicked off first one shoe and then the other before letting his head tumble forward into his upturned palms; shit, shit, shit. Really, what the hell was he thinking of spying on her like that? The curtains are still closed, but he can see that it is light outside. A few birds are singing, and in the distance he can hear traffic humming by on the main road. If it comes to it, he can always deny that he was anywhere near the office building last night. Who is going to be able to prove anything? He sits upright and quickly rubs his eyes. The boy, Rolf, he is probably better suited to her. They no doubt have plenty in common, being strangers in a strange country who are both studying the language and learning to clean up after the natives. The pair of them can laugh about the English and their strange bathrooms, with one tap for hot water, and a completely separate tap for cold water. Clearly this makes no sense, for one can never get warm water unless a decision is made to insert the nasty rubber plug into the bowl. It is all so unhygienic, but this is England. This is what he imagines the young couple thinks of his country, and so let them talk about this together. Perhaps Danuta will grow to love this Rolf and choose not to return to Poland? Perhaps she will go to Latvia? Or perhaps Danuta will stay in dirty England? But not with him, for he knows that his unbecoming obsession is over. This morning marks the beginning of a new resolution, for he must now begin to act his age and stop associating with young girls who one moment appear to be malleable and the next flare with anger.

For two days he secludes himself in the Wilton Road flat and he works eight hours a day on the book. He writes in two-hour shifts, setting the alarm on his mobile so that he knows when his shift is over and he can get up from the computer screen. He chooses coffee over tea, and when his concentration begins to waver he does not distract himself with quick snacks of cheese and crackers, or a microwaved bowl of soup. He walks to the window, and then stretches out his hamstrings by bending forward and lowering his head on to the windowsill. He holds this pose for two minutes, or until he feels dizzy, then he walks purposefully back to his desk. By the end of the second day he has begun to put some substance into the heart of the book, but he is now worried that changing the title of the opening section from 'Motown and the Suburbs' to 'Dancing in the Streets' might be too cute; after all, how many readers will remember Martha Reeves and the Vandellas and recognise the oblique reference to her hit song of the same name? For the moment, he chooses to stay with the original title, for he is determined to steer clear of those annoying self-referential headings that usually burden the academic articles that he has xeroxed and saved over the years. They tend to involve either a colon or parentheses, as though the writer is trying to signal his or her cleverness before the piece has even begun. 'Re-Recording Pain: Black and Blue and Makes Me Wanna Holler.' Or, 'Distant Lover(s): Masculinity, Evasion and the African-American Voice'. Midway through the third day he realises that he is about to run out of food and he will therefore have to venture outside, but this is good timing for tonight he has an appointment that he cannot break. Just two more hours, then he will shower and dress carefully. He already feels some relief, as though he has paid penance for his sins by reapplying himself to his work with such single-mindedness. At least with the work there is no awkwardness to negotiate and no guilt to absorb, for he ties himself securely to a routine which allows him little opportunity to wander in either mind or body.

Annabelle opens the door and quickly looks him up and down without saying anything. He wants to shake his head for there is no subtlety to her greeting. She still does not trust him, despite the fact that he knows full well how to dress appropriately.

'Well,' she says. 'Are you coming in?'

'How about "hello" or "good evening" or something?'

Annabelle throws him a fake smile. 'Hello.'

'Well, I can't just march in. It's your place now, or so you keep telling me. Maybe Mr Documentary Film Editor is in there in his boxer shorts.'

'Very funny.'

She steps to one side, and as he passes by he smells her slightly overpowering scent. He can never remember the name of her perfume, but he knows that it is expensive. No doubt Bruce remembers.

'I'm just saying that "good evening" would have been nice. Has the cat got your tongue?'

'Jesus, Keith, you sound like an extra from some sitcom. What kind of phrase is that?'

He stands at the foot of the stairs as she begins to slip her raincoat on over her blue dress. He hasn't seen this dress before and it looks good on her, but he knows that it is best to say nothing about the dress for clearly she is in one of her combative moods and even the most generous of compliments is likely to be turned against him.

'Well, do you want to say hello to Laurie?'

'Where is he?'

Annabelle tosses her head in the direction of the staircase.

'Laurie, your father is here.' There is no reply. 'He's probably got his headphones on again when he's supposed to be doing his homework.'

'Leave it, I'll speak to him later.'

Annabelle furrows her brow. 'Leave it? I don't think so. I told him you would be coming around.'

She begins to trudge upstairs, but as she does so Laurie appears on the landing with his headphones pulled down around his neck and the thick black cable dangling like a loose thread.

'I was just coming to get you.'

Laurie shrugs, but he makes no effort to come downstairs. 'All right, Dad?'

'How's your schoolwork?'

'You tell me. Isn't that what you're here for?'

Annabelle sighs loudly. 'Are you not going to come down here and talk to us properly? I'll get neck ache if you continue to stand up there.' She looks at her watch. 'Oh Christ, we've got to go anyhow. Are you going to be all right?'

'I'm seventeen, Mum.'

'Which is why I'm asking.'

'Have fun at parents' night. I can't wait to hear what those tossers think.' He pauses. 'Not.'

He looks up at his son.

'"Not"? What kind of English is that?'

'Don't start, Dad. You know what I mean. Check you later.'

They both stare as Laurie slides the earpieces of his headphones up and over his ears, and then turns and shuffles out of sight.

Annabelle shakes her head. She finishes buttoning her coat as she descends the stairs.

'And you don't think there's a problem?'

'He's just styling, that's all. It's what the youths do.'

'"Styling"? What the hell is that? He's not a bloody case study, he's your son.'

He shifts his weight on to his left side and pushes his hands into his trouser pockets. He doesn't want to point, for that always sets her off.

'Listen.' He pushes his hands an inch or two deeper into his pockets. 'I know he's my son, and I know something about what he's going through.'

'Well maybe you could explain it to me because it's not that easy to live with.' She throws a quick glance upstairs. 'Sometimes he looks at me as though I'm stupid. I don't just mean as though I don't understand, I mean as though I'm really stupid, and I'm not sure how much more of this I can take.'

He stares at Annabelle and recognises the symptoms; the faint tremor to her voice, and the ever so slightly buckled lower lip as her anxiety rises. Annabelle becomes quieter as she gets angrier.

'Look, we'd better go and hear what his teachers have to say. We can talk about it afterwards, okay?' Annabelle stares at him. 'I'm not trying to avoid the subject, but you said yourself that we should go, right? I don't want to be late on top of dressing like this.'

'Who said there is anything wrong with the way you're dressed?'

'Annabelle, you looked at me like I was something the dog had dragged in.'

'What's with all the animal references? Don't tell me you've started watching *Zoo Nation*?'

'What's *Zoo Nation*?'

'A programme on the television. But it doesn't matter, you're right. We should go. And I never said anything about your clothes.' She looks him up and down again. 'You look okay.'

'Okay? Just "okay"?'

'Jesus, should I take a picture?'

He opens the door and gestures to her. 'After you, Madam.'

Annabelle brushes by him shaking her head.

'Stop pissing about, Keith. I'm really not in the mood, okay.'

The wine bar is almost empty so they are able to get a booth in the window. The candle flickers crazily, as though caught in a gale, and he watches the flame dance until he can take no more. He reaches in and quickly closes his forefinger and thumb on the wick, which leaves a black mark on his hand.

'You're not even listening to me, are you? No wonder Laurie is the way he is.'

'I'm listening, and what do you mean the way he is?'

'Well, he's not officially ADD, but Mr Hughes seems to think that there is some kind of concentration issue.'

'Mr Hughes?'

'The headmaster. We've just been talking to him.'

'I know. I've not forgotten. I just didn't realise that the pompous prat had a name.'

He removes the bottle of wine from the ice bucket and prepares to refill their glasses. Annabelle quickly picks up her glass.

'I'm fine.'

The bottle creates an unholy noise as he thrusts it back into the mass of ice, and for a moment he can't hear the music, but this is good. He wonders why they always play The Gipsy Kings in wine bars, or maybe it's just this bar that is obsessed with the fake bonhomie created by mimicking the enthusiastic rhythms of Spanish folk culture. The usual crowd of BBC yuppies are not in evidence, probably because of the inclement weather, so he is grateful for this break. As he gets older he finds it increasingly difficult to deal with either excessive numbers of people, or loud music which dominates attempts at conversation. Strange, he thinks, this heightened sensitivity to environment. He sips at his wine, and then replaces his glass on the wooden table top.

'I'm going to take Laurie out tomorrow. And I'll talk to him about everything, okay?' Annabelle looks at him, but says nothing. 'Well, is that okay or not, because I can't tell if you don't say anything.'

'Of course it's okay.' She pauses. 'You know I want you to talk with him.'

'Listen, I don't care what they say about him being difficult, I'm just praying that he gets through his exams and goes to university. That's what he says he wants to do, and as far as I'm concerned that's all that matters. If he's really got some learning problems don't you think we'd have noticed them by now?'

'"We'd have noticed"? You mean you as well as me?'

'Yes, that's what I mean, both of us. "We."'

'If you say so. I don't want to bicker.'

He realises that Annabelle has provided him with a classic opening for an argument, but he is determined to avoid any conflict. The issue is Laurie and he is going to stay focused.

'I don't like how those teachers talk about him at that school, like he's some freak. He's one of the few black kids in his class and I know how that feels. I'm not saying that this prat Mr Hughes, or the other teachers, actually want him to fail, but they don't look to me like they particularly want to help him get through the system. Telling us, "Your son has a problem with this, and your son has a problem with that." I've heard similar crap all my life. The fact is, I'm pretty sure they're not on his side.'

'And what about me? Do you think I'm on his side?'

'Look, there's no need to get all defensive. You know I'm not talking about you.'

'Actually, let me tell you something, Mr Conspiracy Theorist, the truth is I don't know that you're not talking about me. I'm really not sure any more, okay.'

She looks around, suddenly conscious that she might have spoken too loudly.

'Annabelle, what are you talking about?'

She returns her attention to the table and leans closer to him. 'And so when I tell you that there's a problem with Laurie, and you don't bother to call me back, do you think it's just more of the same crap that you've heard all your life?'

The owner appears at the table and he strikes a match against a large economy box and relights the candle. The balding man then places a glass sleeve over the candle so that the flame plumes upwards and flickers neither to the left nor to the right.

'I'm not sure where that draught is coming from, but do let me know if it gets too nippy for you.'

The owner smiles as he thrusts the large box of matches into the pocket of his slightly feminine apron and returns to his station behind the bar. He watches as the owner lowers the open leaf of the bar back into place, and then the man picks up his notepad and continues to take inventory of the wines stacked neatly in the rack behind him.

He turns and looks again at Annabelle.

'Listen, Annabelle, of course I know that you're on Laurie's side. I take whatever you have to say seriously. Anyhow, we're here to talk about Laurie, right?'

'And how do you think he's going to feel when he finds out about your latest mess?'

'My latest what?'

'Spare me the denials, Keith. People talk.' She pauses. 'And don't look at me like that. Do you want me to spell it out? I've never been one to ask what you're doing for sex. Who you're sleeping with. If you're in a relationship. It doesn't matter how nicely or delicately one puts it, you know it all adds up to the same thing, but as far as I'm concerned it's simply none of my business. Until, that is, people start to talk.'

'Who starts to talk?'

'Does it matter, who? I mean people who enjoy seeing somebody fall flat on their face and making themselves look stupid.'

He shakes his head and takes another sip of his wine.

'Yes, stupid. You don't pee in your own bed, didn't anybody ever tell you that?'

'I'll tell you what nobody ever told me. They never told me how vindictive and manipulative women can be, that's what nobody ever told me.'

'Well yippee, you've found out at last. Can I have some of that wine?'

He tops up her glass, and then adds an extra splash to his own, which empties the bottle. He turns it upside down and crunches it into the bucket.

'You've got to protect yourself a little bit, Keith. And if you don't want to do it for yourself, then at least have the common sense to do it for your son. Do you really want him to hear about you sleeping with girls his age?'

'She's twenty-six and a divorcee. She's hardly a bloody teenager.'

'I think you get my point.'

He stares at Annabelle, whose glass is hovering halfway between the table and her mouth. For a moment she seems unsure what to do, and then she slowly replaces the glass on the wooden table.

'Look Keith, I know that in a sense it's none of my business, but it matters to me.'

'What matters to you?'

'I don't want you making a fool of yourself.' She pauses. 'People look up to you. For heaven's sake, don't let some desperate girl drag your name through the mud.'

'I did nothing wrong. She's the one who ought to take a good look at herself, but I know how it comes across. I'm older. She works for me. Apparently I'm the one with all the power. That's what people see, isn't it? That's what it looks like.'

'I don't have to tell you what it looks like, but have you ever tried taking the word "no" for a little walk around your tongue?' She pauses. 'Well?'

He turns and looks out of the window as an elderly couple stroll by. They are bent into the wind, the man with an arm curled tightly around his wife's shoulders as though trying to anchor her to the ground so she won't blow away. That's how it should be, he thinks. Old people with old people are not so old.

He turns from the window and looks at Annabelle, who finishes her wine and then places the empty glass back on the table.

'Shall we go? I can drive you back.'

He calls for the bill, but continues to scrutinise Annabelle. She is still beautiful, despite the lines around her eyes, and the short, grey hair, and he has no difficulty recognising her as the courageous young woman he met over twenty-five years ago. However, he is unsure of what she sees when she looks across the table at him, for that look of respect, which he had once been accustomed to, has long since vanished from her face. He probably last saw it at her father's funeral as they sat together, with Laurie squeezed between the two of them, in the narrow front row pew of the village's Norman church. As the time drew closer for Annabelle to approach the altar and deliver her reading from the Old Testament, he knew that she was stealing sideways glances at him and trying to draw strength from his presence. She required his support, and he was not only proud to be there for her, he was determined that she should get through both the service and the reception at Magnolia Cottage without any unnecessary distress. He knew that his wife needed him, and so he snaked his hand behind their son's back and gently caressed her shoulder as the captain of the local golf club finished delivering the eulogy.

Annabelle's mother took her husband's death badly and, according to Annabelle, within weeks of the funeral she became helpless. It could, of course, have gone the other way, and being suddenly free from the scrutiny of an overbearing husband might have provided a timely boost to her confidence, but he was surprised to hear just how difficult his mother-in-law found it to cope with the day-to-day practicalities of being by herself. Now that Annabelle's work at the theatrical agency seemed to have dried up altogether, she was free to travel to Wiltshire as often as two or three times a week. If she chose to visit at a weekend she generally took Laurie with her, for he seemed to get a thrill from seeing his sunflowers beginning to dominate one corner of the garden and, like himself, starting to shoot up in size. These days nobody called him a 'halfie' any more, and his late grandfather would have been pleased to learn that if they did so they were likely to get a thumping for their impertinence. On the very few occasions that he travelled with Annabelle and Laurie, he was shocked to see for himself the degree to which his mother-in-law's self-assurance seemed to have been eroded by her husband's death. She hesitated over every decision, and even simple things such as where to place a vase of flowers, or whether to have tea or coffee, seemed to mire her in a haze of confusion that was soon complemented by a forgetfulness that quickly became alarming.

It was shortly after he had moved out of their house, and into Wilton Road, that Annabelle telephoned to let him know that she had made the decision to relocate her mother into an assisted living residence. Apparently the Briars was more like a cosy country hotel than an old people's home, or at least that's what they claimed in the advertising material, and by selling Magnolia Cottage, and carefully investing the proceeds, her mother would in all likelihood be well looked after for the rest of her life. Annabelle now had a full-time job at the BBC, so he thought it only fair to ask her what, if anything, he could do to help, but she insisted that she had it under control. She did, however, want to let him know that her mother frequently asked after him, and she always coupled her enquiries with an apology. He asked Annabelle why, but she snapped at him and told him that it was because of her father. 'She's not a fool, you know. She *is* ashamed of how Daddy behaved over the years.' A part of him wanted to say that she should be ashamed, but he held his tongue and chose instead to ask how Laurie felt about visiting the Briars.

'What do you mean, how does he feel?'

'Well, is it awkward for him?'

'He says it's full of dry white people and he doesn't want to come any more, if that answers your question. He wants to see his grandmother, but not there.'

There was an awkward telephone silence and he wanted to say that he couldn't blame his son, but instead he asked her if he should try to persuade Laurie to visit, but Annabelle was adamant that it was just a phase and this was the least of her problems with Laurie.

'So you go alone then?'

Annabelle laughed ironically. 'Are you asking me if I take Bruce?'

'No, I'm asking you if you visit by yourself.'

'You know I haven't told Mummy about our situation, so how can I tell her about Bruce? I don't see why I should cause her any unnecessary confusion.'

'So she still thinks we're together?'

'She has no reason to think anything else, and I believe it's better that way, don't you?'

He held on to the telephone not knowing how to answer.

She finds a convenient parking space across the street from her house and he leans over and quickly kisses her on the cheek. He doesn't want any more conversation and, judging from the silence which had accompanied their journey home, neither does she. As he slams the car door and begins the short walk back to Wilton Street, he resolves not to turn around and see if she is watching, although he is reasonably sure that she will be. He decides that once he disappears beyond the corner and passes out of sight, he will jog the rest of the way home as he is cold and he also needs to use the bathroom. Their drink at the wine bar had not exactly been a success. When the bill arrived they decided to have one more glass, which gave him the opportunity to re-route their conversation away from what Annabelle had taken to calling his 'mess' and back on to the subject of Laurie. However, once they returned there Annabelle only seemed to become more agitated.

'Mr Hughes thinks he might be in a gang.'

He shook his head. 'Mr Hughes wouldn't know a gang if they tried to carjack his bike from underneath him. Is Laurie doing any drugs, or binge-drinking, or carrying weapons? No, he's not, right?'

'Not as far as I know, but it's the type of people that Laurie's involved with that appears to be the issue. Apparently Mr Hughes thinks they are affecting his concentration, and his grades are clearly not as good as they were.'

'Okay, Annabelle, but why didn't this prat say all of this to me when we were there tonight?'

'We only had a few minutes with him.'

'Look, I said I'll talk to Laurie, and I will. But don't you remember when you were a teenager? You took risks and kept secrets from your parents, didn't you? You did things they didn't know about, but you came through it.'

Annabelle sighed. 'Keith, I know. I get it, but I feel as though I might be losing him around the black–white thing. I suppose that's what Mr Hughes is trying to say, for Laurie only seems to want to be with black kids. He's my son and I don't want him to start disliking me.'

He leaned forward and touched the sleeve of her blue dress.

'You know that's not going to happen, okay? Don't worry about that, not for a minute.'

'I'm sorry but I can't drink this.' She pushed the glass of house white away from her. 'We should probably go now. I've got to be in the office early.'

He called for the bill again, and almost immediately the owner emerged from behind the bar and plucked the plastic folder from the pocket of his apron. When they first arrived the owner had told them that it was house policy to take a credit card for each table and they had found this annoying, but at least things would now be quick.

'Everything to your satisfaction?' The owner smiled and blew out the candle at the same time.

Annabelle nodded. 'Lovely, thank you.'

He watched as the man picked up their still full glasses of house wine and placed them on a circular cork tray. Then he turned his attention to the credit card statement and filled in the tip amount and totalled up the bill, before handing the merchant copy to the owner and slipping his own copy and credit card into his wallet. He smiled at Annabelle.

'Shall we go?'

* * *

He switches on the lights in the flat and rushes to the bathroom. Having relieved himself, and washed his hands, he passes into the living room and begins to empty out the contents of his pockets on to the coffee table. First, his wallet, with the receipt from the wine bar that is folded loosely into it, and then he takes out a small handful of change, two £20 notes, and his mobile phone. He lines them up as though there is some sort of organisational logic to what he is doing. It is then that he notices the 'missed call' message on the mobile, and so he sits on the sofa and checks to see who has called. There is no message, but he recognises the number and speed-dials Annabelle and waits. The short trip home should not have exhausted him so much, but he decides that it's a combination of the tension of the walk, plus the nonsense of the school visit, and the conversation with Annabelle, that has left him feeling so depleted. Annabelle's phone goes immediately to voicemail so he leaves a message asking her to call if she needs to, and then he tucks the phone into his pocket and goes into the kitchen where he turns on the kettle. He finds the last Earl Grey teabag in the back of the cupboard and drops it into the empty cup. Then, just as the water is starting to boil, the phone rings. He can hear traffic in the background, and anxiety in Annabelle's voice.

'Keith?'

'Where are you? You sound like you're at a Grand Prix race.'

'I'm by the Westway, and looking for Laurie. He wasn't at home when I got back.'

He turns off the kettle and moves into the living room where the reception on his mobile is a little clearer.

'You mean you don't know where he is?'

'He and his friends like to go to this skateboard park. I'm walking up towards it.'

'A skateboard park? At this time of night?'

'Maybe you'll believe me now.'

'I can get a minicab and be there in five minutes.'

He reaches for his jacket and pushes one arm into a sleeve. He switches the phone from one hand to the next and then wriggles the other arm into the jacket.

'Jesus, it's all right.' He can hear the relief in Annabelle's voice. 'I can see him.'

'What's he doing?'

'Nothing. He's just with some kids on mountain bikes. Laurie's sitting on a park bench.'

'Just sitting by the Westway at this time of night?' He slumps down on the sofa and waits for Annabelle to say something.

'He's seen me.'

'Look, I can still get a minicab and meet you there. Or back at the house.'

'Let's just leave it for tonight. He seems okay.'

'Okay? He's totally out of order.'

'He's walking towards me.'

'Let me talk to him.'

'Look, I'm going now, Keith. You can talk to him when you come over tomorrow. But I mean it. I'm not sure how much more of this I can take.'

The line goes dead, but he continues to hold the mobile to his ear. As long as he holds this pose there is still some communication between himself and Annabelle and their son. He just has to hold the pose.

III

He stands by the gate to the school and studies the scruffy parade of boys trooping out with bags slung casually over one shoulder, ties flapping over the other, shoelaces undone, and hair uncombed. There is no point in his getting too judgmental for, although he would like to imagine otherwise, some part of him knows that he almost certainly looked just as unkempt when he was a sixth-former. And then he sees Laurie, loping across the playground by himself, the same pair of expensive oversized headphones jammed on to his head, and his body gently bobbing to the beat of the music. He knows that his son has seen him, but it is not until Laurie is only a few feet away that he reaches up and literally pulls the headphones down to his neck, and then he gives his father that upward nod that begins with his chin.

'All right, Dad?'

He pats his son on the shoulder, then squeezes. 'I'm fine, son. Just fine.'

He waits on the pavement outside the Cineplex for Laurie to

emerge from the toilets. While they were watching the film it grew dark, and a little chilly, but for some reason the streetlights now seem unnaturally bright. He blinks hard, realising that he is having some difficulty adjusting his vision to the glare of the night, and he wonders if the many hours that he has recently spent at the computer screen have affected his eyes. He turns up the collar on his leather jacket and thinks that it might be best if they simply make a dash for Pizza Express. He had toyed with the idea of taking Laurie to a Greek or French restaurant, somewhere semi-formal so that at least the two of them might have somewhere quiet to talk, but a part of him knows that Laurie will regard any restaurant with cloth napkins and two forks as a pretentious dump. As he waits with the cluster of nervous smokers, he suspects that a longer walk to a proper restaurant would also irritate Laurie, whose patience seemed to be wearing thin for much of the second half of the Will Smith film. Not that there had been much choice, for it was either this, a cartoon featuring talking penguins, or an Italian art movie that looked a little bit too risqué, as he wasn't ready to start watching bedroom scenes with his son. Predictably, the Will Smith film had been little more than a special-effect-laden action feature, with the obligatory light-skinned romance, and he sympathised with Laurie when he noticed him take out his mobile phone and furtively begin texting. As he glances at his watch, he imagines that his son is most likely in the toilets engaged in exactly the same type of clandestine communication.

Pizza Express turns out to be a good choice. Laurie asks for some extra breadsticks while he waits for his 'special' pizza, and he seems happy that his father is letting him drink a small bottle of Italian beer. 'Thanks, Dad.' He slops it quickly into the glass tumbler.

'Does your mother let you drink beer? Or maybe wine. You know, with a meal.'

'Are you losing it? She'd have a fit if she thought I was out boozing with you.'

'Well you're not exactly boozing, are you? Just a bottle of beer.'

'But it's more than she's gonna let me have.'

'Well, maybe she has her reasons for it.' He looks at Laurie, who shrugs his shoulders and takes another gulp of his beer. 'You know, she told me about you getting wasted last Christmas with your mates.' Laurie lowers his eyes and swirls the beer in the glass. 'Listen, it's all well and good drinking too much, but the real problem isn't the headache, or the puking, it's the lines you cross because your judgement is off.' Laurie looks up at him and he can see frustration in his son's eyes. 'The point is, it's the things you do and say when you've been drinking that usually come back to haunt you, because they're not always things that you mean. Am I making sense?'

'I suppose so.'

'Listen, what's done is done, but all I want to say is don't disrespect your mother by coming in drunk, all right. She was pretty upset about what happened last Christmas.'

'Is that the end of my lesson, then?'

'You think this is a joke?'

His son stares at him, and then slowly, almost imperceptibly, he shakes his head.

'No, I don't think it's a joke.'

'Keep control, son. Keep it together. There are enough people out there trying to knock you out of your stride. Trust me, you don't need to be helping them.'

Both pizzas seem too large for the plates. He understands that 'value for money' is supposed to be the special feature of Pizza Express although, to him, it looks like small plates are their real speciality. He watches as his son eats quickly, tearing at the pizza with his hands rather than cutting it neatly into slices, and he realises that there are some things that he cannot talk to Laurie about. It is probably too late.

'So you have no idea of what you would like for a present after your exams?'

'You mean after passing my exams, 'cause you're not giving me anything if I fail them, right?'

'You'll pass. I'm not worried. I thought maybe a trip to the Caribbean.'

'The Caribbean?' Laurie pushes a particularly large piece of pizza into his mouth, and he speaks through the food as he chews. 'Why there?'

'What do you mean "why there?"? Your grandparents come from there. Are you saying you're not interested?'

'Whatever.'

'What's that supposed to mean? You're supposed to know something about where you come from. Or at least be curious. I'm not asking you to go and live there or anything, but at least just take a look. It's the Caribbean, Laurie. How bad can it be?'

'Well how come you've never been there if it's so important?'

'I suppose a part of me was waiting until you were old enough so we could go together.'

'Your dad doesn't want to know, does he?'

'I've already explained to you. He's very private about everything.'

'Weirdo, more like. Sitting up there in that house by himself.'

'Come on, that's not fair.'

'What's not fair? Am I lying?'

He stares at his son and understands that, from his point of view, his grandfather must appear to be a somewhat eccentric man. However, this is not a topic he feels comfortable discussing with Laurie. The one time he took Laurie to meet him, his father simply sat and looked at his twelve-year-old grandson, before abruptly picking up his pork-pie hat and leaving for the pub without saying a word. Annabelle had warned him that she did not want their son to be as upset by his father as she had been on the one occasion that he had introduced her to him. After they had moved to London, the theatrical agency that Annabelle worked for had informed her that they had a play opening at the Crucible Theatre in Sheffield and asked her if she might be free to view it. When Annabelle told him that she would have to travel to the north, he realised that he could go with her and take this opportunity to introduce her and, if truth be told, re-introduce himself to his father after many years of estrangement. However, when he and Annabelle presented themselves at his father's house, the stubborn older man retreated into a silence which resisted Annabelle's quietly expressed appeals for there to be communication and, as she put it, 'fence-mending'. On the train back to London, a pregnant Annabelle sat and stared out of the window with the occasional tear rolling down her face, and although he found this uncomfortable, it was better than the anger he had been expecting. By the time they reached London, Annabelle seemed to have pulled herself together again.

'He's your problem, Keith. You'll have to sort things out between the two of you before he ever accepts me, so I'm going to make the effort not to take it personally. At least I tried, right?' She looked across at him. 'Right?'

He helped her down on to the platform, and then picked up both of their bags. 'I know you tried, and I'm sorry. I told you he was out of order.'

Twelve years later, his father gave him and his son the same silent treatment when they stopped to see him after he had taken Laurie to visit the National Railway Museum in York. After looking at them both for some minutes, and then muttering something under his breath, his father simply picked up his hat and walked out of his own house. Laurie seemed to deal with the rejection better than Annabelle, but five years later, given the unpleasantness of the encounter, he can't argue with his son's description of his father as a 'weirdo'. He watches as Laurie pushes the final piece of pizza into his mouth and then wipes his fingers on the crested serviette.

'Well, this Caribbean trip isn't about your grandfather, it's about you and me.'

'Yeah, I know, bonding. We had to write an essay about it in General Studies.'

'Well? Are you interested or not?'

'In bonding?'

'In going to the Caribbean. Okay, bonding in the Caribbean, if that makes you feel better.'

'All right then, we can check it out. But Grandma gave me some money, so I'm also going to Barcelona. It'll be after the end of the season, but at least I'll see the ground and maybe I'll get to see them train.'

'You're telling me that you'd rather go to Spain, which is just around the corner, than go all the way across the Atlantic to the Caribbean?'

'I told you, I can go to both.'

'Do you want me to come with you to Barcelona?'

'What for? You don't like Barca. Anyhow, I'm going with some mates.'

'No adults?'

'You're not worried about me, are you?'

'Should I be?'

'Get real, Dad. I'm nearly eighteen.'

As they step out of the Pizza Express he sees a group of boys idling on a low brick wall near the entrance to the Tesco Mini-Mart. For a moment he thinks about walking in the opposite direction, for he knows that it will be straightforward to get a cab in the next street, but Laurie seems to know the boys and he shouts.

'Yo!'

He sees his son throw a quick hand signal that elicits a chorus of 'Yo!'s from the loiterers, but he turns away from Laurie and squints anxiously down the street. He flags down a passing cab, for he wants to get away from these boys as quickly as possible. Laurie scampers over to join him, and as the cab moves off he wonders if he should ask his son if he is in a gang. However, if Laurie says 'yes' he is unsure of what advice he might offer him that wouldn't just provoke his son's ire and frustration, so he decides to say nothing. He turns slightly and looks out of the window at the heavy night traffic. So, Annabelle's mother has given Laurie money to go to Spain. More likely that Annabelle has given him the money in the name of her mother, for he is sure that his mother-in-law's dementia has reached a stage where she would not even recognise her grandson. It pains him that he is unable to offer his son another grandmother, or a proper relationship with his grandfather, for he doesn't want Laurie to feel that should anything happen to him then Annabelle's family are all that he has. In a sense, offering to take him to the Caribbean is his attempt to repair this imbalance, but if Laurie prefers to take his grandmother's money and go to Barcelona with his mates, then he should be free to do so. He turns quickly and steals a glance at his son, who has slipped his headphones back into place and is once again bobbing his head to the music which leaks out from his bulbous earpieces. He wants to suggest to his son that conversation might be a good alternative to just cutting himself off in this way, but he decides to leave it. Both the trip to the cinema, and then the pizza, have been a success. At least they have talked, which is what he hoped for, and Annabelle can have no complaints. She can't accuse him of not trying to bond with his son.

He registers the quizzical look on Annabelle's face as she opens the door and stands to one side. Laurie squeezes past her, but he doesn't bother to take off his headphones or greet his mother. His son half turns so that he faces him, but he doesn't break stride.

'See you, Dad. Thanks.'

He watches as Laurie bounces upstairs, easily taking two steps at a time, and when the tall young man eventually disappears from view he looks at Annabelle.

'What's the matter?'

'Jesus Christ, Keith. "What's the matter?" How can you be so casual about everything. Her name's Yvette, right?'

He shrugs his shoulders and makes it clear that she should continue.

'There's some kind of website with a blog on it and people are posting messages. Apparently she's on antidepressants and is barely functioning. That's what's the matter. People are writing about you and her, and I hate to tell you this, but you're not looking too clever.'

'You've got to be joking.'

'Do I look like I'm joking?'

'Well what are they saying?'

'I think you'd better read it for yourself.'

'I don't know anything about this website.'

'Trust me, you will.'

'But it's ridiculous, we're two single people who started to see each other and it ended, that's all.'

'You don't get it, do you? You can't win in these situations, and you do understand that somebody is going to send the link to Laurie, the same way they sent it to me.'

'Who sent you the link?'

'I'm buggered if I know, but somebody wanted to make sure that I saw it.'

He runs his hand quickly across his face, but he realises that he is not thinking clearly.

'You think somebody's trying to stitch me up?'

'Yes, Sherlock, somebody's trying to discredit you further than you've already discredited yourself. And it might not be Yvette, or whatever her name is. It's a blog so anybody can sign in. It's public space.'

'Maybe I should speak to a lawyer and see if I can get it stopped.'

'Well do me a favour, Keith, do *something*, will you? Before your son begins to dislike you too.'

'What do you mean?'

'I mean you don't have a lot of friends on that blog.'

'Including you, I take it.'

'I'm not on the blog.'

He shakes his head. 'You know what I mean.'

'How was it tonight?'

'How was what?'

'Your time with Laurie. What do you think I mean?'

'I had a good time with him. He's changing, that's all. Going through that moody "I'm a man" stuff. But we chatted, and it's fine.'

Annabelle smiles sarcastically. '"And it's fine"? What are you talking about? What's fine?'

He feels anger and frustration rising quickly within him, but he bites his bottom lip hard. He lowers his voice to just above a whisper.

'Laurie's fine. He's passing through adolescence so he's doing the whole awkward thing. What do you expect?'

'And you think that's all there is to it? That's he's not hiding something from us?'

'Look I'm his dad, not his bloody therapist. He seems fine to me. All that ADD crap that the headmaster was talking about is just that. Crap.' He stares at Annabelle. 'All right?'

Annabelle glares at him, but she has clearly decided to say nothing further.

He takes a sip of wine as the computer whirrs and beeps and offers him various upgrades which he rejects with a succession of hurried clicks. He puts down the glass then stands up and takes off his jacket and drapes it over the back of the sofa. As he does so he notices that the two cinema tickets have fallen from his jacket pocket on to the floor, so he stoops to pick them up and tosses them on to the coffee table before stepping back into the kitchen and switching on the central heating. He has been meaning to program the thermostat so that the heat comes on automatically, but this will mean reading the booklet and he's yet to find the time to do so. He re-enters the living room and sits back in front of the screen, but his hands hover for he is still trying to decide whether or not to take a look at the offending website. Annabelle had helpfully written down the address on a piece of paper and shoved it into his hand as he was leaving. But why, he thinks, should he expose himself to something that he knows is going to disturb him, and most likely make him angry? He logs into his email and begins to write to Clive Wilson. He needs to see him urgently. In fact, first thing in the morning. Before he sends the short email he stands up and walks a few paces to the window where he stares out into the darkness. He can see nothing, no people, no movement beyond the gently swaying branches and the flickering light in the lamp-post, but he can hear cars swishing by on the main road at the end of the street. There is no need to explain to Clive why he needs to see him. Surely, Clive Wilson should be able to work that out for himself.

'Here,' says Clive. 'Just drink out of the other side of the cup. No milk and no sugar, right?' He pushes the coffee cup across the desk. 'Whoever heard of running out of coffee. Hang on, you can have your own cup of decaf if you like. I've got some of that.' Clive slides back his chair and prepares to climb to his feet.

'No thanks, Clive. This is fine, we can share.'

He lifts the cup to his mouth and takes a quick sip of the watery coffee, and then he places it back in front of Clive, careful to make sure that the handle is facing the right direction. His boss laughs nervously then clears his throat.

'I promise you, I'll speak to her about the website, but it might not be anything to do with her.'

'Oh come on, you know better than that.'

'Look, I'm on it, Keith. I've already contacted our IT guys, and they've been in touch with some internet lawyers so, one way or another, we'll find out who's responsible. Anyhow, the site's probably already been cleared up. Basically don't worry about the website, that's no longer an issue.'

'Well, can I assume that you don't have a problem with me wanting to come back to work?'

'Well, personally, I'd kill for a few weeks' paid leave. I don't know what the hurry is to get back.' Clive slurps his coffee, but he doesn't bother to push the cup back in his employee's direction. He holds on to the handle. 'I thought you were writing a book or something.'

'More like "something".'

'So it's not going well. Is that why you want to plonk yourself back behind your desk?' He thinks about how best to explain the situation, but Clive continues. 'Lesley's doing just fine in your job. I mean it's a bit of a stretch for her, but she's coping.'

'With all due respect, it's not Lesley that I've come to talk about.'

Clive Wilson sighs and brings his hands together on the desk, as though about to pray.

'Like I told you, Yvette's back now and she's healing. I think that's what they call it. Bloody hell, what kind of language is that? They make it sound like she's tripped up and bruised her knee.'

'Look, Clive, the only way I'm going to put an end to this bullshit is by standing up for myself and confronting the situation. I want my job back. I've got to let people know that I didn't do anything wrong and that it's all finished with.' He pauses. 'It would be better if you could move her to a different department, or transfer her out of the building, but I suppose you've got your reasons for not doing so.'

Clive laughs, and leans back in his chair as he does so.

'Yes, Keith, I've got my reasons all right. She's accused you of harassment and technically she's the innocent one here. I can't just make her disappear.'

'I'm not asking you to have her bumped off or anything, but how can you call her innocent? Harassment? I've never harmed anybody in my life. Come on, this is bullshit, Clive. Whose side are you on?'

Clive leans forward and places his hands back on the desk.

'It's probably best if I forget that I heard that.'

'No, it's all right. You can go ahead and answer. It's about time somebody explained to me just what the hell is going on around here.'

'I had to fight for your job, Keith. I know you don't want to hear this, but it was me who suggested that rather than begin disciplinary proceedings against you, which the local authority were seriously considering, they should give you paid leave which would enable everyone to have a cooling-off period. I can't do much about gossip, and these days people don't just whisper in the corridors or by the water fountain, they do so on websites. It's pretty uncomfortable, but I can't legislate for that. Nobody can, but like I said I think that's been dealt with. But I'm sorry, you *are* going to have to sit tight for a few weeks before I can begin to ease you back into your job, and when I do so Yvette's not going to like the situation any more than you like it now, but that's just the way it will have to be.'

Clive quickly drums the tips of his fingers against the desk with an almost military flourish, and then he sits up straight and stares at his subordinate.

'Can I ask you something, Keith? I'm not trying to be offensive or anything.'

'Ask whatever you want to ask, Clive. You're in charge, aren't you?'

Clive sighs. 'Look, I don't want any unpleasantness between us. Believe me that's the last thing that I want.' He pauses. 'I suppose I just wanted to know if it was serious. On your part, that is. I'm not interested in what she was thinking, I'm just trying to work out what was going on in your mind. Because, if it wasn't serious, have you ever thought about using prostitutes? I mean, that's what they're there for. Quick, simple, easy, nobody gets hurt, and who gives a fuck, right?'

'Is that what you do, Clive? Fuck prostitutes, and you think that makes you better than me? Cheating on your wife with hookers, that makes you smarter than me?'

'Calm down, Keith. I've never been with a prostitute in my life, I was just trying to understand something, but I'm sorry if I offended you. Look, you made a mistake, Keith. I don't want to come over all heavy, but you made a mistake. These are other people's kids that you're treating like this.'

'Other people's kids? She's a fucking twenty-six-year-old woman. She's not some schoolgirl virgin. Can you not get that straight? She's not innocent, and don't you dare talk to me about other people's kids like I'm some fucking sex offender.' He pushes back the chair and stands up. 'Clive, don't fucking patronise me.'

'Please, Keith. Keep your voice down.'

'Fuck you, Clive. "Somebody else's kids"? Have you lost the plot? You really have bought into all of this "healing" crap, haven't you?'

When he reaches the door to Clive's office he turns, but he stops himself as he hears the words of resignation rising to his lips. No, he isn't going to give him the satisfaction. Clive Wilson emerges from behind his desk and walks towards him with an arm extended awkwardly in his direction.

'I'm sorry, Keith but you need more cooling-off time, and I'm going to recommend counselling. It's important for you, I think. And it will also show that you're serious about addressing these issues.'

'Fuck you, Clive.'

'I know you're angry, and maybe I would be too. But work with me on this. Please.'

He leaves the office and realises that he needs to calm down. Another minute and he would have smacked the smug bastard. He decides to take a walk by the river, and because it is nearly lunchtime he has the option of dropping in at one of the pubs on the embankment for a drink and something to eat. He walks purposefully through the busy pedestrian traffic on the High Street, having made up his mind to stop first at a cash machine and then buy a newspaper, but before he gets to his bank it strikes him that wandering alone by the river sounds too depressing.

He dashes across the street and passes into the indoor shopping centre. Shit, maybe he should have shaken Clive Wilson's hand before storming out, for he has now left the fool with the impression that he is simply an angry man. By flying off the handle and failing to keep control, he has allowed Clive Wilson to talk his rubbish about a cooling-off period, and needing to see the bigger picture. He is going to have to email him a note of apology, but he will stop short of suggesting another meeting in his office, or a reconciliatory drink, for that would be to give up too much ground. A simple note of apology will have to suffice and he will leave it up to Clive Wilson to make the next move.

In the sports shop he is faced with a difficult decision. The young tracksuited assistant has spread three Barcelona shirts on the counter top with the back of the shirts, complete with names and numbers, facing up.

'So you don't know who your son's favourite player is?'

The boy speaks as though he feels sorry for his foolish customer.

'I don't really know that much about Spanish football,' he mutters in his defence. 'Do they show it on television?'

'Like every Sunday. And there's a round-up of La Liga on a Monday night.'

He is puzzled, but he doesn't want to ask anything further of the spotty youth. However, tracksuit boy quickly identifies the source of his confusion.

'La Liga. The Spanish League. Like the Premiership.'

He nods quickly and then turns his attention back to the shirts. He recognises the short, aggressive, name of a player he thinks is Brazilian and decides that with a combination of Brazil and Barcelona he can't go far wrong.

'You know the other thing that we can do is to put your son's name on the shirt with his own number. So long as there are not too many letters in his name, that is. He does play, doesn't he?'

The boy is beginning to sound like a minor government official. He looks at the assistant, and hands him the middle one of the three shirts.

'I think this one will do the job.'

'Okay then, no name.' The somewhat disappointed boy takes the shirt and begins to fold it up.

'If your son doesn't like it then you can always bring it back with a receipt, so long as he hasn't worn it.'

'You mean to play in?'

'No, I mean worn it at all. We can't accept returns on soiled goods.'

'You mean if he tries it on it's soiled?'

'Not my rules, if you know what I mean. I only work here.'

He watches as the assistant slips the shirt into a plastic bag, and then drops the plastic bag into a large paper sack with handles. The boy takes his credit card and quickly swipes it and then hands the card back.

'Sign here, please.'

He picks up a fake pen that is tethered to the counter top and scrawls his name on to a plastic screen.

'I'm sure if he just pulls it on over a T-shirt to see if it's the right size then he won't be soiling anything.' The assistant drops the receipt into the bag and hands it to him. 'All a bit stupid if you ask me, but then again nobody ever does ask me.'

He quickly makes his way out of the warm shopping centre, and back on to the frigid High Street. It is the middle of the day, and people are rushing around in their lunch hour trying to pick up a few groceries, or paying bills, or hurrying to the post office before returning to their offices. And then it strikes him again: he does not have an office to go back to. In effect, he has no role, and beyond the occasional fits and spurts of attention that he pays to his book, there really is no cogent purpose to his day or his life. Clive has temporarily cut him loose from his moorings and he is drifting. He sees a bus coming and wonders if he should ride the four stops back to Wilton Road. But then again, what's the hurry? As he walks past the queue at the bus stop, he catches a glimpse of himself in the window of Mr Crusty and is relieved to note that he still recognises the man who is reflected in the glass. But he will have to be careful. Shopping for football shirts in the middle of the day. It makes no sense whatsoever.

Danuta is standing by the door with her rucksack at her feet. She must have rung the doorbell, discovered that he was not in, and decided to simply wait. He calls her name, and as she turns to face him he notices the smile of relief that momentarily brightens her face. He walks towards her and gently places his hand on her arm, for he is sure that she is about to burst into tears.

'Are you okay?'

She shakes her head, but manages to hold back her tears. She takes one last draw on her cigarette and then drops it to the ground and stubs it out with the toe of her scuffed shoe. There are a half-dozen other butts that litter the pathway and suggest just how long she has been waiting.

'You'd better come in, don't you think?'

He transfers the bag with the Barcelona shirt from one hand to the other, then he forages in his pocket for the keys to the front door and ushers her into the ground floor hallway and out of the cold.

He hands her the cup of coffee, which she cradles in two hands, and then he sits opposite her and puts his own cup down on to the glass-topped coffee table. He doesn't want to force her to explain, but he would like to know what has happened. Maybe she has lost her cleaning job, or perhaps there is a family illness back in Poland, or maybe she has been mugged? Whatever it is, he understands that he will have to wait for her to initiate the conversation, but she still appears to be shaken. She blows gently on her coffee, and then she takes a tentative sip.

'Would you like something to eat? I can make you some soup, or I can order food for delivery. Well, Chinese or Indian.'

She shakes her head.

'Or I can leave you alone for a few minutes, maybe that would help?'

'It is Rolf. I think that he is perhaps too attracted to me.'

He looks quizzically at her as she puts down her coffee and finally looks directly at him.

'What I mean is that he likes me, that is all. He is not happy for me to be by myself. He has changed and it is not easy, but I am sorry to come to you with this problem.'

'Has he hurt you in any way?'

She lowers her eyes and does not answer. Her clothes are rumpled, as though she has slept in them, and she starts now to bounce her knee nervously.

'It is important that you tell me if he has hurt you.'

'Why is it important? What are you going to do? Report him to the police? Is that what you plan to do?'

'He isn't allowed to hurt you, Danuta.'

'He has not hurt me. I have hurt him.'

She looks up now and stops bouncing her knee. She swallows deeply, and for the first time she appears to be helpless.

'Perhaps it is possible to stay here for a few days? I cannot go back to Rolf, but if it is not possible then I will understand. I know of a hostel for women. I stayed in this place when I first came to London.' She quickly stands. 'Perhaps it is better if I go there. I am sorry for bothering you with my problems.'

He too stands, but he is careful not to move towards her.

'Look, if you are in danger then you have to go to the police.' She stares at him but says nothing. 'Well, are you in danger?'

'Mr Keith, I think it is better if I go now to the hostel.'

'Do you have money for the hostel?'

'You are a lonely man, but kind.' She looks tired, but she manages to smile as though she feels sorry for him. 'I think you cannot help.'

'Danuta, I'm not putting you out, but is staying here really going to solve anything?'

'I understand, and I do not wish to stay here. You are right, this is my problem.'

'How have you hurt him? You said you hurt Rolf.'

'Please, Mr Keith. I have made a mistake coming here.' She picks up her rucksack from the side of the sofa and then runs a hand back through her loose mop of hair. 'It is better if I go now.'

'But you look so tired. Are you working tonight?'

She shrugs her shoulders.

'You don't have to tell me anything if you don't want to, but at least sit down for a moment. I'd prefer it if you didn't leave like this.'

He listens as the water suddenly stops flowing. She has locked off the faucet in the shower and will now be stepping on to the bathmat and towelling herself dry. He was relieved when the exhausted girl asked him if she could maybe sleep for a couple of hours, and it was his suggestion that she take a shower first for this would give him time to dash into the bedroom and change the bed linen and generally straighten things out. He picked up a handful of old copies of *Spin* magazine from the floor, and pushed them into the drawer where he keeps his T-shirts. Then he drew the curtains closed and turned on the bedside lamp before tackling the issue of changing the bed clothes. He rushed the job, but he managed to square off the pillows, and tuck in the top sheet, before he bent down and collected up the dirty sheets and quickly pushed them into the wicker laundry basket. She knocks on the open door and then edges her way into the bedroom. Her blonde hair is still wet and lank, and although she wears the same jeans and sweatshirt she carries the rest of her clothes, including her underwear, in her hands. He flattens himself against the wall so she will be able to pass by, but having taken a few steps into the bedroom she is now rooted to the spot.

'Come on in. I'll get out of your way and let you get some sleep.'

He gestures towards the bed, and she inches past him as though determined that they should not make contact in this narrow space.

'I'll come and wake you at the end of the afternoon. I'm sorry for asking again, but are you going to work?'

She shakes her head. 'This is not possible.'

He watches as she places her clothes on the floor beneath the window and then, still in her jeans and sweatshirt, she slides into his bed.

'Sleep well. There's a switch on the lamp so you can turn the light off whenever you're ready.'

In the afternoon, he tries to do some work. He has been listening first to the Isley Brothers, and then to the O'Jays, for he has a notion that he can frame part of his book by looking at family history, particularly at singers who have children, or siblings, who are also singers. He decides now to turn his attention to Nat King Cole and Natalie Cole; Cissy Houston and Whitney Houston and, of course, Whitney's aunt, Dionne Warwick. He takes out a sheet of paper and begins to make a flow chart that is soon full of dates and arrows. Three hours pass by pleasantly enough before he readily admits that his doodling is nothing more than a diversion. He confesses to himself that he needs to return to his more orthodox structure if he is ever going to make any progress with this book, and so he gathers up his pens and various bits of paper and packs them away neatly into the bottom drawer of his desk. He lowers his desk chair with a quick turn of the handle, and then promptly raises it again having decided that the higher he sits the more attentive he is to his work. It is getting dark now and he realises that he should wake up the girl. However, before he does so he will make her some soup as he imagines that she must be hungry. He puts on Miles Davis's *Sketches of Spain* and turns up the volume so that it begins to fill the room. He then goes into the small kitchen and pops the plastic lid off a carton of vegetable soup and tips the contents into a deep blue bowl. He sets the microwave timer for three minutes, which guarantees that the soup will be extremely hot, and then he prepares a tray on to which he places a white paper napkin, a spoon, and a few plain crackers. By focusing hard on his book he has managed to avoid dealing with the awkwardness of Danuta's presence in his flat, but as he listens to the mechanical hum of the microwave, which dominates the lilting strains of *Sketches of Spain*, it is clear to him that he now has no choice but to confront the situation and discover just what is going on with the girl.

He nudges open the door to the bedroom with his shoulder, and she slowly turns and opens her eyes.

'Time to get up, I think.'

He sits on the edge of the bed and holds out the tray. At first she does not take it. She stares at him as though trying to remember who he is and why she is in this bed. Then she pulls herself upright and arranges a pillow behind her back.

'Thank you,' she says, as she takes the tray from him and balances it between her stomach and her slightly raised knees. 'You are a kind man.'

He watches as she lifts the spoon to her mouth, and he is surprised how detached he feels, for he neither wishes to touch her, nor to share his bed with her. Strangely enough, he simply wants to protect her, for she suddenly appears to be painfully young and liable to be exploited. He can see now that her navy blue sweatshirt is actually filthy and he is tempted to suggest that she wears one of his, but he decides to be patient.

'Would you like some coffee or tea? Or a glass of wine? It's pretty much that time of day.'

She shakes her head and continues to lift the spoon to her lips.

'So you're definitely not going to work?'

'I cannot go to work. It is not good for me to see Rolf. I told you, he is angry with me because he says that I have not been fair to him.'

'Does it have anything to do with me?' She looks at him but does not reply. 'Perhaps he thinks that something is going on between the two of us?'

'I told him about you, but he is not angry with you, he is angry with me because I do not want to be with him.'

'I see. So you were with him, and now you've decided that you don't want him for a boyfriend and he is upset.'

'Perhaps.' She puts the spoon down on the tray to the side of the still half-full bowl of soup. 'I am sorry, but I cannot eat any more. Thank you.'

He takes the tray from her and watches as she lowers her knees and leans back into the pillow.

'Rolf has never been a boyfriend to me. It is what he wants. It is in his head, that is all.'

'It sounds like he doesn't cope too well with rejection, and maybe he just needs to get over it.'

'I am sorry, but I do not understand.'

He wonders if he should throw the soup away, or perhaps reheat it later when she has gone. After all, she has hardly touched it.

'Let me just put this in the kitchen and I'll be back. Are you sure you don't want any tea or coffee?'

She shakes her head and pulls up the duvet to her chin.

'I'll just be a minute.'

As the kettle boils he realises that he has to say something to the girl. What if Laurie wants to come by? Or Clive Wilson was to drop by to apologise? This is crazy. He should never have allowed her to sleep here, not even for a few hours. And then there is this Rolf, who sounds as though he is capable of doing anything. Danuta is an adult, and she should check into the hostel and start to sort out her life. He can always visit her, or meet her for coffee or lunch. They can go out in the evenings to the cinema, or simply get together for a drink. He knows that she doesn't think much of the local pub, but there are other places that they can go to. They don't have to go to the Queen Caroline. He decides to make himself a cup of instant black coffee, which he knows will taste bitter, but he doesn't want to leave her by herself for too long.

He sits carefully on the edge of the bed, this time a little closer to her as she is no longer balancing a tray and trying to eat. Why does she not go back to Warsaw and her family? She has a job there in a kindergarten, and her English is already good enough. How much better is it going to get if she stays in England for another month or two? After all, she can always come back again later, when things have calmed down a little. She's not an idiot, and she must know that there are plenty of other solutions to her present predicament with this Rolf. He is beginning to feel used, and as he stares at her troubled expression he reminds himself that he owes her nothing, and that he can't risk unmooring his life for her. She shouldn't expect this from him.

'Don't you have any other friends? People that you can talk to about what's going on. I mean people here in London?'

'I do not understand.'

He takes a sip of his coffee, then balances the cup on his right knee and holds it with both hands.

'I think you should talk to somebody about the situation and maybe get some advice. Have you thought about going back to Poland for a while?'

'I do not have the money to go back to Poland. How do I go back?'

'Well, I'm just saying, maybe you should talk with friends and explore all of the options that are open to you. That's just one of them.'

'But how do I go back to Poland? And why should I go back?'

'No, Danuta. I'm not saying that you should go back, I'm just saying that it is something that you might want to explore. If you need money for an air ticket I can lend you the money.'

'You want to buy me a ticket to fly to Poland?'

'Look, all I'm saying is that if you think you should go, and if you don't have the money, then maybe people can help you. That's all.'

The girl pushes the duvet away a little. She still has on her sweatshirt and jeans, and her other clothes remain in a neat pile on the floor beneath the window. She should go now, he knows this, but it is already dark outside and the idea of her tramping off to some hostel is too depressing. He can open a bottle of wine and sit with her in the living room, and maybe they can even watch a DVD. It will be better for her to leave in the morning, and by then she might have had the decency to tell him just what the hell is going on instead of teasing him with these half-snippets of carefully calibrated anxiety about this boy Rolf.

'Listen, Danuta, you can stay here tonight, but in the morning I think you should probably go. I've got things that I have to attend to. To be honest, it's not a good time for me at the moment.'

'You want me to leave in the morning?'

He can hear a mixture of hurt and anger in her voice, so he decides to think carefully about how he is going to phrase his response.

'Look, here's the thing.' He pauses. 'The longer you stay, the more complicated it will be for you.'

'So you are thinking of me?'

'Yes, I'm thinking of you, but I am thinking of me too.'

'I would like to get dressed now.' He looks down at her, but she will not look up and meet his eyes. 'Please, I need to get dressed.'

He stares into the bathroom mirror and then cups his palms together and splashes cold water into his face. It shouldn't take her too long to get dressed, and he has decided that once she has done so, and is ready to leave, the best course of action will be to give her the minicab fare and offer to pay for her first night at the hostel. He imagines a somewhat gloomy dormitory room, full of unwashed European and Australian backpackers, a place where the urge to sleep is not as powerful as the desire to stay awake and keep an eye on one's possessions. He knows that he is doing the right thing, and given her rapid descent into angry silence, she would clearly have only become more irritating with each passing hour. Maybe he should suggest accompanying her to the hostel and checking her in, and then perhaps taking her out to see a film? If there's time afterwards, they might even have a drink together and then he can walk her back to her place. As annoying as she is being, he has no desire for things between them to end on a bad note. As he buries his face in a clean towel he hears the door to his flat slam shut, and then the thumping of feet bounding downstairs. He waits a moment and is then jolted by the crash of the front door, which is followed by a vacuum of ominous silence. He tosses the towel over the side of the bathtub. She has gone. The problem is solved, and he knows that she will not come back and ask him for any help. She has gone.

He is not sure what is happening. He reaches out a hand and presses the button on the front of the digital alarm clock, but the ringing continues. Then he realises that he has left his mobile phone in the living room. He looks at the dimpled white ceiling and waits for the voicemail to pick up. The sudden storm is over and he now rolls on to his side and stares at the wall. Today he will try and do some more work on the book, but he knows that he should soon make up his mind and decide whether to try and get a publisher involved, or maybe even an agent. The truth is, he has been avoiding rejection, but he understands that he needs to put his ego to one side and get some proper feedback and professional advice otherwise the whole thing is in danger of becoming little more than a time-consuming vanity project. The phone starts to ring again and this time he leaps from his bed and dashes into the living room. Somebody is obviously keen to speak with him.

He doesn't recognise the slightly shrill voice, but he decides to buy a little time and pretend that it is a bad connection. He asks the woman to repeat herself.

'It's Lesley. Can you hear me now?'

'Yes, I can hear you. I'm sorry. I think I need a new phone.'

'I left you a message. Just a few minutes ago. You didn't pick up.'

'I was in the shower so I didn't hear the phone, and I haven't checked the messages. What's going on?'

He tries to sound as casual as possible, but he wants to know how she has managed to get hold of his mobile number. Perhaps Clive Wilson, or one of the researchers, passed it on.

'I need to talk to you, Keith.'

'Okay, but I don't have a land line to call you back on. Is this clear enough?'

'No, I need to talk to you face to face. In person. Now.'

He can hear the urgency in her voice, and he realises that she is panicking.

'Do you want to come round here?' The line goes silent, as though the call has been dropped. 'Are you still there?'

'I don't think that would be a good idea. Do you know the Starbucks by the Bingo Hall? Across the road from the bus depot.' She doesn't wait for an answer. 'I'll see you there in half an hour, but it's probably best if nobody knows we're meeting.'

'It's okay, I haven't got you on speakerphone. Do you want me to wear a disguise?'

'Trust me, this really isn't the time for jokes, Keith. I'm trying to help you, okay?'

'Trying to help me?'

'I'll see you in half an hour, okay? Bye.'

He closes the phone and then immediately finds the charger and plugs it in. If he leaves in ten minutes, and walks quickly, he can get there in time. He rushes into the bathroom, where he stares at himself in the mirror. It is not good. His eyes are still heavy with sleep, and he needs to shave, but it could be worse. At least the girl left. He turns on the shower, and while the water heats up he speed-brushes his teeth. He looks again in the mirror. There is going to be no time to shave. Everything else he can manage.

He sees her through the huge pane of glass. She is sitting at a window table with two cups in front of her and idly fidgeting with the string of pearls that she often wears. Then she sees him and her face momentarily brightens as though she is relieved that he has turned up. He's late, he knows this, but only by five minutes or so. As he slides into the chair opposite her, she places a large paper cup in front of him.

'I didn't put any milk or sugar in. I don't really know how you take it.'

'Thanks. It's fine as it is.'

She looks worried, but good. Younger, actually, and he wonders if it's her clothes, or if she has cut her hair. He has never been very good at figuring out whatever it is that older women do to themselves when they change their appearance, but from experience he knows that it is generally best to say nothing.

'Look,' she begins, 'I can't stay long, but I do want to have a quick word with you. Something's been bothering me.'

'Is it about us? I've never told anyone, apart from Annabelle, so you don't have to worry on that score. I'm just sorry that things didn't work out.'

'"Things didn't work out"? Are you taking the piss, Keith? You didn't want to know, or did I miss something?'

'It wasn't that straightforward.'

'No, I'm sure in your head it wasn't straightforward. Somewhat convenient, wouldn't you say?'

'I wouldn't really describe it as convenient. It did break up my marriage.'

She shakes her head in exasperation, and he realises that he had better offer an olive branch of some sort.

'Look, I'm sorry if I caused you any distress. What else can I say?'

'Let's just drop it, okay. I haven't come here to talk about us, or about the past. It's not my place to offer you advice, but I think you should seriously consider resigning. That way you'll at least keep your pension.'

He picks up his coffee, but the paper cup offers no insulation and it is too hot to hold, let alone drink. He places the cup back on the tabletop.

'Well, obviously you know something that I don't know, so maybe you should tell me what's going on.' He pauses. 'If you want to, that is.'

'Listen, I'm pretty sure that they're going to press formal charges. Apparently you've created a hostile work environment for Yvette.'

'You're winding me up, right?'

'Clive is not going to protect you. In fact, I don't know what's gone on between the two of you, but he's not your friend, Keith.'

'Well that much I'd already figured out for myself. He's a totally two-faced arsehole, but then again he always has been.'

'Well, at least we're in agreement on this.'

He stands and carefully picks up his coffee.

'I won't be a second, I'm just going to put some milk in it.'

Fat-free, two per cent, full fat, he doesn't give a damn, milk is milk, and so he presses the nozzle nearest him. He hadn't expected Lesley to be so genuinely concerned. He looks across at her as she stares out of the window at the traffic, her free hand playing idly with some loose strands of her hair. Maybe he should have been more honest with her. After their liaison at the New Forest retreat, he did deliberately avoid her and he made no real attempt to stay in touch. As a result she probably has some reason to be annoyed with him, but she knew full well that the situation wasn't easy. He was a married man, and they worked together, so it was unrealistic of her to actually expect anything to come of it. However, given his present circumstances, an excuse about their working together is the last thing that he can offer her.

He returns to his seat and she turns her attention from the window and looks back in his direction.

'Thanks,' he says. 'I know you're trying to help.'

'Well, I'm not after your job, if that's what you're thinking. I'm just the stopgap till Clive figures out what to do. Anyhow, the amalgamation of the Race Equality, Disability and Women's Affairs units is a stupid idea, and I pity the poor sod who has to keep everything in order.'

'Well, from what you're saying, I suppose that won't be me now.'

'I'm sorry that I'm the one who has to tell you this, but I don't think anybody else has got your back.'

'So that's it then? He's going to get rid of me?'

'I'm afraid that's what it looks like.' She pauses. 'You can probably get another job in the field if you voluntarily step aside.'

He laughs. 'Come on, Lesley, you're not being realistic. We both know that people always think that there's no smoke without fire and all that bullshit. But I can't say I'd be too sad to move on and do something else.'

'You've still got time ahead of you.'

'Jesus, Lesley. Lighten up a bit. You sound like you're writing my obituary.' He shakes his head. 'Maybe you are.'

'For what it's worth, I don't think it's fair.'

'Thank you.'

'But you *have* been stupid.'

'I know. I'm sorry.'

'I don't think you have to apologise. At least not to me.'

She gathers up her coat from the seat next to her.

'I have to go now, Keith.' She stands. 'You know where to find me if you need to talk.'

People are running up the street from the direction of the tube station, with their football scarves flying in the wind and their newspapers rolled up like batons in their hands. He stands and looks on as they pass quickly through the turnstiles, eager to watch the evening match. He had arranged to meet Laurie half an hour ago, but it is becoming increasingly clear that his son must have forgotten. He presses the redial button on his mobile and tries Annabelle again, but her phone seems programmed to go to voicemail without even ringing out. He is loath to leave a message so he quickly shuts the phone and decides that he may as well go in and watch the game. There is no point in trying Laurie's mobile, for when he called him this morning to arrange to see him, his son announced that his phone would be out of credit by the end of the call and he didn't have any money to top it up. He could barely hear Laurie, who was on the bus *en route* to school, but they had arranged to meet at seven o'clock at the Loftus Road turnstiles, and he told Laurie that after the game he would top up the phone for him. Once he finished talking to his son, he decided to order a latte before leaving the Starbucks. No doubt Lesley would already have arrived at work, with her business face in place, but his own shapeless day would continue with him sipping on a latte and thinking aimlessly about what to do with his book. When his latte arrived he asked for it to be placed in a cardboard sleeve so he could hold it without scalding his hands, and as he grabbed a handful of napkins for extra insulation he realised that whatever frustrations he felt with regard to his book it helped to know that at the end of the day he would be spending time with his son. But there is no sign of his son. Laurie probably thinks that Queens Park Rangers against

Sheffield Wednesday is a fixture for losers. The kind of match that he would be embarrassed to admit to having attended. In a way, he sympathises with Laurie, but in the absence of anything else to do he moves towards the turnstiles. After buying a ticket, he is subjected to a full-body search, which he feels is somewhat unnecessary at his age, but he knows that it is best to say nothing to these guys. He stands with his hands up in the air and waits until he hears the predictable, 'All right, mate,' which he recognises as his signal to move off towards the home fans' stand.

At half-time it is nil–nil, and the lamentable quality of the football on display leaves him somewhat relieved that Laurie has chosen to abandon him. It would have been difficult to try and justify this rubbish to a seventeen-year-old Barcelona fan. These two outfits are unquestionably on the decline, clubs that were 'big' when he was a boy, but who now struggle to attract five-figure crowds. He points at a bar of chocolate, pays the money, and then picks up both the chocolate and his pint of lager and shuffles to one side where he discovers some space on a shelf where he can put down the plastic 'glass'. He reaches in his pocket for his mobile and calls Annabelle again, but she still isn't answering so he decides to text her. 'Where's Laurie? Did he forget football?' He keeps it short, for he doesn't want to sound too alarmed. He knows how quickly Annabelle panics, and he has no desire to reveal to her how disappointed he is that his son has not even had the decency to let him know that he has changed his mind. As he tucks the phone back into his trouser pocket, having first set the call feature to vibrate, he notices that the crowd is beginning to file in for the second half. He looks at their down-turned and miserable faces, and he wonders why he should subject himself to forty-five more minutes of this nonsense. Both teams are safely mid-table, and at the moment there is nothing to play for. However, even if there was something at stake, he is reasonably sure that neither team would be competent enough to exploit the situation. In fact, he only suggested coming to this match so that he could spend some more time with Laurie, but without his son's company what's the point? He decides to linger over his pint, and maybe order another. There is a closed circuit television screen behind the bar so it occurs to him that he might as well stay put and watch the game from this vantage point.

It is after eleven when he finally slumps down on to the sofa and kicks off his shoes. The second half was hardly an improvement, and when Sheffield Wednesday scored the winning goal in injury time he quickly downed his third pint and headed for the exit before the rush. The Queen Caroline was busier than usual because of the football, but he found a spot on a threadbare bench seat near the jukebox, and then foraged in his pockets for a handful of £1 coins which he pumped into the machine before returning to the bench seat and listening to the music. For some reason he decided that tonight he would just play reggae, and so he chose songs by Dennis Brown, Gregory Isaacs, Third World and Bob Marley. No doubt those who were not fans of reggae music would have been unimpressed by his devotion, but that was their problem. As he sat in front of his pint he was consumed by his feelings of disappointment and frustration that neither Annabelle nor his son appeared to think it necessary to let him know what was going on. How, he wondered, had he gone from being a husband and a father to this? Mr Bloody Nobody.

He gets up from the sofa and crosses to a precariously stacked pile of CDs. He scans them quickly, then takes out a Peter Tosh CD and slots it into the player. He listens for a moment and then turns the bass up a single point before returning to the sofa.

He doesn't want to disturb the neighbours. What should have been a stress-free evening with his son has turned out to be deeply hurtful, and Annabelle has still not called him back. In fact, the only person who did contact him was Lesley, who telephoned him as he was watching the second half of the match on the television screen behind the bar. She apologised if she had been out of line in summoning him to Starbucks, but he assured her that there was no reason at all for her to say sorry. He didn't tell her that after their meeting at Starbucks he had not managed to achieve anything all day, beyond calling his son and arranging to go to the game with him, for he had been unable to get Clive Wilson's treachery out of his mind. He should, of course, have been thanking her for being so honest and putting him in the picture, but he just listened and occasionally interrupted and reassured her that he really did understand why she felt compelled to contact him and meet up. 'Let me know if you need to talk,' said Lesley, 'I know it's not easy for you, but you've got my number on your phone now so don't worry about calling me. It's fine.'

He gets up from the sofa and lines his shoes up neatly. Then he turns down the volume of the Peter Tosh CD before making his way into the kitchen. Come on, Annabelle, he's not just *your* son. She should at least have the courtesy to put him out of his misery and tell him that Laurie is all right. He takes the solitary bottle of Pouilly-Fumé from the fridge and twists a corkscrew into it, before wrestling both cork and instrument clear. He pours the wine into a tumbler and then puts the bottle back into the fridge. As he slumps down on to the sofa he picks up his phone and dials quickly from memory. He can tell from her voice that she is in bed and probably about to go to sleep.

'I'm sorry, I didn't mean to wake you up. I can call tomorrow if it's better for you.'

For a moment there is silence as she takes in just who it is that is speaking. Then Yvette laughs slightly.

'Have you lost it? Or have you been drinking, is that it?'

'What do you mean "drinking"?'

'You shouldn't be calling me. Not with things being the way they are.'

'Well things are only the way they are because you want it like that.' He pauses. 'Are you still there?'

'Listen, we can't work together because of what went on between us. You know that, right?' She waits. 'Well?'

'We can't work together because you seem to think that it's all right to go putting our business out where everyone can see it.'

'I don't have anything to hide.'

'Certain things are private, Yvette. Don't you realise how bad you're making yourself look?'

She laughs. 'I don't believe it, you *have* been drinking, haven't you? You know what, why don't we just pretend that this phone call never happened?'

'Why don't we pretend that things between us never happened? That'll make it easier for everyone. I mean, this is all messed up. Where do you get off telling people that I've been harassing you?'

'I'll tell you what's messed up, Keith. The fact that if I don't pretend that this phone call never happened then I'll have to tell my solicitor and it's going to sound suspiciously like you were bullying me. So just go to sleep and leave me alone, all right?'

'So you don't see us working together again?'

'Get a grip, Keith. It's gone way too far and you know it. Maybe if they gave me a settlement of some kind then I'd leave, but according to my solicitor they won't. It's easier for them if you step down because it doesn't cost them anything.'

'I see.' He pauses. 'Yvette, why are you doing this? We got on just fine, didn't we?'

'Women don't like being dumped, or didn't anyone tell you that? Maybe I've saved some other poor sod from feeling used and then chucked.'

'You weren't used and you weren't chucked. Things end, Yvette. That's just life.'

The phone goes dead. She has hung up on him, so he closes the phone and puts it down on the glass-topped table with a click. Then he picks up the tumbler of wine. He knows that he shouldn't have called her, but at least he's sure now. He knows where he stands.

Annabelle opens the door. She is still in her dressing gown, and she looks him up and down as though he is a salesman who is attempting to press some unwanted household products upon her. His former wife simply shakes her head.

'You look like shit, Keith. You're not taking care of yourself, are you?'

'Yes, well I didn't come around here at eight o'clock in the morning for your opinion on how I look.'

'Really? Well, I didn't open the door and expect to find a vagrant on my doorstep. So, are you coming in?'

She moves to one side to let him pass, but he does not move.

'Well, are you coming in or not?'

'Is Laurie here?'

'He's asleep. Come on, I don't want to talk to you while you're outside.'

He moves past her and into the kitchen where he sits on a tall stool by the breakfast bar.

'Why didn't you call me yesterday? I left messages. In fact, by the end of the day I was worried sick.'

'I know, it's my fault. I should have called you, but my mobile needed charging.' Annabelle sighs, and then she pulls out a chair and sits. 'And there's something else.' She pauses. 'Look, Laurie got himself in a bit of bother with some boys from school.'

'What kind of bother?'

'Shoplifting. I had to go and pick him up from Mr Hughes's office. Don't worry, I gave him a pretty serious talking to, but he claims that it was all a big mistake, and maybe it's true because the school let all of them off with a warning.'

'All of them? How many kids are we talking about? You make it sound like something out of *Oliver Twist*.'

'Five or six, according to Mr Hughes. Look, maybe you could try getting through to Laurie again. He's staying at home and revising today, so why don't you come back in a few hours and maybe take him out for lunch. But for heaven's sake, smarten yourself up a bit.'

'You know, Annabelle, sometimes you're not real. Laurie is hauled into the headmaster's office and accused of shoplifting, and all you want to talk about is how I look?'

'Mr Hughes is worried about him.'

'And I'm worried about Mr Hughes.'

'And given how you look, I'm worried about you. Did you get any sleep?'

Over the past three years, Annabelle has mastered the art of irritating him with a well-placed comment, or even a look, and he has had to teach himself carefully how not to rise to her bait. He takes a deep breath.

'Look, Annabelle, we're talking about Laurie. This could be serious, okay?'

'I've been trying to tell you for some time now that there's a problem. Laurie's getting by with his work, but no more than that.

But those kids he runs around with, I don't like it. Mr Hughes confirmed to me that some of them are binge drinkers, buying their cider and their alcopops by the case and puking up in the street every day. Jesus, they go to school either drunk or hung over, and you know these kids can buy the stuff twenty-four hours a day in the supermarket and it's cheaper than fizzy water. Sometimes I feel like I'm losing Laurie to his so-called friends. I can't fight it alone and quite frankly you don't even seem to be trying.'

'Annabelle, I'm hearing you, and I am concerned about him, but I've got a lot going on, okay? And, to be honest, you know what I think about Mr Hughes and that school. Most of the kids there learn by downloading information from Wikipedia and all the teachers do is just help them to organise the facts that they've gathered. Don't you remember when he was doing his GCSEs, and the Religious Studies teacher showed them *Spiderman* because it was about "making choices", and then *The Nutty Professor* because it was about "prejudice". I mean, what chance do the kids stand if their headmaster lets teachers get away with lazy crap like that? Hughes is full of it.'

'But it doesn't matter what Mr Hughes says, it's me Annabelle who's telling you that Laurie is in with a bad set. I'm sorry, but those kids that he fraternises with are just not our type of people, and I don't mean anything by it but I can't put it any simpler than that.'

He looks closely at her and begins to shake his head.

'You're serious, aren't you?'

'I'm serious about my son and his welfare, and to my mind that's all that matters. I'm sorry, but I wish I sensed that you feel the same way. I know you've got a lot going on, but I don't think that I can deal with his attitude by myself for much longer.'

He stares at her and swallows deeply. Then he silently counts to five. Are these really her opinions? 'Our type of people'? He hasn't seen or heard of Bruce in a while, but he assumes that the film editor is still in the picture.

'I'll come back later for Laurie. Just tell him to be ready, okay?'

As he climbs from the stool and turns to leave, he can feel her eyes upon him. He knows that she will say nothing further. She has said enough.

Laurie looks bored as the London Eye first hoists, then spins them skyward with its slow circular movement. His son stares down at the pod beneath them where a group of city businessmen are tucking into crustless sandwiches and champagne that is being served to them from a large hamper by two pretty young women in white aprons. Apparently, his son seems to think that the corporate outing is more fascinating than observing the tight switchback patterns of the River Thames, or looking out at the vast panoramic sprawl that is south London. However, now that they near the top, Laurie finally deigns to look interested in the view and he points to the newly refurbished Wembley Stadium in the north.

'Check it out, Dad. You can almost see right into it.'

It does look impressive, particularly the high graceful arch which rises over the whole arena, but he wants to talk with his son about things other than sport. He points east towards the mouth of the Thames.

'You know, if you look over there you can get a really good idea of how London developed as a great port city.'

'What do you mean?'

'Well, fifty years ago, on either bank of the river there was nothing but docks and warehouses, and this river would have been filled with ships from all over the world. Cities have to make money in order to survive and grow, and London made its money out of shipping. That was its business.'

Laurie shrugs his shoulders. 'Well, the business is all mashed up now, right?'

'Well, there's no shipping industry, as such, but there's still business. Banking, insurance, high technology. I mean, London's business infrastructure is pretty diversified these days.'

Laurie seems unconvinced and he shakes his head. 'There ain't no business. I know plenty of people who can't get a job doing anything.'

'Maybe they don't want a job.'

'Or maybe somebody doesn't want to give them a job. It's not always as simple as it looks.'

'Is this your way of telling me that you still don't know what kind of career you want?'

'What's that got to do with anything?'

'Nothing, I suppose. But have you thought any further about what you might do after you finish at university?'

'I've got to get in first.'

'Are you worried about your exams?'

'No, I'm not worried. Are you? Anyhow, it's only November and I haven't even done my mocks yet. The real thing's not for another six months.'

'I remember.' He pauses. 'I did them too, although it was a while ago.'

Laurie sucks his teeth. 'You're telling me.' His son turns away from him and from the expanse of the river to the east, and refocuses his attention on Wembley Stadium.

He looks to the west, where the sudden bend of the river creates the illusion that Battersea Power Station is floating on the water. A camera flashes and he realises that their photograph has been taken, and then a voice on the speaker system announces that at the end of the 'flight' they will be able to purchase a souvenir snapshot. He looks again at Laurie, whose eyes remain firmly fixed on the football stadium to the north, and he resists the urge to continue his history lecture, which is of course a veiled attempt to persuade Laurie that this is his city too. And then it occurs to him that it's possible that his son already knows this, and that there is no reason for him to acquaint Laurie with what he already possesses. His son is probably quite at home with the Tower of London and the Palace of Westminster and Waterloo station and St Paul's Cathedral, all of which are clearly visible from this vantage point. In fact, Laurie is most likely circling in the London Eye wondering why his old man is banging on like some demented tour guide about his city, the city of his birth. He looks again at his son, whose deep brown eyes remind him of Annabelle's, and he wants to give the boy a reassuring hug, but he knows better than to spoil the moment. He is also, if truth be told, unsure as to which one of them is in need of reassurance.

Earlier in the afternoon, when he returned to Annabelle's house, a sheepish-looking Laurie was already sitting downstairs and waiting for him. His son glanced up and muttered 'What's up?' but when he asked the sprawling boy what he wanted to do for the afternoon, Laurie shrugged his shoulders and avoided taking any decision-making responsibility. He suggested to Laurie that it might be relaxing for them to go into central London and walk by the river, and so the pair of them ambled silently to the end of the street where he flagged down a taxi. He thought about saving some money and taking the tube, but Laurie seemed impatient and he had no desire to waste time ambling to and from train stations with a reluctant son. The taxi had only just pulled away from the kerb when Laurie stopped fiddling with his seat belt and began to mumble an apology for not having shown up at the football.

'We got into some bother at school, but it was nothing. Some guys jumped us and there was a bit of a ruck.'

'I thought it was shoplifting.'

'The guy who runs the mini-mart near the school complained about us to the head. He said we'd been nicking stuff, but that wasn't the main thing. Mr Hughes wanted to talk to us about the fighting, but it was nothing.'

'What do you mean it was nothing? Why didn't you just walk away?'

'Walk away? Look Dad, you can't walk away if somebody jumps you. It's too late. It's all over, right?'

'So this was nothing to do with shoplifting?'

'Like I said, the guy from the mini-mart made a complaint but Mr Hughes would have suspended us if we'd been shoplifting. He was more concerned about the ruck.'

'Did the other gang hurt you?'

'What do you mean "other gang"? I'm not in a gang.'

'You know what I mean.'

'I've just got a few bruises and stuff, but it was handbags.'

'Handbags?'

'A bit of name-calling and thumping and all done. The other kids were muppets, but Hughes is a real drama queen.'

He was suddenly conscious that the driver was listening to their private conversation, for he could see the man's eyes in the rear-view mirror. He decided that for the moment it was probably best to say nothing further. Fifteen minutes later they stepped out of the taxi at the back of the Queen Elizabeth Hall, and he turned to his son and asked him if he'd like to go up in the London Eye before they set off on their walk. Laurie shrugged, which meant that there was no serious opposition to the idea.

As the Eye continues to turn, and they start their descent, he notices that his son has a cut on the back of his right hand which has clearly been bleeding. He decides to say nothing, leaving it up to Laurie to tell him about it if he so wishes, but he suspects that his son will choose to remain silent about the source of his injury.

He steps out of their pod and is relieved to feel terra firma beneath his feet. He puts a hand on Laurie's shoulder.

'Have you ever been inside the Houses of Parliament? I mean on a school trip or something?' Laurie shakes his head. 'Let's take a walk to Westminster Bridge. We probably can't go into the actual parliament at this time of day, but you get a great view from the bridge.'

They stand together on the bridge and look across at the back of the Palace of Westminster. He realises that the best view is probably from the south of the river, but it is too late now. They are standing in the middle of the bridge, directly over the water, and Laurie is clearly waiting for his father to say whatever it is that is on his mind.

'Does this mean anything to you, Laurie?' He gestures with his arms in a somewhat grand manner, hoping that the flamboyance of his motion will suggest a kind of ownership. He then drops his arms and places both hands on a low stone wall and leans forward slightly.

Laurie shrugs his shoulders. 'I'm not sure what you're on about.'

'All of this is yours if you want it, but to get it you'll have to work harder than your mates. You've got to prove to your mates that you're better than them, and you've got to remember that nobody is ever going to give you anything.'

It is apparent, from the puzzled look on his son's face, that he should either be clearer about what he is saying or else he should say nothing further.

'You're not really sure what I'm talking about, are you?'

'I haven't got a clue.'

'No, I didn't think so. It's my fault.' He pauses. 'I'm worried about you, Laurie. You're a young man now, and I don't want to tell you what to do with your life, but I can help you, if you want me to help you that is. But it's up to you.'

'How can you help me?'

'I can talk to you. Or you can talk to me.'

'You want me to talk to you?'

Of course he wants his son to talk to him, but he understands why his son feels a little distant. Sons can be unforgiving towards those who they believe have hurt their mothers. He knows this from his own life.

'I'd like nothing more than for you to talk to me, but I don't want to force you to do anything. I know it doesn't work like that.' He reaches into the black leather knapsack that hangs from his shoulder, and he produces a plastic bag. 'Here, I got you this.'

Laurie takes the bag from him and pulls out the blue and red striped Barcelona shirt.

'Man, that's cool. Cheers, Dad.' As he speaks his son keeps his eyes firmly fixed on the shirt. 'Thanks.'

'But you're sure that there's nothing that you want to talk about? The fight, for instance?'

'I thought you said that you weren't forcing anything.'

Of course, Laurie is right. He will have to take his son's word that he is telling the truth about the scuffle with the other boys, for he knows that if he comes on too heavy then Laurie will simply tune him out.

'Well, we can talk whenever you're ready. It doesn't have to be now. Your mother is trying her best, but there are some things that she can never really know about.'

'You mean because she's white?'

'No, I suppose what I really mean is because she's not black.'

As the words come out of his mouth he wants to kick himself for he knows that he sounds annoyingly glib.

'Look, what I'm trying to say is that I know it's not exactly straightforward for you out there on the streets. Who knows, maybe this is something that you might find easier to talk about with me. After all, there are some things that I've been through myself as a black kid growing up in this country and I think I can tell you what I know without it coming over like a sermon.'

His son seems momentarily embarrassed and he wonders if this is the right time for him to drop an arm around Laurie's shoulders and for them to leave Westminster Bridge and begin their walk along the embankment. He looks at his son's confused face and he realises that, on second thoughts, maybe they should just head straight back to Annabelle's house. He turns from Laurie and looks down at the water and decides to leave the decision up to his son, but the silence deepens and it is becoming increasingly uncomfortable.

'The thing is, Dad, I don't know if things are the same now as they were when you were my age.'

He continues to gaze down at the river. At least his son is talking to him. He looks up and turns so that he is facing Laurie.

'So tell me then, how are they different?'

'It isn't just about discrimination and stuff. I know that's important, and that's your job and everything, but it's also about other things.'

'Other things like what?'

'It's got a lot to do with respect. You can't let people just large it up in your face and disrespect you. A man's got to have respect or he's nothing better than somebody's punk.'

Respect? What has Laurie, or any of his friends, achieved in their lives that makes them imagine that anybody should respect them? What have they done to *earn* respect? How pathetic he must seem to his son, blathering on about a career beyond university, and how he will have to put in more effort and try twice as hard as anybody else, and all the while his son is obviously thinking what a square tosser his dad is. However, what his exasperated father is trying to say to him boils down to one sentence that he knows he can't say. 'Laurie, act your age, not your colour.' Both he and Laurie are trying hard not to cause each other any upset, but after three years of living apart it is evident to him that they are woefully incapable of conversing casually.

'Can we go now?' Laurie speaks quietly, as though he feels sorry for his father. 'It's getting a bit cold.'

'Don't you fancy going for even a short walk along the South Bank? We don't have to go far.'

'You mean down there by the water?'

'You can't be that cold, are you?'

'It's freezing, man.'

'Have you got something else to do? Or someone to meet?'

Laurie shakes his head and then gently begins to punch the toe of a trainer-clad foot against the wall.

'Let's walk for a little while and if you're still cold you can always put on your Barcelona shirt.'

Laurie gives him a fake smile, which leaves him in no doubt as to what his son thinks of his suggestion. He decides that they will walk down as far as the Tate Modern, most likely in silence, and then he will hail a taxi and drop Laurie off at Annabelle's. At some point he will try and speak further with Annabelle, and reassure her that there is no reason to panic about Laurie, but Annabelle is not as calm, nor as patient, as she used to be. As they descend the stone steps that lead to the wide pedestrian walkway that hugs the meandering line of the river, Laurie withdraws into a silence that is unmistakably sullen. His mother has taken to describing these moods as his 'big man' behaviour, and he is now experiencing for himself just what she has been referring to. They turn left and begin to saunter along the river, but he decides that they will walk only as far as the National Film

Theatre and then hail a taxi from there. He sees no point in subjecting either one of them to this strained atmosphere for a moment longer than is necessary.

He begins the email for a second time. The use of the phrase, 'waiting for the other shoe to fall', seemed a little too colloquial and clumsy, but having deleted it, and read back over everything that remained, he decided to start afresh. After dropping Laurie off at home, he managed to work on the book for a couple of hours until he finally confessed to himself that he did, in fact, need a total break from it, for he was beginning to lose sight of the book's purpose. He breaks off from the email and pours a glass of wine. He returns his attention to the computer screen, and then he begins to write anew to Lesley, but this time in a manner that he hopes will strike a better balance between the formal and the informal. He doesn't want to insinuate any real friendship with her, but at the same time he doesn't want to come over as being cold and detached given the nature of their last meeting at Starbucks. He simply explains that he will be going away for a few days and he would appreciate it if she could keep him in the loop if there are any developments. He thought hard about this last phrase, and although it's not perfect it somehow makes more sense than referring to shoes falling. He is asking her to help him get ready for any move that Clive Wilson might try to pull, including pressing formal charges, although he has no idea what he will do should it come to this. However, a little advance warning can't hurt. He suggests to Lesley that she might contact him if she hears anything, but he tries to make it clear that email is his preferred mode of communication for he worries that requesting a telephone call might be misinterpreted as a sign of collaborative intimacy.

He gets up from the computer and crosses to the coffee table where he pours himself a glass of Perrier water. He returns to his desk and for a second time he deletes the entire email, unsure of the phrasing and whether this is even a good idea. But there is nobody else he can ask to look out for his interests. He wonders, if things were to go really wrong, who would be there for him? Laurie? Maybe at some point in the future, but certainly not at the present time. A daughter would probably have been better suited to the role of looking after dad, but there is not much that he can do about this. He opens a new email document and begins to type, having decided that it is best to do so quickly and without too much thought. He is simply asking Lesley to follow through on what she has basically suggested herself. He is asking for her help, but not in a way that should make her feel obligated, nor in a manner that should make it appear that he is desperate. He signs it, 'Best wishes,' and sends the email off without reviewing it. He gets up and takes both his glass of wine and the glass of water and sits on the sofa. He should have done this before, instead of hanging about London and becoming frustrated with the book, and then almost getting into trouble with Danuta. A break will do him good, and by the time he is ready to return to London he will hopefully be able to deal with things in a more decisive fashion. Maybe he should call Annabelle and let her know that he is going away? Or perhaps call Laurie and let him know? Not that he can be certain that either of them will care. It's just information, right?

In the morning he stuffs a Nike sports bag with a few shirts, a pair of jeans, socks and underwear, and some softcover non-fiction, but nothing about music. He decides to pack as though he will be gone for only a few days, knowing that if he decides to stay longer then he can always buy additional things. He double-locks the door behind him, and then tumbles down the stairs and out on to the street. He takes a tube that is crammed with semi-comatose commuters who squeeze up next to each other and idly scan the back of other people's newspapers, while those lucky enough to find a seat simply slump and allow their heads to bounce gently in all directions. Once he reaches King's Cross, he realises that if he hurries he can catch a train that leaves in ten minutes. Unlike the tube, the train is relatively empty and he imagines that most of the commuting is in the other direction, into London. The view out of the window is not particularly interesting as they lumber past the back of endless rows of houses, but eventually it begins to rain lightly, and the drizzle spatters the window of the now speeding train so that a hundred rivers soon run in all directions on this map of an unnamed country. He closes his eyes and tries not to worry about the fact that Lesley has chosen not to reply to him. Maybe she hasn't yet looked at her emails or, despite all his efforts, perhaps she has taken offence at some perceived impropriety in his tone or phrasing.

The ticket inspector wakes him up by pushing his shoulder with the palm of his hand.

'Look, mate, you better get off unless you're ready to go back to London.'

He looks around at the empty carriage, then climbs quickly to his feet and retrieves his holdall from the rack above his head. The station is an old Victorian edifice, with huge vaulted ceilings where the birds are constantly disturbed by the roar of train engines and fly in crazy circles. Once he passes out on to the concourse he joins the long line for a taxi and pulls his jacket tight around himself, for the rain is bucketing down. The taxi driver listens quietly to the local BBC news station, while he sits upright and alert in the back seat and looks at what should be familiar streets. However, with each passing year the streets are becoming increasingly difficult to recognise for there seems to be a vogue for replacing the old brick buildings with tall structures of steel and glass. These days his city appears to be trying hard to reinvent itself as a modern hub of commerce and opportunity, but the evidence before his eyes leaves him unconvinced for the people pounding the streets seem to be the same folks as before and, as far as he can see, all that has changed is the scenery. However, he doesn't live here any more and so he feels no necessity to debate the issue, even with himself.

He knocks a second time, but he knows that his father probably can't hear him above the noise of the television set. He takes two steps to his left and taps on the living room window, but it is impossible to see anything through the discoloured net curtain. His father's hand pulls back the yellowing material, and his unshaven face is now visible in the window. He can immediately see that the older man has aged. His father is clearly baffled to see his son standing before him but, furrowing his brow, the bemused man points towards the door.

'All right, Dad.'

His father is not yet dressed, but he holds the door wide open. His pyjamas hang loosely from his thin body, and the socks on his feet are full of holes. He stares at his son as though unsure of what to say.

'Well, you're not going to leave me standing outside in the rain all morning, are you?'

'You can't call and tell me you're coming?'

'I wanted to surprise you.'

'Well you managed that all right.'

He pours the water on to the teabag and waits for it to steep. There's no getting around it: the house smells as though it hasn't been cleaned or aired in a long while. From the kitchen, he can hear the studio-based morning chat show on the television, and he imagines that his father has settled down to resume watching. The topic for the day is teenage pregnancies in schools. Apparently there is an epidemic of them, particularly in the so-called immigrant communities. He removes the teabag and stirs three spoonfuls of sugar into his father's tea, before carrying the mug through into the living room. He places the tea on an old wooden stool that is clearly a substitute for a table, and then he collapses down into the shapeless armchair to the side of the sofa. It is nearly two years since he last visited, and that was only because he was in the north of England for a conference and it seemed somehow wrong not to at least stop by and say 'hello'. The greeting back then had been equally unenthusiastic, but at least his father and the house had appeared somewhat presentable. As his father continues to watch television, he looks around and is alarmed to see the decline in both his father and his living conditions.

'What happened to your helper?' He tries to ask the question without it coming across as accusatory.

'She says she wants some time off, and so I say fine, then go. The council don't send anybody else yet, but I'm doing just fine for now.'

'Well I can give you a hand, if you like. Let me just put my stuff upstairs then I'll start to give things a going over.'

'Why don't you just relax yourself and things can fix later on? No big rush. Anyhow, the less I have to do with those people from the council, the better. They think that I don't know what is going on. First, they send some stupid little man around saying that he is part of the "befriending scheme". You know, they pay them five pounds an hour to come and talk with you, or take you to the pictures or to some park, like you is too stupid to think for yourself. Then the next thing you know the damn council want to take what little money you have and push you into some place like the Mandela Centre.'

'You mean supported living?'

'I don't care what fancy name they give it, it's a home and they jail you up in a little flat. The place is full of crazy people wandering the corridors looking for relatives who abandoned them years ago. What the council don't take from you the other residents thief from you when your back is turned.'

'But there are people there to look after you and give you medical care. Anyhow, I don't see what your problem is with the Mandela Centre. Half of your friends are in the place and you go down there, don't you?'

'I go down there to pass the time, but I don't reach the stage yet where I need to be locked up and looked after. I already had enough of that in my life as it is.'

His father looks directly at him and he can see in his eyes that he is fiercely resolute.

'Listen, Dad, nobody is locked up, right. Everybody has the keys to their own place and you're free to come and go as you please. You know that. I see a lot of Associations for the Elders in my line of work, and the Mandela is one of the best. There's no stigma attached.'

His father continues to glare unblinkingly.

'Look, I know I mentioned it as a possibility when I was last here, but did you at least think about it?'

'Yes, I think about it.'

'And?'

'You know, for a man with such a big education you can sometimes act stupid. I think about it, and two years later you come back and find me still living at home. You really need to ask me what conclusion I did reach?'

He takes the few clothes from his sports bag and lays them out on the bed. He realises that, despite his father's stubbornness, he will have to sit him down and raise the subject of the condition of the house and once again tentatively explore the possibility of his father moving into the Mandela Centre. As he was doing the washing-up he noticed mouse droppings on the kitchen counter top. He cleaned them up with a paper towel and then rinsed and dried his hands before yanking open the fridge door, where he was greeted by half-eaten plates of food that had long been abandoned, and rancid packets of cheese and butter that had passed their sell-by dates. It isn't just that things are disorganised and untidy: his father is living in conditions that represent a health hazard. Having emptied the few clothes from his bag, he opens a double wardrobe and tosses the holdall into the bottom of it. On the top shelf of the wardrobe, where one might expect to find a pile of folded sheets or neatly balled up socks and loosely stacked underwear, he is surprised to discover a cardboard box that he lifts clear of the shelf. The box is full of photographs, but they are mainly black and white shots of people that he doesn't recognise. There are some of Brenda, and a few of his father as a younger man, presumably shortly after his arrival in England. The fashions seem to suggest the sixties, and although in every photograph his father and his friends appear to be cold, they also seem surprisingly content. He wonders if he should take the pictures downstairs for this would, of course, be a legitimate way to encourage his father finally to talk about the past. He holds the box out in front of himself, as though making an offering, and then he decides to replace it in the wardrobe having realised that it might be more politic to raise this subject later, after his father has had time to adjust to his presence. He hoists the box up and on to the shelf and then pushes it to the back and out of sight.

In the evening they sit together in the pub, his father nursing a pint of Guinness and still sporting the pork-pie hat that he always wears on stepping outside his house. His father has made it clear that he knows that there are some photographs in a box somewhere, but he is unsure of their exact location, and he doesn't understand why his son wants to look at them with him. He decides to say nothing further, but tomorrow, or the next day, he will just hand the box to his father and see if the evidence of the photographs provokes a response.

'So what about the book that you was telling me that you want to write. A book about music, right?'

'I'm surprised you remember.'

'You think I don't have no memory? Two years ago, when you was last here, you couldn't shut up talking about it, so I imagine it's this that you've been doing all this time.'

'Well, I've got a job so there's only so much that I can do. You know how it is.'

'Me, I don't have no job, so I don't know how it is any more.'

His father sips at his Guinness and then returns the glass to the watery circle on his stained beer mat. He watches the old man reach into his pocket for a pack of unfiltered cigarettes and then, with slightly shaking hands, he takes one out, lights up, and then drops the book of matches on to the table.

'I know you don't like me to smoke, but what am I supposed to do at my age? It don't make no sense to give up now, and the landlord turn a blind eye. I better off going straight ahead and finishing off what I started.'

He pushes back his chair from the table and picks up his own empty pint glass. He waits for his father to drain his pint, and then he takes up the second glass.

'Same again?' He speaks more to himself than to his father.

When he returns to the table his father is concentrating deeply on his cigarette, the ash of which is hanging precariously from its end. He places the pint in front of him, and then pulls two packets of crisps from his trouser pockets.

'Cheese and onion or Bovril? Whichever one you want is fine by me.'

'I don't want no crisps. At least not yet.' His father gestures to the two packets with his cigarette, and the ash falls off. 'I maybe take a crisp later so you can leave me one packet right there on the table.'

This cheerless pub has been his father's haunt for more years than he can remember, and he suspects that a large percentage of the money that his father has earned in England has flowed across this bar. Although he has never enjoyed coming into this grimy place, for his father it obviously feels like an extension of home. These days the pub appears to have been abandoned by all but a few dedicated drinkers, who seemingly come here in search of company. He is shocked to realise that his father is one of these drinkers. Five years ago, the local university had pensioned off his father, and all the other blue collar janitorial staff, as they decided to outsource their labour needs to private companies, but he had hoped that his father might find part-time work back at the university, or in some other organisation that needed cleaners. Either that, or find a hobby to occupy himself and provide him with a new lease of life. However, during his last visit, he could clearly see that his father had made no effort to re-engage with the world of work in the wake of his redundancy, and it now appeared to him that his father was in danger of embracing a premature inertia that was laced with a hint of reclusive bitterness. He realises that he is both worried and sad to think that this is what his father's life has become: mornings spent watching television at home, and afternoons and evenings given over to the pub. Because the television in the pub appears to be permanently tuned in to a quiz show of some description, he imagines that the only thing that might cause his father to vary his routine would be cricket. No doubt a Test Match, or a one-day international would convince his father that he should remain at home and spend the day staring at his own television set instead of venturing into this dispiriting place.

'So how is everything with the social work then?'

'Well, these days I'm mainly tied up with policy-making, but I can't say I'm too interested in it.'

'Making policies about what?'

'About race and inequality and those kind of things, but the truth is it's boring. However, it's what I do, so that's that.'

'Well, I never did understand why a man of your qualifications would go into this line of work. Just because you're black don't mean that you have to work with black people.'

'I don't just work with black people.'

'I think you know what I'm saying.'

His father stubs out his cigarette and then takes a sip of his pint of Guinness.

'So tell me,' he says, 'if you're so busy doing all this policy-making, then how it is that you're here with me? And how long it is that you're planning on staying here?'

This is the second time that his father has asked him how long he intends to stay, and it irritates him that his father doesn't seem to be able to relax and adjust to his presence. He can't admit to the situation at work with Yvette, but obviously his father senses that something is the matter. He looks at the creased lines on his father's face, and his surprisingly soft eyes, and he watches as the older man slowly shakes his head and then lowers his gaze and takes another sip of his Guinness. He decides that it is probably best if they finish their drinks in silence and then go back to the house.

He lies in the single bed that he used to occupy as a child, and he stares at the black sky through the uncurtained window. In the street he can hear the late night noises of people wandering back from the pub, their voices raised in excitement, and their loud peals of laughter that are occasionally punctuated by the sound of a broken bottle. When he was a child, Brenda used to come upstairs and tuck him in, and she would always tell him a story, usually one that involved castles and princes, but he never seemed to hear the end of it, for her soothing voice always encouraged him to drift quickly off to sleep. He imagined that after he had nodded off, she would noiselessly get up from the edge of his bed, turn off the light in the hallway, and then tiptoe back downstairs and wait for his father to return from whatever pub or club he had been to that night.

When his mother left he didn't understand how radically his life was about to change. How could he, for he was only six years old. One day he came home from school and the slender lady was not there and the unshaven man was waiting for him with a packed suitcase. He took him on a train to another town, and then to another house where he met a woman named Brenda and a man who was introduced to him as his father. To begin with, whenever he was left alone with this Brenda he would cry. If the woman suggested taking him out to the park, or to the shops, more tears would begin to roll down his cheeks. His father spoke to him, and tried to reassure his son that everything would be all right, but in his heart he already sensed that he would never again see his mother. As the days passed he began to accept the sweets and small gifts that Brenda gave to him in an attempt to win his favour, and eventually he stopped asking his father about his mother and began instead to ask Brenda, whose standard response was, 'don't you worry your head, pet, I'm here for you now.' And the more Brenda repeated her cheerfully reassuring sentence, the more he gradually realised that she meant it and that she would look after him.

A whole summer passed, and he turned seven years of age,

and his sad anxiety was slowly replaced by a guilty peace with the reality of his mother's absence. One morning his father reached down and ran his hand through his son's hair, and then sat him in a living room chair and told his boy that he would never again see his mother as she had gone to sleep. By now he felt an attachment to Brenda, but the memories of his mother came flooding back and he could not stop the tears from beginning to stream down his face. His father paused and swallowed deeply before telling his son that his mother was in heaven, but she still cared deeply for him. Then, as though appearing from nowhere, Brenda came into the living room with an ice-cream cone and suggested that the two of them go for a walk. He took the ice-cream in one hand, and slipped his other hand into Brenda's, and together they left his father standing by himself in the middle of the room.

Once they reached the park, they walked through the main gates and directly to the pond, where they found a seat on a bench. For a few moments, they sat together and watched the children sailing boats on the pond, and then Brenda began to explain that although she had never wanted to replace his mother, and she understood that this was not what he wanted either, she would try to bring him up as best she could. She squeezed his hand.

'No matter what happens between your dad and me, I just want you to know that I promise I'll always be there for you, Keith. You do understand, don't you?'

He nodded as he finished his ice-cream, and then he let her wipe his face with a handkerchief. Judging by the way people were looking at them, he imagined that they appeared strange together, but Brenda never seemed to mind how people stared at them.

'Are you going to marry Daddy?'

He could see from the look of surprise on her face that she

was not expecting this question. She smiled, then laughed nervously.

'You do come out with some things, don't you?'

But later that year she did marry his father, but the son was not invited to the wedding. Instead, he stayed with a neighbour until the newly married couple came back from wherever it was they had been, and then life went on as if nothing had happened. Every day he thought about his mother, and sometimes he would wake up in the middle of the night and stifle his sobs in the pillow. He knew that his father was working hard, but he could never be sure of exactly what he did, and then the arguments with Brenda began. At first it was just his father's voice that he heard, and then Brenda began to answer him back, and then they both began to shout.

Eventually, one night the police came to the house. The flashing red and blue lights lit up the bedroom window and woke him up. Downstairs he could hear his father yelling, and then Brenda started to scream and he heard his father ordering her to be quiet. He slowly opened his bedroom door and crawled out on to the landing, where he hid behind the banister. He poked his head around the corner and was able to see straight down the flight of stairs to where everybody seemed to be bunched in the small space in front of the door. It was a policeman who first saw him, and the man nudged Brenda and pointed in his direction. Brenda snatched herself out of the grip of another policeman and she began to race up the stairs towards him. As she came closer he backed away, but it was too late.

'Everything's all right, Keith, love. Your father's just going back into hospital for a while, but he'll be back.'

He had no idea that his father had ever been in a hospital before, and he wondered what kind of accident he'd suffered.

'I don't want him to go.'

He tried hard to hold back his tears, but he couldn't help himself. Brenda quickly pushed a hand into her pocket and pulled out a fresh packet of tissues. She ripped the plastic apart and gave one to him and encouraged him to blow his nose.

'I don't want him to go either, but it's best for everybody. Don't worry, he's not going far, and he might be back home before you know it.'

'Can we go and see him?'

She stroked his cheek with the palm of her hand and smiled. Then she leaned forward and kissed him on the forehead.

'Of course we can. Now then, you be a good boy and get yourself off to bed.'

Later that night, after all the commotion was over and the policemen had gone, Brenda came upstairs. He tried to block out the noise of her footsteps as she tiptoed closer, but then he heard a squeak as the doorknob to his bedroom began to turn. He instinctively rolled over and faced the wall and pretended to be asleep. Brenda opened the door and then paused. He listened as she took a couple of steps inside the bedroom and then she paused again. He knew that she wanted to say something to him, but he didn't want to talk to her. Eventually the door closed and he heard Brenda making her way to her own bedroom. In the morning, a sad-looking Brenda dressed him for school and prepared his breakfast, before taking his hand and walking him all the way to the school gates. He remembered that he had nothing to say to her for he remained confused and hurt, but somewhere inside himself he knew that his father had been unkind to Brenda.

He looks through the same window that he used to stare through as a child. After his father came back from the hospital, the West Indian man from whom they used to rent decided to sell his father the house at a cheap price. Apparently, even though five years had passed by, the man was still upset at what Brenda had done to him, and so once his father regained custody it was this house that a thirteen-year-old Keith had to reacquaint himself with. His father is snoring in the room next to him, and it occurs to him that perhaps it was not such a good idea to leave London and come up north. After all, they passed the last hour or so in the pub in almost total silence, which pretty much summed up the nature of their relationship since he left to go to Bristol University as an eighteen-year-old. Nearly thirty years later, his father remains as much a mystery to him as he was back then. He had sat in the pub and watched the older man polish off another two pints of Guinness, but having done so his father looked as though he was going to fall asleep and so he had suggested to him that they leave the pub and make their way back home. During the short walk he tried to make conversation by talking about what they might do tomorrow, but his father seemed irritated by his questions and suggestions and so they re-embraced silence. Once they reached home, he simply followed his father into the cold, empty, house and then wished him goodnight before climbing the stairs to his bedroom.

He waits for his father to finish reading his *Daily Mirror*, and empty the second pot of tea, before he suggests that rather than watch television they might go out for a walk.

'Where?' asks his father, who now looks again at his newspaper.

He stands and begins to collect up the cereal dishes and stack them in the sink.

'Just to the park.'

'You want me to go walking in the park with you?'

He decides to do the dishes later, and so he wipes his damp hands on the front of his jeans and looks across at his father, who is now staring back at him over the top of the newspaper.

'Look Dad, I want to talk to you.'

His father lowers the *Daily Mirror*, but he doesn't say anything.

'I'm not suggesting anything drastic or bad, Dad. I'm just saying that we should talk, okay. Let's just go for a walk and it'll give us both a chance to stretch our legs.'

The park is empty, considering what a pleasant day it is, but he also notices that it seems far smaller and scruffier than when Brenda used to bring him. He understands that one's memory plays tricks, and that the park is exactly the same size, and just as unkempt as it always has been, but he is still disappointed. The pair of them sit side by side on a wooden bench by the small boating pond and he decides to tell his father about the situation with Yvette. He explains that she works for him, and that they started to see each other, and once he broke it off she began to make things both difficult and ugly. He doesn't stray far from the facts of the story, and he tries not to complicate things by mentioning either Clive Wilson or Lesley.

'The woman sounds like a bitch.' His father speaks without turning to look at him. 'Are you blaming yourself for this situation? Is this why you're telling me about it?' He sucks his teeth and doesn't wait for an answer. 'Man, women can be treacherous, but I suppose at this stage of your life I don't have to tell you, right?'

He wants to ask his father about Brenda, and why he still can't accept that she did what she thought was best for both of them. He also wants to ask his father about the women who seemed to drift in and out of his life during the few years he spent in his father's house before university. And why, for that matter, does he think it's all right to call Yvette a 'bitch'? She isn't his favourite person, but he wouldn't call her *that* name. Across the other side of the pond, a boy is trying to fly a kite, while his somewhat desperate mother attempts to help by pointing in the direction that she thinks the wind is blowing. However, the wind is gusting so she keeps changing her mind, and the boy seems to be getting the string in a tangle. He sneaks an oblique glance and notices that his father is also watching intently, as though this sideshow relieves both of them of the responsibility of continuing their awkward exchange. And then his father slowly turns to face him, and he can see that his eyes are red and damp.

'Boy, you're not feeling the cold? You're like a true Englishman able to sit out here without a hat or scarf and acting like the weather ain't bothering you at all.'

'We can go if you like. I just thought it would be nice to have a walk.'

'Have you finish whatever it is you want to say to me?'

'I want to talk to you about how you're living, Dad. I just don't think that it can go on for much longer. I hate to say it, but I don't want to get some phone call telling me that they've found you passed out in front of the television set, okay?'

'So this is what you want to talk to me about? I thought you come up here to see me so you can tell me about the girl at work.'

'To tell you the truth, Dad, I'm not even sure why I came up here to see you. Maybe I did want to tell you about Yvette. I haven't really had a chance to talk to anybody about it.'

'And you think that I might be able to give you some advice, is that it?'

'No, that's not it. I just needed to get out of London, and I wanted to see you too. But now that I'm here, and I've seen how you're living, I'm worried. Do you want me to pretend that I'm not?'

'You ever have people who tell you that maybe you should mind your own business? Well?'

He looks at his father, whose shrinking frame seems small and inadequate beneath his big, heavy, overcoat.

'Look, I cold. If you want to keep talking then maybe we can walk and talk. I tell a few of the boys that I will see them down at the centre.' His father gets to his feet. 'You want to come with me?'

The Nelson Mandela Community Centre is essentially an old people's home, although nobody calls it this. Above the dayroom, with its television, its CD player, and its neatly stacked puzzle books, dominoes, packs of cards and unused board games, are twenty-four one-bedroom flatlets from which the residents occasionally appear if they feel like being sociable. The management is sensitive to outsiders, but they don't mind one or two people coming in during the period between lunchtime and six o'clock in the evening, which is when dinner is served. His father is clearly a regular visitor, for he appears to be on a first-name basis with the staff and residents alike. 'You all remember my son, Keith.' His father sits with his three friends at a Formica-topped table and waits to be dealt into a dominoes game with Ronnie, Baron and Boysey. The three men barely look up from their dominoes as they nod and mutter greetings in his direction. His father claims to have known these men since arriving in England nearly fifty years ago, and it amuses him to see them now, at this juncture of their lives, still finding the energy to revel with what he imagines to be the spirit of their Caribbean youth.

'He say he come back home to keep an eye on me. I look like a man who need somebody to keep an eye on me?'

The men all laugh, and his father winks playfully at his son.

'Keith don't know how to relax and just enjoy himself. Which don't make no sense now that he get rid of the wife.'

Baron looks up at him and arches his eyebrows. Of all the men, he is closest to 'Uncle Baron' who, when he was growing up, seemed to be the most sensible of his father's drinking pals. More importantly, he was the only one who ever remembered his birthday or bought him a present.

'Keith, you get rid of the nice white lady?'

He shrugs his shoulders. 'She's still a nice lady, but you know how it goes. Sometimes you're just not seeing eye to eye. It's difficult with women, particularly if they're the mother of your child.'

Baron laughs. 'Man, I have a few of those knocking about the place.'

'Mothers or children?'

'Both, man, both. They come together like a package deal. Trouble always like company.'

As Baron throws his head back and laughs, he notices that his 'uncle' has lost his front teeth, which gives him a more mischievous appearance.

'Son, don't take it so hard. Listen to Baron, for he is telling you the truth. Women is nothing but trouble. You leave your wife, but you still got your health and that is all that matters. Plenty more fish in the sea.'

He looks at his father and wonders what on earth goes on in this man's mind. One moment he is cold and aloof, barely communicating at all, the next minute he is smiling, and sorting out his dominoes, and acting as though he is the life and soul of the party.

He sits with his father for an hour, watching him laugh with his friends, but this one table aside, the centre is not a place of joy where men and women at the terminus of their lives can relax in comfortable surroundings. The television that is bracketed to the wall in the far corner of the room seems to be permanently tuned to soap operas, and a group of men in dressing gowns and bedroom slippers sit silently on plastic chairs in an obedient row and gawp helplessly at the screen. He has never been beyond this dayroom, so he has no idea what the flatlets are like, but he suspects that they too are most probably joyless. The centre radiates an aura of communal depression, and the attendants appear to behave more like watchmen than skilled helpers who have been trained to assist the elderly. However, in the absence of close family members, most residents have little choice but to seek admission and accept shelter, and thereafter go about the business of spending what little money they have saved from their working lives in England in order that they might make it to the end with some vestige of dignity. He looks at his father and realises that he clearly has no intention of leaving his game of dominoes any time soon, and so he stands and tells his father that he is going for a walk and he will see him back at the house. His father nods almost imperceptibly, for he remains focused on his hand of dominoes. The older man does not bother to look up as his son leaves the community centre.

It is after seven o'clock in the evening when his father finally walks in and clumsily hangs his coat over the back of a dining chair. His hair is now the shape of the pork-pie hat that he has just removed and dumped on the table, and he is clearly in need of a shave. He looks at his father, and then he picks up the remote and turns down the volume on the evening news. He gets to his feet and passes into the kitchen where he begins to fill the kettle, then he cranes his neck so that he can see his father.

'Can I make you a cup of tea?'

His father rubs his stubbled face with the palm of his hand and nods before sitting down heavily on the sofa.

'You look done in. Must have been a serious game of dominoes.'

'I had to wait for the blasted bus, but I get fed up so I start to walk.'

He plugs the kettle in and then crosses to the door of the kitchen.

'You're not telling me you walked all the way back home? You can't be serious?'

'No man, I didn't walk all the way back. I'd be dead if I try to do that. But I walk about half the way and that is more than enough for me.'

He spoons two sugars into his father's tea and stirs, before rejoining him and handing him the cup. His father lifts the cup to his mouth and sips noisily at it, and then quickly sets it down on the floor. It is too hot.

'Would you like me to make you something to eat?'

His father begins to laugh.

'You can cook?'

'Well, not exactly, but I went to the shop and bought some things. Stuff that's easy to cook.'

'I didn't think you can cook. You looking to poison me, is that it?' His father continues to chuckle. 'Boy, I don't need no food. I ate something at the centre. The people know me good so sometimes they let me take a six o'clock dinner with the boys.'

His father picks up the tea again, and this time he swallows a mouthful before setting it down and leaning back into the sofa. His father closes his eyes and he can tell that the exhausted man has fallen asleep.

Earlier in the day, having left his father playing dominoes at the Mandela Centre, he took a bus to the cemetery. He got off a stop early, having remembered that the short row of local shops included a greengrocer's, and he bought what the Chinese guy behind the till described as 'a mixed bunch'. He told the man not to roll the flowers in a tube of decorative paper, and he took them from him in their plain cellophane wrapping. The afternoon was cold and overcast, and as he passed through the gate he saw an elderly lady with a terrier on a lead, but this lady and her dog aside, the place appeared to be deserted. He was surprised how easily he remembered the location of Brenda's grave, and once there he stood over the simple marble slab and set down the flowers.

After his thirteenth birthday, when he went to live with his father, he began to visit Brenda after school, and at weekends, for his father's house was only a twenty-minute bus ride away. If he and Brenda were watching television and it got too late, or if things between himself and his father were not so good, then he would stay overnight in his old room at Brenda's. The usual source of contention between himself and his father was the number of strange women who seemed to pass through the house, and his reluctance to call them 'Auntie'. Father and son did attempt to maintain some kind of cordial relationship with each other, but as he grew older they mainly strove to keep out of each other's way. He never asked Brenda directly about what had happened between herself and his father, but Brenda let him know that his father had suffered two 'breakdowns', one shortly after she met him, and then a second, bigger one after they were married and the three of them were all living together. It was she who had made the decision to call the police and section him the second time, but Brenda was adamant that his problems were not all of his own making. 'He's sick, Keith, so you have to be a bit easy on him. Hospital changed him, both times, from a quiet man who used to read all the time, and who kept himself to himself, into a depressed and anxious man. But the doctor told me that's the risk with the shock treatment. You know, the electricity. They eventually get better but they change. I'm sorry love, but he changed and I suppose we all had to just move on with our own lives, but your father never liked the fact that I was ready to move on.' Brenda's reference to moving on still disturbs him, for during the years on the Whitehall Estate he had not been aware of any other man in her life beyond himself. His father was convinced otherwise, and had bitterly accused her of infidelity while he was in hospital, but as a teenager this was not a subject that he wished to discuss with his father. However, he had twice come home early from school and noticed a maroon Ford Capri parked by the back gate. Instead of coming in he had chosen to walk around the estate for an hour and come back when the car was gone and, of course, he never mentioned anything to Brenda about the mystery Ford Capri. Brenda once made reference to his mother, in a way which suggested that she knew more if he wished to know more, but he already understood that this was a subject that he and his father would have to sort out between them. As much as he cared for Brenda, he had no interest in learning about his mother from her, and she never brought up the subject again.

At the start of Brenda's final summer, he was able to introduce her to Annabelle, and the two of them spent time alone upstairs talking, although he never asked either one of them what it was they had talked about. After his girlfriend had taken her photograph, and left to catch the train south in order that she might begin her summer job at the *Wiltshire Times*, he took Brenda a cup of tea and sat on the edge of her bed.

'Cancer, darling. Trust me, it's a bugger.' She laughed. 'It's even more stubborn than I am.'

He smiled weakly at her, but he remained too shocked to say anything in return.

'Don't look like that. I'm not going anywhere yet. It'll take more than some stupid tumour to finish me off.'

'Does my dad know?'

She laughed now, the kind of large expansive laugh that she always produced when she was at her happiest.

'Let's just say, I don't think he'd be too interested, do you?'

For a moment he wanted to suggest that despite his own prob-lems with the man, his father maybe wasn't quite that heartless, but he didn't want to argue. Brenda took his hand and demanded to know everything about Annabelle, and about university, and she pressed him about what he might do after finishing his degree, but his reeling mind was only able to half-concentrate on her words.

Six weeks later Brenda was dead. The funeral was a miserable affair, attended by a handful of her relatives, some of whom he had heard of but never met, and a small delegation of Brenda's colleagues and clients from the hairdressing salon. Predictably, his father chose not to attend, and after the coffin had been lowered into the ground, and the priest had said his few words then closed his book, he made his way back to the train station and then back to university without bothering to visit his father. As his father sleeps on the sofa, the cup of tea on the floor having long gone cold, it frustrates him to think that the two of them have never had a proper conversation about the woman who became a second mother to him. He understands that his father's unforgiving attitude towards Brenda has always been fed by his conviction that she betrayed him by calling the police to take him away, despite the fact that even he remembers that his father's response to any disagreement was to strip half-naked or bury himself in a book. What else was Brenda supposed to do? Over the years his father's negative feelings have, of course, been further informed by his stubborn belief that during his second stay in hospital Brenda habitually slept around, but this woman looked after him. It was Brenda herself who told him that when she went to see the doctor about the situation with her husband, the man suggested committing her husband and then having the child fostered, but Brenda remembered her promise to him and told the doctor to 'fuck off'. Nobody was taking 'her Keith' from her. He leans forward and shakes his father gently by the shoulder and asks him if he is ready now to go up to bed. His father does not answer, he just gets to his feet and then sneezes. He passes his father a paper tissue, which he waves away, and then his father pulls a crumpled handkerchief from his back pocket and again he sneezes and noisily blows his nose into the handkerchief.

'Do you want me to bring you anything upstairs? Another cup of tea, maybe?'

'No, the walk finish me off, and I just need to get a little sleep then everything is going to be just fine, okay?'

He watches as his father begins to slowly drag himself upstairs. Eventually he hears the bedroom door slam shut, and then he turns up the volume on the television remote and tries not to think about his father's predicament.

In the morning, he tells his father that he went to the cemetery and put flowers on Brenda's grave. His father barely looks up from his *Daily Mirror*, he simply nods and continues to read.

'Would you rather I hadn't told you?'

His father puts down the newspaper and looks closely at him for some time before answering.

'The truth is, I don't care what you feel you must do about Brenda. It don't have anything to do with me, and I don't have no feelings for the woman.'

'Brenda was like another mother. I can't ignore her.'

'Who is asking you to ignore her? You have a different relationship with the woman than I do, so you must do what you want to do.'

'Don't you ever think about her? I mean, she was your wife.'

His father folds his newspaper in half, and then in half again, but he keeps a tight grip on it. 'I was working hard to make some money so that things can be better for all of us, but she don't want to listen. She get a ring on her finger and then suddenly she have her own ideas. And then she gets rid of me, and takes you away, and when I get out the hospital and I hearing all kinds of things about her seeing other men and you think that this is decent or even respectful behaviour? I don't see why a man, including this man, should have to put up with it.' He tosses the *Daily Mirror* on to the table and shakes his head. 'I'm grateful to Brenda for looking after you, and she did a good job and everything, but my wife is not supposed to be climbing into another man's bed, do you understand? Anyhow, this is a long time ago, and I move on, and she move on, and that's just how it is with big people. You learn to get on with your life and put both good and bad behind you. Anything else you want to know?'

He knows that he has to say something further for he fears that once his father closes this conversation it might never again be opened up.

'Don't you ever miss Brenda?'

'A woman is supposed to look after her husband, not have the police come to his house and take him away.'

'Yes, I know.'

'Then what is your damn point?'

'I'm not sure that I've got a point.'

His father shakes his head. 'Women can say whatever they like, and do whatever they want to do, and they get away with it. And if you don't know that by now then I feel sorry for you.'

'I don't want you to feel sorry for me.'

'Boy, there's no reason for you to get upset. I going down the centre for a while. You want to come and help out? Today they do form-filling and so forth.'

He looks quizzically at his father, who slowly climbs to his feet and picks up his pork-pie hat.

'They fill out paperwork, and everyone helps. Paperwork for

pension cards, bus pass, social security, passport, anything you can think of. They choose one day a week on which they can just get everybody together to do it. Maybe you can help instead of trying to bite off my blasted head about Saint Brenda.'

He says nothing in response to his father.

'Well, you just going to stare at me?'

He sits with Baron, who has no idea what to do with the tax exemption form that he has filled in as best he can. He takes the pen from the older man and quickly checks the right boxes, and then pushes the form back in front of Baron for his signature.

'Don't bother with the date. I can fill that in.'

'So I'm going to get some money from the people?'

'I don't know about that, but you shouldn't be getting any more tax demands.'

'I just throw them away anyhow.'

He dates the form and then hands it back to Baron, who tucks it into the torn and sellotaped pocket of his brown leather jacket.

'Your father seem all right to you?'

'The house is in a hell of a state.'

'Your father is difficult like a mule, and lonely too. He long ago finished messing around with the ladies.' Baron smiles a broad toothless grin. 'All of us put those days behind us, but it's not good for him sitting alone in the house. He can get a flatlet upstairs like the rest of us and at least we can keep each other company. He can even go back to pretending he's still reading plenty of books and nobody will laugh at him like in the old days. I can make sure of that. What do you say? I always understand your father a little better when I see how he is around you.'

'What do you mean how he is around me?'

'Well, Earl likes your company. The man is always boasting

off about you, and how you're doing this big job and in charge of all kinds of people in London.'

He looks closely at Baron to see if he is making some kind of a joke, but Baron's eyes narrow and his face becomes increasingly serious.

'When your mother decide to birth you and leave him out of everything, it really break the man's heart. She was the one who did him wrong, and no wonder he end up in the hospital. And then again, later, after your mother die and send her husband to deliver you like a parcel, your father is angry and suffer all over again, which is why he end up back in the hospital. Your father is not an easy man, but life has dealt him some wicked blows. However, the man can get himself some peace of mind if he just sign up for a flatlet and come and live here among the boys, but for the life of me I don't know what goes on in that man's head.'

'Pride?'

'Pride about what, Keith? Look at us. The sons of Empire. The men who came to this country to make life better for ourselves. What have we got to be proud about, aside from the fact that we're still alive? Have we made this country a better place for you? You can be honest and tell me, have we? And look at how we're living after all these years. When your mother and father come to this country, you really think that either one of them expect to die here?'

He looks around at the men and women in the room, some filling in forms, others watching television, some medicated and asleep, and Baron's words make sense. But he knows that this is not the whole story.

'What about the children, Baron? Some of us have gone on to college or university and we're doing okay.'

Baron laughs quietly to himself.

'Keith, you aside, you see any children here? Man, the kids don't give a damn, and I don't blame them. I got daughters and sons and so on, but we don't really keep in touch, or anything like that. A lot of the kids doing just fine, and some of them getting through in spite of us, not because of us. Why you don't ask your father what he thinks of his time in this country?'

He looks across at his father, who is trying to help a man with a passport form. Baron is right. He should ask his father what he thinks of his time in England. In fact, there remain a lot of questions that he should ask his father, but this morning's outburst does not fill him with hope that his father will ever talk honestly with him on any subject.

They are sitting quietly together watching *EastEnders* on the television when his mobile rings. Aside from texting Annabelle on the first night to let her know where he was, he has had the phone turned off as he wanted to leave London behind. However, after they returned from the Mandela Centre he decided to check and see if he had any messages and he realises that he has obviously forgotten to switch it off again.

'Is that Keith?'

Annabelle sounds unsure of who she is speaking with.

'Annabelle? Just hang on a minute, okay?'

He stands and leaves his father alone in front of the television. He shuts the kitchen door behind him, and turns on the kettle before taking his hand away from the phone.

'What's the matter? Is everything all right?'

'Not really. Look, I think you might want to come back to London.'

'Well, I can come back in the morning. What's the matter?'

'Can't you come back now?'

'Now? What's going on?'

'Laurie's down at the police station, and they're questioning him and his friends. Somebody got stabbed.'

'Stabbed? But Laurie's okay, right?'

'He's fine, but they're saying he was involved. Look, I think you should come back.'

'Oh Jesus. I'll get my things together and call you when I'm on my way.'

'Are you still with your dad?'

'Where else am I going to be?'

'Look, hurry, will you? I'll wait to hear from you.'

He closes the phone and takes a deep breath. It is probably too late for a train, but he knows that the buses run till well after midnight. As he steps back into the living room he sees his father staring up at him with a look which suggests both curiosity and indifference.

'That was Annabelle. It looks like I've got to go back to London.'

His father sucks his teeth and shakes his head, making it clear that he doesn't understand why his son is obeying a woman to whom he is no longer married.

'It's Laurie,' he says. 'Annabelle says he's got into some kind of trouble.'

His father tosses his head slightly. 'The woman don't know how to raise a black child.'

He shifts his weight from one foot to the other and decides to ignore his father's comment. 'Listen, Dad, I'm sorry we didn't get to talk more.'

'You had something more you wanted to talk to me about?'

He sits by the window of the half-empty bus, and stares across the central reservation at the traffic that, even at this hour of the morning, is charging in the opposite direction and away from the capital city. Initially, the bus was cold, but a woman sitting near the driver made a fuss of putting her coat back on, and then her scarf and gloves, and then eventually getting up and speaking with the driver who turned up the heating so that it is now positively tropical. He suspects that his father is not well, for he can see it in his eyes, but he knows that there is only so much that you can say to a man such as his father. He continues to stare at the bright, undimmed, car headlights that flash by in the opposite direction and he chastises himself for not remembering to search in the cardboard box for a picture of his mother. The bus begins to slow now as they approach the end of the motorway, and he stands up and takes his bag down from the overhead rack. He could always send his father a stamped addressed envelope and ask him to mail a photograph to him. This would minimise the awkwardness, and his father might even feel inclined to respond, although the more he thinks about it the less likely it seems that his father would ever bother to go into his son's old bedroom and deliberately re-engage with his past.

He stands in the lobby of the police station with a distressed-looking Annabelle. He feels somewhat tired, but he is also irritated for although it is three o'clock in the morning these people haven't bothered to provide any chairs where they might sit down. Annabelle has been here for six hours. She told him that she has repeatedly gone out to the car to try and calm herself down, then come back in to talk with the officer on duty, who keeps repeating the same nonsense about Laurie already having a lawyer with him, so he can't have anybody else in the interview room. Sensing her frustration rising, he touches Annabelle on the arm.

'Look there's a KFC down by the green that's twenty-four hours. Let's have a coffee in there.'

He turns to the young officer on duty, who looks as though he is barely out of the academy.

'You've got her mobile number, right?' The young officer nods. 'And you'll call if anything happens? We're not going to be more than twenty minutes or so.'

'Don't worry, sir I'll call. Go and have your cup of coffee.'

They are the only ones in the KFC, and he carefully balances both cups of coffee on the tray as he sits heavily on the plastic seat opposite her. The slick floor has recently been mopped so the smell of cleaning fluid is overwhelming.

'Looks like your taking Laurie to the South Bank and talking to him didn't help much.'

'You make it sound like it's my fault.'

'That's not what I meant.' She shakes her head. 'Keith, I don't know how much more of this behaviour I can take. No wonder I had to get out of social work.'

'Well we're not his social workers, we're his parents.'

'For Christ's sake, Keith, I know that. I was just making a point about dealing with stress and young people. Why are you being so difficult?'

She sips at the coffee, then screws up her face in disgust.

'Do you need more milk?'

'I don't think anything is going to help with this stuff. It must have been sitting there for days.'

'What do you expect from KFC?' He pushes his coffee away. 'Are you sure they're not going to charge him?'

'That's what the young man on the desk told me. It appears that two boys have confessed to stabbing the lad, but Laurie is some kind of friend of theirs.' She pauses. 'Anyhow, he told me that he didn't do anything, and I believe him, but he simply shouldn't be hanging around with hooligans like that.'

Annabelle takes a sip of her coffee, and then she opens another sachet of sugar and slowly stirs it into the drink with a wooden stirrer.

'Look, Keith, I don't know what else to do with Laurie. Except, I was thinking, what about going on holiday with him?'

'Who? You and him?'

'No, the three of us. We could maybe take him somewhere over Christmas and try to show him something else.'

'You mean that we care for him?' He pauses. 'Annabelle, there's no need to look at me like that. You're the one who keeps implying that since we split up he seems to have got lost somewhere between the two of us.'

'Look, all I'm saying is that we should consider taking a break together, but if you don't want to then that's fine. If Mummy wasn't so out of it I'd have probably suggested that she join the two of us on a skiing holiday or something, but that's no longer an option so I'm trying to be sensible. I'm trying to include you, Keith.'

'What about Bruce?'

'That's pretty much over.' She pauses. 'Are you happy?'

'It's none of my business.'

'I don't care what you say, he's a nice guy. But I've got other priorities, as should you.' Again she pauses. 'Our son, Keith.'

'Don't patronise me, Annabelle.'

'Well pay attention.'

'Listen, we're both tired. Can we talk about this in the morning? Right now let's just go back to the station and get Laurie. This coffee stinks and I'd like to be there when they let him out.'

They step out of the KFC, and into the eerily quiet street. Right outside the twenty-four-hour kebab shop, he notices a badly parked top-of-the-line Mercedes which strikes him as strangely incongruous. As they pass by he can see that the alarm is primed, for an energetic sequence of flashing red and amber lights illuminates a monitor on the dashboard. Annabelle's phone begins to ring and she dives quickly into her handbag and retrieves it. He watches as she listens and nods her head, and then she flips the phone shut.

'Apparently he's ready to go home now.'

'Was that the officer on the desk?'

She shakes her head. 'No, the lawyer. He says there are no charges, but he'll wait until we're there to explain more fully.'

'Jesus, that's big of him.'

'Keith, do me a favour and try to go easy on Laurie. He was scared when I saw him earlier. He's not as tough as he makes out. In fact, he's still a boy in lots of ways.'

'What are you saying?'

'I'm saying he's not you, Keith. We didn't bring him up like you were brought up, remember? No white working-class estate and National Front kids on every other street corner. In fact, sometimes I don't think he's very streetwise at all.' Annabelle looks closely at him, and then she opens her arms wide. 'All right, I admit it. I can be a bit of a wimp. In this sense he's my son, I get it.'

He nods, and then notices the light on her face. She is standing directly beneath a lamppost.

'The truth is, I just don't want you to forget that he's my son, too, warts and all, and that makes him softer, okay?'

He lies in his own bed for the first time in three days and he thinks of Annabelle standing beneath the lamppost. She is still a beautiful woman, even though her black hair is now totally grey, and the veins on her neck and on the backs of her hands seem to be much more prominent than in the past. As far as he is concerned, Annabelle still looks like the posh teenager he met all those years ago on that night at the theatre. Serene, composed, and long before she leaned over and began to speak he had an idea of exactly what she would sound like.

When he and Annabelle reached the police station, Laurie was clearly surprised to see his father with his mother.

'You all right?'

Laurie looked at his father and nodded in response to the question.

'You must be knackered.'

Again his son nodded, and then Annabelle hugged Laurie tightly. He turned to the young officer on duty.

'We can go now, right?'

'Yeah, you can take him away. Your lawyer had to dash off. He says to call him in the morning.'

He stared at the officer, and wanted to say something in response, but for the sake of his son he decided to leave in silence.

Annabelle opened the passenger door and let Laurie climb into the front seat. She shut the door after him and then turned to face her former husband.

'I can give you a ride home, if you like.'

'Don't worry, but thanks. I'll have no problem walking it.'

'Are you sure?' He nodded then lifted his sports bag up and on to his shoulder. 'So, what time can you come by tomorrow?'

'You mean to talk to him again?'

'Keep your voice down.' Annabelle glanced quickly at Laurie, who was slumped in the passenger seat. 'I don't know what else to suggest, Keith. I'm going to have a sit down with him in the morning, but he really needs to hear it from you. And I don't mean going to football or to the cinema. I mean really sitting down and talking to him.'

She turned from him and looked again at their son, who had tilted back the front seat and balled up his jumper into a temporary pillow.

'Maybe take him to your flat.' She paused. 'It's only a suggestion, but we have to do something to keep him in our sphere.'

'"In our sphere?" What kind of talk is that? He's not an orbiting planet, you know. He's our son.'

'Keith, I'm too tired to play semantic games with you. You know what I mean. He maybe needs to spend some time with you. Maybe he needs to stay with you for a while.'

'Of course I'll talk to him.' He paused. 'I'll come over in the morning, but it won't be early.'

'Look, I should get him back home.'

Annabelle smiled quickly, and then she turned and climbed into the hatchback. The sound of the door slamming echoed ominously, and then lingered. He watched the lights snap on and then he heard the engine sputter to life. Only after she had pulled away, and passed out of sight, did he turn and begin to walk slowly through the gloomily silent streets of west London. As he crossed Uxbridge Road he saw a young couple on the other side of the street that, judging by the way they were laughing and looking at each other, had clearly just made love. They were still naked although they were now fully dressed. He tried to look inconspicuous, but then it occurred to him that they hadn't even seen him. He moved his bag from one shoulder to the other and tried to stay out of the early winter gusts as he ducked his head and pressed on towards Wilton Road.

IV

He sleeps late, but it is the sound of somebody practically leaning against his doorbell that finally wakes him up. He rubs his eyes and then throws back the covers. Who the hell could it be at this hour? People don't just drop by unannounced. Well certainly not to his place. When he lived with Annabelle the postman would occasionally call with boxes of manuscripts for her to read, but even he seemed to understand that it was best just to leave things on the doorstep. Stretching out a hand, he picks up the alarm clock, and he is surprised to see that it is now nearly twelve noon. He pulls on his T-shirt and his boxers, before opening the bedroom door and passing into the living room. He crosses the room and looks out, but unless he actually opens the window and leans forward it is impossible to see who is at the door. The sound of the doorbell is still ringing in his ears, and so he drowsily grabs a pair of tracksuit bottoms and then steps into his training shoes without bothering to undo the laces. He lumbers down the stairs and opens the front door, and he immediately recognises the man standing before him as Danuta's friend, Rolf, but it is difficult to know if the agitated individual is frightened, or slightly crazed. His hair is ruffled and matted, as though he has not slept in days, and his thin khaki anorak is clearly inadequate on such a bitterly cold day.

'Danuta is gone. Do you know where she is?'

So, the young man has no time for introductions. For a moment he thinks about chastising him, but given the distracted look in Rolf's eyes he deems it politic to just answer.

'I saw Danuta maybe three or four days ago. Is she all right?'

'This is a serious matter.' Rolf takes a small step forward. He raises a finger. 'Do you know where she is?'

He now understands that there is no possibility that he will be inviting this hot-tempered man inside, so he makes sure that he can slam the door shut if necessary.

'I've just explained, I haven't seen Danuta in a while. She told me that she was going to check into a hostel, apparently the same one that she stayed in when she first came to London. Have you tried there?'

'She spent one night there, but nobody has seen her since then. Did you go somewhere with her?'

'Go where with her?' He laughs now. 'I'm here. I've been away, but it had nothing to do with Danuta.'

The man takes another half-step towards him. 'I come here every day to look for both of you. Because you are a rich man, you think this is funny?'

'Look, Rolf. It is Rolf, isn't it? Maybe she's gone back to Poland. Have you checked with her friends or family back there?'

'Do you think I am stupid?'

Rolf speaks with an accent that becomes heavier and more difficult to understand the angrier he becomes.

'Nobody said that you were stupid.'

'She gave me a telephone number in Poland and I called. Apparently, her husband and three children left Warsaw last year. The people who answered the telephone had no address for them, and they did not even know that Danuta was in England.'

'She has a husband and three children?'

'You are just as foolish as she said you were.' Rolf laughs and then he shakes his head. 'Of course she did not tell you.'

'What do you mean?' He opens the door a little wider. 'I don't think I'm following you.'

'She told everybody at the language school that you were in love with her and also obsessed with some stupid book about music.' Rolf points. 'Maybe she took your things too?'

'Took what things?'

'I let her stay with me, and I slept on the floor next to her like an idiot. She pays no rent. I buy all the food, I buy presents for her, and then she takes my wallet and my credit card and disappears. I am not a rich man like you. I work in a building site and to begin with I am a rough sleeper in England. Anywhere so long as I can sleep, under bridges, in the park, I do not care. But then I get a room. A room with a divan, and I wash, cook, eat in this one room, but this is not civilised even if it is how the English do it. Then I must get a second job as a cleaner to pay for the stinking room, and so I invite Danuta to share my room and come and help with the cleaning job, for she is not happy. I help her, but then she takes everything. I thought she had come to you, or maybe she has done the same thing to you, I don't know?'

The Polish girl did nothing to him, except provide a distraction. He was tempted. Can he admit this? Will this make him Rolf's enemy?

'I asked her to leave, but not because she took anything. Look, do you want to come inside?' He moves to one side, but Rolf stares blankly at him.

'Come inside for what?'

'Well, it *is* cold.'

Rolf shrugs his shoulders. 'I am not cold.'

'Well I am.' He looks at Rolf, who continues to stare back at him. He can see that the teeth of the plastic zip on Rolf's anorak are misaligned, so that the front of his jacket is poorly secured and exposing the overwrought young man to the biting wind. He decides that he will not bother to point this out to Rolf. 'So she used to laugh at me?'

'Well, you waited outside the language school for her.'

'Only once. Perhaps twice, but I didn't know that she was married with children.'

'Danuta uses men. She is not a respectable woman.'

'I see. Well what about the police? You could report her as a missing person. They must keep files on such people.' He can feel Rolf's eyes boring into him. 'Well she *is* missing, isn't she?'

'I just want my things. My CD player, my DVDs, my sunglasses, my watch. She took one thousand pounds of my money from a cash machine and now she is gone. I have only my clothes, but why should the English police care what one foreigner does to another foreigner? She is probably somewhere in Poland with her family, so what are your English police going to do? I will tell you the truth, English attitudes disappoint me. Do you know what it is like to stand in a shop with money in your pocket and discover that nobody wants to serve you? Telling you with their eyes before you are even asking for anything. Do you know what this is like or how it feels?' The man points to his head. 'Can you imagine this?'

He wonders if he should offer Rolf some money, but maybe this is part of some elaborate ruse that Danuta and Rolf have concocted together. He looks again at Rolf, who exudes both anger and hangdog confusion in equal part. A watery line of sweat decorates the young man's upper lip. No, he is sure now that Danuta has stolen from this Rolf, and that the poor fellow is not going to get his money back. One moment of weakness, such as offering to let her stay at Wilton Road while he went away, or even falling asleep while she was under his roof, could have led to his being the one who was frantically charging about London in a futile attempt to track down his possessions. Finally, he has been the recipient of a stroke of good fortune, but it seems somewhat insensitive to revel in the moment while poor Rolf hops anxiously from foot to foot before him. He decides that he should offer Rolf a few pounds to help him out, but before he can frame his proposal in a manner that suggests kinship as opposed to charity, Rolf offers a hand, which he shakes.

'Okay,' says Rolf. 'I will leave you now. I am sorry to disturb you.'

'It's not a problem. I'm just sorry this has happened to you.'

Rolf looks as though he is going to say something further, but the distressed-looking blond boy simply turns on his heel and half walks, half runs down the path and then disappears from view leaving him marooned on his own doorstep.

He pours the hot water on to the instant coffee granules and stirs vigorously, then he carries the steaming cup into the living room. At least crazy Rolf has enabled him to get out of bed before any more of the day is wasted. He pushes the magazines and articles about hip-hop to one side and he rests his cup of coffee on the table. He had deliberately left the research material there before going north to see his father, his rationale being that the sight of the books and papers might give him a rolling start back into the book once he had returned, but suddenly he is embarrassed. This book will never be written. He hears himself say the words out loud. This stupid book will never be written. He wants to pick up the magazines and articles and dump the lot of them in the tall swing bin in the kitchen. Just clear every-thing out right now and stop messing about. It's not as though he has been getting out of bed in the morning with a burning desire to revise what he has done the previous day, before enthu-siastically pressing on to a new chapter. This has happened maybe twice, or at most three times, but during the past few days with his father he hasn't given the book a second thought. Now that he is once again faced with the evidence of his self-appointed task he feels slightly nauseous. He stands and gathers up the magazines and articles, and then he opens a drawer and pushes everything in. It is a sort of halfway compromise between actu-ally throwing the stuff out and temporarily getting it out of his sight, but having made the material disappear from view he now feels relieved. The books that are stacked like a precarious chimney on the floor beside his desk will have to wait. They are not so easily dispensable. He picks his watch up from the coffee table and he is startled to be reminded of the time. He will take a shower and get dressed, and then he knows what he must do.

He arrives at Annabelle's house feeling slightly light-headed. On the way over he stopped in at the Queen Caroline for an early afternoon pint of lager, having felt the need to steady his nerves after the unannounced visit from Rolf. He understood that narrowly escaping being ripped off by Danuta should be seen as a wake-up call, reminding him that he has to drastically change his behaviour, but he remains confused. If Danuta really has a husband, does this man know what she gets up to in England? Probably not, he decided, but then again, how does she manage to dupe him, and everybody she meets in England? There must be some small oasis of honesty and integrity in the woman's life. Attending the language school in Acton, and pretending that she's learning English so she can open an international kindergarten, and claiming to have to hold down a cleaning job at night to pay for all of this, are most likely familiar lies that she is used to spinning. There must be all sorts of desperate men who are eager to restart their lives and who would give anything to do so with a striking woman like Danuta by their side. Not just good-looking Latvians such as Rolf, but wealthy Arabs from the Middle East, and even Japanese business types. He carried his pint of lager from the bar and found his familiar seat in the corner of the pub, but immediately realised he would have to tune out the noise of two lads seated nearby who were trying to program their mobiles to ring to rap ditties from a menu they were busily sampling. The pit bull terrier at their feet sat impassively, with one Doc-Marten-clad boot clamping the dog's lead tight against the beer-sodden carpet. It is hard for him to see where, exactly, he might fit into Danuta's scheme of things, but Rolf was probably right when he claimed that she was just fooling with him and waiting for the opportunity to rob him. But she didn't take anything, which means that it is still possible that some part of her simply liked him for who he was. A mobile phone Frisbee-ed across the pub and clattered into the wall, and the two lads collapsed into a heap of uncontrollable laughter. The pit bull terrier sprang to retrieve it, but the lead remained trapped beneath a booted foot.

He will have to change his behaviour, which is not an altogether comfortable thing to admit, but it is true. He is in his late forties, and shamelessly flirting with young women is bound to land him in trouble. For over an hour he sat and quietly sipped at his pint while he thought idly about how to make changes to his life, and as he did so he half listened to somebody else's questionable jukebox selection. He remains open to being persuaded that contemporary pop music has some virtues, but whatever they might be they continue to reside beyond him. Having finished his pint he stood up and, carefully avoiding the dog, he crossed to the bar and returned the empty glass and then, politely declining the barman's routine offer of a top-up, he walked out.

Annabelle opens the door and he can see that she has been crying. The delicate skin beneath each eye has darkened as though bruised, and her eyes are moist.

'He's gone out.'

'Gone out where? I thought we were going to have a talk with him.'

'Do you want to come in?'

She leaves the door and walks back into the house. He wipes his feet on the doormat before stepping inside and quietly closing the door behind him. Annabelle has already disappeared, and so he walks down the short corridor and into the kitchen, where he discovers her leaning against the cooker.

'He just said that he had to go and sort something out and so he left. I told him to wait for you to come round, but he said that he didn't have time and that was that. Off he went.'

Annabelle looks exhausted, and her bottom lip begins to tremble as though she wants to cry again. He knows that she should be at work, but he assumes that she has already phoned in and informed her colleagues that the BBC will just have to manage without her today.

'Do you want me to go and look for him? Maybe he's hanging out by the Westway where you found him with that group of kids with mountain bikes.'

'And if he's there what are you going to do? Smack his bum and bring him home? He's seventeen, nearly eighteen. I just want to know that he's all right, that's all. Is that too much to ask? But nothing ever changes, does it? He's always got to do things his own way. Even as a baby, he always slept soundly, but never when I wanted him to. No wonder I always felt tired or ill.'

Annabelle snatches a pastel-coloured tissue from a box on the kitchen counter top and she quickly dabs at her eyes and then blows her nose.

'So you don't think I should bother going to look for him then?'

'I don't see the point. I've called and he's not picking up, so I suppose we'll just have to wait here until he comes back. Would you like a cup of tea?'

'Thanks.' He sits at the kitchen table and watches as Annabelle switches on the kettle. 'Did the lawyer bother to call you?'

'He just confirmed that they've charged the other two boys with grievous bodily harm or something like that, and he said that the police know that Laurie wasn't involved. I suppose that's something to be grateful for.'

'You "suppose"? That's like dodging a speeding bullet. He could have screwed up his chances of university. Maybe six or seven hours in a police station will have scared some sense into him. I know it would have set me straight.'

Annabelle drops two teabags into a plain red pot. 'Earl Grey all right with you?' He nods. 'I meant to ask you, did Laurie ever mention a girl called Chantelle?'

'Who?'

'Chantelle. A tall doe-eyed thing. She turned up last night at the police station and asked for him at the desk. I was standing by the noticeboard so she didn't see me, but I heard her say that she wanted to see Laurie. The young officer on duty just pointed at me and so she turned around and saw me standing there.'

'Is she his girlfriend?'

'Well, I wasn't going to ask her that, was I? She seemed a bit nervous, but then she said that she wanted to know if Laurie was all right and would I tell him that she'd been by to see him. And then she left.' Annabelle paused. 'High carriage, like a model.'

'That was it? She didn't wait?'

'So when we got back last night I told Laurie that Chantelle had dropped by the police station and he just nodded, you know how he does, and then he went up to bed.'

'Well, she's obviously his girlfriend but neither of them knows how to deal with the situation. It's probably not cool to have a girlfriend.'

Annabelle fills the teapot with hot water and then sits down at the table with him. 'What's awkward about having a girlfriend?'

He laughs. 'Come on, you're asking me? We got together when neither one of us was living at home. We were at university, with our own rooms and everything, but once your parents were in the picture, "awkward" would be a nice way of putting it, don't you think?'

'But I don't have any objection to Chantelle. In fact, she seemed like quite a nice girl.'

'Of course you don't have any objection to her, but like I said that's not the problem. They both live at home and it's probably not hip to be coupled any more. These kids like to just hook up.'

'Hook up? What the hell's that?'

'Well what does it sound like?'

'I'm sure I don't have to tell you what it sounds like, but my son is not an animal. You really don't know what it's like, do you? Going off to watch football in Barcelona is nothing compared with some of the things that Laurie wants to do. He comes home asking me if he can "hit the road" with his mates and go off to some music festival or other, living in a tent and sloshing around in mud and rain. I do my research, you know. It's all about mosh pits and drinking and drugs, and I've not mentioned the carbon footprint so there's no need to look at me like that. You know I don't approve of piles of abandoned tents, and thousands of flushing toilets, and all those idling cars, but I'm not giving you some green tirade now, I'm just talking about protecting my son, and remember I'm the one that gets the glares and the door-slamming. Admit it, Keith, you really don't know what it's like, do you, because you've conveniently missed the past three years holed up in your stupid little flat.'

'Have you finished?'

'Actually no, I haven't finished. You're not the one having the horrible conversations with him about wanting to monitor his email and check the websites he visits, are you?'

'Come on, Annabelle. They invent personalities, you know that. It's not real.'

'Well, the internet's been real enough to get you into hot water. Or is this Yvette girl really a nun who is just pretending to be a cheap prostitute?'

'Have you finished?'

'There's a serious point here, Keith.' She pauses. 'Sometimes I feel like the only way to retain proper control over our son would be to install bloody CCTV in his room. It's not been easy, and for the last three years, while you've been playing Mr Eligible Bachelor up the road, it's bloody well me who has had to deal with Laurie.'

'I said, have you finished?'

'Yes, I've finished, but sometimes you just disappoint me.' Annabelle pours the tea, but refuses to make eye contact. 'I suppose I haven't gotten over the fact that the sensitive young man I knew during my last year as a teenager bears so little relationship to the man who twenty-five years later bloody well left me. But then again, why should you be the same person?'

'And do you think you're the same young woman?' He pauses. 'Well?'

She looks at him as she places the cup of tea in front of him. 'I'm sorry, you're right.'

'I don't know why you're suddenly biting my head off.'

'I said I'm sorry, okay?'

'I heard you.' He pauses. 'Look, it doesn't make sense to be snapping at each other like this.'

'Is the tea all right?'

'Yes, it's fine. Thanks.'

He looks at Annabelle. 'Is the tea all right?' Really, that's it, right there in a nutshell. 'Is the tea all right?' No real attempt to take any responsibility for whatever she's venting about, it's just a quick middle-class shuffle and all the unseemly hostility is swept under the carpet, and they can once again proceed with civility. 'Is the tea all right?' Did he imagine her anger? And she has yet to talk to him about the tears in her eyes when she opened the door, but Annabelle appears to have calmed down and he is disinclined to raise anything that might once again disturb her. Twenty-eight years ago this girl found the courage to lean over and speak to him during the interval of a play. Yes, this girl, the one in front of him, the girl from Ashleigh who is concerned about the Earl Grey tea. He stares at her and he feels the question rising within him.

'Do you still think about going to live abroad?'

Annabelle looks closely at him over the top of her cup of tea. She places it back in the circle of the saucer. 'What made you think about that?'

'Well, I just wondered. You remember how we used to talk about it back then.'

'Jesus, Keith, another ten minutes of living under Mrs Thatcher and I'd have willingly moved to Timbuktu.'

'The more I think about it the more I wonder about this place.' He pauses. 'I mean, Britain. It's not like it's done a lot for Laurie.'

'Really? So where do you think we should have brought him up? The West Indies, your imaginary homeland?'

'I don't know, Annabelle, but I'm done with all this, okay? I simply can't be doing this any more. I'm so bored with myself, and fed up with what's become of my life. And maybe you're right about the Yvette thing. Maybe I am behaving recklessly in order to get some kind of thrill because I'm just bored. I'm forever waking up in the morning and feeling that I'm stuck. I can't put it any better than that. Some part of me knows that there's a lot more ahead, I really believe that, but I can't quite work out how the hell I got stuck here.'

'Sounds like you've become middle-aged.' Annabelle begins to laugh. 'Welcome to the club. And I told you, don't look at me like that. They're your words, not mine.'

'I've been thinking about my mother a lot recently. Wondering if this is the grown-up son that she imagined.'

Annabelle puts down her cup of tea and looks up at him. 'Keith?'

The truth is, he has no clear memories of the woman who was his mother, just fleeting images of a slender lady and a man, and himself as a very young boy, and all three of them living together, one on top of the other, in a small room that was always cold because the fumes from the paraffin heater made him sick. As a result, the unshaven man never took off his heavy cardigan or his trousers, but the man was kind to him, that much he remembers. Often the two of them would be left alone while his mother went out to work, and the man would give him large sheets of plain paper and a pencil and encourage him to draw, but he remains disturbed by the fact that he doesn't remember ever leaving the cramped room until he was old enough to go to school. By then it was his mother who was spending most of her time with him in the room, while the man went out to work, and it was his mother who used to talk incessantly about a man called Mr Littlewoods who she hoped would send them back home, but he was practically an adult before he was able to cast his mind back and realise that this Mr Littlewoods was, in fact, the pools coupon, and that only by marking down ten draws on the coupon would this Mr Littlewoods grant his mother her wish and send them back to the West Indies. However, while his mother talked to Mr Littlewoods, he started to go to school where he learned that he had other names besides Keith, most commonly 'chocolate drop'. In the afternoons he would come home from school and meet his mother still lying on the bed in their attic room and it was his job to take food from the cupboard in the corner and go down one flight of stairs to the communal kitchen and ask whoever was in there to boil up something for his mother to eat. And then later the unshaven man would come back, but usually with his eyes and nose running, and he would sit on the end of the bed, and take off his brown shoes, which always seemed to be damp from the rain, and carefully rub cream into his dry elbows and his aching feet and promise his mother that one day they would get out of this one room and start living like English people until, that is, the morning when he discovered dogshit smeared all over the bottles of milk on the doorstep and he stopped talking about getting out of the room and living like English people, and with his mother too poorly to say anything, and the man now seemingly reluctant to say anything at all, his world began to go quiet and maybe it's this sudden silence, which fell on him like a heavy blanket and smothered the light and life from his world, which accounts for the fact that to this day he has no clear memories of his mother. And then one afternoon he returned from school and discovered that his mother was no longer in the bed and the unshaven man was standing in the room with his coat on,

and a packed suitcase by his side, waiting for him. The man
didn't even give him time to put down his school satchel, he
just took him by the hand and the next thing he remembers is
a train journey to another town, and then a ride in a taxi, and
by the time the man knocked on the door to the strange house
he was beginning to understand that he might never see his
mother again. The next morning the new woman wiped away
his tears with a white handkerchief which she then pushed into
his pocket. She suggested that they go for a walk, and the woman
held his hand tightly as they walked past buildings that were
coated black with soot and through streets that were dense with
fog. She told him that it was mild, but he didn't know what
mild was. He knew hot and he knew cold, but this was a new
word for him. Once they reached the shops she bought a big
bag of jelly babies, and as they walked back in the direction of
the house she started to talk. She told him that his father had
put on weight because of the tablets that he was taking, for
England had hurt his head. She laughed: 'He prefers books to
people. Except you, that is, and perhaps me when he's in a good
mood. Trust me, though, he's happy to see you, love. Since he's
come out of the hospital things have been difficult for him, and
even the smallest upset makes him disappear inside himself, so
it's best not to take it personally, that's how I cope. You have to
understand that it's not always you that he's upset with, it can
be something he's just remembered from the West Indies, or
something he's read in one of his books. He's sensitive like a
petal, which is why I fell for him, but he has got a bit of a
temper, although I shouldn't let that bother you. They told me
at the hospital that if they released him into my custody then
I'd have to keep an eye on him and make sure that he takes his
medicine, but he's stubborn like an ox, your dad is, and it's as
though he prefers to be depressed and anxious rather than take

a few tablets and get better. He can give you some gubbins about how he's taken this pill and that one, and then I look in the bottle and has he heckaslike. He says not only do they make him fat, but he feels like he's swallowing his tongue, and he does go on about it. These days it's two buses for me after work, so I'm sometimes late, but you'll soon get used to the idea of being around him and he'll appreciate having you in his life. I'm hoping that he'll soon be able to find a job and get out and about again, but if he doesn't hurry up the Pakis will have all the jobs. But one thing at a time, eh?' He remembers walking with one hand in the woman's hand, and the other hand in his pocket holding on to the bag of jelly babies, and the woman never stopped talking. 'We've got a gogglebox so you can watch television, but only after you've done your school work. You'll be going there tomorrow, love, but let me tell you now, if they call you names you just let them have it. "Ginger" or "Shortie" are one thing, but even that's not nice, yet I imagine they'll be laying it on thick with you. I try to remember that there's good and bad everywhere, but I won't have name-calling, and neither should you.' When they got back to the house his father was sitting quietly at the table reading a newspaper. He stood by the door and looked at his father, but what should he say to this man who seemed to be ignoring him? He knew that the kind unshaven man, who gave him paper and pencils to draw with, would not be coming back, and then again he felt the tears welling up in his eyes. Brenda took his coat and hung it up, and then she removed the bag of jelly babies from his pocket and handed them to him, but he didn't want any. He began to cry for he couldn't remember what his mother looked like. He knew that he had a mother, but her face was already lost to him. The slender lady was gone.

'Well?' Annabelle sounds impatient. 'Why think of her now?'

'I don't know.' He pauses. 'What are we both turning into?'

'Speak for yourself, I'm not turning into anything.'

He is not talking about her looks, but presumably she knows this. And if so, why this resistance to change? Change can be good, if you remain vigilant about the direction you are moving in. His problem is a lack of vigilance. He hates to admit it, but he sometimes feels as though he's lost his bearings.

'You look like you're drifting off again.' Annabelle claps her hands. 'Hello, anybody there?'

'The other day I found that Grover Washington CD that we used to listen to at university. Well, cassette tape back then. We pretty much lived together for our second and third years.'

'Is that why you're asking about living abroad?'

He nods. 'Probably. When we finally got to go Inter-Railing at the end of that second year, I felt happy. Charging around all over the place. One day we're in southern Spain, then we're riding a funicular in Norway, then we're in the red light district in Amsterdam. I worried the whole time about going back and having to deal with your father. I thought he might make you change your mind.'

'You're not serious, are you?'

'Well, he'd sent you that letter about your "irregular liaison" and how he wasn't in favour of colour prejudice in England, he just wanted an end to the thing that caused colour prejudice. In other words, immigration. So bloody clever.'

'And you thought I'd fall for that?'

'I didn't want to lose you, and everything seemed so perfect just riding the trains. We were free, whatever that means.'

'Yes, well the sustaining fiction was that we were somehow escaping the problem, wasn't it?'

'Is that all it meant to you?'

'It was the best holiday of my life.' She pauses. 'Ever.'

'Really?'

'Keith, my parents used to go on Christian group holidays, if they bothered to go anywhere at all. To the Isle of Man, or looking at churches in Austria. I hated it. And when I was a small girl, and Daddy was stationed overseas, you know how it was. Just me and Mummy, trapped in some stupid little seaside town. Travelling around Europe with you was amazing, and you were so careful and thoughtful.' She stands up and begins to clear the cups and saucers from the table. Then she laughs. 'What happened to that sensitive boy?'

'Very funny.' He stands and picks up a tea towel, and as she washes the dishes he begins to dry them. 'Remember the chef at the *posada* near Lisbon where we arrived really late that night? He made us tomato soup with an egg in it, and then carried the two bowls from the kitchen to our table. And later, I remember when we were taking the ferry from Boulogne back across the Channel towards Dover. You were asleep on a bench downstairs, but I stood up on deck and watched as the ship edged closer to England and I knew that we both had to go back to Bristol and do our third year, but I didn't want to come back. I didn't feel like I had any reason to come back to England, aside from the degree that is. If you'd have come upstairs on deck and said, "Keith, let's not bother with our final year," I'd have taken the next boat back to France with you, no questions asked. But you continued to sleep, and you didn't come up on deck, and I just kept watching England come closer and closer, and I kind of knew that it was going to get bad with your parents, but what could we do?' He pauses. 'I suppose that Grover Washington cassette helped a bit. *Winelight*, that's what it was called. We really wore it out.'

Laurie rejects his father's offer of a glass of beer and continues to stare out of the window. Annabelle looks across at them, her arched eyebrows asking if it would be better if she left the kitchen, but he quickly shakes his head and then takes a long swig of beer from the bottle. The pair of them had been waiting for almost two hours when they finally heard the front door open and then crash shut. They looked up as Laurie walked into the kitchen and grunted a circumspect 'hi'. He seemed tired, but the only unusual thing about him was the fact that he was without his headphones.

He stared at his son and tried to remember the last time he had seen him 'undressed' in this way, but it was obviously quite some time in the past. Annabelle leapt from her seat and offered to make Laurie coffee or tea, but their son shook his head before slumping into a chair at the table, his body language suggesting that he knew full well that his parents were keen to talk with him. Annabelle reached into the fridge and poured herself a glass of Perrier and then passed him a bottle of beer. He looked at Laurie.

'Would you like a glass? Or do you want something else?'

Laurie stared at the beer, then at his father, and then he turned and looked out of the window.

'No thanks.'

Annabelle coughs quietly into her hand and clears her throat. 'You know, we've been worried about you.'

'Mum, please.' Laurie speaks without turning to face either of them.

'Your mother's right. Where were you?'

'Just out.'

He can hear the tone of defiance in his son's voice, but he knows that this is not the time to be coy. 'Out where?'

'Like I said, just out.'

Annabelle reaches over and touches Laurie's shoulder, but her son shrugs away from her and she is forced to hang on.

'Laurie, your father and I need to know where you've been.'

Laurie turns now to face them both. 'You mean you want to start checking up on me? You don't trust me, is that it?'

'Last night your mother called me to come and get you at three o'clock in the morning from a police station. In case you haven't noticed, that's not normal and it doesn't inspire a lot of trust. So let's get this straight, okay? Where were you? Were you with those two partners in crime of yours?'

'I didn't commit any crime, they did. And they're not my partners.'

Annabelle lowers her voice to a whisper. 'But they're your friends, right?'

Laurie looks at his mother. 'They're not my friends. Well, not any more. And you can tell Grandma that I won't be going to Barcelona. Not with those two anyhow.' Laurie once again turns away and stares blankly out of the window.

He readjusts his position on the kitchen chair and pulls himself more upright.

'Well, I'm glad to hear that. Who are they anyhow?'

'Just two guys from school. Easy Fingers and Armani Lite. Their real names are Gladstone and Stuart.'

'And you think that's funny, do you?'

'Am I laughing? I told you, they're just two guys from school.'

'Two guys who happen to carry knives.'

'That was nothing to do with me. I thought they just did dinner money. You know, hassle-free pickings. I saw them after they'd done the guy, but I shouldn't have let them leave the knife with me.'

'You didn't have to take it, Laurie.'

'What, so they could do me too? You can get stabbed in this town for just looking at someone in the wrong way. It don't matter if you know them or not. That's why I don't like to leave my postcode, right? And I don't like public transport neither. It isn't safe. Anyhow, I left the knife with a friend of mine and when the coppers picked me up she gave it to them.'

'Well I'm glad one of you had some sense.'

Annabelle takes a sip of her water and then she once again clears her throat. 'I met Chantelle. Last night. She seems very nice.'

'Yeah, well now she's in bother for grassing the pair of them up.'

'Laurie, they're in police custody so there's nothing they can do to her.'

Laurie turns and looks at his father. 'It doesn't work like that. They're in a posse and soldiers look out for each other. At least I took the blade so they're not vex with me.'

'Son, tell me the truth. Is she in danger, because if so we ought to do something about it.' He pauses. 'Well? The only way out of this is to just tell the truth.'

'I've told everybody the truth. You, the stupid police, the lawyer. What else do you want from me?' Laurie turns from his father and looks down at his designer training shoes. 'I wish I'd never met the two of them.'

'Did the police abuse you in any way?'

Laurie looks up at his father. 'What?'

'I'm talking about racial abuse. Did the interviewing officer verbally abuse you in any way?'

'What are you on? The copper who interviewed me was black.'

Laurie looks across at Annabelle, who throws him a quick, sympathetic smile.

'Can I go up to my room now?'

'Laurie, are these boys actually bullying you?' He pauses. 'If so, this is something that you can't deal with by yourself, do you understand?' Laurie continues to ignore him. 'I'll ask you one more time.'

'They've got some issues with me, I think, but it's over now, okay?'

'So where have you been? With Chantelle?' Laurie turns to face him. 'Well, have you been at her place?'

'What?'

'Don't say "what?" Your mother and I didn't bring you up to be so rude.'

'Okay then, pardon.'

'Well, is she all right?'

Annabelle leans forward. 'We just want to make sure that you're both coping.'

'Look, it's got nothing to do with either of you, right? I shouldn't have taken the blade and it's a bit of a mess. But it's sorted. You're treating it like it's some big tragedy. Can I go to my room now?'

Annabelle sighs, and again she touches her son's shoulder. 'Look, Laurie, it *is* something to do with us.'

'Leave it, Annabelle. If that's how he wants to play it.'

'Look, Laurie, your father and I have been talking. Would you like to spend some time with him?'

'What do you mean? I already spend time with him.'

'You tell him, Keith.'

'Shouldn't we talk about this a bit more?'

Annabelle holds up her hands in exasperation. 'When?' She pauses. 'Well?'

He turns to face his son. 'What your mother means is that maybe you could come and stay with me at the flat for a week or two. So we can talk and just figure out what's what.' Laurie looks blankly at him. 'You don't have to decide now. How about if I come back this evening and we go out for dinner?'

'Tonight?'

'Well yes, unless you've got some other plans.'

'I don't really want to go out tonight.'

'Well we can always stay in and talk. Or do you want to think about everything for a day or two?' Laurie looks him in the eyes and slowly nods. 'Okay then, we can leave it just now.'

Laurie gets to his feet. 'Can I go now?'

Annabelle smiles. 'Of course you can. I'll give you a shout later when I've made something to eat.'

They both watch as Laurie leaves the kitchen, and then they listen as their son trudges his way up the stairs. He finishes his bottle of beer and then climbs to his feet. He doesn't want a war with Annabelle or his son, but something has gone wrong.

'Look, I should probably leave you to get on with things.'

'Do you think we should tell the police?'

'Tell them what? That Butch Cassidy and the Sundance Kid are about to gun down this girl? The police don't give a damn. They waste most of their time trying to prevent under-eighteens from buying cigarettes or fireworks, or looking into so-called fraudulent benefit claims. Real crimes? Not their priority, is it? They don't care.'

'Great.' Annabelle stands up. 'So you're on his side now, are you?'

'Annabelle, I'm on no one's side. I want things to work out as much as you do, but Laurie's right. Life out there on the streets is different for these kids.'

'Okay, then you pop off home and leave me to worry myself stupid.'

'Well, do you want me to stay and talk more with you?' Annabelle glares at him. 'No, I didn't think so. We'll go to his school in the morning. I don't know what else we can do at the moment.' He pauses. 'Well, do you?'

* * *

He sits in silence on the sofa and stares into the middle distance. The flat is cold, but he can't be bothered to get up and turn on the heating. He thinks about what else he might have said to Annabelle. For instance, he didn't leave her after twenty-five years, she was the one who wanted him to go. As for his being a disappointment, he could have pointed out to her that during the past couple of years, and certainly since she started seeing Bruce, she has developed a tendency to behave with that mean and slightly smug, green-wellied, middle-class sense of entitlement that he was so surprised, and pleased, to find her devoid of all those years ago at Bristol University. Anyhow, he can't help feeling relieved that her relationship seems to be over. He knows full well that behind Bruce's lapsed socialist prattle, he is a man who would have been pleased to help usher Annabelle in a direction in which she might feel inclined to start dressing like her mother in midcalf-length skirts of heavy material, and begin wearing discreet jewellery with plain, dull stones. This would have enabled Bruce to inch closer to joining the world that he claims to have spent his youth railing against, but he understands that people like Bruce never rail, they just blow. Although he is tempted to put on some music he decides that it is probably best to avoid anything that might remind him of his temporarily abandoned book. Through the window he can see that the late afternoon light is fading, and only the familiar hum of cars passing at the end of the street, and the distant cry of a police siren, disturb the peace. He tries to imagine how it might be to have his son staying in this flat with him, and he finds himself wondering again why Annabelle chose to share with their son the idea of his spending time here at Wilton Road. The two of them had only just raised the possibility, and suddenly it was as though Annabelle was trying to force Laurie upon him.

He knows that Annabelle feels that children ought to spend

time with both of their parents, particularly if the child is without siblings. After all, he remembers how upset she becomes when she wistfully recalls lonely seaside holidays spent with her mother while her father was away on duty in Ireland, or inspecting troops in Germany, or in some long-forgotten outpost of what remained of the empire, such as Gibraltar. Her mother would sit in a deckchair and read a magazine while Annabelle played in the waves or collected shells, or waded in rock pools. Occasionally there might be a donkey ride, but the holidays were essentially miserable affairs, and ever since Laurie was born Annabelle has been adamant about his need for two committed parents, as though some deeply unconscious part of herself feared that she might replicate with Laurie the type of unhealthy dependency that has developed with her mother. However, her recent tendency to accuse him of deliberate absenteeism during the past three years is a bit rich. As soon as she'd ejected him from the family house, she started to spend practically every weekend with her mother in Wiltshire. His access to Laurie was limited to after-school visits and the odd Friday night excursion to McDonald's, but fortunately things did become a little easier once her mother entered the Briars. He looks across at the thermostat and finally admits defeat. Levering himself off the sofa, he realises that he had better turn on the heating before he starts to see his own breath clouding before him.

It is clear to him that Annabelle's anxiety over Laurie has been exacerbated by her own complicated feelings of guilt about her mother's situation. While they waited for Laurie, Annabelle spoke about her mother's continued confusion, to the extent that she sometimes barely recognises her daughter when she visits. Apparently, in among her semi-coherent ramblings about seeing white girls dressed as Arabs on the streets of London, and her conviction that there is a war being fought in the village of

Ashleigh – a misunderstanding which apparently dates back to Annabelle's childhood when an unexploded German bomb was discovered near the Norman church, and the whole village was evacuated for a night and day – her mother, according to Annabelle, did have one recent moment of clarity when she again apologised to her daughter for how they had treated him. 'They', of course, was her mother's way of referring to her late husband, but Annabelle told him that although she always assured her mother that *she* had nothing to apologise for, her mother's 'apology' did make her think again about the complicated bond between mothers and only children, especially when the mother begins to age. Annabelle swallowed deeply and seemed to tumble into a momentary reverie. 'Once upon a time it felt like it was only Mummy and I, and in some ways, as you know, we grew too close and now I don't think I'm coping very well with the responsibility. I know that Mummy needs me now, more than ever, but it's difficult to watch her become little more than a nervous old fuddy-duddy. Her confidence has gone, and she does get very irritated when she is found out for having forgotten something. Her hands start to shake, and she weeps so easily, and I simply don't know how to respond. The other day she wept like a baby and kept telling me that they're all being kept alive so that like old fruit they can just rot. "It's not fair" she said. "There's no dignity to it" and I'm beginning to wonder, Keith. Really I am.' Annabelle stared at him as though embarrassed that she had said too much, and then she gradually came to herself. 'You know, spending some time with Laurie might help straighten you out too.' He looked at her, but decided to let her comment go. The next thing he knows, Annabelle is raising the prospect directly with their son instead of finishing the conversation with him.

He looks around the living room and realises that should Laurie come here then his son will most likely take his bedroom and he will be relegated to sleeping on the sofa. And what, he wonders, of those days when Laurie is at home revising for his exams? The flat isn't big enough for them to stay out of each other's way, and he can already predict what his son's reaction will be should he suggest that Laurie decamp and work at the undeniably grotty local library. It would have been better if Annabelle had said nothing to Laurie about the possibility of spending more time with his father, but given his son's palpable lack of enthusiasm it is highly unlikely that he will have to grapple with these practical issues in the immediate future. He leans back, stifles a yawn, and listens to the wind whipping around the roof and rattling the window panes. Tomorrow morning he and Annabelle will have to face the annoying Mr Hughes. Rather than stay up late watching television it would probably make more sense to go to bed and try and get a decent night's sleep. He looks at his mobile and can see that nobody has called him, but he decides to take no chances. He picks it up and adjusts the ring tone to 'soft'. He will carry the phone through with him and leave it by the side of the bed, just in case.

He stares at the headmaster, whose permanent smile is beginning to irritate him. Annabelle can barely bring herself to look at the man, but he knows her well enough to understand that although she may be smouldering inwardly, she will do her best to avoid any overt conflict.

'Let me put it this way.' Mr Hughes stops playing with the stapler and pushes it to one side of his desk. The space in front of him is now clear. 'If Laurie works hard, or should I say harder, then there's every possibility that he can still go to university. When he applies himself he's a very able boy, and in the top twenty per cent of this school in terms of ability. But the key is *when* he applies himself.'

'I don't understand.'

Annabelle looks up. 'No, I'm afraid neither do I.'

'Why are you suddenly talking about our son as though university is something that he might miss out on? He's at home revising for his mocks. Nothing's changed since we last spoke to you.'

Mr Hughes seems surprised. 'He's at home?'

'He's got time off to do his revision. They all have, don't they?' He looks across at Annabelle. 'Isn't that right?'

Annabelle nods. 'It's their revision week.'

Mr Hughes rocks back in his chair and uncaps, then recaps, the expensive fountain pen in his hands, before tucking the instrument back into his breast pocket.

'Fair enough, although I must say I wasn't aware of this, but so be it. However, the point is that things have changed since we last spoke. I'm afraid that back then there was already some concern about his lack of appetite for study, and the slipshod manner in which he was applying himself, but I think you'll agree that recently things have gone a little downhill. Shoplifting and brawling, and now time spent under investigation in a police station.' The headmaster looks directly at them both. 'We are doing all we can at our end, but when it comes to shepherding a boy through these difficult years then there must be some kind of partnership between school and home.'

'Are you suggesting that Annabelle and I are not doing our bit?'

'Heaven forbid.' Mr Hughes laughs now. 'Of course not. All I'm suggesting is that there is only so much that we can do from our end. We are extremely careful about monitoring social networking sites like Facebook for signs of gang activity. On school property we have zero tolerance with regard to bandannas or colours, and carrying a weapon of any kind leads to immediate expulsion. We don't allow top of the range mobile phones, and all coincidental absences are investigated, as are any reports of over-sexualised behaviour or dress on the part of the girls. What else can we do short of bringing in airport style scanners and random searches? But if, for instance, drugs were to become a problem, then of course we would have no hesitation in really clamping down. That said, we are a school, not a prison system, so we have to be a little open, which is why we rely greatly upon the vigilance of parents. After all, we're in the fight together against this culture of adolescent silence.'

He looks at Annabelle, who has again chosen to avert her eyes and is now staring across the school playground at the tall brick wall which surrounds this Gothic Victorian structure. They never discussed sending Laurie to a private school, although Annabelle's parents made their feelings clear. An inner city comprehensive was not what they had imagined for their grandchild, but then again they had not anticipated somebody like Laurie entering their lives. Annabelle had been predictably stoic in the face of their displeasure, but she has never successfully disguised the fact that this school, with its loutish pupils and ill-mannered parents, has been a source of great disappointment to her.

'I'm still not clear what you're saying to us.' He realises that he should probably lower his voice. 'Laurie's not in a gang or doing drugs. I feel like we're being lectured, and I'm not too happy about it, okay? Is there something that you would like us to do, or is there something that you think we're not doing? If so, just say it.'

'No, no, no. Nothing of the kind. I suppose I just wanted to meet with you to reassure you that we're doing all we can from our side. My door's always open, and if there's any way in which we can partner with you with regard to young Laurie then let's explore it.'

Annabelle picks her bag up from the floor. 'Is that it, then?'

Mr Hughes smiles directly at her. 'Certain lifestyles are more attractive to juveniles, and there's no denying the cultural cachet of the ethnic way of life. It's just that I don't want Laurie to lose his focus any more than you do.'

'You don't want what?' He feels Annabelle's hand on his arm.

'We have to go now.' Annabelle stands up and gestures that he should also stand.

'We must work together if we're going to arrest this issue of Laurie's academic free-fall.' Mr Hughes continues to smile. 'Laurie's an intelligent boy, but like so many of today's youngsters he's confused about the options that are open to him. He needs to be nudged gently down the right path. They all do.'

Annabelle loops her arm through his and guides him towards the door. She looks over her shoulder.

'Thank you for your time, Mr Hughes.'

Before he has a chance to say anything further, he finds himself outside the headmaster's office and Annabelle is pulling the door closed behind them.

'He's not worth it, Keith. Pick your battles, okay?'

He sits in the pub around the corner from the office and waits for him to arrive. A large flat screen TV hangs on the wall, but for some reason it appears to be tuned into a German sports channel and is presently showing table tennis. The place is full of the type of suited men who think that it is acceptable to parade up and down airports or train corridors bellowing business details and dinner arrangements into their Bluetooth attachments for everybody to hear. Mercifully, it is the end of the working day so these buffoons are now clutching their expensive glasses of plonk and braying directly at each other with their champagne-coarsened voices, but it makes them no less offensive to his eyes and ears. He made sure that he had first ordered a pint, and found a seat, before taking out his mobile phone and dialling the number. Clive Wilson seemed somewhat taken aback to be receiving a call, and he could hear him trying his best to appear calm and friendly as he agreed to pop around to the pub in about twenty minutes. He wasn't entirely sure how he was going to play things with his boss, but it was clear that after their last encounter there needed to be some kind of resolution. Clive Wilson had not indicated that he would call, but he was disappointed that, in spite of the way in which their last meeting had concluded, his boss had not seen fit to seize the initiative and mend bridges with a senior executive. He takes another mouthful of beer, and then looks at his watch, and then suddenly Clive Wilson is standing before him and apologising for having turned up a few minutes late. His boss offers his hand, which he shakes. He moves to get to his feet.

'No, no. Sit down, Keith. I'll get myself a drink. You take it easy. I won't be a second.' He watches as Clive Wilson fiddles around in his pocket for money, and then his boss turns and begins to jostle his way to the bar.

After the encounter with Mr Hughes, Annabelle had suggested that the two of them grab a quick coffee at a French pâtisserie around the corner from the school. He agreed with her that he needed to calm down, and once they reached Le Fumoir he secured them both a table while she went to the counter to order their lattes. As he waited, he looked around and found himself formulating a short spiel for Annabelle about how the place appeared to be full of media types who looked like they were discussing whether this year they should go white-water rafting in Tanzania or off-piste skiing in Chile, but he decided that given the present circumstances it was probably best to bite his tongue and keep his cynicism to himself.

'Well?' said Annabelle, placing the coffees down on the table and then looking directly at him. 'That was pleasant.'

The lattes were served in what appeared to be skinny fluted vases and he stared at them and tried to work out whether to overlook this nonsense or demand a proper cup.

'Is everything all right?'

'Yes, no problem.' He decided that there were bigger issues at stake than the coffee cups, but he made a mental note that he wouldn't be coming back here. 'I was just thinking, maybe we should take him out of that bloody school.'

'And do what? He's only got six months to go and you want to move him to prove what exactly? That you won't be spoken down to?'

'You really think Laurie is being helped by that kind of atmosphere? That guy's a jerk.'

'Keith, we're not moving him, okay. We need to do something, but not that.'

'Well then you're right, he should spend some time with me. But a few days isn't going to do anything. I should start looking for a bigger flat, and if he's serious about not going to Barcelona then I *will* take him to the West Indies. Maybe over Christmas?'

'You don't have to do all of this, you know.'

'I'd like to.' He pauses. 'Maybe this will give you time to get back together with Bruce.'

'I beg your pardon? Is that meant to be funny? Because if it is, I have some news for you.'

'I'm sorry.' He paused. 'I just don't know how you could have been with a guy who seriously thinks that we need a set of citizenship rules, or whatever it was that he said. All that bullshit about reclaiming patriotism for the left. He comes over like a member of the BNP.'

'You only met him once.'

'And that was enough.'

'Have you finished your rant?' She stares at him. 'Well?'

'It's not a rant.'

'Good, then I'll assume that you've finished. Do you think that we might talk about our son?'

'That complete arse of a headmaster was trying to shift responsibility from his lazy, ignorant teachers and put it on to us, the parents.'

'Well not all the parents are paragons of virtue. Hitting their children right outside the school gates, or not bothering to dress them properly for school, or not even caring if they go to school at all. And that time when I tried to say something at the PTA meeting they practically lynched me.'

'You mean the black parents practically lynched you.'

'I didn't say anything about black or white.'

'Well it didn't help that you stood up and started talking about kids kissing their teeth and how you couldn't understand their accents, or have you forgotten what you said? Maybe you'd prefer if the kids were all called Fergus or Becky, and their mothers spent all their time chasing between Sainsbury's and the gym?'

She stares at him. 'Why are you doing this? Turning it into something that it isn't. All I'm trying to say is that some of the parents are pretty damn useless, and almost all of them are time-poor.'

'"Time-poor"? What does that mean?'

'It means they're too busy to put their kids first. They're not our type of people.'

'There you go again! "Our type of people?" Are you deliberately trying to wind me up?'

'I can't put it any simpler than that, so if you don't like it you'll just have to take it on the chin. I don't mean anything offensive, and I'm certainly not defending that idiot Mr Hughes, but it's unfair to suggest that there are not a few good teachers who are trying. All kids need some kind of help at home, but some of the kids in that school have no bloody supervision, and no wonder Laurie finds himself having to mix with delinquents.'

'You know, Annabelle, sometimes I wonder what that clown Bruce turned you into.'

'How dare you be so condescending!' She looked around and then lowered her voice. 'He didn't turn me into anything. I'm telling you what I feel and if you don't like it I'd prefer if you would at least credit me with enough intelligence to be able to form my own opinions.'

'And they're really your opinions?'

'Yes, they're *my* opinions.'

He leaned back in his chair and sighed deeply. 'Look Annabelle, I've known red-faced tossers like Bruce all my life, in their pink and black hooped rugby shirts, sitting on barstools pontificating about how we've carried the jocks for years despite the fact that they've got oil, and how we need our traditional friends, meaning New Zealand, Australia, and Canada, not these fair-weather Johnnies in Brussels.'

'Don't you think you've said enough?'

'No, I don't actually. Why don't you credit *me* with some intelligence? I don't want my son around arseholes like Bruce.'

'Well as long as our son is in *my* custody then he'll be exposed to my judgements on people, not just yours.' She paused, then snorted in disgust. 'You can really be an arrogant bastard when you want to be, can't you?'

'You're entitled to your opinion.'

'Thank you.' Annabelle shook her head. 'Was he that much of a threat to you?'

'Who?'

'Listen to yourself. It's pathetic. You know exactly who I mean. Bruce. Or do I have to spell it out for you?'

His phone began to vibrate in his pocket. He was about to answer it when he thought he should check first with Annabelle, for he had no desire to further antagonise her. He reached into his pocket and held up his still vibrating mobile.

'I don't know who it is.'

'Well, then you'd better find out, hadn't you?'

Baron sounded hesitant and slightly unfamiliar with the telephone.

'Keith? It's you? I get your number from your father.'

'Is everything all right?'

'Good, good, man. It's all right, but I'm staying by your father's place as he has some chest pains. I tell him that I will let you know, so that's all. I'm just letting you know that I'm staying here tonight.'

He looked across at Annabelle, who was averting her eyes and making a clear effort not to listen.

'I didn't call you to make you take off time from work or anything. I know you is a big man in a big job.'

'No, it's no problem. I'll come up in the morning. Just tell him that I'll be up in the morning, okay?'

'You didn't hear me? I said I have it under control. You just go along with the work business.'

He waited until Baron hung up, then he switched off the phone and placed it on the table. Annabelle looked back in his direction. She glanced down at the mobile.

'Are you expecting another call?'

'I hope not. That was my Uncle Baron, one of my dad's friends.'

'Well? You never told me how it went up there.'

'Well other things kind of got in the way, like picking up our son from a police station. But it was pretty much just as you might imagine it.'

'A laugh a minute then.'

'Exactly.' He paused. 'So what do you think we should do

about the school? You're happy for him to stay there with the hoodlum children of the time-poor parents?'

'"Happy" might not be the best way of putting it.'

He tried hard to concentrate on his conversation with Annabelle, but he found it difficult not to worry about what exactly was behind Baron's call. His father's friend was saying all the right things, but for Baron to ask his father for his son's number, and then take the trouble to actually pick up the phone and call, suggested to him that his father must be in some kind of trouble.

'Would you like my help looking for a larger flat? I can look online while you're away.'

'Away where? Who says I'm going away?'

'Well, excuse me, didn't I just hear you say that you would "come up in the morning"?'

'But only for a day or so at most.'

'So I should just leave it then?' He stared blankly at Annabelle. 'Hello, Keith. Anybody at home? Do you want me to look online or not?'

'Thanks, but I'm not sure how much money I have.' He took a sip of his latte and then shook his head. 'Renting in this city is tough, and it's probably a lot more expensive than it was when I signed the lease on Wilton Road.'

'Do you have any savings? And don't look at me like that because I'm not prying.'

'I'll have to figure out the whole money thing. I'm just not sure what's happening.'

'Is everything all right?' Annabelle looked quizzically at him, but he suddenly felt overwhelmed as he realised what his next move would have to be. 'Well, are you okay? You seem to have gone mental walkabout.'

'I'm fine.' He rubbed his eyes. 'Really, I'm fine, just a bit tired, that's all.'

'Another coffee?'

'No thanks. Honestly, I'm fine.'

He watches as Clive Wilson edges his way back from the bar with a pint in his hand, and then his boss sits opposite him.

'Cheers.'

He knocks his own glass against that of Clive Wilson and then takes a drink.

'I might as well come straight to the point, Clive. I'm resigning, okay.'

'What do you mean "okay"? It's not okay with me. I told you, these things take time and this one's a bit tricky. However, I can now see some light at the end of the tunnel. I'm pretty sure that Yvette is going to be transferred.'

'Is that what she wants?'

Clive Wilson laughs out loud. 'What's it got to do with what she wants? It's better for everyone if she moves on. It's a sort of sideways shift, with a more senior title, and the girl seems okay about it. This might happen next week, and then we can see about your coming back. To tell you the truth, I could really use you around the place at the moment. It's a bloody nightmare trying to understand all this new red tape baloney.' He reaches into his jacket pocket and pulls out a piece of paper, which he unfolds. 'Listen to this. I just got this email directive saying that as service providers, we have to "recognise the needs of diverse communities and provide facilities that are genuinely multi-cultural, being aware that different facilities might be needed for people with specific religious, cultural, or dietary needs". All this rubbish just in case I start getting hassle from a one-legged Muslim who likes burgers and feels like the council isn't paying enough attention to his needs?' He tosses the piece of paper on to the table. 'What am I supposed to do with garbage like this?'

'I've got no idea, Clive.'

'Nobody really understands this guff, except you that is.'

'Well, that's not quite true, but I still think that I should resign.'

'Are you thinking of your pension? You can only lose it if you get fired and that's not going to happen.'

'I'm thinking of what's best for me.'

Clive Wilson picks up the email and folds it back into his pocket, and then he takes a long swig of his beer. 'I don't know what to say. Except, of course, you've blindsided me. What are you going to do?'

'I've no idea, but I'll think of something.'

'Are you going to write that book of yours?'

He laughs now. 'I don't think so, Clive.' He stands and points to Clive's glass. 'Another one?'

'I'll have another one. Why not?' Clive Wilson hands him the empty glass. 'But you are going to stay in the business?'

'Social work?' He smiles. 'I don't know. Maybe it's time to do something different with my life. You know, before it all gets a bit monotonous and predictable.'

'You mean like my life?'

He continues to smile, and he notices that Clive Wilson is looking perplexed.

'So you think your life is monotonous, do you, Clive?'

'Like watching bloody paint dry. Sometimes I think I should go out and get myself a young bird. Put a bit of spice back into things.'

'And you think that'll do the trick?'

'Can't hurt, can it?'

He stares at the computer screen and scrolls down the list of flats to rent in his area of west London, beginning with the three-bedroom flats, his thinking being that he can set up an office while he and Laurie can each have a bedroom of their own. The problem is the price of renting in London, which, as he feared, seems to have gone up significantly since he signed the lease for this one-bedroom flat. His rent is hardly cheap, but three years ago he was more concerned with the trauma of the break-up than he was with money. However, after a miserable week in the Travelodge, during which time it became clear that Annabelle was serious and had no intention of changing her mind, he convinced himself that this was an unexpected opportunity to begin anew, and he might as well seize it and pay the exorbitant rent. The recently decorated flat smelt of paint, and there were dustballs in the corner, and bits of sandpaper and twiglets of electrical wiring on the floor that the workmen had left behind. However, the space was his for him to reinvent himself as he saw fit, and although he remained somewhat confused and hurt by Annabelle's rejection of him, he eventually made peace with his situation. But having his son move in with him is hardly a new adventure, more like an obligation that he knows he should fulfil, but without a job he is having difficulty figuring out how he can realistically make this work.

He quickly accepts the fact that he will most likely have to set up a work-station in his bedroom, and he scrolls down to the two-bedroom flats. While they are significantly cheaper, they are still prohibitively expensive and it occurs to him that maybe he should have tried to negotiate some kind of pay-off deal with Clive Wilson. However, given the manner in which they left things, it is now highly unlikely that his former boss would be receptive to any more overtures from him. He took Clive Wilson's pint glass and crossed to the bar, where he ordered a lager. Once the barman had pulled the pint, and he had paid for it and received his change, he carried the pint of lager back to Clive Wilson and placed it on the table before him.

'Where's yours, Keith?'

He looked down at Clive Wilson. 'So you're really sorry that I'm leaving, are you, Clive?'

'I told you, nobody understands all this gobbledy-gook about brand-repositioning better than you do. The new regulations make no sense, and the language is impossible. Anyhow, there's still time for you to reconsider.'

'Let me ask you, Clive. Do you know how to spell "hypocrite"? It's not a hard question.' Clive Wilson looked up at him with his hand eagerly gripping his new pint of beer. 'Pride yourself on running a tight ship, do you? Well you need to look around yourself a bit for I'm not the only one who thinks that you're a sad tosser. That's t-o-s-s-e-r in case you're still struggling with "hypocrite". They're both applicable.'

He turned and left before Clive Wilson could reply, but as he pushed his way through the crowd of briefcase-wielding after-work drinkers he knew that at least he'd done the decent thing and bought his boss a pint.

As he left the pub he saw a bus approaching, so he quickly dashed across the street to the stop outside the West London Internet Call Centre, a place that seemed to specialise in calls to Somalia, Bangladesh, or Pakistan. The girl ahead of him in the bus queue was wearing flip-flops as opposed to pumps. He remembers Yvette telling him that in London women's feet get too dirty and calloused in flip-flops, but this girl, who was listening to some kind of bhangra music on her iPhone, seemed cheerfully oblivious to this fact. As the doors to the bus concertinaed open, and the line began to shuffle forward, he realised that for the first time since he left Bristol he was now officially unemployed.

He googles another rental agency and begins to scroll down their list of flats, but price remains the problem. Now that he no longer has a job, he will have to think again about this plan of Laurie moving in, for even large one-bedrooms appear to be beyond his pocket. Moving further out of London doesn't appeal, for he has always been scornful of the suburbs and the commuting life, but at the moment the idea of knuckling down and getting another job is also unappealing. He should really start looking at social work job listings online, but he knows that he will be immediately pigeon-holed as an expert on inner city black problems, and be expected to spew sound bites to the media about how gun and knife violence are not black crimes any more than paedophilia is a white crime. However, when he points out to the press that Bangladeshis in Tower Hamlets or white gangs in Essex are committing exactly the same gun and knife crimes, he will immediately be viewed as part of the problem itself. Some years ago, shortly after they left Birmingham and moved to London, he suffered his first, and only, instance of media backlash when he stood up at a national conference on drug trafficking and pointed out that a young teenager who had £10,000 in his pocket should not be liable to be arrested by the police, and have charges pressed against him, unless there was some direct evidence of criminal wrongdoing. Apparently, according to the *Daily Mail*, this made him an apologist for drug-dealing. Without even looking at the jobs that are available he knows that with his experience and complexion, and given the national push towards more racially polarised community monitoring, he will undoubtedly find it hard to land a job that doesn't place him in the firing line of the press on race issues. What he finds even more galling is the fact that even the most senior job in this area is likely to pay him less than he was earning as an executive policy-maker with the local authority under Clive bloody Wilson.

The ringing of the doorbell interrupts the gentle clatter of the keyboard as he once again changes the parameters of his flat search. He glances at his watch and can see that it is going up for ten o'clock. He picks up his mobile phone from the messy desktop and makes sure that nobody has been trying to get hold of him, but as he does so the discordant sound of the doorbell again cuts through the silence and so he quickly grabs a track-suit top and makes his way downstairs. Lesley stands before him with her hands pushed deep into the pockets of her winter coat.

'I'm sorry, I know I should have called. If this isn't a good time then we can always speak in the morning.'

He stands to one side and smiles in an attempt to disguise his surprise. 'It's fine. Come on in. I'm just playing about on the computer.'

He closes the main door behind them and decides that whoever gave her his phone number must have also given her his address. Lesley doesn't look distressed, which might excuse her behaviour. In fact, there is an air of impatience about her manner, which leads him to believe that they are about to have a confrontation of some kind. But does he truly care? He knows that some friendships cannot be dissolved little by little, they require an indelicate blow. She follows him upstairs and into his flat, where he takes her coat and hangs it on the solitary hook in the cramped entrance hall. He then ushers her into the living room and encourages her to take a seat on the sofa, while he crosses to the computer and closes down the open window. He assumes that she will not be staying for long so he does not log off. He offers Lesley a glass of wine, but even before she can formulate an answer he moves back in front of her and goes into the kitchen where he pours them both a glass of the only wine he has left, a some-what overpowering Australian Chardonnay. Before he shuts the fridge, he makes a note that there are two more bottles lying on the bottom shelf, in addition to the one he has just returned to the holder behind the door. He carries the two glasses back

into the living room and decides not to apologise for the wine
in case it sounds as though he is being pretentious. Instead he
just passes Lesley a glass and then takes a seat opposite her.

'So,' she begins, having taken a sip of her wine. 'You've done
it then.'

'Well, I suppose he told you.'

'Oh yes, and everybody else. He said you really lost it. Black
rage.' She takes another sip of wine. 'Well, he didn't actually
use that term, but that was what he was getting at. You know,
where you get all loud and illogical and he's the calming paternal
figure.'

He starts to laugh. 'And you believed him? I mean, do I look
like I'm out of control?' He opens his arms and gestures, although
he is careful not to spill his wine. 'Do I look like some nutter
who's about to push somebody off a tube platform?'

'You could have calmed down, I suppose.'

'Yes, and I could have held up Lloyds Bank this afternoon
with a sawn-off shotgun but it's just not me, is it? That's the
point. He says something and everybody suspends disbelief and
goes along with it? Makes me feel glad I jacked it in.'

'I never said I believed him. In fact, most people haven't got
any time for him, but you already know this. However, the problem
is, Keith, I wish you'd have spoken with me first. Given me a
chance to let you know what was going on.'

'Hang on a minute.' He stands and crosses to the kitchen
where he removes the bottle of Chardonnay from the door of
the fridge. He once again takes up his seat and pours himself a
splash more, before putting the wine down on the floor to the
side of his chair. 'I'm listening.'

'Did he tell you that Yvette's taking the matter to a tribunal?'
She pauses. 'No, I didn't think so.'

'I thought she was getting promoted.'

'Shunted to one side, and she didn't like it and so she's been threatening to go to a tribunal, which means it will probably be all over the papers.' Again she pauses. 'He didn't tell you, did he?'

'Apparently not.'

'Look Keith, what it means is that your resigning is irrelevant in terms of bringing an end to things. In fact, it's probably about to kick off for real now.'

'For Christ's sake, who told her to go to a tribunal? Her lawyer, I suppose.'

'I can't help you there, but you might have been better sticking with the job and going head to head with her, rather than throwing in your cards now. It makes you look weak.'

'Weak? Guilty more like. As though I'm running away from something.'

'I do wish you had talked with me first.' She holds up her glass and he reaches to the floor and picks up the bottle and pours her a refill. 'Look, am I keeping you from something? Or someone?'

'No, I told you, I was just doing some stuff on the computer.'

She kicks off her shoes and tucks her legs up underneath her on the sofa. He watches as she swirls the wine around in the glass, and for a moment he worries that she might smell the bouquet and pronounce her verdict.

'You know, it's still possible for someone to have a word with Yvette.'

'You mean for you to have a word with Yvette?'

'I really don't think she's getting sensible advice. To go to a tribunal isn't good for you, but it might not be good for her either. She's been offered a pay rise and promotion, but I imagine her lawyer is just focused on the harassment issue and dangling some imaginary big cash settlement in front of her. It's such bullshit.' She sips at her wine and then looks up at him. 'Would you like me to talk to her?'

He can hear the BBC morning news. Even before he opens his eyes he realises that he must have fallen asleep with the television set on. He knows that in all likelihood he is on the sofa for he has no television in his bedroom. His mouth is dry, and tastes like a discarded ashtray. He tries to licks his lips but he has no saliva. He rubs his eyes and then sits upright. The light bulb in the desk lamp is shining directly in his face. On the coffee table are two empty glasses of wine and an empty bottle lies on its side on the floor. There is no sign of Lesley, and he has only a vague recollection of her leaving the flat. He does, however, remember her asking him if he had any regrets about what had happened between them in the New Forest. He had seen this question coming for some time, but when it arrived he still had no carefully constructed answer with which to defuse the situation. He need not have worried for Lesley didn't give him an opening to answer. 'You see,' she insisted, 'I've never regretted acting along the lines of how I feel. I suppose it's only when I don't act that I regret it.' He remembers looking at her and thinking that of course she has no regrets because she had nothing to lose. He on the other hand has plenty of regrets for he should have been responsible not only to his wife's feelings and her dignity, but to her life, to her journey, to the fact that he had met her parents, and it was not possible for him to simply pat himself on the back and prioritise being in tune with his feelings over his sense of responsibility. Of course he had regrets about what had happened between them, which is why he eventually blurted it all out to Annabelle, although a part of him still can't understand why such a brief and inconsequential act of infidelity should have mattered so much to her. Lesley was not a threat to their marriage. It was a mistake, and Annabelle was not being abandoned, and they were not trapped in a sexless marriage. For Christ's sake, the whole thing meant nothing. Their marriage may not have packed the passion and the lust that it once did, but it wasn't broke and wasn't his confession a testament to this? He had no desire to compartmentalise at his wife's expense, for there were already too many secrets hanging over his life, and so he did the decent thing and he admitted his guilt, but still she jettisoned him. Jesus, it didn't seem fair. After all, he had embraced the myth that one person was all that he needed, and he had tried to be loyal to the myth, to live by it, and to accept the notion of the myth as the basis of his life, and it had, if truth be told, given him many rewards. But by betraying it just one solitary time, everything had collapsed and this woman wanted to know if he had regrets? Sitting with him in a one-bedroom rented flat on a cheap sofa drinking bad wine, she seriously wanted to know if he had regrets? He remembers drifting into the kitchen and opening another bottle of dodgy Australian Chardonnay, and then avoiding her questions, and physically keeping his distance from her, but the tension of the evening, and endless glasses of wine must have eventually taken a toll for he still has only a hazy memory of her leaving. But leave she did, and if he remembers correctly she again stressed, at least once, that she might be able to talk to Yvette, but by this stage he didn't give a damn. By the time he poured the final drop of wine from the last bottle, he couldn't care less about a potential tribunal, or a newspaper scandal, or his being sacked, or the withholding of his pension. He no longer cared about the whole pantomime of his fancy job and the consequences of his so-called inappropriate behaviour. None of it held any interest for him. He remembers looking at a bleary-eyed Lesley, her face twisted with righteous concern, and thinking, let them do with him what they wish. Let them make an example of him, humiliate him, who cares, he was sick of it all. And yes, he did have regrets, especially staring at her podgy face. He regretted going to the conference, he regretted going to the local pub in the forest with her, he regretted the quick fumble, he regretted everything. Was that clear enough?

By nine o'clock he has finished tidying up the flat and he has packed a bag. Outside he can hear a helicopter buzzing overhead like an intoxicated insect, and he imagines that there must be a drug bust on the local council estate, either that or there is an appalling traffic snarl-up at some junction, but what's new? These days, nobody in London ever gets anywhere on time. The laundry has been done, the bathroom and kitchen have been cleaned, the sofa straightened out, and all his papers and bills neatly filed and arranged. What remains to be organised has been simply pushed into a drawer and out of sight. He is not sure how long he will be gone, but it is important to him that he comes back to a neat place. The sink is full of soapy water, but as he searches for stray items to wash he realises that there is only an odd cup and a single glass left to take care of and then he will be ready. He pulls out the plug and listens to the water spiralling away. An hour ago, as he still lay on the sofa piecing together the night before, Laurie had called and asked if he should come round to see him. He had told his son that he was more than welcome to do so if he wished, and that he shouldn't feel that he had to ask, but then Laurie confessed that he didn't really have much to say at present, and he was sorry for all the trouble and worry that he was causing. Maybe they could do something later in the week? He found himself listening to his son's suggestion, and then saying 'sure', like some gum-chewing cowboy from the movies. 'Sure, Laurie.' His son seemed relieved, and he promised to call back in a day or two, but he didn't bother to tell Laurie that he would be gone. He decided that once he knew how long he was likely to be away then he would phone Laurie and set something up. He tears off some sheets of paper towel and begins to wipe out the sink where the suds have gathered. Then, having disposed of the wet paper, he crosses to the fridge and makes sure that the ice-making machine is turned off. He will actually call Laurie once he gets to his father's house, for there is no reason at all why he should leave things up in the air for a minute longer than is necessary. He will speak to Laurie, and figure out what his son would like to do. At the very least, he owes his son the courtesy of attempting to play the part. He fully understands that Annabelle has probably encouraged Laurie to call him, but unless Laurie wanted to speak with his father then he wouldn't have picked up the phone. In this sense, Laurie has made the decision by himself. His son called him, and so he will set up something specific with him. During the past three years there have already been too many casual plans made, and too many casual plans broken, and as the grown-up it is his responsibility to change this pattern of behaviour between them.

V

The sharp, acrid smell of the hospital ward alarms him. The noise of the machines that beep with metronomic precision, and the sight of people laid out in various states of helplessness is unsettling, but it is the high stench of cleanliness that truly disturbs him. Suddenly he is desperate for fresh air, but it is too late now. He walks slowly towards the far end of the ward where he can see his father lying prostrate in the cot under the window with his eyes closed, an intravenous drip needled and taped into the underside of his forearm, and his heartbeat, a neon green parabola, blipping away on a small screen. His father is asleep, but his brow remains furrowed, which suggests that this is not a painless slumber. He looks down at the surprisingly wizened face that is lined like a walnut, and he can see that his father seems to have aged a whole decade in the space of a few days. Near the end of the bed there is a plain metal fold-out chair which is set at a watchful angle, and so he sets his bag down to the side of the chair and then sits heavily and stares at the sleeping man. Were his father to open his eyes he is not sure what he might say to him, so he is grateful for this moment of silent contemplation.

The train had once again picked up speed and was flashing through the countryside of the midlands when his mobile rang. His diary was open before him as he was planning a time to see Laurie, but he soon realised that the diary was unnecessary as he was unemployed and pretty much available any time. Flanking his diary on all sides were a whole mass of print-outs which detailed the specifications of various one- and two-bedroom flats. There was nobody seated next to him, or in the two seats opposite, and so he was able to scatter his documents across the tabletop without inconveniencing anybody. He panicked for a moment, for he knew that the phone was somewhere underneath these papers, and then he found it and quickly flipped it open. Baron was characteristically blunt and to the point. 'Your father is in the hospital with a heart attack. I call the ambulance this morning when I notice he can't catch his breath, but they have him stabilised and everything. They say no danger as we get him there in time, but it don't make no sense for you to go by his place. You better come straight to St Joseph's and you'll find him there.' For a moment he didn't know what to say to Baron, but then he caught a reflection of himself in the window of the train, with the phone in one hand and his mouth hanging open and foolish. 'Keith, you still there?' He tried to adopt a casual tone as he let Baron know that he would take a taxi from the train station straight to the hospital. But he couldn't help checking. 'But you say he's all right?' Baron laughed the low rumbling laugh that he remembered from his childhood. 'They just keeping an eye on him, or whatever it is they does call it. Monitoring him.'

Once he hung up on Baron, he busied himself for a few minutes tidying up the print-outs. He folded them in half, and then he tucked everything into his diary which he then pushed into the holdall on the seat next to him. The train began to amble and so he stared out of the window as the countryside was replaced by the outskirts of yet another grim industrial town that was too insignificant for the train to stop at. He snapped out of his daydreaming, then picked up the phone and dialled Annabelle. He could tell from the background noise that she was driving and not fully concentrating on what he was saying. She asked him to speak louder. 'I said, I'm going straight to the hospital. He's had a heart attack, but apparently it's not serious.' Annabelle said nothing in reply so he couldn't be sure if she had heard him. And then she spoke with a clarity that took him by surprise. 'Hold on, I'm just pulling over.' Again he turned his attention to the window, as the train began now to pick up speed and leave the red-bricked town behind. Returning to the countryside was a welcome relief, but these fields differed from the previous ones for they were decorated with cows and sheep. He had never really understood how this worked. Who owned the animals, and how did you prevent them from running away or getting mixed up with other people's cows and sheep? 'Is he all right?' He reassured Annabelle that everything seemed to be under control and that Baron didn't seem too worried. 'Should I tell Laurie?' On this he was adamant. 'No, don't tell him. I'll call him myself. He should hear it from me, but there's probably not much to tell him.' Even as the words came out of his mouth he found himself wondering why, if this were the case, he had called Annabelle. In the silence, he could hear her car engine idling, and then what sounded like a lorry roared past. He had no idea what else to say to her.

The harried-looking nurse asks him how his father's health has been of late. He shrugs his shoulders and tells her that he lives in London, but he saw his father just recently and he seemed fine.

'He lives on his own, does he, love?' He nods and watches as she writes on the clipboard file that she cradles in the crook of her left elbow. 'The other feller wasn't that much help. He did say that your father was retired, can you confirm that?' He nods, but not wanting to be thought of as unhelpful he continues.

'Yes, he's been retired for a few years now. He worked at the university, as a janitor. And yes, he lives by himself.'

'Well,' says the nurse, without looking up, 'that never helps, to be honest with you, but at least we can rule out any possibility of elder abuse.'

'Of what?'

'There's more of it than you'd believe.' She finishes writing and looks across at the monitor. 'Anyhow, I don't think you've got anything to worry about, he's stable. You can come back in a few hours. Maybe between six and seven when we'll wake him up for something to eat.'

He wants to ask her if Baron is due back, but her no-nonsense manner suggests that she will have little sympathy for his question. Only now does the nurse actually deign to look in his direction. She is a reasonably attractive woman, but some make-up would help. Or would it? She looks like she has recently tightened her grip on the world of clipboard authority, having arrived at the age where a single woman becomes a spinster.

'You're welcome to stay, if you like. You can sit here, or we've more comfy chairs out there in the reception area.' She points towards the far end of the ward. 'And there's a cafeteria downstairs if you want tea or coffee. It's up to you, but I'll warrant your father will not be opening his eyes for a good few hours yet.'

There is nobody on the door to the Mandela Centre. He walks into the lobby area and stares at the noticeboard, which boasts an airline poster of a beach in Barbados and a monthly schedule of events. In among the coffee mornings, and the bingo sessions and the occasional fish and chip supper, he can see that this afternoon the residents are being offered chair-based exercises, which he assumes take place in the dayroom at the end of the hallway. The walls of the corridor are decorated with drawings that are evidently the result of some therapeutic course. Prominent among the infantile stick figures, and the crayoned sunsets, is a large sheet of white cardboard that is framed with thin bamboo strips and upon which are stencilled the words, 'Have a Positive Encounter With Yourself.' He hears the country music before he enters the dayroom, but as he opens the glass-panelled door none of the half-dozen or so residents look up from their chairs. Before them sits a matronly woman who turns and eyeballs him, but she continues to flex her elbows and ankles to the jaunty rhythms of Tammy Wynette.

'I can help you with something, dear?'

'Sorry to interrupt, but I'm looking for Baron. I thought he might be here.'

'Well, you don't see him here, so I suggest you pass upstairs and see if you find him in his flatlet. You know where to take the lift?' She points. 'Just down so at the end of the corridor. You related to him?' He shakes his head. 'No, you don't favour him. Your face too sweet.'

Baron answers the door dressed in an overstretched red tracksuit that hangs loosely around his stout frame. On his head he wears a baseball cap that is set at a comically rakish angle, and his bare feet are unslippered.

'So you finally reach.' He swivels away from his guest and speaks now with his back turned. 'You better come in.'

The flat is stiflingly hot and cramped, but Baron picks up a pile of old tabloid newspapers from the sofa and drops them on to the carpeted floor, thereby making space for him to sit.

'Me, I don't stand on no ceremonies here, so you better just squat down and make yourself at home.'

He sits and looks at the photograph of a smiling Lady Di above the mantelpiece, and then at the wooden walking stick that is leaning up in the corner beneath a crucifix that has been clumsily nailed to the wall. For some reason the crucifix has a washcloth hanging from it. The oddly shaped, almost circular, television set is the centrepiece of the room, and an afternoon game show holds Baron's attention. Balanced precariously on top of the television is a vase that is stuffed with an outlandish array of exotic plastic flowers.

'I can get you something? Tea or coffee? I eat downstairs with the others, but my kitchenette always have the basics.'

He shakes his head. 'No thanks. Maybe later.'

Baron's rumbling laughter begins slowly, then starts to rock his whole body. 'Later? How long you planning on staying? You don't think I have things to do?'

He can feel the powerful surge of heat coming from the radiators, but he assumes that the residents' bills are either partly or wholly subsidised. Baron sits in a battered armchair, and above his head a leash hangs from the ceiling. He knows, from having made site visits to similar facilities, that this is the emergency pull in case of any problems. Again he notices Baron's feet, which are calloused and chalky, and he watches as Baron vigorously rubs them together as though trying to flake off an outer layer of skin.

'I take it you never been in one of the flatlets before?' He shakes his head. 'Well, I'm a man who likes to keep myself to myself. I don't go knocking on doors asking to borrow teabags or anything, but if I have something I will share it. People around here is generally friendly, but you bound to get a few of the types who just go to church so they can change clothes and shoes and show off and look at women, and then you get the crazy ones who wander the centre at night looking for their children, the same children who get a council assessment against them and force them into this place. The Mandela is what they call supported accommodation, but you know this already. And it's here that you must make your father come when they let him out of the hospital.'

He looks at Baron and shakes his head. 'I don't think I can make him do anything that he doesn't want to do. You know how it is with him.'

'Your father's situation is better than most people. Look at me. I am a twin, which means there's two of me. One of me is back in Jamaica living good, and me is here on medication and so no point in going home for I can't afford the medicine back there to keep me alive. My pension just about work here, but back there the pension can't pay for my pills. I don't have no choice but to be here and I know I never going see my twin again. I'm understanding that. We don't even correspond. But your father is lucky for he just get a scare. However, if he go back to trying to cope with everything by himself, then who knows what happen the next time?' Baron pauses and looks at his television game show. Then, as though suddenly remembering that he has a guest, he turns back towards him. 'He need to be among people. His own people. I live next door to English people for forty years, but I had enough. They don't want me, then I don't want them. However, a man must have some kind of people, but your father's head is hard. Ever since Brenda call the police to drag him away and get him locked up the second time, your father don't like to be too close to nobody. But remember, he come to take you from Brenda when he get out. The man's head is hurting bad from two times in hospital, but at least he make the effort for you. Then after you gone off to college he just get more stubborn and he don't want to get involved in no palaver with women or anything that can hurt him again and so he choose to remain free, but life don't come free. Look at me. Look at all of us.' Baron laughs. 'Freedom don't look so clever now. I used to tell your father that marriage is just possession and obligation, and the real thing is wild, but because most men want both the possession and the wild they end up running two women, but your father ain't suited to either style.' Again he laughs. 'But like I say, freedom don't look so clever now.'

He hears his mobile begin to ring in his trouser pocket and for a moment he thinks about ignoring it. Then he realises that it might be Laurie so he arches his body and takes it out. He can see from the screen that it's Lesley, so he quickly pushes the phone back into his pocket and returns his attention to Baron, who once again seems fixated on the game show.

'Sorry about that.'

Baron turns from the television screen and grins toothlessly at him. 'No reason for you to be sorry. I know you is a busy man.'

'Well, thanks for taking the trouble to stay with him and get him to the hospital.' He pauses and looks again at the washcloth that is dangling from the crucifix.

'Keith, listen to me. Your father is a proud man, but he has a lot of pressure on his soul. A normal man would have seek out some kind of church guidance, but your father is not a normal kind of man, so church ain't going to help.'

He looks at Baron, and then at his bag, which sits on the floor next to the pile of old newspapers. The game show is over and the theme music is bellowing out, and the light from the television flickers and illuminates the sombre room. A part of him wants to thank Baron and then take a taxi to the station and catch a train back to London and simply forget this whole mess. He should let his father just live out his life in whatever fashion he wishes, but he knows that if he goes back to London now he will, in all likelihood, never return. Baron leans forward slightly and reaches into his trouser pocket and then holds out his hand.

'Here, you going need the keys to your father's house.'

He takes the keys from Baron and folds them into the palm of his hand. Baron continues to stare at him.

'You love your father?'

He looks closely at Baron, but he is unsure how to answer this question.

'Keith, whether you love the man or not, the fact is you're doing this for him, not for you. At this stage of his life who else can he talk to?'

On the way back to the hospital he sits on the lower deck of the bus close to the front door. The bus has been parked for ten minutes now, and the driver is still arguing with two youths who want to bring their KFC on board. The driver is insistent. 'You can poison yourself all you like with that crap, but I'm not having smelly food on my bus.' One lad defiantly eats a piece of chicken in front of the driver, while his friend seems to be increasingly aware of the fact that they are holding up a bus full of people eager to get home after a day of work. 'Come on, guy. You're being a mentalist now.' He looks away from the turmoil and out through the window of the bus, and then he takes out his mobile phone and dials the access number to his voicemail. Lesley sounds matter-of-fact, but she is letting him know that she did as promised and spoke with Yvette, who has agreed not to go before a tribunal. Apparently, Yvette has fired her lawyer and decided to take the settlement package that Clive Wilson has offered her. 'I think she was seeing the lawyer. Not that it means anything, but I suspect that her relationship with the lawyer was the hold-up.' She pauses. 'She didn't mention you, in case you were wondering, it was all about the lawyer. But she sounded good.

Well, you know, relieved.' Again Lesley pauses. 'Look, I won't be calling you again so no worries, okay? Well, that should be the end of it.' The awkwardness of the phone message seems to be intensifying and then she laughs. 'Bye, Keith.' He continues to hold the phone to his ear. It is the commotion of the police car pulling up, and the two youngsters swiftly jumping from the bus and bolting away in the direction of the concrete and glass shopping centre, that suddenly jars him back to life.

His father props himself up in bed, and the no-nonsense nurse hands him the cup and saucer before turning her attention to the task of filling in her patient's chart.

'You see what I've turned into? A bloody Englishman sharing a cup of tea and a biscuit with you.'

'Nothing wrong with a cup of tea.'

'So, I have a son who thinks that there's nothing wrong with an English cup of tea.'

'Do you want a son at all?'

'What do you mean by that?'

'Not every man wants to be a father.'

'Well, I didn't plan to have no kids, but your mother was a woman, and women have their own ideas about these kind of things. Anyhow, you're here, and I don't have no problem with that.' He pauses and sips his tea. 'Nothing can change that.'

Does this obstinate man not realise that after thirty years spent sweeping out lecture halls, and cleaning blackboards and emptying dustbins, his pitiful life has been reduced to drinking by himself in a depressing pub, or making the occasional trip to a community centre to play dominoes, or else falling asleep in front of his television set while programmes about people attempting to sell the junk from their attic blare out until he once again wakes up and crawls upstairs to bed. This is the life that he is trying to rescue his father from, but the man's feistiness hardly suggests gratitude.

The nurse finishes filling in the chart, which she now hooks on to the foot of the bed. She feels the older man's forehead with the back of her hand, but his father ignores both the nurse and his son and stares out of the window where it is pitch black. Winter nights are upon them.

'Mr Gordon, I'm going to love you and leave you, all right? I'll be back later to check up on you, but you can give me a call if you need anything, okay?' She pauses. 'You'll be all right, will you?'

He realises that the nurse is now talking to him, but she has caught him by surprise. The nurse looks at him as though she is expecting a reply, but then she swivels on her heels and squeaks her way down the polished linoleum floor and in the direction of another patient's bed. His father puts his tea back down on the saucer with a clatter.

'That one's just playing nice.'

'She seems okay. I suppose they're overworked.'

'You think so? I take it Baron phone you and tell you what happen?' His father coughs violently and reaches out for a tissue. He picks up the box and places it in his father's lap.

'You were asleep when I arrived so I went round to see Baron and thank him for looking out for you.'

'I feel like I have water on my chest, and I don't mean a drop or two, it feel like a whole pail full of water is pressing down on me.'

'Do you want me to call the nurse again?'

'Call her for what? We just get rid of the woman.'

He watches as his father looks for somewhere to discard his tissue, so he lifts up the wastepaper basket and offers it to him. He has already decided that he won't bother to bring up anything to do with the Mandela Centre, beyond mentioning his visit with Baron, for his father's belligerence cannot disguise the fact that he is still weak and in need of rest.

'Shall I leave the bin by the side of the bed?' His father nods, and so he places the wicker basket on the floor. 'Maybe you should get some sleep.'

'I don't know why I'm so tired. I can hardly keep my damn eyes open.'

'Well you've just had a heart attack. The next few weeks you'll need to rest up and let these people do what they have to do.'

His father snorts in disgust, but he can see that the older man's eyes are closing like curtains.

'You really believe these people know what they're doing?' He looks up at his son. 'Maybe they give me something to make me sleep? I don't feel normal.'

He takes his father's hand in his own and squeezes gently.

'Just rest, okay.'

'Rest?' His father laughs. 'This is no time to rest. Me, I want to go home.'

'Home? Maybe in a few weeks, but what are you going to do there by yourself? You know it doesn't make any sense to be living all alone in that house.'

'You don't understand me, Keith.'

He looks at his father's weary face and wonders if maybe this is, in fact, an appropriate time to revisit the idea of his father taking a flatlet in the Mandela Centre. He doesn't want to bring social services into the picture and force a move upon his father, for he understands that to do so will inevitably trigger painful memories. But having visited Baron, and seen the accommodation for himself, he is now adamant that his father will not be returning to his house. Tomorrow he will go back to the Mandela Centre and pick up the necessary paperwork which will ensure that when his father is discharged from St Joseph's he will be going directly to a flatlet.

'You listening to me?'

He looks down at his father's face.

'I want to go home, Keith. I don't mean to some stupid English house. I mean home. Home, home.' His father stares up at him. 'You understanding what I mean? I'm not from here. I land in England on a cold Friday morning. It is April 15, 1960, and only three weeks before this I put my father in the ground. It seem to take forever to pass through the Bay of Biscay with its rough, rough sea that is so bad that at night not a single person want to play dominoes, or organise a dance, or any of that kind of thing for everybody is suffering hard, but then eventually all the pitching and rolling and vomiting come to an end and suddenly the sea is smooth like a slack water pond, and I find myself gawping upon land. But even before I get off the boat England deliver a big shock to my system. Looking down from the deck I see plenty of white men in dirty clothes hurrying this way and that way up and down the dock, pushing wheelbarrows, and spitting on the ground and shouting at each other. These people don't look like the type of white men I used to seeing back home wearing club blazer and tie and walking about the place ramrod straight. Jesus Christ, I don't know England have such poor white men. I'm only twenty-two years old, in a thin jacket and foolish straw hat, and people on the boat arguing about whether spring reach or if it's still winter but I feel cold invading my body like it don't care if it throw me down and finish me off right there and then on day number one, so even before I get off the damn boat England punishing my mind and my body and teaching me a hard lesson about what kind of place it is. I remember, soon after we leave the West Indies, two Trinidadian fellars fall into the habit of sitting out on deck in the afternoon and talking all singsong about what to expect when we reach England. It turn out the two of them get demobbed from the RAF after the war and they take off back to Trinidad hoping to make a go of it, but after fifteen years' hard scrabbling they coming back to England with big ideas about how much money they going make, and chatting foolishness about how they understand everything about England and so if we want to make good we should shut up and listen to the pair of them running their mouths about how you have to dress for the cold because England have icy wind and sleet and snow that can bite your backside hard, and they telling us that in England everything is dear, and whatever you do don't show off to these people, and Lord have mercy you better learn to queue because the English relish nothing more than making a queue in an orderly fashion, and in England you have to learn double-talk, because if they ask you to please stay a bit longer, they want you to leave, and they love a sweet clock because everything have to be punctual and on time, and all ship-shape and proper, and English people don't like noise or any kind of trouble with the neighbours, and you must get accustom to the fact that everywhere is a sea of white faces, everywhere you turn you always looking on a sea of white faces and they don't know nothing about you, or where you from, or who you be, and they don't know the difference between a Jamaican and a Bajan, or where is this West Indian island, and they never hear the name of that West Indian island, so while you know everything about them, daffodil, king this and queen that, poet and lyrical feeling and so forth, Sherlock Holmes, Noel Coward, this statue and that statue, castle and tower, Robin Hood, Lord Nelson, what-ever question they care to test you on you have England under control, but the truth is most of these people don't know a blasted thing about themselves so every question pointing at you but if you want to shame them you just turn it round and ask them about themselves and their own history and you soon going see how quickly they stop talking. Mark you, the one thing they all know is they don't care much for the foreigner and that is you, man, that is always you, but don't call them prejudice because that will vex them, and don't tell them you don't want to hear them talking like you is savage and they come missionaries whose job is to educate and civilise you because this is just going to heat up their blood. What you must do is play the stranger because it make them feel better; play the part of the stranger and nod and smile when they ask you if you know what is a toilet, or if you ever see running water coming from a tap. Look upon their foolishness like a game you winning and the stupid people don't even know that you busy scoring points off their ignorance. Play the damn stranger and you can win in England and maybe you don't run crazy, but it don't matter what the two Trinidadians on the boat say, because when I finally reach England I not ready to deal with everything that I seeing, beginning with the scruffy white men with the wheelbarrows going in all directions up and down the dock. I know then, right there at the start, that serious pressure reach my head because my mind don't understand what my eyes looking upon, but I have to keep this worry lock up inside of me so nobody can tell what it is that I feeling. Back home people know me as a quiet fellar, and they respect the fact that I keep to myself, especially my sister Leona and my best friend, Ralph. They know me, but I also know them, and because this is the situation we all just get along fine with one another. But even before I get off the boat I looking at this new place and I feel my heart pounding, for what I looking down upon don't make no sense, and the hurting in my head begin right there, and I find myself standing up on the deck and leaning against the rail in my thin jacket and straw hat and trying hard to act like nothing in the world is the matter even though I feel hungry and light-headed but I fight back the hunger and the fear and I follow everybody down the walkway and straight into the immigration office where I wait and wait and then eventually I show the man my British passport and he speak fast to me with a voice like a gun (*got a job have you, son?*) and I shake my head and he hand me back my passport and then I take the train to London in a carriage that is full of people from the boat so I don't really meet England proper till I reach London and I have to change train stations. I make my way across London town in the back of a taxi that I share with a man from Barbados, who say that he also need to find this King's Cross station, but from the moment we get in the car neither one of us say a word and we just stare out of the window with big, big eyes like we standing up outside a bakery and neither one of us eat properly for a week. Even though it's still late afternoon, it already look to me like night reach, and then I see the place called Hyde Park which is big like a rainforest, but I take it that all the trees must be dead for hardly any leaves on them. As we pass through the centre of the city the lights from Piccadilly Circus burn my eyes and make me feel giddy, and noisy double-decker buses choking up everywhere I look. I see all the people rushing about and London seem like a place where opportunity must knock and knock again and keep a man awake with all its possibilities for the city is big and crazy like I imagine America must be big and crazy, and it make me think of my brother Desmond, and what he must be going through in whatever part of America he finally decide to live in. In truth, London don't seem real but this taxi man is driving me through the place in the direction of King's Cross station at a hell of a lick and I want to lean forward and say to the man, take it easy now because I want you to set me down safe and sound, but I don't say nothing to the man because it's his town and he must know what he's doing.

'A year before I reach London I find myself sitting in the bar down by the harbour looking upon Ralph, who is slumped over the counter like a long fish. Through the open window I see bright moonlight on the surface of the sea, and I watch the small launch still taking passengers out to the boat. Soon it will be time for my best friend Ralph to pull himself together and make a start on his big journey to England, and so I nudge the man's cardboard suitcase to one side with the outside of my shoe, and then I kick at Ralph's stool and the man jump to attention and quickly rub his face with an open palm as though the man's hand is some kind of small towel. "What happen? I miss the boat?" I don't study him, and I ask the barman to open up two more bottles of beer so we can fire one for the road that Ralph will be crossing for the next two weeks until England show herself. According to Ralph, once he make it to England he say he will travel to the north of the country because some friend of his godfather promise to find him a job in a factory casting iron and the man claim a West Indian can make big money doing this kind of work. However, Ralph say that after five years he coming back home to open up a garage and establish himself in business as a mechanic. He already have the slogan for the advertisement that he say he going to put in the newspaper: "Bring your auto to the Car Doctor Ralph for he going fix it up nice, nice." I remember it don't rhyme or nothing, but it still impress me, and back then I suppose I feel a little jealous toward Ralph because the man talk about his plans with such confidence and I sure he can make anything happen. Me, I don't have no plans to speak of. Since my mother die, and my pregnant sister Leona leave the house to marry the son of Mr Williams, the taxi driver, it's just me alone working five days a week in town in the heat and noise of the sugar factory, and then come night I riding the bus back to the village and taking care of my father whose health don't seem to be getting no better. Even though I don't have no plans, I still have my dreams, and my dreams all locked up in the law book and the dictionary that I used to carry everywhere. I hold on tight to these two books and when the fellars at the sugar factory take a lunch break I sit on an upturned pail underneath a big tamarind tree and read, and when they start to play dominoes and get boisterous I just continue to read my law book and my dictionary and I don't study them even when they pitch stones at me and hail me up as "Lawyer Earl". Back then it is always tall Ralph who stand up and tell them to leave me alone, and it's Ralph who walk with me to the bus stop at the end of the day and if he don't have business in town with his woman, Sonia, it's Ralph who will ride back to the village with me and sit and take a drink at the Bus Stop Bar before we both wander off to our parents' houses. Sometimes we talk about getting a room together in town so we don't have to trouble with the bus journey in the morning, and then again at night, but this talk just stop at talk, and then my mother die and my sister get pregnant and so I'm the only one left to watch over my father and after this neither Ralph nor me ever say another thing about rooming together because we both know that come night I don't have no choice but to go back to the village, and then one day out of the blue Ralph decide that he is going all follow-fashion and taking himself off to England to work, and he reach this decision without so much as a "What do you think?" He's going and it seem like Ralph don't want any discussion. So I sitting in the bar down by the harbour and I look at Ralph and ask him if he trouble himself to tell Sonia that he going to England, but he just take a swig of beer and then thump the bottle back down on the bar top and start to laugh. He tell me that I don't really understand women, because if I did then I would know that once Sonia realise that he gone then it only going take a day or so before she find a next man because women can take a blow and push up their lips and move on like nothing happen. "Maybe Sonia come looking for you with your damn books and your head stuck up in the air like you always thinking about something." I tell Ralph that I not interested in a fast woman like Sonia, and besides I already have my village thing with Myrna, but he tell me again that I must stop hitting it with Myrna because every man dipping his bread there and maybe I going catch something. I tell him that Myrna don't mean nothing to me, and so she don't cause my head no anxiety, but he laugh out loud and insist that no matter what I say he know that something always causing me to worry. Ralph drape his long arm round my shoulders and the man behind the bar reach up and turn on the electric bulb which hang over the counter. The sounds of the night begin to come louder now, particularly the noise of the waves lapping up against the wooden pier and the rush of the wind passing through the leaves of the palm trees which line the harbour road. I remember, Ralph take his arm from my shoulders and pull out a coin which he tap against the bar and tell the man that we need two more beers. Then he turn to look at me and tell me, "I know, I know, then I have to gone." The barman disappear to the backyard then soon return with a fresh crate of beers. The man uncap two bottles and push them across the bar, and I find myself thinking about my father, who I know will be lying in the dark waiting for me to come back and feed him up, and then help him to get ready for sleep by rolling him a quarter turn over and on to his side. But tonight he will have to wait. I look across at Ralph and I wonder if I ever going see my friend again, because inside of me I know that Ralph don't be coming back to this small island in five years, or ten years, or one hundred and ten years, because we both know that Ralph and the cardboard suit-case leaving the island for ever. Ralph swivel round on his stool and look me full in the face. "So you never hear from Desmond then?" I tell Ralph that once upon a time my father get a card from somewhere in America, but my brother don't send an address so it ain't possible to write back or anything like that, but I tell him that my father still have the card tucked away someplace. Ralph slowly nod but like the rest of the village Ralph already know that my father place all his faith in his eldest son who, ten years ago, take off to Florida promising that he would come back, but Desmond never come back. Everybody know that after ten years Desmond, the chosen one, is never coming back, but my father continue to torment himself with hope, and when the man look at me and my books his face always turning sour, but part of me want to remind him that at least I stay back so the man have somebody to care for him. Ten years earlier, I remember standing in short pants at the end of the pier, sheltering from the wind behind my sixteen-year-old sister, Leona, and annoying the hell out of her because she want to be left alone so she can play the fool and giggle and so forth with the son of Mr Williams, the taxi driver, a boy who is squatting uncomfortably like a pelican on top of the fence that line the harbour wall. Again Leona pushes me: "Boy, move nuh man so I can get some peace." I'm enjoying tormenting the girl since the alternative is to stand up next to my long-faced parents and watch the boat slowly pulling out the harbour. My mother is a thin woman, like a piece of cane, and her figure is silhouetted against the night sky. Her eldest son is going to pick oranges in Florida, but it's the husband who is troubling her head because the man staring at the boat as though he losing some big part of himself. Once the launch reach back, and the crew start to move off in the direction of the bar, my mother turn and look sharply at her budding daughter, who continue to make eyes at the pelican-boy. Mr Williams lean up against his taxi and wait in the shadow of the large treasury building ready for his family of passengers to let him know when it is time to return to the village. Mind you, as long as it's possible for my father to still see the boat on this side of the black horizon I know we don't be going nowhere. Later that evening, I stare out the window of Mr Williams's taxi as it trace its slow way along the island's one road, a narrow piece of tarmac that hug the coastline tight. On this main road no light coming from neither moon nor streetlamp, and at this time of night the island seem dead, so much so that it difficult to think of the place as being inhabited with people. I turn from the blackness outside the window to my mother, who is resting up gently against my father, and then I look upon my sister Leona who is trying hard not to fall asleep and the girl's eyes fixed on the back of Mr Williams's son's head. The boy is sitting up front in the passenger seat next to his father, while the four of us squeeze into the back, but eventually is me, not Leona, who start to nod. That night, I lie in bed and listen to the frogs outside in the darkness, and the breathing of my sister in the narrow bed next to my own. Between us a pile of schoolbooks is organised in a way that make sense to me, and behind the door my mother already hang up my school shirt for the next day, all wash and iron. I look away from the shirt and close my eyes. The island have only one scholarship for studying overseas at university and at least six boys in my class have parents who can pay for extra lessons, and all of these town boys have new textbooks. Even if I study day and night and don't bother with sleep I still can't catch these boys, but my mother don't believe this. I'm sure that part of the reason Desmond gone off to America is to escape the attention that I getting, and maybe this is why he start to behave bad. In the village, people always running their mouths about Desmond saying he's a bad john, and talking about how he put a woman in the next village with child, and how the woman's husband threaten to cut Desmond with a machete, and so leaving to pick oranges in Florida is maybe just an excuse. In the morning I hear my mother shouting at Leona, who like to linger by the gate in the shade of the star-apple tree and talk foolishness with the village boys instead of bringing back the pail of water inside the house. My father long ago gone off to work in the fields, but my mother waiting for the water so she can make some tea for me before I go to school. Leona finally bring the water, then she come into the bedroom and tell me to turn my back while she make herself ready to go off to typing school. Once my sister gone I drink the tea and prepare for school, and soon after Ralph appear at the gate without any books and the two of us walk up the alley and wait for the school bus and I'm watching Ralph idly kicking at stones and messing up his good shoes. That morning he ask me if Desmond truly gone, and when I tell him yes, my brother truly gone to America, he just start to laugh and tell me that Desmond won't be coming back, but I don't say anything to Ralph because I already know this and so I just move my books from under one sweaty arm and place them under the next one and shrug my shoulders because I don't see what it is that Ralph trying to prove. And ten years later, in the semi-dark of the Harbour Lights bar I find myself sitting with the same Ralph and staring at the naked light bulb that brighten up the gloom of the place, and suddenly my best friend looking unsure as to whether he really want to leave for England. I feel sure he want to order another bottle of beer, but Ralph know I watching him good and so he stand up from the stool and reach for the cardboard suitcase. "Well, you want me to write you and let you know how things going over there, or you want me to do you like Desmond and just disappear?" Ralph laugh like he convinced he say something funny. "Man, no need to look at me so. I already tell you, five years then I back. Five years at the most, you hear me?" He pauses. "Well, what happen, somebody glue your backside to the stool?" Ralph throw out an arm like he's vex with me. "You just going sit?" I remember looking at him, then smiling and I tell him, "Better you just walk out of here like you gone from the bar for the night and I going see you tomorrow. That way it can all seem fine and natural?" Ralph look at me in surprise, then he start to shake his head and tell me how this book learning must have seriously mess up my mind, but I notice that maybe Ralph drink one beer too many because my friend look a little unsteady on his feet. "Look man," I say, "you better go before Sonia come down here searching you out. Go ahead, England waiting." Ralph hesitate like he want to shake my hand or something, then he stop himself and the man seem puzzled. "You really want me to go to England just so?" Now it's my turn to laugh, "Yes man, just like so, because this way I know I going see you again. No big goodbye or nothing, you just go along." I turn away from him and signal to the barman to open a next beer and out of the corner of my eye I see Ralph walking slowly out the bar like a jumbie, but I don't look up. I just keep my eyes focus on the scratched-up bar top and then a beer appear in front of me and I reach down and feel the coldness of the bottle and wonder if I should stop by Myrna's place for I don't see the woman for nearly a week. I sit in the bar by myself and listen to the sound of the sea, and I realise that without Ralph the island going seem empty. And then, two months after Ralph leave for good, my father die, but he do so all casual and easy. One night I bring him some tea and a piece of bread, and I help him to make himself upright in the bed. Recently the man's eyes seem to have grown big, and his stare is intense like he's accusing me of something, but on this night the eyes seem normal again and he looking at me like he want me to give off some conversation, but I don't know what to say so I keep one hand steady behind the man's back, and I feed him the bread with the other hand, and outside it start to rain and the water beating down hard like a hammer on the tin roof and making any kind of talking difficult. In the morning I take my father a glass of water but I can see that he no longer breathing, and his eyes are closed, and to begin with I convince myself that maybe he just fall into a powerful sleep and I must simply shake my father to wake him up. I push the man's shoulder once, then twice, but nothing happen so I place a hand to his nose and mouth and finally I'm accepting the situation. I sit on the side of the bed for I feel it personally like my father leave me but he can't trouble himself to say anything, and I thinking if my mother is alive then she would know how to cope with this confusion. Long ago she forgive me for not winning the island scholarship, and she forgive me for ending up working at the sugar factory, but she tell me no matter what anybody say about me being a failure I must never give up my reading. My mother always know what is the best thing to say and do, and when my father shout at me and tell me that he don't know what a grown man doing living under his roof when I working a job, and he don't understand why all I do in the evening is just read book to no purpose, it's my mother who tell him to hush up and mind his business, but now I see my father lying on the bed like a piece of board and I confused about what to feel and what to do and I think maybe I should talk with Leona because my married sister now living in the next village but one. Two years earlier, when my mother die, I know what to feel. Although I hurting bad, it's a relief that she finally escape the disease that has been eating out her body and already reduce the woman to a skeleton, but this thing with my father is strange and come too quick. The next thing I know I standing next to my sister and I watching as four men lower my father's body into the ground and I trying like hell to work up some feeling for the man, but my father never recover from Desmond leaving, and he never care much for either me or Leona, and I steal a quick glance at my sister who is dealing with her two children and she too look like she is don't have no feelings for the proceedings. It seem like the man going into the ground cold and without a tear shed, but I don't feel it's my place to pretend and so I just focus on some goats standing nearby who cropping the short grass and keeping the cemetery all shipshape and tidy. Later that same afternoon I sit on the hardback chair in my father's bedroom and watch Leona open every cupboard and every drawer, but my sister don't search through anything she just open and open as though she making ready to unpack the man's life but she don't know where to begin. Leona pick up his Sunday suit and she hook the hanger over the back of the bedroom door. My sister look closely at the man's only suit before unhooking it and hanging it back where she find it. "You want anything of his?" I just shrug and tell her, "Take whatever you want for your husband, or give it away to the church. I don't need anything." On the bedside table is a bible, and sticking out from the side of the book is the card that I know Desmond send from America. I thinking to myself, so this is where my father keep the thing. On the front of the card is a picture of some trees and a town square with a big clock, but when you turn over the card only a few scratchy words written there. My brother telling his father to let everybody know that he is "just fine". Nothing about when he might come back, and nothing about how we doing, just he is "fine" and a signature that make it clear that the card is from Desmond. Leona take a seat on the edge of the bed and she ask me what it is that I going do now, meaning now that the man is dead and I don't have no reason to play nurse any more. "You planning on staying here and growing old in this house?" I look round and realise that the house have nothing for me except bad memories. "Look," say Leona, "why you don't take yourself and your books to England. I can sell the house and send you the money to pay back the price of the boat ticket. No point you staying here and feeling miserable. Me, I can't go no place with two children because England is for people without no obligations, but if you stay here then you just going get catch by Myrna or some other woman and then what will become of you? Think about yourself, Earl. Think about what you can do that will improve your situation." I looking at Leona, whose eyes make it seem like she upset with me or something. She stand and turn away and slam a drawer shut with a big noise. "Earl, you're the only brother I have left so this not easy for me, but nothing is here for you. You want to live your life just dreaming and growing old in this two-room house and eventually dying on the same bed that take both our parents?" Outside I can hear the village children squeezing the last drop of playtime out the day, but I know the light is gone and the children just chasing shadows. I also know my sister is right. I want to say "thank you" or something, but instead I look through the open window and watch a chicken backscratching in the dirt beneath the guava tree. The fowl is throwing up a cloud of dust, and then something frighten the bird and it shriek and open its wings and disappear from view. I decide that the next day I going come home from the sugar factory and call on Leona and we can talk properly. Maybe tomorrow brother and sister find it easier to look each other in the eye, but not today, for today things is difficult because we are the two who been left behind. We sit next to each other on the bed and listen to the stubborn children playing outside in the dark, but neither one of us say another word.'

He pushes the key into the lock but he cannot open the door. After trying a second time to twist the key in both directions, he puts down his bag then slips a hand into the letterbox. He takes a grip which enables him to pull the door towards himself and turn the key at the same time. The key swivels and he shoves open the door and steps inside. The unpleasant smell of mouldy food wafts through the darkness and his hand scrambles up and down the wall until he finds the light switch. He retrieves his bag from the doorstep and closes the door behind him with a resounding clatter. He coughs then cups his hand to his mouth and nose, before moving into the kitchen where he sees that Baron has neither cleared the pots and pans from off the top of the cooker, nor has he done the washing up. However, he can't blame him for he must have been in a rush to get his father to the hospital. He looks at the mess, but in spite of his own fatigue he knows that he won't be able to relax until he has cleaned up. When the nurse had suggested to him that he leave now so that his father could rest, he hesitated and thought about insisting that he be allowed to remain seated in case the patient woke up and wanted to keep talking, but he realised that the stern-faced woman would have none of it. 'Will you be wanting me to tell you a second time?' He continued to look at the slumbering man, whose pursed lips suggested a quiet determination, but he realised that, in fact, he was the one who needed to rest. He stood up from the metal chair and stretched. The neon green parabola continued to blip away reassuringly on the small screen to the side of his father's bed, and he wanted to ask the nurse if his father was 'stable', whatever that meant. 'If you take my advice you'll be away to get some sleep. No point in the two of you being sick.' The nurse was now leaning over her patient and busily applying extra tape to the needle that was attached to his father's arm. He looked at her and decided that it was best not to argue with, or even question, the woman. Everything could wait until tomorrow.

He slides the cardboard box of photographs to one side and clears a space on the table so that he is able to put down the mug of tea. He has not only washed up, he has dried and put away all the crockery and utensils and carefully wiped down the counter tops. However, he will have to drink his tea black, for the milk in the open carton that he found sitting next to the kettle is curdled. Baron must have forgotten to put it back in the fridge. He can see that there are still some photographs in the cardboard box, but the majority of the black and white prints are scattered on the tabletop like jettisoned invitation cards to the past. His father must have taken the box from his son's room and started to look through them, and maybe Baron was helping him to remember faces and names, but clearly there was no time to complete the task or tidy up after themselves. He wants to call Annabelle, but he is reluctant to say anything further to her about his father's condition; he just wants to hear the reassuring sound of her voice. However, his reticence will be transparent and she will know that something is amiss, and so he decides to forget this idea. Through the uncurtained window he can see a cluster of stars in the sky and he contemplates stepping outside and staring up at the heavens. But what's the point? It's cold outside and he's seen stars before. He slips his mobile out of his pocket and thinks about texting Laurie. 'Are you okay?' Or is that 'R U OK?'? There's no way he's going to start bashing the English language in this way. And what if Laurie texts him back? What's his excuse for not breaking off from texting and giving him a call? He can't think of anything that he wants to say to his son so he decides that it's best not to text. Or call Annabelle. Or do anything, including standing outside in the dark and staring up at the sky. It's not going to happen, is it? The moment when his father's anger turns to tenderness and a touching acceptance of his situation. He's wasting his time hoping that the man's face might be transfixed by the gentlest hint of a reconciliatory smile. After all these years, why now? He looks again at the sea of photographs and then picks up his mug of tea. Just what, if any, connection do these people have to his own life, let alone that of Annabelle and Laurie? His father's silence has meant that his son has never been able to properly explain himself to anybody. For a moment he is tempted to gather up the photographs and toss them all into the box and then push the cardboard receptacle into a cupboard and out of sight, but unlike the pots and dishes these photographs have considerable weight. He can't bring himself to pick them up, or even touch them. Not now, not at this moment. He will just have to be careful as to where exactly he places his mug of tea when he sets it back down on the table.

His father is cautiously spooning a breakfast of stewed prunes into his mouth, but his shaking hand means that the spoon hovers for two or three beats before he quickly dips his head towards the implement. He sits opposite his father with a carefully folded napkin in his hand ready to offer it to the older man should he need to mop up any spillage, but his father appears to be well-practised. This morning he left his father's house and walked to the Mandela Centre, where he asked the caregiver on duty if she would give him an application form in order that a family member might apply for a flatlet. The woman took her time rifling through various filing cabinets, and having found the form she made a performance of folding it in half and inserting the form into an official-looking brown envelope. He silently urged her to hurry up, for the last thing he needed was for Baron to wander downstairs and discover his presence and start to ask him about his father. A quick in and out was all he wanted, and when the caregiver finally handed over the envelope he was already on his feet and pointedly glancing at his watch. 'Thanks,' he said. The woman asked him if there was anything else she could do, or maybe he would like a tour of the facility but, looking again at his watch, he politely declined her offer and moved quickly out of her carpeted office and into the hallway. His eyes fell upon the bamboo-framed poster which read, 'Have a Positive Encounter With Yourself'. The eager woman followed him out of her office and for a moment he was tempted to say something to her about the crassness of the slogan, but he could see the enthusiastic gleam in her eye and so he smiled and once again thanked her for the form before hurrying his way out of the centre.

He takes the empty bowl from his father and sets it on the bedside table, and then he rearranges the pillows behind his father's back so the patient is once again propped fully upright. As he moves to sit back on the metal chair he takes the brown envelope from his inside pocket.

'I'm going to leave this envelope for you on the table. You can take a look at it later.'

'Later when? You going abandon me like last night?'

'You were asleep.'

'I sure these people giving me something to make me sleep like a donkey. It ain't normal.'

'Anyhow, I've left it there for when you're ready.'

'There where?'

He had a sneaking suspicion that his father's vision was impaired for, unless something was right in front of him, his father appeared to be having difficulty seeing objects. And now he is convinced. The envelope is just to his left, but clearly his father can no longer see anything out of his left eye. When his father next falls asleep he will have to find the nurse, or a doctor, and question them about it.

'It's there. On the table.'

'What do I want with a blasted envelope? Last night I was

talking to you, remember? One minute saying something to you, and the next minute you gone. You don't want to hear what I have to say?'

'Of course, I do.'

'Well then listen to me instead of this damn envelope business. After I arrive in England, and the taxi drop me off at King's Cross station, I make my way into the place and ask a white man in uniform where I can find the proper train to take me to the north of the country. He point me toward a platform, then laugh and tell me I must first buy a ticket. I thank the man, and touch the brim of my straw hat, but the man continue to laugh, but for the life of me I can't see what the joke is. I want to ask the jackass, "Mister, what exactly it is that is amusing you?" but I just turn my head and walk off because I don't want to put a foot wrong. Eventually I get on to the right train and pass into a small compartment full of English people who don't pay me no mind. As the train leave London and begin to journey out into the countryside, I decide to keep my nose pressed up tight against the glass and look at the small fields, but I can't see no pasture, just everything organised and sliced up small and neat. One other West Indian man is in the compartment with me, crouching down beneath his sharp hat and pretending to read the English newspaper and fit in with everybody, but he don't fool me because I can see the man's reflection in the window and he falling asleep. I have to look twice at him, because to begin with I think the man favour Leona's husband and I wonder if maybe the fellar is family to the Williamses, but I sure somebody would have tell me if Leona have people in England so I just study the resemblance and let it go at that. The English people in the carriage all reading their newspapers for true, and smoking, and it seem to me that they trying hard to ignore the pair of us, although an English man in a grey suit sitting opposite keep raising up his eyes to look across but I just stare out of the window and make sure that my feet don't touch up against his own in the little space that we have to share. Sometimes the train leave the countryside and pass into a town where I can see the buildings all close together, and everywhere chimneys pointing toward the sky with smoke coming out so at first I thinking they must be factories but it don't make no sense because I sure they don't boil so much sugar in England. However, I soon realise that these places is houses where English people live, and even from the train I see that the English like to walk fast and these people don't trouble to look up at each other and smile or something like that, and the man must have been watching me all this time because without any warning he fold up his newspaper with a big noise and lean forward and offer me a cigarette in a way that make it clear that he is hoping to take part in some kind of conversation. I accept the man's cigarette and I watch him take hold of his umbrella, which is balanced upright between his knees, and the man stand up and place it on the overhead rack before opening up his briefcase and he reach in and pull out a package. The man close up the briefcase and place it on the seat, then he hold open the compartment door and I realise that it is expected of me to pass out into the corridor with him to smoke the cigarette. I stand and edge my way past the other passengers and the man follow me and slide the door closed after himself. At first the man don't say a thing, and he don't even light my cigarette, he just open up the package of greaseproof paper and offer me a sandwich. "Tuna paste" is all the man say, so I take one because I know that it is rude not to do so, and I bite into it and the man does the same with his own sandwich. "Somewhat crowded in there," he say. "Just arrived, have you?" I nod at him, but my mouth is too full to answer so the man just continue. "Student?" This time I shake my head and wait a moment before telling him that I will be looking a job. "I have a friend who say he is going to help me." The man seem to approve and he nod his head. "Well, the weather's not too good at the moment, but if you can cope with this then I imagine you can do well here." The man finish off his sandwich and then he light his cigarette before lighting my own. I try to look cool, and I take a long hard pull, like in the cinema, but my head start to feel strange and I explode in a fit of coughing that only manage to embarrass the hell out of me. "You can throw it out if it's not to your liking. I won't be offended." The man hold open a small window at the top of the glass and I quickly drop the cigarette down on to the track. "I'm sorry, but I'm just not used to the English cigarette." The man don't give me any time to say anything else and he start to pat me on the back. "Are you, in fact, used to any cigarette? You see, in this country you don't have to pretend. Just be yourself and I'm sure you'll do very well here. Can I get you some water?" I look closely at the man and I shake my head, but he just smile at me. "Do you have a wife or a girlfriend?" Again I shake my head. "I imagine you'll be quite popular with some of our girls, but a word of advice. Don't be getting too saucy. Some of you boys do take liberties and it does stir up bad feelings. I mean, there's no reason for you to be giving white girls babies, is there? Or tapping them on the shoulder at 'Excuse me' dances. I fought for two years in the jungles of Malaya along-side you chaps. If you're good enough to fight and die with us then you're good enough to live on my street. Same with the Jews and the Irish. Everybody's the same in my book. Come along, there's a good chap. Let's get back inside and out of this nasty draught." Once we pass back into the compartment I close my eyes and try to sleep, but the noise of the engine, and my worries about whether I going find Ralph, mean that my mind can't turn off. The train arrives with a big carnival of shouting and whistling and I open my eyes and blink against the bright light. The man opposite me is standing and holding his briefcase in one hand, and his rolled-up umbrella is tucked underneath his arm, and the man reach out with his free hand. "Take this loose change, please. If you have any difficulty using the telephone system then you can always request that the charges be reversed and that way you won't have to pay. However, if you remember my instructions then you should be fine. I do hope that you locate your friend." I take the man's change for this is the quickest way to get rid of him, and I watch the man disappear into the corridor. I wait and let the others go before me, including the West Indian fellar who decide to keep quiet throughout the whole journey, and I am the last to leave the compartment. When I find a telephone box I follow the man's instructions and dial the number slowly and I'm waiting. I hear an English woman ask me, "Hello, can I help you?" and I panic because I'm expecting to hear Ralph's voice and I sure that I must have call the wrong number. "Excuse me please, but I'm looking for Mr Ralph Henry." There is a brief pause and then I hear the woman make a big sigh as though she annoyed. "Who is it that I should say is looking for him?" I tell the woman to let him know that it's Earl, and that I just arrive, but having discover who I am the woman decide to tell me that Ralph is not "at home" but I can find him at the Red Lion pub, but of course I don't know where to find this pub. She ask me, "Are you at the train station?" However, before I can answer the woman say that I should take a taxi and tell the driver that I need to go Randolph Lane and he will know exactly where to carry me. "If Ralph's not there then you can call me back, but you'll find him at the pub, I'm sure of it." I watch the taxi driver hard, trying to make sure the man is driving in just one direction and not seeking to rob me by making circles. However, outside is dark, and I don't know these streets, and so I have to trust him. Eventually he turn into a narrow road that have more of these joined-up houses crammed together on both sides of the street, and then it start to rain and the man switch on the window wipers and I see him look at me through the rear-view mirror. "It's just up here on the right, mate." Having parked the car, the man turn round in his seat and he look at me. "Let's call it two bob." I hand the man half a crown and wait for my change. "Are you not planning on getting out? You can make it in there without getting wet." I smile at the taxi driver and continue to hold out my hand, but the man just stare back at me. "Listen, sunshine, you getting out or what? I have got other jobs, you know." The first thing I notice when I open the door to the pub is the noise. It hit me and nearly knock me down, and then there is the smoke, which is so thick I can barely see a damn thing. Once I step inside I happy to see plenty of coloured men in the pub so I don't feel so out of place, and then it occur to me that maybe this is where all the West Indians in the town come, so if you want to meet some-body then you have to find yourself here. That's when I see Ralph in the far corner sitting with a heavy man who looking closely at a newspaper and making some markings upon it with a pencil. As I walk closer to Ralph, I can see my friend is tired and that he don't shave for days, but the bright eyes are the same. He look up at me and smile. "Well, what the hell is this coming in from the cold?" Ralph don't bother to stand, he just pat the seat next to him to let me know that I must sit down. "I have no idea what time to expect you or I would have come to the station myself, but I take it you speak with Mrs Jones?" Ralph don't wait for no answer. He point to the man on the other side of him who still have his head buried in the newspaper. "This is Baron from Jamaica. He been in England since forever. Maybe longer than this." So here we are on a Friday night just drinking some bitters and chatting about home, and Baron following the form of the horses because the man look like he prefer horses to people. I'm listening to Ralph but I not really hearing the man's words because I still trying to work out how this tall shabby-looking man is the same man that only a couple of months earlier stagger out of the Harbour Lights bar to take the boat to England. "Man, I'm seeing you good now," say Ralph. "Since when was the last time you get any sleep? It look like you can barely keep your eyes open. Your body don't know what time of day it is, right?" Ralph laugh loud and hard, and then he stand and pull a ten shilling note from his trouser pocket and tell me that he is going to fetch me a next drink at the bar and I should just wait. "Baron can keep you out of trouble till I get back." However, Baron seem occupied with his newspaper business and he don't look as though he have much to say to anybody, especially to a man fresh off the boat. I'm sure that this Baron don't want to hear about my father's funeral, or how my sister move herself and the two children into my father's house before I even leave the island, or how Sonia create a stink and tell everyone that Ralph abandon her for a woman in England, or any of the things that I trying to remember that I must tell my friend. Later that night I follow Ralph up a dark staircase, but I stay three or four steps behind him because Ralph already slip twice and I frighten that he going tumble backward and come crashing down on me. At the top of the house we reach a door, but Ralph have trouble getting the key into the lock and my friend begin to curse under his breath. Ralph eventually manage to push open the door, and I follow him into the attic room and wait while he scratch round for the light switch. Having turn on the bulb the man fall down on a single bed and point to a mattress in the corner and tell me I must sleep there and be grateful I have a roof in England because finding a place to sleep at night is the biggest problem that everybody have. I look around and I see dirty clothes drape every-where, and unwashed cups and plates on the floor, and an empty bedpan in the middle of the room, and I surprised to find my friend living like this. I watch as he haul himself upright on the bed and pull out a pack of cigarettes and light one, and then Ralph blow out a big cloud of smoke. I ease out of my shoes and line them up, then I lean back on the mattress and look up at the ceiling because I can feel sleep rushing into my body. I hear Ralph start to laugh. "You know I was hoping that you coming to England would make home feel closer, but the truth is you here now and it seem like you making home feel even further away. Sometimes I can be walking down the street, or riding a bus, and suddenly I see somebody who remind me of somebody I know back home, and I close my eyes and find myself thinking of the sea, or the taste of grafted mango, or the smell of saltfish frying, and then I come back to myself and open my eyes and realise where I am. Lord man, I'm in a place where people give me a form to fill out and then ask me if I can read, and on the bus they prefer to stand rather than sit down next to me. I travel all this way for what? To see England with her pants down and her backside hanging out? But nobody tell me that I must leave for England and cut up my life like this. I swear, five years and then I going back to open up a garage, you believe me?" I don't say anything, but Ralph not studying me anyhow. "Man, England is good, but you soon going to find out that England ain't easy. Sometimes I just can't believe that people back home selling tools, and furniture, and borrowing money, and putting themselves in big debt, and all for this, to come to a place where people eat on the street out of a piece of news-paper full of chips and vinegar. People mashing up their lives for this? A West Indian can't afford to be sensitive and decent in a country like this. Let me tell you, man some of them like to mess with you, asking you for a cigarette then reaching for the whole pack, and if you refuse they crowd you and start to kick you, but I don't play that game. Next time a white man want to mess with me he better be ready, you hear? He can call me "nigger" and "spade" and box me one time, but just one time, because if he come again he better be ready for the next time I going have something for him." I watch Ralph turn to one side and reach for a bottle from beneath the bed and tip it up to his mouth and drain it. Two minutes later he is slumped over the bed and he don't say goodnight or anything and he just start to snore. Then I hear a knocking at the door, then a silence, then more knocking and a woman's voice call out "Ralph, Ralph!" I recognise the voice as the same woman who speak to me on the telephone, but I just keep quiet because I not sure what kind of trouble is going on and eventually I hear the firing of the floorboards as the woman move away from the door. So this is my first night in England, and I cold as hell and I don't know where I am, and I want to use the toilet but I don't know where to find it, and I sure I not going to get any sleep with Ralph making so much noise with the damn snoring. Things don't look so good, but I trying to put a confident face on everything or else what is the point of coming all this way? That is what I telling myself, that I have to simmer down and believe that everything is going work out to my satisfaction and I have to be positive about things, otherwise what is the point?

'The foreman looked upon me as though he's looking at an animal that he thinking of buying. He turn back to face my friend. "Bloody hell, Ralphie where do you find them? This one's got no meat on him. He'll probably melt if we put him anywhere near the furnaces. Thin like a piece of liquorice, he is." Ralph already tell me that this man don't have any prejudice like most of the others who, according to Ralph, say they don't want to work with us because we're too friendly with their women, or they claim our hands are too rough, or they can't share the same lavatory with us, or they frighten that when the tea break come we might use their mug, or they say we blow our noses when they passing by and we won't take off our hats indoors, but I already know the truth is they just can't tolerate being close to a coloured man but they will take us as a last resort if no Englishman will work for such low wages. However, Ralph tell me this man is a good man, and Ralph squeeze my arm and laugh and promise the foreman that he will make sure I eat plenty Yorkshire pudding and roast beef, but I not laughing and I looking hard at the English man and remembering what Ralph tell me about these union men who like to talk big about the import- ance of the empire, and everything is brother this and brother that, and I only been in England for a few weeks but already I have to leave two jobs because these people like to trouble your mind because in one breath they talking all this brother foolish- ness with a smile, and with the same smile they tell you it is better if you only bring English food to eat at break because some people don't appreciate foreign muck and if they don't like your name, or if they find it too hard to pronounce, they quick to call you Jim or Sam or something that is supposed to make you know your place, and Ralph tell me that these are the same men whose children like to dress up in the drainpipe trousers and fancy jackets and carry flick knives, and when they go out "nigger hunting" they wear motorbike chain necklaces and carry iron bars and starting handles and talk about "Keep Britain White" as they leave the pub and begin a "nigger run" for the night, but they always make it back before last orders and laugh about how many spade heads they crack and somebody will sing "Bye Bye Blackbird" and the landlord's bell will ring out and if they catch you on the street after the pub close then they going pelt milk bottles and bricks at you and the "nigger run" begin again right there and then. So I'm standing up straight and Ralph is feeling my arm and talking stupidness about roast beef and Yorkshire pudding and I look at the man and I want to ask him if he have any Teddy Boy sons, or maybe a daughter who he teach to spit on the ground for good luck when she see a coloured man, but I don't say anything and the man run his big hand across the top of my head and he tell Ralph that "at least we won't have to prescribe Amplex for this one" and if he can find a pair of overalls into which I don't disappear then I can start work on Monday and he shake my hand and tell me welcome to the factory and promise me that if I keep my nose clean and my head down they going treat me just like everybody else. Ralph is jumping from one foot to the next and he say "thank you" and I looking at Ralph and wondering what the hell is going on inside the head of my friend because he carrying on all skittish and telling the man that he never see me without a book and how I always studying, and I want to tell Ralph to relax because this is a factory job and as far as I can see book learning don't have nothing to do with working in an iron foundry. After all, it's Ralph who tell me that work start at eight, but nothing is done before nine except reading the newspaper and smoking, then at eleven everything stop for tea, then again at one for lunch, then tea again but this time with cake, and then people go home at five, so the thing is not like real work, and I don't think a man's brain have anything to do with this job, but I don't say nothing although inside my head I begging Ralph to stop off his talk about me and the blasted books.

'A week later I find myself sitting in front of a man who is looking upon me with a strange smile on his face and his two feet propped up on a desk. Underneath one shoe is covered in mud, and the man is stroking his short beard with his right hand.

Then the man stop doing so and drop both hands together in his lap and begin nodding as though answering a question, although as yet I don't say a thing. The man is wearing a thick brown jacket and I'm studying the pieces of leather on the cuffs and elbows because I never look upon a jacket like this before. Then I find myself gawping at the shirt and tie and pullover, which bulk out the man's small frame, for this is the first time in my life that I see anybody wearing so much clothes inside a building. Eventually the man stop dreaming and he reach into his breast pocket and pull out a pipe which he hold carefully in the cup of his palm. His fingers poke about in an envelope of tobacco and he begin to push a clump of weed into the bowl of the pipe before putting the thing in his mouth and lighting it. He haul up some smoke, then he take the pipe from his mouth and begin to use the thing to point. He ask me, "So to what exactly do I owe the pleasure of your visit? The department secretary said that you wanted to see a professor." He smile. "Well, I'm afraid I'm not a professor, I'm merely a lecturer, but I hope I'll do." I thank the man and tell him I want to register at the college to take classes, but if this is not the right place then I can come back at a more convenient time and speak with a next person. I don't tell him that the ignorant woman at the front desk ask me what I want, and when I say I want to study she look surprised and tell me that it is half-term but she will see what she can do. However, she tell me like she want me to know she doing me some kind of big favour. After a few minutes the woman come back and say, third door on the right, and that I am lucky because this morning Dr Davies is in the office and he have a few minutes to spare. I put down the magazine that I holding and thank the woman, but she don't have no time for me. "Well go on," she say, "he won't bite." Dr Davies swings down his feet from the desk and he lean forward and ask me if

I have any idea of what subject it is that I wish to register for, but I tell him that I don't know, and I looking good at this man because I not sure if he on my side or if the man just amusing himself. "I'm sorry," he say, "I seem to have forgotten my manners. Would you like a cup of coffee or something?" I shake my head, but then I remember my own manners and say "no thank you," but the man continue to stare at me. I tell him that I pass all my school exams, but not so high that I can take the scholarship, and then I confess that maybe I want to try for law. The man is listening with a kind of pretend smile on his face so I decide I better tell him everything. I tell him that I work at the factory with my good friend, Ralph, but I can work in the day and still plenty of time to study in the evening. I try to convince the man that I ready to take the college exams or whatever it is that you must do to gain entrance into the place. The man wait a second or two and then he ask me all calm and easy if I can truly work and study at the same time, and I tell the man the hours at the factory are eight to five but I don't have to go to the pub after work with the other fellars because I prefer to study. Dr Davies look pleased, and then he tap his pipe on the desk and push in more tobacco and light it up again. He say that he hope I don't mind that he is asking, but why it is that I think so many of us are coming over. "Opportunity or adventure, or a combination of both?" I look at Dr Davies and wonder if this is some kind of examination question. The man look kind enough, but a part of me is ready to get up and go and find Ralph. I watch him begin to smoke the pipe, and then the man tell me he favour Commonwealth migration, particularly as it seem as though we prepared to make a big sacrifice and abandon our lovely sunshine. He say he understand the situation because his sister is a nurse in Ceylon, and before this she is in Nigeria. "But look out of the window," he say, "look at the blessed weather. Who would want to flee paradise for this, for heaven's sake?" I know the man don't really be talking to me so I just watch him and wait for him to turn back and look me in the face, which he eventually decide to do. Dr Davies ask me if I have any family in England, but before I can answer the man is talking to himself again. He rest down the pipe and sigh. "You're all so bloody young. Remarkable really, but you're all just kids when it comes down to it, just kids."'

The new, younger, nurse gently touches his arm and he lifts up his head from the tabletop and slits his eyes against the bright light.

'I'm sorry, Mr Gordon, but your father's awake now and he's asking after you.'

He looks around and realises that he is in the cafeteria. The television set is bracketed high in the far corner, where the walls meet the ceiling, and he can see that it is broadcasting the nine o'clock news with subtitles.

'We've tried to bed him down for the night, but he keeps asking after you.'

He squints up at the woman, then shields his eyes with a raised hand and pushes back his chair. This one is prettier, and he likes her manner more than the other one. He remembers the first nurse ushering him away from his father's bedside, insisting that the older man needed a wash and an afternoon rest, and pointing him in the direction of the cafeteria. Once there, he ordered fish and chips, with a portion of peas and bread and butter on the side, but as he took his place at the Formica-topped table he realised that he didn't feel much like eating. He dialled Annabelle's number, but the phone went straight to voicemail and so he quickly ended the call. He remembered that this morning he'd gone to the Mandela Centre for the application form, and deliberately tried to avoid Baron. He wondered if he should call Baron and let him know how his father was doing. He could even nip round to see him and have something to eat with his father's friend at the pub, instead of consuming the rubbish that he had just bought, but he assumed that Baron would only expect to hear from him if his father's condition took a turn for the worse. Baron was probably giving father and son some time together. He recalled staring down at the fish and chips and pushing the meal away from himself to the far side of the table. He let his head fall forward into the cushioned pillow of his folded arms and closed his eyes. And now the young nurse is standing over him and waiting patiently for him to follow her back to his father's bedside.

His father watches him take a seat on the metal chair and then he slowly twists his body to one side and places the brown envelope back on the bedside table. The older man grimaces with the effort, and the new nurse gently massages the underside of his arm where the intravenous drip is needled into a thin vein. Having done so, the nurse stands with her arms crossed before her and watches carefully before speaking to the son in a half-whisper.

'I'll be going off duty at midnight, but I'll stop by from time to time before then. It'll be all right for you to stay so long as you're both quiet. But don't overdo it. He's weaker than he thinks.'

He nods appreciatively, but it is only after she has turned and started to walk away that he realises he still hasn't raised the subject of his father's eyesight.

'Why is the girl whispering?'

'It's getting late and people are sleeping. She's just trying to be respectful of others.'

'You want to sleep?' His father looks hurt. 'You want to sleep, then sleep. I don't be stopping you sleeping.'

'I'm not tired. I was listening to you.'

'Well, I was telling you about meeting this man, Dr Davies. You remember?'

'I remember. The college lecturer.'

'Well nearly a month pass by since I have the meeting with this Dr Davies, and one night I find myself sitting with the fellars in the pub when suddenly Baron fold up his newspaper with a big performance and he stand and push the thing into his coat pocket. He announce that he gone for the night. My eyes follow him across to the door and I watch as he leave the pub. This is the third time this week that Baron get up from the table for he can't listen any more to Ralph shooting off his mouth about what he will do to the next teenager who try to push him off the pavement. Ralph return from the bar with three pints of bitter balance in his two hands and set them on the table before he drop back down into his seat. My friend continue to talk as though he don't notice Baron gone. As Ralph lift the new pint to his mouth, I can see the bruise on the side of his face where the English boy punch him in the head. "You know," he say, "they still have pubs in this town that don't let us in at all. We barred, and like I tell you, don't bother going to any dance club without a girl, coloured or white. They don't care what kind of girl you bring, but what they don't want is no single coloured man prowling around the place sniffing up the women. They believe all this inter-racial business begin in the dance hall, but what they can't deal with is when the English girls begin sniffing back and that's when you hear them start talking about not wanting a country full of half-castes. They think all of us is ponces looking to prey on a piece of white thing that we give a drink to, or a bit of dope, then we breed them and put them out on the street. Well, you know that's what they saying, don't you?" I'm listening to Ralph, but I hear the speech already because every night since Ralph start seeing an English girl who work on the buses, my friend getting drunk and loud and saying the same thing over and over. Tonight, as he walking the girl back to her place from the bus depot, the girl's brother ambush him and Ralph beat the boy and take a knife from him and pitch it down a drain, but not before the boy thump him hard. The girl decide to stay with the brother, who shouting that he going get Ralph and calling him a coon and a sambo and other things that Ralph say he can't understand because the accent is too thick, and Ralph seem upset that the girl would want to stay with the brother even though I tell him that blood is thicker than water and he should realise the brother don't mean nothing and the boy is just trying to save face. Every night since Ralph get sweet on Doreen from the bus depot my friend drinking too much. Ralph say the brother have big sideburns like he think he a man, and he wear stupid thick, thick shoes, but Ralph claim that he show him who is the man and he is sure the boy not coming back for a next beating. Ralph empty his pint in one and my friend move to get up from the seat but he fall back. "Jesus Christ, man, you know these people want a colour bar here so why they don't just get on with it and make it legal. But where does that leave the Cypriots, you tell me? They let them run a café here and there and everywhere, but are the Cyps coloured people? They look coloured to me, don't you think?" I watch Ralph lift up his paper mat out of a puddle of beer, and then he put down his empty glass on it. "They seriously think they can lynch me? They think they can do me like Little Rock? Don't make me laugh. I know them, smiling at us at work and then ignoring us when they see us in the street. Man, I know them, I know them good, and if I can't walk home a decent girl like Doreen in peace and quiet then what the hell is going on, you tell me that? Man, this place is a joke."

'By the time the summer reach, and the nights are warm and long, Ralph start to carry on bad and he encouraging me to do the same. I press up even harder against the girl, like I trying to drive her into the tree, and as I do so she reach down and open up her coat a little wider, and then her legs, and then the girl begin to liven up her cold performance and start to maul me like she must think I'm her pet monkey. She whisper crude things into my ear but I know she just want me to finish quickly so she can be on her way. Eventually I peel away from the girl who quickly close up her coat and ask me if everything is all right, but a part of me want to laugh because how can everything be all right if I leaning up against a tree in a park with a young girl to whom I just pay cash money in exchange for a few minutes with her body? Everything is not all right and, although this is the third time that Ralph sweet-talk me into coming to the park with him and looking for skirt, I already know that I won't be troubling with this type of business no more for it's no good for a man like me. I going have to reason with Ralph about this woman-against-the-tree caper, and about the fact that I paying half the man's rent to sleep on a mattress on the floor, yet every Tuesday and Friday, when Mrs Jones's husband on night duty, he put me out in the hall with a blanket and Mrs Jones pay him a visit and collect what Ralph like to call the "extra rent money". I starting to feel that if I going do any serious studying then I must find a place by myself, and maybe it's time to give Ralph back his privacy, so I start asking around to see if anybody know of a room that I can rent. It seem like everybody in the factory, and everybody in the pub, saying the same thing about how is only prejudiced landlords in England, and these same landlords who insist on "European Only" keeping back the coloured man from progress because without a decent place to live then we can't bring over our wives or girlfriends and start to live properly. Every coloured man in England is waiting on decent housing to open up, and in the meantime every coloured man not only putting up with prejudice at work, but when he try to find some place to rest at the end of the day he meet more big problems there. The girl finish buttoning up her coat, and I watch as she unwrap a piece of gum from its foil paper and then fold it into her mouth as she speak. "What about the money? You haven't paid me yet." She push a finger into my chest. "You lot have to pay a coloured tax, didn't anybody tell you that?" The girl must think I straight off the boat, so I remind her that I already paid the damn money and she should just fix up herself and move on. When I turn to leave the blasted girl grab hold of my arm and start talking about how she have three kiddies and no money, and then she bite down on she bottom lip and her eyes begin to water, and I thinking about maybe giving the girl another shilling but I'm wanting to ask Ralph first in case it mess up things for the other fellars. That's when I hear Ralph's voice, and I turn and see him pelting toward me, and three white boys chasing after him, and so I turn and start to run. After a minute or so I look back and see that Ralph decide to swerve off to the right and my friend running down the hill toward the main road and the three boys following him and nobody following me, but I still run until I reach the small stone wall that surround the park, and I jump the thing and I pleased like hell to see plenty of traffic and people everywhere. I stop to catch my breath and then turn up the collar on my jacket and I start to walk fast, but I taking care to keep my head down. I don't know where the hell I am, but I too frightened to stop and ask any question and so I just keep walking. Eventually I see a bench near a bus stop and I take a rest for a minute and then realise that I'm looking upon a canal. I like the quiet water, but the noise of the traffic troubling my head, especially when a bus pull up at the stop. For maybe an hour I just sit and stare at the water, and wonder if once I figure out where I am if I should go seek out Ralph at the pub, or maybe he gone back to Mrs Jones's house, but I know for sure that my friend bound to be at one of these two places and I want to make sure that everything all right with him because the three white boys running seriously hard after Ralph.

'It's late by the time I decide to abandon the bench by the bus stop and go and search out Ralph, but when I finally reach the Red Lion all I see is Baron by himself in the corner with a copy of the *Racing Post* and a stub of pencil behind one ear. He tell me that he don't know where Ralph is, and as usual the man don't have much time for conversation so I decide no point in staying for a drink and I move off. At this time nothing really worry me because I expect to find Ralph back in his room and lying on the bed with a bottle to his mouth ready to tell me everything with plenty of exaggeration. However, as I walk toward the front door of Mrs Jones's house I hear groaning coming from the bushes and so I step off the path and discover Ralph, whose face is covered in blood and the man's mouth moving but no words coming out. I pound on the door and Mrs Jones open up and ask me if I lose my key, but I point at Ralph and the woman look frighten and she say that she will ask Mr Jones to call for an ambulance. I ease past Mrs Jones and into the house and fill a cup with water which I bring back for Ralph. I prop up my friend's head and start to feed him some water from the cup, but his lips can't form a funnel and everything dripping down the man's cheek and all the time I speaking to him, take it easy Ralph, take it easy man, you know everything going be just fine, just take it easy. Maybe fifteen minutes later, I watching the ambulance man rub some ointment into the head wound, but the blood continue to flow so the man quickly put on a fresh piece of bandage. As he does so he lose his balance because the ambulance take a hard right and the tyres squeal before we straighten out again. I hold on to Ralph's hand, but I can't bring myself to look again into the man's face because

I know the nose is broken and squashed flat and cotton wool is pushed up into each nostril. One eye closed up tight, and the other only half open, and Ralph's lips big like two red balloons. The ambulance man try to move one of my friend's twisted legs, but Ralph cry out in pain and so the man stop what he is doing and ask me again if I am with Ralph when the attack happen, and if I see the men who beat him, but again I tell him I just see three boys chasing Ralph out the park, and I'm running the other way, and that is all. After the ambulance arrive at the hospital, I wait for the night nurse to pass back into the empty visitors' room, and when she does so I climb to my feet and ask the woman if she have any news, but the woman say the doctor will come and talk with me but in the meantime I must sit back on the hard wooden chair and wait. I ask if she have change for a shilling as I need to make a phone call, but the night nurse shake her head then take out a threepence from her purse which she give to me and ask if I know where the phonebox is. The first week I arrive in England, Ralph hand me a piece of paper with the number of his sister in Manchester saying if anything happen to him then I should let her know. I can't imagine anything going happen, but for some reason I keep the number safe and sound in my wallet where I can find it. Shirley know who I am, but she talking down the phone like she don't trust me, but then I realise that I must have woken her up and so she bound to be a little suspicious. I tell her what happen and I can hear the worry in the woman's voice. Shirley say she will make the arrangements to come over tomorrow at the end of work, and I tell her that if I can meet her at the station I will do so, but in the evening I have to go to college. I say this hoping to impress the woman, but all she say back to me is "thank you" and that she will see me at the hospital and then she hang up and the woman leave me feeling foolish with the receiver in my hand. I fold up the piece of paper with

Shirley's number and push it back in my wallet, and I go back to the empty visitors' room where the clock on the wall telling me that it is past one in the morning. Again I take up a seat, and the double doors swing open with plenty urgency and the doctor come forth with some papers in one hand and the other hand pushed down in the pocket of his white coat. The man move quickly toward me as though he is going to arrest me. He ask me what happen to my friend, but I tell him that I don't know because I'm not there, and he say he must file a report with the police because it's the law in England and so I say fine. I still waiting for him to say something about how Ralph is doing, but the man just look at me and slowly shake his head which make me anxious, but if the man don't want to talk then the man don't have to talk, and I can't force him to say whatever it is that is on his mind.

'The next day I ask the foreman if I can leave early because of what happen to Ralph. The foreman assume that I going to the hospital and so he say, "yes, of course you can go and see your friend," but instead of going to the hospital I decide to go to the train station and I get there just as the Manchester train is pulling in. It's two or three years since I last see Shirley, but she don't change much. Even the heavy coat can't disguise her sweet figure. She smile when she see me, but on the bus to the hospital she don't say a word. Once we reach the hospital I find a seat in the visitors' room while Shirley alone go in to see her brother, but at least other people waiting in the room. After twenty minutes the same doctor come out to speak with a man who is sitting across from me, but when the doctor sight me he just nod then continue with his quiet quiet conversation. Once he finish talking to the man he come over and drop a hand on my shoulder and tell me they doing all they can for Ralph. I remember the doctor smiling as he say this, but before I can ask him what he mean by "doing all they can" the doctor turn and leave. Maybe an hour later, Shirley come out through the double doors but the woman looking sad as if she been crying. I tell her if she not planning on going back to Manchester tonight then she must stay in Ralph's room and I will sleep on the landing. Shirley don't say anything in return and so I ask her if she hungry, but the woman shake her head without looking up at me. Once we get on the bus, I ask Shirley if she want to go straight back to the room or if she want to do something else. The truth is I prefer not to take Shirley to the pub, because I know the pub is no place for a woman like this, and I looking at the brightly lit streets and thinking it will be a shame to go straight back to the miserable room, so when Shirley say she would like to go to the pictures I glad. I'm trying hard to think of where I can find a film place, but Shirley tell me she notice a cinema across the square outside the train station. "A big place that is named Majestic," she say. When the film done, and the name of the people begin to come up on the screen, it's then that I realise I going have to move myself. For the past two hours my leg been accidentally resting against her own leg, and I can't concentrate on the film but at the same time I don't want to move. Now the film is over and I not too sure about what I must do. Then the national anthem start to play and this solve the problem because now I must stand up, and then after the music finish we leave the cinema. Shirley don't say a thing as we walk to the bus stop, and I thinking that she must still be upset about Ralph and the film don't make no difference to her mood. Back at the room I bring a cup of tea from the kitchen and I set it down on the small table beside Ralph's bed. I tell her, "I put in three sugars, but if you need more I can go and get more." I also tell her that everything is straighten out with Mrs Jones, the landlady, so the woman is not going get a shock if she run into Shirley in the bathroom or in the kitchen. It's then that I notice Shirley still not taken off her coat. "I sorry if you cold," I say, "but the paraffin heater take time to warm up." I pick up some clothes and a blanket and pillow from the mattress on the floor, and I balance everything in my arms. I tell Shirley that if she need me then I going be outside, and I mention that in the morning I will take her back to the hospital before I go off to work. She look at me and ask me why it is that tonight I don't go to college. Before I can answer Shirley tell me that this is the first time she ever see me without a book in my hand. "I surprise you don't already come a lawyer." For a moment I not sure if the woman is making a joke, and then she smile and say that she not tired yet and maybe I want to talk. I look at her and decide to set the bundle of clothes, and the blanket and the pillow, back down upon the mattress. I sit on the floor with my back to the wall and stretch out my legs in front of me.

'Maybe a week after the attack on Ralph, Mrs Jones make it clear that I have to find a next room. The English man who own the house, and advertise the room, just throw open the door but he don't bother to turn on the light bulb. He gesture with an arm but I find myself watching the ash on the end of the man's cigarette. "Well? It's a double room like I said, with a small gas stove. You got your privacy in here, pal. You share a lav in the basement, but no hot water though. However, it doesn't seem to bother anyone. Two pounds ten shillings a week for the room, no questions asked, just be sensible with the visitors and respectable girls only. I don't want the house going down. A shilling for a shower at the local baths, which is three streets away, and that's a coal fire, but you'll have to get a guard. Well, you want it or not because it'll go? I wouldn't hang about because there's plenty of people looking for a roof for the night, you do know that don't you?" The man take a deep draw on his cigarette, then he stub it out on the wall and I watch the ashes flake

down on to the nasty carpet. Back on the street I can see that
these houses had once carried some style, but these days they
broke down and paint peeling from them and the tiny front
garden just pile up with rubbish. My head is hurt bad, and I
push the scrap of paper with the addresses of the rooms to rent
back into my pocket and I keep walking. Me, I done look at my
last room for the day. Mrs Jones tell me I must leave because
after what happen with Ralph her husband say he don't want no
more coloureds in his house. It's not that he's prejudiced, she say,
it's just that he can't take any bother with coppers. And so I
walking in London town, and the night smog starting to itch
my eyes, and I can't see more than ten yards ahead of me. The
streetlights don't help with the fog, because they just make everything look like ghosts everyplace. In my head I can hear people
talking to me, but I try not to listen and I keep my eyes down
and walk quickly until I find myself outside a restaurant. I go
into the empty place, but as soon as I sit down the two men who
work there look hard at me and start to talk to each other in
their language. The scruffy, younger, man come over and hand
me a dirty piece of paper with the menu printed on it, and I say
thank you very much but I already know what I want. I just need
a plate of rice. "Just rice?" Yes, I say, just plain white rice. The
man take back the paper and I watch as he go into the kitchen
with the older man. A few minutes pass and I stare out of the
window into the black night, but I find nothing to see and nobody
is walking by. These days, it dark going out to work and dark
coming in again, and I try to think about this but it no use for
the people in my head still talking. For a week now I been hearing
these blasted people in my head, but nothing they say make any
sense and I can't seem to make them stop. Tomorrow I going
look at some more rooms, because Mrs Jones don't have to ask
me twice. I'm not a dog or a cat. Nobody going put me out at

night. The younger man come back through from the kitchen with a plate of rice which he put down in front of me and the man move off to one side and wait by the door. It's then that I reach down in my pocket and take out the tin of sardines and start to open it with the metal key, carefully curling back the tin lid, then I tip the sardines on to the rice and stir them in good. I pick up the salt and pepper and flavour the food. By now the older man come out from the kitchen and the two of them staring at me. They come to my table and the older man start to wave his hands and shout. "Oh no, sir, this is not possible. You cannot do this. It is our food that you must eat." I just keep eating and I ignore the both of them.

'Three months later I follow Shirley into a Wimpy Bar and find a seat by the window. Shirley barely speak a word since she see me waiting by the factory gate as she come out from work. She stop and say something to the woman she is with, and the woman look up at me before saying goodnight to Shirley and walking off. Only when the woman pass out of sight does Shirley start to drag herself toward me, and it's she who suggest that we go somewhere and talk. I can't see why Shirley is treating me like this, because once she telephone my workplace I agree to do the right thing and come over to Manchester to meet up. We sitting in the crowded Wimpy Bar and I drop a lump of sugar into my tea before picking up the spoon and stirring it in. I tell her that after Ralph die I move out of Mrs Jones's house and I now have my own room. I tell her I need the privacy if I going to study properly. I'm still working at the factory casting iron, but I want the woman to understand that at night I have some serious college work that I must do. I watch Shirley spread butter on her toast with two long passes of the knife, then she bite into the toast and look me in the eye and ask me if I need my privacy more than I need a wife and child because I better make up my mind as to my priorities. I swallow deeply and turn from the woman and stare at the back of a stranger's head. The last time I see Shirley is at Ralph's funeral, but I trying hard not to look anybody in the eye because I too upset. The wind start to blow the pages of the vicar's bible, and for some reason the man clamp down his hand on the pages instead of just shutting the book for he already finish with it. Then I hear Shirley crying, and I mean real powerful crying not womanish sobbing, and I feel for the woman. The coffin-bearers start to ease down Ralph's casket at an awkward angle, and soon after everybody step forward and begin to toss dirt on the box so it sound like rain falling hard. I'm thinking, Jesus Christ, Ralph must be frighten by all this noise. Why people can't throw dirt quieter? I know that Baron and some of the boys soon heading off to the Red Lion, but I don't know if I should go with them or stay and look out for Shirley. I know she won't want to come with the fellars to the pub, but as people move off I find myself standing by the grave not able to make up my mind as to what I must do. It's then that I see Shirley walking away without so much as a "so long" to me and now everything come clear. Me, I'm going to the pub. I reach and everybody in the lounge talking loud and carrying on with plenty drinking, but my spirit can't take it and so I go in the public bar. It's then that I notice Dr Davies from the college and I see the man is carrying some leaflets and moving up and down the place giving them out to people. The young woman behind the bar staring at me and waiting for me to say what I want to drink. The woman smiles, first with her lips and then with her eyes. "Well, what's happening, love? You waiting for your premium bonds to come up? Concentrate dear, you look like you're in Cloud-cuckoo-land." I *am* concentrating and I trying to make myself small and hoping that Dr Davies don't see me because I never been anywhere near the blasted college since the time I go to see the man with his feet up on the desk. Luckily he pass out of the bar without noticing me and so I order a pint of bitter from the woman who ask me if I belong to the wake in the lounge. I say "yes," and then she tell me they call it a wake because nobody can sleep through the damn noise. The woman laugh and point at the door through which Dr Davies just leave and she ask me if I trying to avoid the chap from the college. Before I know how to answer she tell me that she don't blame me for the man is always acting like a bloody nuisance with all this research into immigrants. Then the young woman just move off to serve somebody else. When I reach my room that night I find myself wondering about what happen to Shirley, but I realise she must have decide to go back to Manchester and that is good because I don't want no repeat of the confusion of the night when Ralph is in the hospital, and especially not on the day that my best friend from home is going into the ground. But here I am sitting in a Manchester Wimpy Bar and the woman telling me that she is pregnant with my child and eating toast and drinking tea like it's me alone who create this situation. I'm trying to be decent, I trying hard, but her behaviour simply don't impress me. The woman finish with the toast and wipe her hands on a paper napkin, then she screw the napkin into a ball and push it under the rim of the saucer, and then she look across the table at me. "Well?"

'It take me nearly a year before I find the courage to ask out Brenda. I used to go into the public bar after work and sit and talk with her, but I'm trying to do so in a way that people won't think that something is going on with the two of us. But, of course, I know that some people beginning to wonder if I don't have any other friends. I do, but these fellars are in the lounge. Baron is a good man, but he's not a man to say much, and the other people remind me of Ralph too much and I don't want no reminder of my friend because the police still don't prosecute anybody and every time I think of Ralph my head hurt like hell and the voices start up again. So, three or four nights a week I find myself in the public bar and I talk with Brenda who tell me how she is from Bradford, and how she meet her husband there, and when he join the army they station them near some place called Ripon. Brenda tell me that at first things is fine, but when the doctor say she can't have babies the husband change and start to get mean, and then he begin to raise his hand to her which is when she say she decide to run off and find a job. She can't go back to Bradford for the husband have family there who will tell the man where she is, and so she renting a bedsit near the city centre and she take a job in a hairdresser, and in the evening she work in the pub, and according to the woman she just about getting by. I listen to her, but I don't have no story to offer in return, and it never occur to me to make one up, so I just listen and when this Brenda done with the conversation I try to get her to tell me a next story, and then a next one, but the woman just keep asking about me, and the situation getting uncomfortable and so I start to drop by the pub only two or three times a week and then she begin to ask me where I been and so I ask her if she ever take any time off from the bar work and if she does then maybe one night we can go to a restaurant together. She look at me and start to laugh. "I was wondering when you were going to ask me out. I'd nearly given up on you." The place I take her to is the same Indian restaurant that I was foolish enough to think might treat a coloured man good, but for some reason I think maybe things will be different if I walk in with an English woman. But it don't turn out so. From the moment we enter the place I feel everybody looking down on me and I can tell that the Indian people are talking about Brenda. I know that Brenda can sense it too, but the woman just keep behaving as though nothing is the matter, and she never take her eyes from me, but I can't concentrate, and I'm looking at the curry and rice in front of us, and Brenda is still talking, and I can hear the voices in my head making all kind of loud noise and so I just lean over and push the rice bowl on to the floor and watch it break into pieces and Brenda stop talking, but everybody else in my head still talking, including Ralph, who is talking the loudest, and I just wait for the people to come and clean up the mess, but the Indian people slow to come so I shout, "Hey you people, you can hear me? Clean it up, clean up the fucking mess now!"

'Maybe a week pass before they say I can get up from the bed, and that's when I start to get the visits from the doctor. Every time the doctor come into the hospital room he make me sit in a chair and shine a light in my eyes with a small torch and ask me how I feel about this and how I feel about that and if I happy in England. I'm looking at the man and I don't want to annoy the fellar so I give off the answers I think he expecting and I try to smile at him, and after weeks of these blasted visits I want to ask the man when he think I can leave this place and go back to my rented room, but I know the doctor not going to answer me truthfully so I keep the question to myself. The other people in the place seem fine, but sometimes things can be difficult because I don't know if these people are talking to me or if they talking to themselves, for the thing about this hospital is that nobody seem to mind if a man decide to talk to himself. The only thing I don't care for is when they take me to the room where they strap me down on the bed and attach the wires. Not only does it hurt bad, but afterward they feed me tablets that make me sleep for days, and even when I'm awake I feel as though I'm asleep. Brenda start to come to see me every weekend and when she arrive they put me in a clean shirt and take me to a reception area with big windows so everything is bright and the two of us sit together. Brenda tell me all the different things that she done in the week, including babysitting, but when she say this I have to tell her that I never hear of this word and so she explain it to me, but the woman laughing hard because she can't understand that I don't know what is babysitting. Brenda tell me everything that happen at the hairdresser's and in the pub, and she give me all the chat that the fellars have, and I know that she is doing so in order that I don't have to feel no pressure to say anything because what is there for me to talk about? She know I don't go no place. Every week I look at Brenda and wonder why it is she trouble herself to come to the hospital, but I never ask the question in case I scare her away. One day I see the doctor and the man ask me if I know how long it is that I been "with them". I look at the doctor, but I don't say anything. Then he put his hand on my own hand, but he do so suddenly and I find myself pulling away from him. "I'm sorry," he say smiling. "I didn't mean to alarm you. Over five years," he say. "It's been a long time but we think that you're ready to go now. Are you ready?" I smile. Yes, of course I'm ready. I mean, what kind of foolishness is this? Five years is a big piece of life. Ralph claim that he is going home after five years. Five years is plenty of time so yes, I'm ready. "Perhaps your friend can help you settle into life outside. Is this possible?" The next weekend I sitting in the reception area and listening as Brenda tell me everything that happen that week at the hairdresser's and in the pub. Apparently Baron decide that he don't want to speak with anybody, but nobody seem to notice. Then I ask Brenda if she will consider marrying to me as soon I going be leaving the hospital. I let her know that I hoping to get back my job at the factory and maybe we can set up a house together. I know that the medicine make me put on some weight, but when I start to study again I sure that the weight going drop off. Brenda don't say anything, so I

tell her that if she already have a mister then I will understand
and she must just forget that I ever say a thing. I confess that I
don't like to think of her with a next man, but if she don't have
anybody special in her life then perhaps she will consider me.
Brenda just keep looking at me and so I keep talking and I tell
the woman that I'm not going home. I tell her that I don't have
nothing to go back to, not after all this time. Only my sister,
Leona, and I never hear from her. Brenda is staring at me, and
then she start to smile.

'I don't see you till you was six. Some coloured man come
knocking on my door and the man ask Brenda if I living in the
house. Standing behind him is a small boy in a blue school
uniform and with a sharp parting in his hair and wearing glasses.
I think you know the boy. Brenda call me to the door, and the
man tell me that Shirley finally die of the lung infection that is
making it difficult for her to breathe, and that he can't keep
Shirley's son as the boy should be with the father. This is how
I find out that you are now my responsibility, and suddenly I
find myself being asked to play the role of the father. Brenda
usher both you and the man inside, and then she put on the
kettle. Me, I sit down heavy in a chair and wonder how the hell
I'm supposed to play this role. I marking you sitting in a corner
and screwing up your face like you trying hard not to cry, and
Brenda come to sit with you and she start talking soft and offering
you sweets, but still you can't hold back the tears. The man tell
me that he marry to Shirley before she even have you, but the
pair of them never pretend with you that this man is your father.
The man insist that it's Shirley who tell him that if anything
happen to her then he must give you to me, and I watching the
man sipping at his tea and making a loud noise, and then the
man look up and catch me watching him and he just shrug his
shoulders. That night I lie in bed with Brenda and tell her that

I don't see how we can afford a child. Between her work at the hairdresser's and the bar, and my work at the factory, we have just enough to cover the rent payments on the house. I don't have much in the way of vices; I smoking a little, and drinking a few beers when I go down to the pub to pick up Brenda at the end of a night, but I already discover that if a man is living in a house, and not just one room, then paying bills in England is a serious business. I see Brenda watching me, but she don't say a thing. She wait until I finish talking then she put out the cigarette in the ashtray to the side of the bed. The woman turn to look at me. "He's your child, Earl. It doesn't matter what you think of Shirley, or if you believe she tricked you. The only thing that matters is he's your child and you better face up to this fact, okay?" When Brenda finally fall asleep I get out of bed and creep along the corridor and open up the door to the bedroom in which you're sleeping. I go inside and look down at you lying there with your mouth open and your nose slightly blocked up with cold, and I'm thinking to myself that nobody can say that I don't do nothing with my time in England. I lose my best friend, and then I get fooled off by a woman, and then I find myself living with an English girl, but at least I have you. But I'm not ready for this. It's not you that I don't want, son. I just don't want this life, because England already hurt me enough as it is. It seem like every time I think I discover some peace of mind then something else come along to trouble my head. But it's not you that I don't want, it's this damn life. I looking at you lying so still and peaceful and I want to bang my head on the wall because I just don't have any idea how to go forward with my life. I watching you sleeping on the bed in front of me but I just not ready. A part of me want to turn back the clock and find myself in the Harbour Lights bar with Ralph, and I want somebody to give me back my law book and my dictionary, and I want back my mother and

my father and Desmond and Leona. Your face is so peaceful and
I looking down at you, Keith, and I want to tell you about tall,
crazy Ralph, who you never going to meet, and how the two of
us sit together drinking beers and listening to the wind passing
through the palm trees and the two of us thinking of England.
The idea of England is fine. I can deal with the idea. You understand me, son? I can deal with the idea.'

The young man seated two rows in front of him on the bus is
watching an action film of some kind on his iPod. The youth's
baseball cap is turned backwards on his head so that despite the
mid-afternoon gloom he can just about make out the faded logo
of an American sports team. He can also hear the screeching of
tyres and the popping of gunshots as the action film climaxes in
some sort of car chase sequence. He is still not sure why he
decided to take the bus back to London instead of the train, but
he suspects that some part of him imagined that the longer journey
would give him more time to turn things over in his mind, but
as the bus hustles its way down the M1 all he can think about
is the time when his father came to see him, the week after the
thirteenth birthday visit, and abruptly announced to Brenda that
he was taking his son to the pictures. Brenda shrugged her shoulders and told him to go upstairs and get ready, while she stood
calmly by the door and waited with his father. He couldn't be
sure if Brenda was standing guard to prevent his father from
storming into the house and causing confusion, or if she was
worried that his father might disappear without waiting for him.
Either way, he hurried upstairs and grabbed his coat and scarf,
and then he ran back down, not because he was eager to go to
the pictures, but because he didn't want to leave Brenda alone
for too long.

'What time will you be bringing him back?' Brenda ruffled

his hair as she spoke, and then she encouraged him to fasten his scarf into a knot around his neck. 'Not too late, all right?'

'Whatever time the film finish.'

'Look, Earl, I'm not planning on going out anywhere, but he has got homework to do this weekend.'

He looked up at his father, who was visibly annoyed, but he could also see that his father had now made a decision to remain silent.

'Well, can you give me *some* idea of a time?'

His father turned to leave, and he understood that this was his cue to step forward and join him.

Brenda called out. 'I'll see you later, love.'

The film was an animated Disney cartoon, and from the moment it began he found himself caught up in the plot. He had been to Saturday morning children's matinées before, but this was the first time that he had been to a proper late afternoon screening. He couldn't remember if his father bought him any sweets or anything to drink, but he clearly recalls that when the film was over he followed his father out of the darkened auditorium and back into the lobby. Through the huge glass windows, he could see that outside it had got dark, and that car lights were on. He could also see that it was snowing and huge white flakes were tumbling down out of the sky and coating the pavement white. His father held up his coat for him and he pushed one arm into a sleeve, and then fished around looking for the other one. He finally jammed his arm into the hole and threaded it through but he couldn't take his eyes from the snow. His father offered him his hand and even though he felt too old for this he took it, and together they left the warmth of the foyer and stepped out into the bitterly cold evening. They began to walk back in the direction of the bus stop, past the parked cars that were already clad in snow, and as the flakes continued to fall on their bare heads he could feel his hand tight and safe in his father's hand. He looked behind him and saw two sets of footprints where they had walked, a large pair and his own smaller ones, and then he gazed up at the sky where a sudden surge of wind buffeted the flakes so that the snow began to swirl feverishly. As they turned a corner, he tugged his father's hand. His father looked down at him and smiled. He pointed to the sky. 'Look at all the snow!' His father continued to smile.

Brenda opened the door and quickly beckoned him inside.

'I thought you two might be building an igloo or something.' She paused and looked at his father. 'Would you like to come in for a warm before you head off?' His father shook his head.

'I have everything with the lawyers so that I can get my son back with me. They say you will hear from them next week.'

Brenda sighed. 'Look, Earl, it doesn't have to come to this. Have I argued with you? He's your son, you just have to make sure that you've got a proper place for him and then we can come to an arrangement, that's all.'

His father ignored Brenda and looked down at his son. 'I better go now before the buses stop running.' His father leaned over the threshold and hugged him, although the older man was clearly somewhat uncomfortable with the gesture. Once his father released him he stepped outside the house and into the snow, and he looked on as his father gingerly picked his way down the path in search of some form of transportation that might convey the snow-furred pilgrim back to wherever he lived. As he walked, his father left behind a single set of footprints, and he remembered lingering by the doorstep and watching closely as the falling snow steadily erased all evidence of his father's presence.

As the speeding bus continues to careen its way down the motorway towards London, most of the passengers are trying to doze. However, he notices that the young man with the iPod is now busily selecting another film whose ambient soundtrack will no doubt torment his neighbours for what remains of the journey. This morning the familiar older nurse had pushed his shoulder somewhat aggressively, and then she stood over him until his blinking eyes began to focus.

'That's not the best chair to fall asleep in, but you were obviously shattered after listening to him.' She paused. 'Older people often have a lot to say. We see it from time to time.' Again she paused. 'After he'd finished his chatting we thought it best to leave you both, and eventually you nodded off too.'

He could feel that both of his shoulders and his back were aching because of the angle at which he had fallen asleep, and so he pulled himself upright on the metal chair. He then realised that he could no longer hear the sonar beep of his father's machine. In fact, the hospital bed was empty.

'I'm sorry, love but about half an hour ago we moved your father to intensive care as his vitals were failing. That's when I first tried to wake you, but it was an emergency so we had to rush. And then we lost him. He just slipped away in his sleep so he wouldn't have known a thing about it.'

He looked up at this woman's face in disbelief. What was she trying to tell him?

'I'm very sorry, but it happened quickly and quite frankly there's not a thing that you could have done or said. I've just come back from over there.' She paused. 'Intensive care, that is.'

'Is that where he is?'

'They'll be moving him now. We've left a message for his friend at the Mandela Centre is it?'

'Yes, the Mandela Centre. His name's Baron.'

'We know, love. He checked your father in so we have all of his details.'

'Yes, of course. I'm sorry.'

'Sorry for what? I take it that you'll be going over to your father's place and starting to sort things out as you're the only family we have registered.' He nodded. 'And can we reach you there, or do you have a mobile number that we could perhaps have?'

He couldn't remember his mobile number so he took out the phone and checked. He wrote down the number on the back of an old receipt and handed the piece of paper to the woman. The nurse gave him a sympathetic smile, but it was apparent that the woman had nothing further to say and she hovered awkwardly. He sensed that he was keeping her from something. Fearful of any more platitudes, he climbed to his feet and began the long, confusing, walk down the length of the ward away from his father's empty bed. So that was it? His father had 'slipped away in his sleep'? Slipped away? The words echoed in his mind like a pedalled note. That was all she had to say? That was her explanation?

The bus begins to slow down and bully its way across the motorway and into the inside lane. As they bear left and take the service station slip road, the driver announces that this will be a very short stop and they will leave in five minutes. Only those who need to disembark the bus should do so, the others should remain on board. 'Sorry, but there'll be no time for the games arcade or the food emporium as we're running behind schedule.' They cruise past the entrance to the car park, and the family picnic area, before swinging extravagantly into the bus parking zone and coming to an abrupt halt. He left the hospital knowing that he would have to go back to his father's house, but he is still not sure how he found himself at the central bus station buying a one-way ticket to London. He remembers putting the key in the door and then lumbering upstairs and grabbing his bag, before trudging back downstairs and looking at the photographs that remained scattered on the kitchen table. For a moment he lingered, but it was too soon to even think of beginning the process of sifting through the evidence of his father's life and so he turned his back on the house. He remembered to lock the door behind him, and he now finds himself just over an hour away from London and he realises that he should probably call Annabelle. He wants to do so before the driver starts up the thunderous engine, and so he arches his still aching back, and squeezes the mobile phone out from his trouser pocket and hits Annabelle's speed dial number. She sounds fraught.

'Keith? I was worried about you. In fact, I left you a message last night.'

He has not checked his messages so it's now his turn to be worried. 'What's the matter?'

'Are you sitting down?' She doesn't wait for him to answer. 'It's Chantelle. She's pregnant.'

'For Laurie?'

'Well, yes, who do you think?'

'Well, hang on a minute, I don't know. I've never even met her.'

'Well they're both coming over to explain things to me. Their words, not mine.'

'I'm on my way back. I should probably come over too, right?'

'I thought you were going to be away for a few days? Is your dad okay?'

'Yes, no problem. Why?'

'Are you sure? I mean, why the change of plan?'

'No reason really.' He pauses. 'Do you think it's best if you see them by yourself? I can be there in a couple of hours at most.'

The doors to the bus close with a cushioned sigh and the engine rumbles to life. He lowers his head and cups his hand around the phone so that he will be speaking directly into the microphone, and then he feels the bus beginning to lurch its cumbersome way out of the service station parking zone.

'Well that would be brilliant, if you're really on your way back. I won't start talking about anything until you're here.' She pauses. 'Are you sure you're all right? You sound a bit stressed.'

The iPod-playing youth has now located yet another shoot-em-up film and he seems to have increased the volume on his iPod to maximum. Annabelle is right, he is stressed, but he understands that sleep is the best remedy and, although it appears to be a long shot at best, he will try to block out the noise of small screen murder and mayhem and grab a quick nap before they reach London.

He stands in line at the newsagent's intending to buy chewing gum, but these days they seem to have converted these shops into places where you simply wait your turn to purchase lottery tickets. Traditional transactions, such as buying a newspaper, seem to take forever. Just as he is about to give up, the young man behind the counter, who sports the faint shadow of a moustache above his top lip, reaches out a hand and takes his money while continuing to process a lottery request with his other hand. Back outside on the pavement, it is both dark and windy. He stuffs a piece of gum into his mouth and then hoists his bag up and on to a shoulder, but he does not move off. He stands and stares across the village common at the row of Victorian terraces where Annabelle lives. These houses are now highly sought after, despite the fact that they open up right on to the street, but when they moved here from Birmingham, this area was hardly fancy or trendy. Today, outside the self-consciously designer shops, there are increasing numbers of basketed bicycles chained to purpose-built bike stands with a variety of unlikely locks, but back then if you were reckless enough to leave a bicycle chained anywhere for five minutes you would be lucky to find its skeletal remains. At the weekend there is a farmers' market, and any stall vulgar enough to sell non-organic products is likely to find itself picketed by what Laurie calls his mother's 'Green Posse'. Other parts of London seem to have made peace with Pound shops and Somali-run internet cafés offering to unlock your phone for a fiver, but not this little haven on the common which boasts a gymnasium for children called Cheeky Monkeys, and pubs which feature foreign beers served in breast-shaped glasses and a female clientele who wear long skirts and shooting jackets and walk soft-mouthed dogs, while the guys, if not English, are Mediterranean types who like to tuck their hair behind their ears like Premier League footballers. The truth is, he liked the area better then; in fact, he liked his life better back then. He remembers moving to London in the eighties as an exciting time for them both. Annabelle was beginning to think about a new career in the media, and he was finally going to be able to be the type of social worker who wouldn't have to spend most of his time listening to pleas for Saturday schools for under-performing black kids, or fielding applications for black theatre workshops where kids could learn the cultural importance of playing steel drums. His new job in London meant that he could leave behind the discomfort of being the black guy with a suit and briefcase, whose job seemed to principally involve him going into Afro-Caribbean centres and being taunted by angry dread-locked men as a 'baldhead'. Coming to London represented a new start and a new challenge, albeit in an unfashionable part of west London, but as he slowly chews gum outside the newsagent's shop across the common from Annabelle's house, he realises how dramatically things have changed, and not only in this now-fancy part of the city. So that's it then? His father has gone and now there's nobody ahead of him. Nobody higher than him on the tree. The traffic suddenly dies down for a moment, and he stares across the common and finds himself enveloped in a pocket of silence. He feels exposed and vulnerable. Small. That's it. Small. An accelerating lorry blasts by, and then another. So that's it then?

Annabelle ushers him into the kitchen, where he can see that Chantelle and Laurie are both about to leave. They have on their hats and coats and they are standing by the kitchen table. He puts down his bag on the floor and then smiles at them.

'Dad, this is Chantelle.'

The girl is tall and pretty, with large hazel eyes. Her hair is cut short and close to her head and she is the type of young woman who could easily end up modelling clothes for a career. She holds out a slender hand, which he shakes.

'Pleased to meet you, Chantelle.' He turns to Laurie and is surprised to see no sign of the headphones. 'If you're both going out then I don't want to keep you. But from what your mother's told me we should talk at some point.'

Laurie looks directly at him and shrugs his shoulders. 'We can talk now if you want. I was just going over to Chantelle's house to tell her mum and dad. They don't know yet.'

Annabelle starts to fill the kettle. 'It was Laurie's idea that they go over there together.' She looks at Chantelle. 'It's obviously going to be a bit of a shock for your family, isn't it?' Chantelle glances quickly at Laurie, then turns back to face Annabelle. She nods. 'Well, it was a bit of a shock for us too.'

'Look, Dad.' Laurie looks at the holdall on the floor. 'I'm sorry that it's twice now that you've had to come back because of me, but I want you to know that me and Chantelle are going to get it sorted. We both want to go to university so we're not going to let it get in the way. Well, you know what I mean. I don't want to sound too heartless or anything.'

'No, I know what you mean. You're right.' He pauses. 'Look, there's no point in everyone hanging about your mum's kitchen like this, so why don't the two of you go off and have the conversation with Chantelle's parents. We can talk later, or tomorrow, okay?'

Annabelle sees them to the front door and then comes back into the kitchen just as the kettle starts to boil.

'Aren't you going to sit down?'

She places the cup, with the teabag still in it, in front of him and then opens the fridge and takes out a carton of milk.

'She's a nice girl, and well-mannered. And Laurie seems to like her a lot.' Annabelle looks at him and then sits down opposite him at the table. She puts the milk to one side.

'What is it, Keith?'

'Nothing. I'm just tired.'

'But you've come back already. What's going on?'

'I told you. Nothing. I just wanted to come back.'

'Did the two of you have it out?'

'Something like that.'

Annabelle pours the milk into the tea, and then she picks up a spoon from where it rests on a paper napkin and she stirs. 'Why don't you go upstairs and lie down before Laurie and Chantelle come back?'

'Upstairs?'

'You'll have to walk it. I don't have a lift.'

Annabelle gets up from the kitchen table and turns on the halogen lights that illuminate the granite counter tops. She stands by the sink and looks across at him.

'You look like a couple of hours of sleep wouldn't hurt you. Leave the tea there if you like. I'll bring you up a fresh cup at about eight or so.'

When he opens his eyes he realises immediately where he is, but the room seems different, and he feels like a stranger in his own bedroom. He finds the tight envelope of sheets claustrophobic and so he pulls and kicks the top sheet until it is untucked. And then he looks around and sees Annabelle's things where his should be and he remembers what has happened. The door creaks opens and bright light from the hallway floods the room. Annabelle is holding a tray.

'I've got no hands. Can you turn on the bedside light?'

He leans over and takes the small switch between finger and thumb and squeezes it one turn clockwise before hauling himself upright.

'What time is it?'

'Nearly ten. I've brought you some tomato soup and some crusty bread.' She sits on the edge of the bed. 'I came up at eight but you were out for the count so I thought I'd let you sleep.'

'You should have woken me up.'

'What for? Do you have somewhere to go tonight?' Annabelle places the tray in his lap. 'Your mobile was ringing but I left it downstairs with your bag. Would you like me to bring it to you?'

He shakes his head. He realises that he has not eaten all day so he starts to spoon the soup up to his mouth.

'Laurie's back. Apparently it didn't go down too well with Chantelle's parents, although I can't say I'm surprised. Seventh Day Adventists.'

He stops eating. 'Where is he?'

'He's fine. In his room with Chantelle. I told her that she can stay on the sofa tonight. No need to look at me like that. She needs somewhere to stay, but I haven't exactly got used to the idea of my son having sex yet, let alone having sex under my roof. I said she can stay on the sofa, and I mean the sofa.'

'So they've kicked her out?'

'That's how most people would feel if their teenage daughter fell pregnant. But they'll get over it, and in the meantime she's welcome here. I was going to bring you some cheese to go with the bread. It'll only take a minute.'

'No thanks. I should get back to the flat and leave you to it.'

'What's that supposed to mean? Are you expecting somebody?' He shakes his head. 'Well, you don't look like you could make it to the end of the street, let alone back to your flat. Just give me the tray and go to sleep, all right?'

'I don't understand.'

'Just give me the tray. I'll take it downstairs and I'll be back up in a minute. We can talk about everything else in the morning.'

He watches as Annabelle opens the door with the outside of her slippered foot and closes it behind her by hooking the door shut with her instep. He listens as she carefully descends the stairs to the kitchen. He looks around the bedroom and his eyes alight upon a framed photograph of her parents that sits prominently on the dressing table. Her father is looking confidently into the lens of the camera, while her mother's gaze is altogether more mournful. It is not his bedroom. He belongs at Wilton Road. When she comes back up he will tell her this. He should get dressed and go home and then tomorrow he can come back and they can talk. He is not ill or incapable. There is no reason for him to spend a night here in this small terraced house with all these people. He will tell her this when she comes back upstairs. He lies back on the pillow and listens as downstairs Annabelle turns off the lights and closes all the doors. Then he hears her footsteps as she begins to walk slowly up the stairs.